...

THE
TRUST

...

. . .

ALSO BY RONALD H. BALSON

Karolina's Twins

Saving Sophie

Once We Were Brothers

...

THE
TRUST

...

Ronald H. Balson

St. Martin's Press

New York

THE TRUST. Copyright © 2017 by Ronald H. Balson. All rights reserved. Printed in the United States of America. For information, address St. Martin's Press, 175 Fifth Avenue, New York, N.Y. 10010.

www.stmartins.com

The Library of Congress Cataloging-in-Publication Data is available upon request.

ISBN 978-1-250-12744-0 (hardcover)
ISBN 978-1-250-19023-9 (international, sold outside the U.S., subject to rights availability)
ISBN 978-1-250-12746-4 (ebook)

Our books may be purchased in bulk for promotional, educational, or business use. Please contact your local bookseller or the Macmillan Corporate and Premium Sales Department at 1-800-221-7945, extension 5442, or by email at MacmillanSpecialMarkets@macmillan.com.

First published in the United States by St. Martin's Press

First U.S. Edition: September 2017

10 9 8 7 6 5 4 3 2 1

To my wife, Monica,
and a lifetime of mutual trust

ACKNOWLEDGMENTS

• • •

The Trust is a work of historical fiction. The cast of characters portrayed herein are products of my imagination and do not refer to any actual person, living or dead. Nevertheless, Northern Ireland's rich and complex history plays a substantial supportive role. I have tried to draw upon the history of the Troubles as authentically as I could, insofar as that setting supports the fictional story. The existence of the organizations mentioned—the Irish Republican Army, the Real IRA, the Ulster Volunteer Force, and the Ulster Defence Association—is indisputable, but their role in the story is purely fictional. The political parties and the police services—Sinn Fein, the Ulster Unionist Party, the Police Service of Northern Ireland, and the Royal Ulster Constabulary—were accurate references, though again, their connection to the story is fictional. The Rape of the Falls, the Orange Parades, and descriptions of the violence during the Troubles are unfortunately accurate. The Good Friday Peace Agreement and its provisions for early release of prisoners is also factual.

I am indebted to the wonderful people of Northern Ireland and their beautiful country. I am especially grateful to the staff of the Ulster Museum, the staff of the Dunluce Castle, and the staff of the Titanic Museum, and for the wealth of history they were willing to share. My special thanks to historian Gerald McGlade, who graciously took us on a hands-on journey through the Belfast neighborhoods. As Liam would enthusiastically concur, I urge everyone to include Northern Ireland in their bucket list.

Once again, thanks to my supportive group at St. Martin's Press: my editor, Jennifer Weis; my publicist, Staci Burt; Brant Janeway, Sylvan Creekmore, and Jordan Hanley. Thanks to NaNá V. Stoelzle, for her talented editing. Thanks to my agent and good friend, Maura Teitelbaum.

As always, my heartfelt thanks to my cadre of readers and their invaluable advice: The Honorable John T. Carr, Cindy Pogrund, David Pogrund, Linda Waldman, Rose McGowan, Richard Templer, Katie Lang, and Lawrence and Benjamin Balson. And my deepest gratitude to my indefatigable wife, Monica, who read the pages as they came out of the printer. She must have read and edited the story a thousand times and always stayed upbeat and positive.

Finally, a toast to the lads at Robinson's.

...

THE
TRUST

...

PREFACE

...

In the sixteenth century, the British Crown, mindful of the bourgeoning thirst for independence on the predominantly Catholic island of Ireland, instituted a landgrab policy referred to as the Plantation of Ulster. Catholic farmlands in the northeast sector of Ireland were confiscated and handed over to thousands of Protestant settlers from England and Scotland who were willing to pledge loyalty to the Crown. As a condition of ownership, the new landowners were prohibited from employing Catholic workers. Hence, the native Catholic population in the six northern counties was institutionally deprived of its lands, its income and its political status. Centuries of conflict ensued but failed to diminish the hold of the Protestant ascendancy.

In 1920, the English Parliament passed the Government of Ireland Act, partitioning the island into two entities: Southern Ireland and Northern Ireland. The twenty-six counties of Southern Ireland would become the Irish Free State in 1922. The six northeast counties of Antrim, Armagh, Down, Fermanagh, Londonderry and Tyrone would become the country of Northern Ireland, and remain a part of the United Kingdom.

By 1969, Catholics numbered a third of Northern Ireland's population, but had not a single Catholic cabinet member. Judges were uniformly Protestant and civil servants were required to swear allegiance to the British crown. Public works and housing, administered by the Protestant-controlled government, directed economic benefits to Protestant neighborhoods. Living conditions for Catholics in the larger cities of Belfast, Derry, Portadown and Antrim were bleak and oppressive. Health care was poor and male unemployment exceeded 70 percent.

Catholics began to organize protests and stage civil rights marches often ending in violence. The Irish Republican Army (IRA) and its political arm, Sinn Fein, advanced the Catholic cause, often by violent means. The Ulster Volunteer Force (UVF) and the Loyalist Volunteer Force (LVF), with their political arm the Ulster Union Party (UUP) took up arms in opposition. Civil order in the six counties disintegrated and led to a bloody civil war that would last for thirty years. That war was known as the Troubles.

ONE

...

L IFE'S DIRECTION IS EPHEMERAL. Something as common as the ring of a telephone can knock it off its course. Simple as that, but I didn't see it coming this time. I had just arrived at my office, set my coffee on my desk and was starting to unfold the morning *Tribune* when my phone rang. Since I make my living as a private investigator and my assignments typically begin with a phone call, the ring was not unwelcome. But this turned out to be a call I didn't expect and I certainly didn't want.

It's not that my life was so predictably calm, but lately I'd settled into a comfortable routine. I had a new baby, a happy marriage and a solid investigation practice. Then the phone rang, and like the switchman in a railroad yard, it redirected my life. First I'm going north, now I'm going east.

I lifted the receiver. "Liam Taggart, Investigations."

"Liam? It's Janie."

The call I didn't expect. I sat there staring at the phone.

"It's Janie. Your cousin, Janie. The cute one. Holy Mother of God, Liam, have you lost your senses? Do you not remember your own family?"

I winced. Janie was one of a dozen cousins I had back in Northern Ireland, a clan I hadn't seen since the late nineties. She was seventeen then, a lively little dark-haired colleen. Deep expressive eyes. Little turned-up Irish nose. Full of spunk. Her voice brought back old memories. Memories I had locked away sixteen years ago.

"I'm sorry, Janie, it's just that your call took me by surprise. How's everyone back in the North?"

"Uncle Fergus died last night."

My heart sank and I swallowed hard. I feared this day would come and I knew I'd better make amends before it did. But I hadn't. Damn the call I didn't want. Fergus and I, we should have never left it like this. We had unfinished sentences, incomplete paragraphs. I could have gone to see him. We could've raised a pint, cleared the air, restored our relationship. Hell, it might have been as easy as a damn telephone call. We'd shared too much to let it end like this. Now he's gone and it's too late.

No longer locked away, memories flipped through my mind like pages of a photo album. A smiling Fergus Taggart, my father's brother and a giant of a man. Me, riding on his massive shoulders. Us, fishing in a wooden boat on the Lough Neagh. Me, sound asleep in a booth at McFlaherty's Public House, my head upon his lap. Him, slipping a fifty-pound note into my jacket pocket the day I left for America. And the pure joy of Aunt Deirdre's Sunday night dinners.

Who was it that said hours pass slowly but years fly by? It was just sixteen years ago that Fergus said the last words he'd ever speak to me.

"I don't think you and I have anything more to say to each other, Liam. You best be off now."

They were never supposed to be the last words. They were just words to end the day. Maybe the week. There would always be time to make amends. To find other words. Did Uncle Fergus believe those would be the last words or was he, like me, waiting for the inevitable reconciliation? I guess I'll never know.

"I'm sorry to hear that, Janie, truly I am. That's such sad news. How long had he been ill?"

"The funeral's Thursday. We'll talk about it when you get here. Please come."

I took a deep breath. Three days. "Oh, I don't know, Janie, I'm scheduled to—"

"Mass is at St. Michael's in Antrim, Thursday morning at eleven. The family needs you. Uncle Fergus needs you."

I furrowed my forehead at the odd remark. There would surely be no loving summons from my estranged Irish family. And Fergus wouldn't know one way or the other. I nodded to the phone. "I'll see what I can do. I'll have to get back to you."

CATHERINE MET ME AT the front door with her finger on her lips. "Shh, the baby's sleeping." She gave me a kiss. "What are you doing home so early? Are you feeling okay?"

I nodded, hung my coat on the rack and went straight to the kitchen for a cup of coffee. "I got a call from a cousin in Northern Ireland," I said over my shoulder. "My uncle Fergus died. They want me to come to Antrim for the funeral."

"Oh, I'm sorry," Catherine said. "Was he sick?"

"I don't know. I asked Janie and she gave me a cryptic answer—we'd talk about it when I got there. I mean, if he died of a heart attack, wouldn't she tell me?"

"I would think so. That's a strange answer. You and your uncle were very close at one time, weren't you?"

Close? At a critical time in my life Fergus was the most important person in the world. When my mother became ill, I was sent to live with him. He and my aunt Deirdre took a scared little four-year-old boy in short pants into their home and raised and nurtured me for six years. Close? I loved him with all my heart. Still do. I needed him and depended on him and he was there for me. I blinked a few tears and nodded my head.

Catherine put her arm around my shoulders. "I'm so sorry, honey. When's the funeral?"

"In three days. It doesn't matter, I can't go. I have appointments scheduled later this week."

"Can't you reschedule them?"

"Maybe I could, but that's not entirely it. I think if I were there it would be uncomfortable. Not just for me, but for everyone. I didn't leave under the best of circumstances and I haven't talked to any of them in sixteen years. I had a falling-out with my uncle, returned to America and shut them all out of my life like they didn't exist. I'm sure the family harbors bitter feelings and who could blame them? They deserved better from me. I should have taken the initiative, stayed in touch, but I just didn't know how to start the conversation. Now it's been too many years."

"You left because you had a falling-out with your uncle? Seems to me that it takes two to have an argument."

"No, Cat, this one was all my fault. I was living a lie and I got caught. I never should have put myself in a position where I had to lie to my family. It was foolish of me to accept a posting in Northern Ireland that was bound to end in a betrayal. I don't know why I did it."

"Maybe because it was the right thing to do? And you were young, Liam. Cut yourself a break."

"At the time, I thought it was the right thing to do. It was 1994 and I was a young recruit with the CIA. I'd only been with the Agency for a year when a position opened up in Northern Ireland and I jumped on it. For one thing I hadn't seen my Irish family since I was a young child and for another, Northern Ireland was the decade's political hotspot and I wanted in on the action.

"The Troubles was always front-page news for me. I followed it every day. In January 1994, President Clinton decided to get involved in the peace process. He invited Gerry Adams, the IRA's top politician and the UK's public enemy number one, to visit D.C. He arrived to rousing crowds and shook hands at the White House. It wasn't exactly what Tony Blair and Bertie Ahern had in mind, but Clinton was an effective peacemaker.

"As expected, Clinton directed the Agency to assist on the ground in Northern Ireland. Because I had family in County Antrim and could move about in the nationalist community, the Agency granted my request and posted me there. So in the summer of 1994, I returned to a grand reunion. My uncle Fergus was so happy to see me, it was like I'd never left. He gave me a bear hug so strong I thought he'd break my bones. As far as he and I were concerned, not a single minute had ticked off the clock since I was ten years old. There was my aunt Deirdre, with tears in her eyes and her arms wide open, the woman who warmly and unselfishly took me in and gave me a mother's love when I was four years old. There was my uncle Robert, always a broad smile on his rosy face. There was my aunt Nora and my wise old Uncle Eamon. They couldn't wait to welcome me back. And me, I was the undercover spy who was going to help bring an end to the war. What I didn't realize was that I had chosen a path destined to alienate me from the family I loved.

"The job directed me to use my family to spy on the Catholic community. At first, all the Agency asked me to do was to hang out in the various clubs and organizations and pass along information if I thought it was important. What's the buzz in the nationalist circles? What rumors have you heard from the republicans? Is there anything going down that we should know about?" "My uncles were prominent in republican circles and because of them, I could freely come and go in those organizations and I learned quite a bit. Some of my information saved lives, Cat. Make no mistake, I did some real good while I was there.

"Right up until the end, I was enjoying strong bonds with my family. I loved them all dearly and they loved me. Aunt Deirdre would cook these marvelous Sunday dinners and the whole family would come and gather around her long kitchen table. More often than not, there'd be an extra chair for a single girl that my aunt Nora 'just happened to know' and 'wasn't she a darling?'"

Catherine raised her eyebrows. "I'm not sure I want to hear about the darling single girls."

Catherine was right about that. Most of the girls were just passing encounters, but not Annie. Just thinking about Annie and the year we had together brought all those feelings back to the surface—feelings that needed to stay locked away where I put them sixteen years ago. What would my life have been like had I not had that falling-out, had I not returned to America in 1999, had I stayed with Annie? What would my life have been like had I not been blindsided? Had the rug not been pulled out from under my feet? I had no desire to revisit those memories now, nor did I wish to discuss them with Catherine.

"Nothing came of the darling girls," I lied. "But everything ended in 1999 when my uncles learned who I really was and what I had done behind their backs. I was the great deceiver. I was a fraud. I had betrayed them."

"Seriously, Liam, aren't you going a little overboard? What did your family think you were doing in Northern Ireland? Didn't they have an inkling that you weren't a liquor salesman?"

I shook my head. "Absolutely not. I certainly couldn't divulge that I was working for the CIA. I was sent there to secretly gather information. For five years I pretended to be working for a whiskey exporter. I even negotiated contracts for delivery of Uncle Fergus's crops to an Agency front.

"You sold your uncle's wheat to a phony CIA distillery?"

"Barley. It was barley. Single malt stuff. We brokered it to Jameson."

"And they never figured out you were CIA?"

"Not until the end. Oh, one time Uncle Fergus caught me talking to my station chief, Jim Westerfield. It was right before one of the Drumcree marches and I thought my uncle was suspicious. He questioned me about Westerfield, but Westerfield had credentials as a whiskey distributor and my uncle was satisfied. He trusted me. And of course, there we have the crux of the matter. My uncles trusted me."

Catherine nodded. She understood—it was all about trust, or lack thereof.

"Cat, my family took me in and loved me without qualification and I conned them. I played them for information. And when they learned the truth in 1999, it ended very badly. We haven't spoken since I left. I should have called. But every time I thought about it, I didn't know how to start the conversation, and every day that passed made it more difficult. Now I think it would be too awkward to go to the funeral. There are bound to be a lot of bad feelings."

"Well, staying in touch is a two-way street. He could have called you as well."

I shook my head. "Not the way it ended. I had to be the one to make the first move. And I didn't."

"What really happened in 'ninety-nine? What was so earth-shaking that it destroyed your relationships?"

I took a sip of coffee and a deep breath. "It all started with a guy named Seamus McManus. He was a technician, an IRA bomb maker. He designed and set off a petrol bomb in the Belfast Arms Hotel in 1975, killing twelve people including three children. Two years later he was arrested, tried, convicted and sentenced to life in prison by a judge who called him a monster. He sat in Crumlin Road Prison for twenty-two years."

"Don't tell me they released him."

I nodded. "In 1998 the Troubles officially ended with the signing of the Good Friday Peace Agreement. I say officially because there were still plenty who wanted to keep fighting. The GFA called for the release of four hundred prisoners, and McManus was one of them. He was paroled in 1999.

"One night, barely a month after his release, with his bones full of hate and his belly full of Guinness, he clubbed a Protestant aid worker to death with an iron pipe. He was rearrested and thrown into the Antrim jail. Westerfield got word that McManus was part of a plot to set off a bomb at the Orange Parade. He wanted to plant someone in the cell with McManus to pump him for information. I volunteered. They gave me the identity of Danny Foy and threw me into the cell with McManus. My cover story was that I was arrested for plotting to shoot up a Protestant lodge. I spent two days with McManus and I got it all. Everything. The where, the when, and the names of all the conspirators that McManus was plotting with. As a result, eight men were rounded up and their guns and bombs were confiscated. The planned attack never went off. The eight terrorists got life sentences. I did my job and I was damn proud of it."

"So what was the problem?"

"Later in the week, after one of Aunt Deirdre's Sunday dinners, we were sitting on the front porch—Uncle Fergus, Uncle Eamon and me—when suddenly, out of the blue, Uncle Fergus turns to me and says, 'Kevin Donnelly told me that he saw you coming out of the Antrim jail last Tuesday with Mr. Westerfield. What the hell were you two doing there, Liam? Selling whiskey?'

"I hesitated. I couldn't tell him the real reason. I tried to bluff my way through it, but I must have had guilty written all over my face. 'Nothing,' I said quietly.

"'Nothing?' he said. 'Nothing at a jail? You weren't sitting in there talking to Seamus, were you now?'

"I don't know how he knew. My uncle had deep contacts everywhere, so he must have found out. 'I can't tell you about it,' I said. 'I'm sorry.'

"Uncle Fergus stared at me. He looked right inside of me. He bowed his head and slowly shook it back and forth. 'How long, Liam?'

"My charade was over. My disguise was gone and I stood naked before my uncles. And even then, at that moment, I couldn't own up to it. I was too afraid to answer, too afraid of losing their respect, their love. Too afraid of being cast out, as indeed I would be.

"'How long for what?' I stammered.

"'C'mon, son. The U.S. intelligence service. How long have you been snooping for 'em?'

"I let out a deep breath. There was nowhere to hide. 'Since I got here,' I said. 'Since 1994. Seamus McManus was a killer. He told me an attack was coming down in Portadown. He knew everything—the time, the location, the names of all the raiders and where the arms were stashed. I was planted to get the information and I got it. And I'm not sorry. I saved a lot of lives, Uncle Fergus. People would have died. I interceded and that's what I've been doing here in Northern Ireland.'

"'No liquor distribution?'

"'No, sir. I lied to you.'

"My uncle closed his eyes. 'All this time you've been gathering information, your so-called *intelligence,* from me and Eamon and Robert?'

"I nodded.

"'And using it to arrest republicans?'

"'The bad ones.'

"'For all these years, Liam, you've been dishonest with us?'

"I nodded again. What could I say?

"My uncle pursed his lips, looked at Eamon and stood to dismiss me. There were tears in his eyes. "Of all the people I know . . . I never thought it would be you, son. I don't think you and I have anything more to say to each other, Liam. You best be off now.' I walked off the porch, turned around, looked back and saw him hanging his head. That was the last thing he ever said to me."

Catherine took a seat at the end of the couch, tucked her legs and patted the cushion for me to come sit beside her. Her blond hair lay gently on her white cable-knit. Her smile was warm and kind. I looked into her blue eyes and drew comfort from them. I've been enamored of this woman since we were in high school and I considered the fact that she was now my wife and the mother of my son to be an ongoing daily miracle. "Come sit," she said.

"'You best be off now,' my uncle said, and I lost the best friend I ever had. The only father figure I can really remember. He was the only link to my early childhood, back when we all lived within a few blocks of each other in Belfast's Lower Falls."

"Before you moved out to the farm?"

I nodded. "I left the Falls when I was four and I don't have many memories of those days. I can barely remember my house and the room I shared with my sister. We all lived in terrace houses—narrow town houses all linked together with common walls on each side. They were called 'two up, two down' because they had two rooms on the first floor and two bedrooms on the second.

"The Lower Falls was a battlefield, but I was too young to know what was going on. I remember hearing gunshots, seeing British soldiers running down the street with their rifles and watching as they busted down our door and screamed at my mother. I didn't know why. I just knew it scared the hell out of me. In 1975, my dad died, my mom was hospitalized and I was sent to live with Uncle Fergus on his farm outside of Antrim."

"You said you had a sister. What happened to her?"

I shook my head and sighed. Memories buried away were now bubbling up. Catherine was opening too many floodgates. I got up from the couch, put down the coffee, grabbed a beer from the fridge and stood at the windows watching the neighbor water her parkway.

"I did have a sister," I said after a few minutes. "Her name was Molly. She was a couple years older and she died the same year as my father. I don't know the circumstances and my mother never wanted to talk about it. It was a subject I was never permitted to raise with my mother. I don't have many memories of Molly, but I do recall she was a happy child. She danced around the house and giggled a lot. She had long, curly red hair. She died before I moved out to Antrim."

Catherine's eyes glistened and she blinked away a tear. Simpatico. Cat and I share the same wavelength and it didn't take much imagination for her to surmise what had probably happened to my sister.

I tried to shrug it away. "It was Belfast, Cat. Life was cheap and fragile. That's why we all ended up in Antrim. But the grass wasn't much greener and relations between Catholics and Protestants weren't any more cordial. My mom finally gave up and packed us off to Chicago."

"But you didn't come to Chicago right away. You said you lived with your uncle," Catherine said.

"That's right. For six years. My mother was sick and didn't come out to the farm for several years. When she did, it was just to get us ready to move to America. We moved in 1981. She had cousins in Chicago, in the Bridgeport neighborhood. She closed the door on Ireland and never looked back. She didn't take any furniture, any pictures or memorabilia. Nothing. She put it all behind her like a bad dream. She cut off all communications."

"How did he die, your dad?"

"I don't really know the details. I was only four. They said he died in an accident. He was visiting someone and was killed in a car accident."

"And your Uncle Fergus was his brother?"

I nodded. "There were five Taggart siblings. Eamon was the oldest. Dad was second. Then Fergus. Aunt Nora was four years younger than Dad and died in 1999. Robert was the baby. I remember being scared, lost and alone when I was sent to Antrim but they took me in and loved me like a son, Cat, all of them.

"When I came back to Antrim in 1994, we reconnected like we'd never been apart. The love was still there, strong as ever. But five years later, my duplicity destroyed it all and I left under bitter circumstances. As the years went by, I should have made amends. At least I should have tried."

"Liam, don't beat yourself up. You made a courageous choice to accept a post in Northern Ireland and you did it for the right reasons."

"I don't know if it was courageous or foolish or ambitious. Are any of those acceptable reasons for lying? I betrayed my family."

"You did what you were sent to do. You were a spy. By definition, spies deceive people. Surely, you knew what you were getting into. The fact that it ended as it did, as we lawyers would say, was an assumption of the risk. Your motives were good, but you had to accept the possibility that members of your family were active in the Troubles. I mean, isn't that why you got the job?"

The Agency sent me to gather information, which made me professionally dishonest. Had I told my uncles the truth, they would have kept me out of the loop. I had no business taking the assignment. Nothing justifies lying to your family. Was I filled with some mixture of arrogance, conceit and self-importance? I had just come out of the marines, spent a year at Langley, and put in for the transfer, certain that I could help make a difference in my native land. Didn't I consider the possibility that I would be lying to my family? I shrugged at Catherine. "I didn't give it as much thought as I should have."

She reached over and gave me the medicine that only she could dispense. She hugged me tightly. "I understand," she said softly. "And it's okay. I still believe you did the right thing."

"I loved my uncle Fergus, Cat, and I don't think he ever forgave me. We never spoke again."

Catherine squeezed my hand. "I know you feel guilty, but *they* called *you* today, Liam. They want you to come to the funeral. Maybe they realize, like you do, that it's time. You're letting sixteen-year-old bygones get in the way. You should go. Go see your family. Go say good-bye to your uncle Fergus. Go see your aunt Deirdre. Make your amends. I know wherever Fergus is, he'll be listening to you. You'll be sorry if you don't go."

She was right.

"Want to go with me?" I said. "I could use the moral support."

She gave me an *I'm sorry* smile and shook her head. "There are too many arrangements I'd have to make. It's too sudden for the baby and me."

"It's too sudden for me too."

She gave me a kiss to end the conversation. "You should go."

Two

· · ·

THE SEVEN-HOUR AER LINGUS flight gave me time to reflect and compose responses to the questions I knew would be coming once I arrived. Why did it take a funeral to get me back here? Why haven't I called? Am I still with the CIA? Or maybe they'd get right to the point—why did you do it, Liam? Why were you a stool pigeon? How could you turn on your own people? Or, maybe they'd put it more graphically: how could you sleep with the flippin' RUC? By the end of the flight I'd come up with no answers.

The phone rings and life's direction changes. What if I hadn't picked up the phone? Would Uncle Fergus still be alive? What if I had called first? Would that have changed history? Would he have answered the phone? Could I have made amends? Damn you, Fergus, for dying before I could make amends.

Uncle Fergus knew me in diapers. People like that—parents, grandparents, aunts, uncles—they are the repository of precious memories. They are the keepers of family history. Now who will remember for me? Who will prompt me about the time I got the fishhook stuck on my leg and I cried and cried, not because it hurt, but because I had put a hole in my new trousers? With Fergus gone, who will engage me in conversations about the time I was chased by a baby goat, and who will laugh until his sides hurt? My father was gone, my mother was gone and now my Uncle Fergus. Family deaths cut off the highway to treasured memories.

"I don't think you and I have anything more to say to each other, Liam. You best be off now."

I should have made amends.

W E CIRCLED DUBLIN BAY and set down shortly after 6 a.m. I was tired. I hadn't slept and I was dreading the reunion and how to explain the vagaries of my past behavior. Most of all, my heart was heavy with the loss of my beloved uncle. What did Janie mean when she said we'd talk about his death when I got here? Why was she evasive? I hate to think of the alternatives.

I picked up an Audi at the rental agency and reacquainted myself with driving on the left side of the road. A few tire scrapes on the shoulder curbs and I was good to go. Actually, I didn't need to rent a car at all. Janie had offered to pick me up. But I respectfully declined, wanting to preserve the freedom to come and go on my own. I was unsure of the upcoming reception and I needed the ability to claim exhaustion or some other lame excuse and not be tethered to Janie.

My route to Antrim took me up the coast and through the middle of Belfast, capital of Northern Ireland, second largest city on the island and ground zero for the Troubles. I was taking my time. I didn't want to be the first one at the church, standing there greeting my estranged relatives one by one as they arrived. I intended to keep a low profile, sit in a back pew and fade into the woodwork.

I arrived in Belfast at eight thirty and Antrim was only forty minutes away. To kill time, I parked the car and strolled over to the Titanic Quarter, Belfast's sparkling waterfront development, all new since I'd last been here. Gone were the old shipyards where the White Star Line built its storied ocean liners. In their stead were high-rise apartment buildings, tony shops, cafés, offices, a harbor marina and a ten-thousand-seat indoor arena. Rising above it all was the *Titanic* Museum, ninety feet high and covered with brilliant metal panels.

I strolled along the walkway and stopped in a café. "I'd like a cup of coffee, a little cream, a little sugar."

"Americano?" said a young girl in a green T-shirt and matching cap.

"Who, me?"

"No, the coffee. Do you want a cup of Americano?"

I groaned. Welcome to Europe. "Can't I just get a cup of regular coffee? A little cream, a little sugar?"

She closed her eyes and exhaled through her nose. She was dealing with an idiot.

"An Americano is a shot of espresso with hot water added."

"I don't know why they call it Americano. No one in America drinks espresso and hot water."

She shook her head. "Here's a cappuccino. It's the best I can do." She didn't wait for me to answer. It was one pound forty.

I pointed to the museum. "When does it open?"

"The Iceberg?"

"Iceberg? I thought it was designed to resemble the prow of the *Titanic*."

She nodded. "It was, but everyone calls it the Iceberg. It doesn't open until eleven."

I thanked her and took a walk around outside of the museum. Because I would soon face my family, I felt a kinship with the *Titanic*. Both of us were fated to sink soon after leaving Belfast. I took a seat on a park bench to watch the seagulls and ruminate over hurtful discords exchanged before I left. All these years and not a word. Out of touch. Systems down. All connections lost. Sixteen years and it suddenly felt like yesterday. *Of all the people I know . . .*

I retrieved my car and took a slow ride through the old neighborhood, just to see if it had changed as much as the waterfront. It was a quiet sunny morning, but the serenity was deceptive. There was a turbulent undercurrent beneath the still waters. To emphasize the point, the ominous Peace Wall stood before me, twenty-two feet high, marking the border—Falls Road to the left and Shankill Road on the right. Mostly ornamental now, the wall divided the Catholic and Protestant neighborhoods. Forty-eight so-called "peace walls" still stood in Belfast, Derry and Portadown, with the majority of them right here in Belfast. Supposedly, plans call for their demolition by 2023, but as I made my way through the Falls, there they stood. Still operational if the need arose.

On either side of the wall, symbols of allegiances were boldly displayed, letting you know, should you be amnesic, upon whose turf you were treading. On the Shankill side, the Union Jack flew from lamp-posts and front porches, loudly proclaiming, "You are in loyalist territory." Murals on the sides of houses still depicted armed and hooded UVF soldiers with shoulder patches reading, "For God and Ulster."

Turn the corner onto the Falls Road and the Republic of Ireland's tricolored flags of green, white and orange fluttered in the morning breeze. This is nationalist turf, they said. Murals on this side depicted IRA martyrs, like Bobby Sands.

I pulled over at the corner of Albert and Falls Road. Here in 1997, Westerfield and I failed to prevent a unionist firebomb that took the life of a Catholic family. We knew about it, we phoned it in, but the RUC couldn't get there in time. It was a failed mission that resulted in the arrest of four unionists, but didn't prevent the slaughter. The black residue from the firebomb still stained the bricks beneath the front window, metaphorically reminding me that the Troubles cannot be washed away.

I drove slowly through the Lower Falls and stopped in front of my childhood house on Cairns Street. Here, on the sidewalks where I rode my trike, my memories came out to greet me. The Reilly twins next door. The ice-cream cart in the late afternoon. My dad coming home from O'Shea's with a metal bucket full of Guinness. I could see them all and they brought a smile to my face.

Then I remembered the armored trucks that came speeding around the corner and the packs of soldiers who jumped out with rifles pointed. And the mothers who rushed out of their houses to kneel on the sidewalk and bang their galvanized garbage can lids as hard as they could on the concrete to sound the alarm—the Brits, the RUC, they're here, beware.

I could hear the neighborhood melodies, the cacophony of the Lower Falls: Irish tunes, portable radios, childhood chants. And the ominous sounds as well: claps of rifle fire, women and children screaming and the uniformed members of the Royal Ulster Constabulary standing over cowering mothers shouting, "Tell us where the guns are stored and we won't hurt you or your babies." I remembered my mother holding me close and burying my head in her body so I would not see. But I could hear. I hear still.

I drove out of the Lower Falls, out of Belfast, and meandered along the southern route toward Antrim, through the pastoral countryside, all in an effort to waste more time before arriving at the funeral. It was August and the fields were awash in in hues of barley, wheat and oats. I pulled off and stopped for breakfast at Grainger's Mill.

A pretty young waitress with a loose ponytail and a flowered apron set out a place mat and silverware and smiled. "You're not from around here, are you?" she said. "I can tell, you know. What I recommend to you is the Irish breakfast. It's what the locals'd order." She bit her bottom lip in a cute, coy expression.

"Who says I'm not from around here? I'm an Irishman."

"Go on about you," she said with a squint and a smile that dared you to test her.

"I am in truth an Irishman," I said with my hand on my heart. "But I've been away."

She flashed her infectious smile at me. "Well then, Mr. Irishman, will you have the Irish breakfast today?"

"Why not?"

I knew why not when she brought it to the table. Healthy portions of bacon, sausage, black and white pudding, eggs, potatoes and Irish soda bread served on three plates. I stared wide-eyed, mouth open, and she giggled.

"As I suspected, you're not from around here. Nor are you up to eating a hardy man's breakfast, are you now?"

I shook my head. "I'll not argue with you."

"Around here we say, 'You eat your breakfast like a king, your lunch like a prince and your dinner like a pauper.'"

"I think I'll just be a minor administrative assistant today."

I ate my eggs and soda bread, drank my tea, tipped her most generously, for which she was demonstratively grateful, and left to attend the funeral of my beloved uncle.

"I don't think you and I have anything more to say to each other, Liam. You best be off now."

S T. MICHAEL'S, A FIVE-HUNDRED-YEAR-OLD GOTHIC church, sat perched on a hill beside a river named Sixmilewater. The car park was nearly full when I arrived and the moment I pulled in I saw Janie. She was standing alongside her car in a black jersey dress, having a smoke. When she saw me she flipped her cigarette, walked quickly over and threw her arms around me.

"So glad you're here, Liam." She slipped her hand in the crook of my elbow and led me toward the church. "Everyone will be so pleased to see you."

"Maybe not everyone."

"Anyone who's not will have to answer to Janie," she said forcefully.

We walked into the vestibule where the congregants had quietly gathered around my uncle's casket waiting to follow him into the nave. My aunt Deirdre, a black veil covering her head, held her hand firmly on the casket. She would hold on as long as she could to the man she'd loved for so many years.

My arrival turned a few heads and some acknowledged me with a nod. We stood off to the right, next to my uncle Robert, Janie's father. Normally, he was the jovial Taggart, with cherry cheeks, a generous paunch and a beer in his fist. Today he had dark circles under his eyes. He warmly shook my hand. "Welcome back, Liam. It's good to see you."

"Good to see you as well," I answered. "I just wish it weren't under these circumstances."

"As do we all."

I leaned my head sideways and whispered to Janie, "How did he die, Janie? What did you mean we'd talk about it?"

"He was killed, Liam. Murdered in cold blood."

Somehow I knew that was coming, but all the same, her statement resonated in my bones. I wanted more information but then the organ sounded its somber chords and the pure white pall was draped over the coffin. A soloist began a wistful rendition of "Danny Boy" and we silently filed into the church, taking my uncle to his final repose.

Once in our seats, I whispered to Janie, "How? By whom?"

"He was shot in the chest. And we have not a clue."

"No suspects? What do the police think?"

"Who knows? There's no love lost between Uncle Fergus and the local gendarmes and we don't expect much effort to solve the crime." Then the mass started and she put her finger to her lips.

So that's what Janie meant when she said the family needs me. She could just as well have said, "Let's put aside your past transgressions, Liam, we need your skills. The Police Service of Northern Ireland, the PSNI, cannot be counted on to bring the murderer to justice. You may have been a turncoat, but we want your investigative experience to solve the crime." I hoped not. I hoped she wanted me here because she considered me family.

The mass turned out to be rather lengthy, with many taking to the pulpit to say a kind word. Fergus had lived in County Antrim for over forty years and owned a pleasant patch of farmland south of Antrim town. Within his Catholic community, he was well respected, notwithstanding the animus they probably held for me, and they praised his memory. There were also Protestants, friends of Fergus's, business associates and town leaders, who came to pay their respects and honor him. But the most poignant eulogy was delivered by his brother, Uncle Robert.

When it was Robert's turn to speak, he walked slowly to the pulpit, his head bowed. In his right hand he carried a handkerchief and he used it often to blot the tears. In his left, he held a handful of notes that he never consulted. It took him a few moments to get himself together.

"I thank all of you for coming and joining me in taking my brother to his eternal rest. And here we gather in this church, as we've done so many times before, to bury yet another precious soul, yet another good man, yet another victim of our country's violent, sectarian hate. And you have to ask yourselves, why is this still going on? Didn't we sign a peace agreement almost twenty years ago? Didn't we lay down our arms in 2005? Fergus has led a peaceful life for decades," he said, pronouncing my uncle's name in Irish dialect as *Fearghus*. From time to time Robert's voice would catch and he'd stop to compose himself, but he delivered his address with resolve and grace.

"A man of peace he was, even back in times of discord and hostility. He always counseled peace. Some may say he was deeply involved with the IRA, and to that we'll not argue, but his was the voice of peace. I can still see him as a young man on the corner of Divis trying to calm the angry ones and separate those who were there to fight."

Uncle Robert stopped and wiped his eyes. "We all know that my brother lost his darling Margaret to an Ulster mob when she was only twenty-four, leaving him with two wee lads. Did he have cause for a lifetime of retribution and retaliation? Did he have justification? Aye, that he did." He nodded solemnly. "But that was forty-five years ago. Those were the so-called bloody days when retribution and retaliation were the daily news. Not *now*. It's not supposed to be happening *now*. We're at peace.

"My brother was able to put those days behind him; why can't others? Why can't the devil who did this?" Robert paused and his voice quavered. "I'm sorry. My brother only wanted to live out his days in peace. And now, with deep sadness, those of us who loved him so, gather in this church to wish him the peace that eluded him on earth." He took a step down from the platform, stopped and said in a faltering voice, "Are we never to be done with those days?"

In silence, we all watched Robert slowly take his seat in the pew beside us, and the silence continued for several minutes before the eulogies resumed. But the words "retribution" and "retaliation" lingered in my mind. Had a long-dormant seed now germinated? Did a deeply rooted retaliation choose this time to burgeon? Were we truly not done with those days?

I'm sure that many other good things were said about Fergus during that morning service, but my thoughts were otherwise engaged. The professional side of me wanted to know when the murder happened, where it happened, what happened the day before, the month before and who were the possible suspects? Was this a dispute leftover from the Troubles? Was this a latent payback for an old IRA attack? I didn't think that Fergus had much money or property, a common motive to kill an elderly relative. Why did someone want to murder my uncle?

My distracted state must have been apparent because Janie patted my arm and whispered, "There's a meeting tonight. The family will all be there and we'll talk about what should be done."

Following the service, Janie walked me down the hill to the cemetery. It was there that Uncle Fergus was laid to rest. Several of us stood in the misty rain. Robert wrapped his arms around Deirdre and the two of them sobbed heavily. Other than the liturgical prayers offered at the graveside, very little else was said.

THREE

...

THE GATHERING OF FAMILY members was held at Doogan's, a small stone public house on High Street. I knew it to be one of my uncles' haunts. Doogan closed the bar for us, and depending on one's preference, he'd pour a pint of Guinness or a tumbler of Jameson. Or both. On the house.

Doogan tapped the bar and raised his glass, "May that dear old rascal *Fearghus* be safe in the arms of heaven before the devil learns he's gone. *Sláinte.*"

"*Sláinte,*" was the echo.

"Aye," said Robert. "And here's to me brother. To live in the hearts we leave behind is never to die."

The family was strewn about at several tables and booths. Janie and I had been the last to arrive and she made the introductions. "For those of you too young to remember, this is your cousin Liam from Chicago. He lives in America now, but he's an Irish Taggart through and through."

"Bah," I heard someone say under his breath.

True to her word, Janie snapped back. "There'll be none of that. We're all here for the same reason, and we'll not disrespect Uncle Fergus's memory." She raised her voice and a tumbler of whiskey. "And we will unearth the bastard that committed this heartless act and bring him to justice."

"Hear, hear," echoed the room.

She continued. "It was me that called Liam, and it was me that insisted that he come, though I'm sure he would have anyway. If any of you are disturbed by his presence, blame me. But I have this to say, the past is past. I know two things for sure: one, Uncle Fergus loved Liam like a son, and two, Liam Taggart is the finest private investigator in America. We'd be fools not to ask for his guidance in helping us find the murderer."

There were nods and grunts of approval, but I heard grumbles as well.

I stood and shook my head. "Look, I'm not America's finest anything. I came here to join my family and say farewell to Uncle Fergus. I didn't come here to be a detective. I'm happy to give you my two cents, but I'm afraid it'll hardly be worth any more than that."

Robert took center stage to lead the discussion, but his words were often sent in my direction. "Deirdre found him in the field on the side of the house. When he didn't come in for lunch, she went after him and saw him lying out there. At first she thought he'd passed out from the sun, but when she got closer and saw the blood, she called me right off."

Robert conveyed the scant facts that were known and those that weren't. The medical examiner confirmed the time of death at 10:30 a.m. Fergus was found lying faceup. There was a powder burn on his shirt, indicating he was shot from very close range. No weapon was found, there were no witnesses, and as of late, there were no suspects. The local police said the investigation would be ongoing and they'd appreciate any tips. Robert's tone was soft and somber, and he added, "I stand with Janie in welcoming my nephew Liam from America and in asking for his help to find the foul demon who killed me brother."

I turned and faced my family. "I know I've been gone a long time and some of you may harbor ill feelings, and I don't blame you. I'll give you what help I can, but I live three thousand miles away with a wife and a child and a business. I can't spend that much time here. I appreciate the confidence, but you don't want me to take the responsibility of leading an investigation. That should be left to the police."

"Well, we're truly grateful for whatever time you can spare, Liam," Robert said. "We hope you can find it in your schedule to give us a few days, because, you see, we don't have a lot of confidence in the constabulary."

Constabulary, PSNI, Gardaí, guard or coppers, call it what you will, my family had no use for the Northern Ireland police. Robert's soft-spoken statement, while I'm sure it was well intentioned, laid a heavy guilt on me. My extended family, all sitting there looking at me, and I'm telling them I'm too busy to help them find my uncle's killer. I swallowed hard. I had responsibilities at home, but I couldn't just walk away. I sat at the bar and poured another two fingers of Jameson.

"What do we know about the murder scene?" I asked.

Robert nodded. "Fergus was killed with a single shot to his chest, a nine millimeter. There were two sets of footprints, but there were no signs of a struggle. No bruises, no scratches, no defense marks on his body."

"Did anybody see a car, hear a noise or see someone running?"

"No." Robert was in every sense Fergus's counterpoint. Where Fergus was strapping, Robert was round and chubby. Where Fergus was a power, Robert was a thinker—the contemplative brother. His cheeks were plump and they bunched up when he smiled. His laugh was hearty and true. He displayed a perpetual warm smile and the deep lines around his eyes and mouth were there to prove it. Yet today, his eyes were bloodshot and bore testimony to the depth of his bereavement.

Doogan's was filled with my relatives. Fergus's older brother, Eamon, who I remembered from my childhood as robust, sagacious and a bit cranky, sat off in the corner. His beard was thinner now and he showed the frailty of age. As far as I knew, Eamon never married and had no children.

Fergus's youngest son, Riley, sat an adjoining table. When I was young and sent off to live on Uncle Fergus's farm, Riley became my best friend. Though a year younger than me, we were as close as twin brothers. In fact, Riley was closer to me than he was to his older brother, Conor. When I was back here in the nineties, Riley was living in Dublin working for some banking firm. Janie told me that he now worked for an investment house in Belfast in one of the downtown commercial buildings.

Some of my younger cousins, who were now in their twenties and thirties, were only brief acquaintances during my service years. I recalled them only as boys and I wouldn't have recognized them without an introduction.

"Is it possible this was a random killing?" I asked. "A robbery? Does anybody know of any motives?"

Robert answered with a flick of his hand. "'Twasn't random or a robbery, that's for certain. My brother was found with cash in his pocket, his watch on his arm and his wallet in his pants pocket with all of his cards."

Riley agreed. "Shit, Liam, my father was lying on his back with his mouth wide open." His voice cracked. "The police took crime scene photos. Maybe they'll let you see them."

"Were there any recent threats? Known enemies?"

"Ha!" Uncle Eamon said, standing to make his point. "A million enemies and then some. But nothing in the last twenty years. God knows, my brother was a marked man during the Troubles. You yourself were rattin' on him, Liam. You oughta know."

I hung my head. I knew this was coming. Time to face it. "Can we clear the air on our past differences, if for no other reason than to turn the page?" I said quietly. "We all know I was working with the CIA. We all know the Agency was supporting the peace process, and—"

"Aah, the bullshit," Conor snapped. "You were a foockin' rat, Liam Taggart. Ya cannot deny it."

Janie bounced to her feet and pointed. "He doesn't have to deny anything, Conor. Didn't you just hear him? He acknowledges he was with the CIA, he doesn't deny a damn thing. I begged him to come and he's here, ain't he? You want to find out who killed your father, Liam's our best bet. You want to leave it to the PSNI? Half of 'em are former RUC. How anxious do you think the Ulster Protestants are going to be when it comes to finding Uncle Fergus's killer? Hell, they probably wish they did it themselves, and maybe they did. They'll make an official report that'll say, 'Killed by his own IRA. Good riddance.' And then they'll close their files. Myself, I'm counting on Liam."

Eamon shook his head. "Conor's not wrong, Janie. He did snoop on us."

That was enough for me. "I own up to it. Okay? I was a professional spy. Everybody happy now? I worked for the CIA and I used information I got from you and everybody else to save lives and help bring the goddamn war to an end. I'm not proud I lied to you, but what I did was right. If that pisses you off, I'm sorry. I'll take the next plane back."

"What's past is past," Robert said quietly. "Let it go, Conor."

"Uncle Robert's right," Riley said. "Liam's offered to help and I for one am going to accept his offer."

Eamon nodded sharply, looked around the room and stepped to the bar. The stiffness in his eighty-year-old joints made his gait unsteady. "I'll take your hand, son. I can't forget, but I will forgive." His grip was firm.

"Thank you, Uncle Eamon. That means a lot to me. I'm sorry I haven't stayed in touch. I should have, I should have taken the initiative, but I didn't and that's on me. The sixteen years I could have connected with my family are lost to me. I regret it deeply." Turning to the group, I said, "You all knew Uncle Fergus well, and spent time with him. To the extent I can provide any help, please let me know if any ideas, motives or suspects come to mind."

A tall, young man, in a red T-shirt raised his hand. "I don't know if you remember me, Cousin Liam, my name is Sean. I'm Conor's son."

I smiled. The last time I saw Sean he was a freckled-faced boy. "Sure I do. You were a little smaller back then."

"If we come up with something we think might be important, I mean any of us, what are we supposed to do? When you're in America, who's going to coordinate this? Are we supposed to give it to the police?"

"Good question. It's never a bad idea to give information to the police, but among yourselves, I leave it up you. Janie might be a good choice."

Janie shrugged her shoulders and nodded.

While we talked, I kept an eye on Conor, sitting off in a booth by himself. He was maybe forty-eight now, with an athletic build and trendy clothes. A pricey bracelet hung on his wrist. From time to time he'd curl his lip in disgust like all this was leaving a sour taste in his mouth. Although I hadn't seen him since 1999, I remember Fergus's oldest son as an unpleasant, arrogant pain in the ass. We never really got along. In fact, I'd witnessed many a heated, gloves-off argument between Conor and his father. Now he started shaking his head. I decided to flush him out. "What's on your mind, Conor?"

"I've listened long enough to this whodunit bullshit," he said. "We all know you're a detective in Chicago, but this ain't Chicago. We don't have any gangsters here. This wasn't done by some corrupt politician. Janie's no more a coordinator than the man in the moon. Everybody knows she can't even coordinate her own relationship. Why don't we hire a real private detective, one who works here in the North? An Irishman. To be frank, Uncle Eamon, I'm not ready to forgive Liam for betraying my father and the family. I'd just as soon he board his plane and get his two-faced ass back to Chicago."

Robert interrupted him. "That matter is closed, Conor, and we'll not bring it up again. If you don't want to participate, we'll move on without you. But we'll accept no interference and they'll be no more insults thrown in Liam's direction."

With that remark, Conor threw down the rest of his whiskey and said, "Then you can all play your make-believe detective games and be junior coppers, but I'm looking into getting us a professional. In my business, I know plenty of them." He turned and walked toward the door. "And don't give me this *participate* crap. I'm his oldest son, you'll not cut me out. If anyone's calling the shots, it's going to be me." And he walked out.

In a booth along the inner wall, Aunt Deirdre sat alone. She held a white handkerchief in her hands and frequently covered her eyes. As Conor left, she hissed and said, "Good riddance."

Janie leaned over and spoke softly to me. "She's in bad shape. She and Uncle Fergus were together for more than forty years and now she seems lost. She doesn't accept any solace and she doesn't want to open up to anyone."

Although thinner than I remember, she was still very lovely and every inch a lady. "I always loved her," I said. "For six years she was my mom. Truth be told, she was warmer to me than my mom ever was. I've missed her dearly. I'm ashamed that I haven't called her, but I always assumed she felt the same way as my uncle and I didn't know how to start the conversation."

"You're going to have to get over that. They both loved you. You need to go to her."

Robert watched Conor leave, and sadly shook his head. Then he turned to the rest of us and announced, "My brother's solicitor, Malcolm O'Neill, will be reading the will tomorrow at two o'clock. He's in the Union Building on Railway Street. If any of you want to attend, you'll be welcomed. Liam, we'd like you there." With that, the meeting ended.

In the parking lot, I asked Janie if I could get into Fergus's home. She shook her head. "It's cordoned off. There's yellow tape around it and they've padlocked the doors."

"Have they posted a guard?"

Janie shook her head. "I don't think so."

"Good. I'm going to head over there tonight."

"I'll go with you."

I smiled at her spunk. "It's better that I go alone."

"Well, be careful. The PSNI officer in charge of the investigation is Inspector Farrell McLaughlin. He's a stickler for the rules. He'll lock you up if he catches you in there. He's an old-timer, a wise, shrewd type. When you talk to him, you know that there's a lot going on behind those eyes. He can be gruff, but he's not a bad guy. I met him years ago." She smiled and tilted her head. "His grandson always had a fancy for me."

I had to chuckle, and thought to myself, what young Irishman wouldn't? I gave her a hug and headed off to check into my hotel in downtown Antrim.

FOUR

· · ·

IT WAS NEARLY MIDNIGHT when I pulled up to Fergus's farmhouse, a country cottage of wood and stone nestled beneath a canopy of oak and poplars, set back a couple hundred yards off the road. The area was pitch black but for the faint glow of a crescent moon. As Janie had described it, I found the house cordoned off with yellow tape. The windows were dark and I walked toward the front door holding a small flashlight. It was padlocked.

A walk around the house confirmed that the windows were all locked and the back door had been padlocked as well. Then, remembering my childhood, I went around to the side facing the pasture. Behind the evergreen bushes I found what I was looking for, the metal covering on the abandoned coal chute. I lifted it open and lowered myself into the basement.

I hadn't been in my uncle's house in sixteen years, but I knew where everything would be. There were tools hung against the wall and storage boxes stacked beside the furnace. Same boxes in the same places. I climbed the stairs and opened the door to the kitchen, surprised at how time had managed to stand so still. Was I opening the door to 1998? To my right was the long wooden table where Aunt Deirdre would serve her family dinners. Where I'd first met Annie. And standing right before me was the spirit of my uncle frying eggs and sausage for my breakfast, standing tall, his suspenders over his white T-shirt, a proud smile on his face. A vision that disappeared when I smelled cigarette smoke. Someone was in the house.

In the darkness of the living room, off in a corner, I could barely make out a solitary figure.

"Well, well, Liam Taggart, I should have known. You startled me, son."

"Aunt Deirdre."

"Came in through the coal chute, eh? Pull up a seat," she said in a voice weakened from crying. She struck a match, lit a candle and emerged from the shadows. She was settled deep into a tufted wingback chair, her legs crossed, a cigarette in one hand and a cocktail glass in the other. An open bottle of Bushmills sat on the end table. She picked up another tumbler, poured it quarter-full and handed it to me.

I threw my arms around her and hugged her like I was ten years old. And there was never a doubt that she'd hug me back just as strong. Even when I was a child and I'd crossed the line, broken a rule, I could always return to her embrace and it was never withheld. Tears were flowing and she whispered, "I've missed you so, son."

"Please forgive me, Aunt Deirdre. I'm so sorry."

"There's nothing to forgive and you'll not bring it up again."

She was that kind of woman.

"What are you doing out here tonight, Aunt Deirdre?"

"What am *I* doing here? I live here. This is *my* home. Has been for forty years." She was still wearing the same black dress she wore at Doogan's. "No inspector's going to tell me I can't sleep in my own bed."

I nodded and took a sip of whiskey. In a fight between McLaughlin and Deirdre, my money's on my feisty aunt.

"I'm guessing you didn't jump down through the coal chute," I said.

She chuckled. "The back window. It never locked right. I suppose you're out here to look around for some clues or something?"

"Are there any here?"

She shrugged. "Might be, if I knew what to look for. But you're better off coming during the day when you can see what you're looking at. Can't see crap at night. They turned off the electric."

I laughed a bit. "I brought a flashlight."

"Come during the day. No one cares. McLaughlin's a good cop, but the PSNI's not going to waste any time looking into Fergus's homicide. We don't kid ourselves. They don't give a damn. Fergus is just another republican casualty. A statistic. Today they'll say isn't it a shame, and tomorrow they'll go on about their business and Fergus will just be someone who used to be." She covered her eyes and her intermittent sobs made her shoulders twitch. I sat down on the edge of the couch.

"I don't know what I'm supposed to do now, Liam. I don't have any-place to go but here. Truth is, I need to discuss it all with Fergus. He'd have the answers for me. He'd tell me what to do. I could always turn to him."

She took a healthy swallow of whiskey, set the tumbler down hard on the table and glared at me defiantly. "Stop looking at me like I'm some pitiful old woman. I'm entitled to my grief. I'm allowed to wal-low if I want to." Then her lips morphed into a grin and she let out a husky laugh. "Bet you didn't expect to find all this when you decided to come out here tonight."

"No, I didn't and that's for sure. I really didn't know what I'd find. I was hoping just to get a feel for what was going on in Uncle Fergus's life before he died. Maybe I'd come across something that would give me some direction."

"I'm looking for the same thing. Some direction. We're two blind fools in the dark." She sniffled. "It's been a long life for Fergus and me. You know, I first met the man more than forty years ago, the very day I was released from jail."

"Jail?"

She raised her eyebrows and grinned. "Yep." She poured another two inches of whiskey into her glass and swirled it around. "It was July, 1970. The Brits had put Falls Road under a twenty-four-hour curfew. 'Indefinite curfew,' they said. 'Indefinite.'" She put the glass to her lips, took a sip, leaned back to let the memories come to her, and addressed her words to the room as a whole, like I wasn't sitting there. "Twenty thousand Catholics living in the Falls and no one was allowed to go outside the house for any reason. People couldn't go to the store, couldn't get food, couldn't get bread, couldn't get milk. Babies were crying. Anyone who dared go out on the street risked being arrested or worse.

"I was living with my mother on Andersontown Road, a dozen blocks away. As the curfew was going into the fourth day, a buzz started going from house to house. 'Something's got to be done to help those folks,' my mother said. 'We can't let those children starve.' And we knew it had to be us. The women. 'Ladies, come out of your kitchens! Grab a box of eggs, a loaf of bread, a quart of milk. We're going to the Falls and no one's going to stop us.'"

Deirdre smiled, a proud smile. "So, one by one, we came out of our houses, just women and children, carrying milk and bags of food and we gathered together in the street. Thirty, forty of us to start, and then we were hundreds, I'm telling you hundreds, all walking toward the Falls. You've never seen anything like it. Rows of women and children marching straight into the Falls, chanting, singing, all carrying groceries."

She knocked back a solid swig of Bushmills. "The Brits tried to stop us, you know. The soldiers stood arm-in-arm and made a barrier across Leeson Street. Helicopter blades were churning overhead. Rifles pointed. Loudspeakers blaring. Truth is, those young soldiers were more scared than we were, but what were they going to do? Shoot the whole lot of us—women and children? Ha! We had 'em in a fix. They parted and let us pass."

She bit her lip and nodded proudly. "The women broke the curfew that day, Liam. But they arrested over three hundred of us. Threw us all into the center courtyard of the prison. They didn't know what to do with us. It was a nightmare for them, the whole thing, so they let us all go. We had a street fair that night, a celebration, and that's when I met Fergus. Drop-dead handsome, he was." She stopped. Her tears were flowing more freely now, breathing came in gasps and she held a cloth to her eyes. "Forty years. What am I supposed to do now? Tell me. Where am I supposed to go?"

I shook my head. I sincerely hoped that Fergus had made provisions for her in his will. Maybe he left her the house and the farm. Riley and Conor were successful businessmen. They didn't need it.

Then abruptly, she stood, set her glass down and beckoned me to follow. "Bring your flashlight. There's something I have to give you."

She led me into an alcove off the back bedroom that Uncle Fergus had used as an office. "The police haven't searched the house yet," she said. "They're supposed to come by on Saturday. They locked the house to prevent anyone from *disturbing the evidence*." She held up her fingers to put the phrase in quotes.

In the bottom drawer of an old battered desk, she extracted a walnut box. The size of a cigar box, it was highly polished with an inlaid flower design on the top and a brass keyhole on the front. "Fergus kept his important papers in this box," she said, holding it out. "He told me that if anything were to happen, I was to give this box to you."

"What do you mean 'if anything were to happen'? What's that supposed to mean?"

"For some time, Fergus has been on edge. He was like a Doberman that sensed an intruder and stood ready with his ears up. At first I thought he was being foolishly paranoid, maybe a leftover from the old days. But he was serious. You'll ask me why and I'll tell you I don't know. Fergus shut me out when it came to anything dangerous. He said it was for my own good."

She held the box out for me again.

"Why me? Why did he tell you to give this box to me?"

"Of all the people in the world, he trusted you the most. He said, 'If something happens, give this box to Liam.'" She thrust the box into my hands. "The key is on a hook in the basement."

"What's in the box, Aunt Deirdre?"

She shook her head, shrugged her shoulders and turned to walk back to her Bushmills. She was finished with this conversation. She had done her duty.

I followed her. "Why me, Aunt Deirdre? Why not Riley or Conor or one of Uncle Fergus's brothers?"

She scoffed when I said Conor and receded into the darkness of the living room.

"Seriously, why me? The last time Uncle Fergus and I were together . . ."

"I know. I was there. 'You best be off.' It hit him hard, Liam, and he wept for days. Many times he thought about calling you, but he didn't know how to start the conversation. Stubborn bunch, you Taggarts. He even reached out to Annie. You know, the two of them have stayed pretty close through the years, but she said she hadn't been in touch with you either. So now you ask 'why me'? Because he loved you like no other."

When I heard all that, my legs went weak. I wiped the tears with the back of my sleeve. It felt like a golf ball was stuck in my throat and I stood there, numb.

I could have made amends after all. It would have been easy. For either one of us. It could have been done anytime with a simple phone call. And then it occurred to me. There never was a need to make amends. When you love someone that much, bad words, hurtful words, are like a covering of snow. They'll melt away in time.

"Are you going to stand there all night?" she called from the dark. "Or will you have a drink to your uncle?"

We clinked our glasses until we emptied the bottle. I stood to leave, a bit off balance, and Deirdre said, "One more thing." She handed me a white envelope with no writing on it. "I found this in our mailbox the day Fergus was killed."

I opened the envelope and a photograph slipped out and fell to the floor. It was a photo of the remains of a redbrick townhouse, severely ravaged by a fire. I shrugged. "Do you know what this is?"

"No idea. It looks like a place in the old neighborhood, but it obviously burned down."

I studied the picture. Terrace house, two up, two down. Just the shell of a house, just the carcass. It didn't mean anything to me either.

I turned for the door and Deirdre took my hand. "Don't punish yourself, Liam. He loved you strong. There's an old Irish proverb: 'May you never forget what is worth remembering, nor ever remember what is best forgotten.'"

FIVE

. . .

I DON'T RECALL EXACTLY how I found my way back to the
hotel. The next morning I awoke fully clothed with my arms
around the inlaid walnut box and my head throbbing. It took me a
few moments to get my bearings, remember what bedroom I was lying
in and why I had this box sitting on my chest. What was it about the
contents that were so important that they could only be entrusted to
me? Why not Deirdre? Or Riley, or Conor, or one of my uncles? Why
did she laugh when I said Conor? How did Uncle Fergus even know
I'd come back to Antrim? Maybe he shouldn't have taken that for
granted. Maybe he should have called *me* and made amends, just to be
on the safe side. I wonder if any of those scenarios went through his
mind before he died.

The box remained locked and the key was in my pocket, though I
don't remember going to get it in the basement. I was certainly in no
condition to examine the contents the previous evening, having been
grossly over-served in the dark of the living room. I leaned over to
check the clock. Ten thirty a.m. I was scheduled to meet Janie for
lunch at noon, and then walk with her to the solicitor's office for the
reading of the will.

I was curious to see what was in the box, but I had to clear my
head first. A hot shower, two cups of black coffee, and three aspirins
later and I was ready to tackle the mystery. I set the box on the desk
and opened it. No genie, no maps of buried treasure, no star sapphires.

Just groups of papers bound with rubber bands: bank statements, deeds to the farm and the adjoining rural property, stock certificates and yearly investor statements from Global Investments, Inc. I went through a few of the recent bank statements and learned that Uncle Fergus was not just some humble farmer. He had done all right. His bank balances were solid. The farm was owned free and clear. I couldn't tell what his investments were worth, but he appeared to be well off.

There were records of purchases and repairs on farm equipment, some doctor and pharmacy receipts, contracts with local grain storage companies and receipts for delivery of grain sold to breweries. On the bottom of the box was a sealed envelope. "Liam" was written on the face. I opened it to find a handwritten letter.

Liam:

It's been too many years and I deeply regret our separation, though I have never doubted for an instant that our hearts are bound together for eternity. No recriminations will be allowed, my son. We are two hardheaded Taggarts and we'll leave it at that.

If you are reading this, I am dead. Over the past several weeks, I have become alarmed over certain things that I have heard and seen. At first, I thought it was impossible. Now I've come to believe that I'm onto something, a danger that threatens everything I value, the entire treasure of a man's life. I pray that I'm wrong, and for that reason, I'm not going to name any names. I dare not slander an innocent person. But I intend to find out if my suspicions are correct and stop it in its tracks. God help this family if I fail.

I have endeavored to prepare my estate in order to benefit the ones I love. Malcolm O'Neill has the signed and notarized instruments. But here is my last request to you, my dear nephew—before my estate is closed, before anyone inherits anything, the circumstances of my death must be clear and certain. If I died of natural causes, then I guess it was my time. But, if the cause of my death is suspicious or the result of a homicide, then the person(s) responsible must be identified and brought to justice before my estate is distributed. I have given you the honor (or the burden—call it what you will) of seeing that my estate is properly handled. Liam, my legacy is in your hands. Take care, my son. You're the only one I can trust.

My warning to you: be careful and do not trust <u>anyone</u>!

With love,

Your Uncle Fergus

P.S. I have followed your career (including your recent jaunt to Israel to catch that evil jihadist). I've learned that you are married and have a child. I wish I could have met them. Know this: I am mighty proud of you.

I sat on the bed, read and reread the letter, and wept until it was time to meet Janie. What was he digging into? What was so dangerous that in Fergus's words, "threatens everything I value"? Why couldn't he have called me and brought me into this mystery weeks ago?

I MET JANIE AT the Emerald Inn, just up the block from O'Neill's office. She stared at me and scrunched her nose. "You don't look so good. Are you all right?"

"Thanks a lot, Janie. But flattery will get you nowhere."

"No, I'm serious. Your eyes are bloodshot, you have wrinkles on your wrinkles. You looked like you had a hard night in the Belfast pubs. You got drinker's remorse?"

"Something like that. Did Uncle Fergus ever say anything to you about death threats?"

She shook her head. "No. When men get to drinking, they talk about the Brits, the Ulster Volunteers, the paramilitary groups. They talk about their past involvement in the Troubles and we all know it's one part fact and three parts fiction. Back then death was knocking on the door, but things are different now. You think he was killed by an old enemy, the UVF or an Ulster Freedom Fighter?"

"The thought has crossed my mind."

Fergus's letter wasn't exactly informative. *"Alarmed by certain things"* could surely refer to a holdover from the sectarian war. Maybe an Ulster Volunteer or a Loyalist Volunteer who sought revenge for an IRA attack and held Fergus responsible. There could be plenty of them out there. But Fergus didn't say who he suspected. I suppose he could have been killed by a radical member of his own IRA, a staunch Provo seeking retaliation because Fergus wouldn't go along with or support a failed attack. Or was he killed by someone close to him, maybe a good friend or even a member of the family, perish the thought? Still, the thought has merit, otherwise, why postpone the inheritance until the killer is prosecuted? That would justify the comment, *"God help this family if I fail."*

Janie took a bite of her salad, dabbed at her mouth. "Well, who then?"

I shrugged. I didn't want to tell her about what I had read.

"Did you go out to the house last night?" she asked.

I nodded. "You were right. It's all cordoned off."

She looked up from her salad. "Deirdre was there, wasn't she?"

I nodded again.

Janie gave me that all-knowing smile. "She doesn't want to leave. As long as she stays there, she's still with Uncle Fergus. She can come and go every day as she has for the past forty or so years, and dwell in the essence of their relationship. There's still a lot of Fergus left in the house, if you know what I mean. When she moves away, that connection will be lost and she'll be conceding he's really gone, it's over. She's got quite a history, you know? As a young woman, she was a leader in the women's movement to break the Falls Road curfew, what they called the 'Rape of the Falls.'"

"She told me."

Janie nodded. "After Margaret died, Uncle Fergus found himself widowed with two young children. Conor was five and Riley was two. I can only imagine the chaos of a five-year-old Conor and Riley as a toddler. Uncle Fergus must have been a fish out of water trying to take care of those two wild boys. Deirdre stepped in to help him out."

"That was generous of her. She's always been that kind of a woman."

"She's all good. A heart as big as the Connemara. Eventually they moved in together." Janie smiled. "But it wasn't all charity. I don't know if you remember your uncle as a young man, but when he was in his twenties, he was dashing. I've seen the pictures. And Deirdre was quite a looker herself. They made a handsome couple. Still, not to take anything away from her, she did move in and raise those boys. She never had any children of her own. Riley and Conor became her children."

"She raised me too. When did she marry Fergus?"

She shook her head. "They never married. I guess they were the modern type—ahead of their time."

I tried to think of Uncle Fergus as the modern type. It didn't work. "I have no memories of Margaret, I was too young. I only remember Uncle Fergus with Aunt Deirdre and I always assumed they were married."

"Nope. Maybe they didn't want to spoil a good thing."

"Maybe, but they were living in a Catholic community forty years ago. It couldn't have been easy." I shook my head. "Meanwhile, Janie, what's going on in your life? The last time I saw you . . ."

She smiled. "I was in secondary school, a gangly teenager."

I tilted my head this way and that. "Not so gangly, as I recall."

"Liam!"

"You got a beau?"

She blushed a bit with a tight-lipped smile and nodded. "He's on the continent this week, otherwise he'd have been at the funeral. I talk to him every day."

"Tell me about him."

"His name is Charles. He's tall, taller than you, and very handsome. He was a Gaelic football player."

"The rugged type?"

"Sort of, but he's very polished. He owns a company that sells linen. Fine Irish linen. He ships to the continent, the EU, Russia, Croatia, I don't know." She shrugged her shoulders and smiled.

"How did you meet?"

She bit her lip. "In a bar. Six months ago I was with my girlfriends at Robinson's."

"In Belfast?"

She nodded.

I smiled. "I love that bar. Still have great music?"

"Every night. Well, six months ago Charles walked in the door, beelined right up to me and bought me a drink. Just like that. We've been dating ever since."

"That's great. I'm happy for you."

"He was on the continent at some business conference when Uncle Fergus died. When I told him, he offered to cut his conference short and come back, but I told him not to. He should attend to his company, I'd be okay."

"What's the name of Charles's company?"

"Northern Exports." She gave me a mocking glare of disapproval. "Are you going to check him out, Mr. Private Investigator?"

"Of course not," I said with a laugh, but I thought I might if I had the chance.

"Well, I really don't know all that much about what Charles does. His company buys linen from local mills and farms. He ships it to foreign markets."

"Just as long as he treats you well."

"That he does." Janie checked the time on her watch, folded her napkin and placed it on the table. "We have to go to Solicitor O'Neill's. This should be interesting."

I'VE WORKED FOR A lot of giant law firms—hundreds of lawyers, paralegals, secretaries and administrative staffers occupying multiple floors with winding staircases and marble reception areas. I didn't expect that in Antrim, but O'Neill's office was positively Dickensian. Dark, old and filled with antique furniture. The walls of the waiting area were covered in deep maroon wallpaper bordered by ornate wainscoting. A gray-haired receptionist in a dress with padded shoulders sat behind a large wooden desk. She was thin and stern and wore her hair in a bun. She didn't have an upright typewriter or a telephone switchboard with wires to pull in and out, but I sure had the feeling that we weren't too far away from those days.

Mrs. O'Donohue, the humorless receptionist, rose up from her chair as we came in. Her posture was as perpendicular as a fence post. She led us back to a conference room, where a dozen chairs were set around an oblong table. Deirdre, Robert, Riley and Eamon were already seated when Janie and I arrived. Conor entered a few minutes later.

Malcolm O'Neill, a gaunt man with wavy hair the color of tree bark, entered precisely at 2 p.m. His frameless reading spectacles hung on a chain around his neck. He carried a brown cardboard file at least six inches thick, which he set on the table. Mrs. O'Donohue silently took a seat at the far end with her pen and steno pad.

"My name is Malcolm O'Neill. I was solicitor and friend to Fergus Taggart for the last twenty-five years." Mrs. O'Donohue dutifully took down every word in shorthand. She never looked up. "We are here today for the formal reading of the last will and testament of Fergus Taggart. Would each of you please state your name loud and clear so that we may make a record of this proceeding."

As each of us stated our names loud and clear, Mrs. O'Donohue wrote them down.

O'Neill continued, "Are there any prefatory questions relative to the nature or propriety of our gathering this afternoon?"

Conor leaned back in his chair, checked his watch and said, "Yeah. Can we just get on with the reading and not take all day? I've got a business to run."

With his pointy nose in the air, O'Neill responded, "There are legal formalities to which we must adhere. You, of course, are free to leave at any time you wish. Your presence here is not compulsory."

Making sure to get in the last word, Conor added, "Okay, okay, let's just get on with it. Just read the damn will, let us know who gets what and then we'll each be on our way." Conor spoke fast, but not too fast for Mrs. O'Donohue.

O'Neill distributed a stapled set of papers, entitled *Last Will and Testament* to each of us. Then he laid a large manila envelope in front of me. It was sealed shut.

In sonorous tones, O'Neill said, "You'll see from the document before you, that Mr. Taggart instructed his executor, that is *me*, to first discharge the expenses of his final illness, ambulance and hospital care, which were minimal, given the tragic circumstances of his demise. Next, I am instructed to pay the expenses of his funeral, which I have done. Next, I am instructed to pay any outstanding debts and obligations. I have not yet been informed of any lingering debts but there is a statutory period of six months during which creditors may file a claim.

"Finally, the rest and residue of Mr. Taggart's estate is left to a testamentary trust. The designated trustee in whose hands the considerable estate is placed, is Mr. Taggart's nephew, Liam Taggart."

There was a general and immediate consensus of shock. Everyone sat with a stunned expression, except yours truly.

"Liam?" Conor said.

"Quite so," O'Neill said flatly. "The terms concerning the maintenance of the trust assets and the method, means and times of distribution to the named beneficiaries are set out in great detail in the trust document itself, which lays inside the envelope I have placed in front of Liam Taggart. Mr. Fergus Taggart has instructed that the trust itself must remain sealed to all but the trustee, pending the occurrence of a certain condition set forth in the instrument. Any questions?"

The family members all looked at one another and shrugged their shoulders.

"I'm sorry, Mr. O'Neill," Robert said, "but I don't think I understand. Who inherits my brother's property? His house, his money, his stocks and bonds?"

"At this particular time, no individual inherits anything. Your brother's property is to be held by the trustee in trust until a time in the future when all of the assets will be disbursed to named beneficiaries. It's all in the trust document. Quite simple."

"What beneficiaries and what times?"

O'Neill rose. "I'm afraid I'm not at liberty to disclose those details. The trust is sealed."

"What?!" yelled Conor. "What is this shit? What trust? Who are you kidding here? What do you mean, 'sealed'?"

O'Neill looked at Conor as though he didn't understand English. "I mean until the occurrence of the specified event, the terms of this instrument are private, confidential, sealed, secret—how else can I say this?—not open to anyone other than Mr. Liam Taggart and myself."

"What specified event, Mr. O'Neill?" Eamon said. "When will we know the contents of this envelope?"

O'Neill raised his eyebrows and nodded. "Fair question. Mr. Fergus Taggart specified that all assets were to remain in trust and not given to any beneficiary until the circumstances of his death were established. Mr. Taggart instructed that if he were to have died in any way other than by natural causes, then the assets were to be held and remain in trust until the person or persons responsible for his death were apprehended and suitably prosecuted." He smiled and nodded. "That is all. You are all discharged and free to go."

"Whoa, whoa, whoa, Mr. Solicitor," Conor said. "You mean that until my father's killer is caught and prosecuted, nobody gets anything? All his property just sits in limbo?"

"No, sir. It sits in trust. Liam Taggart, as trustee, will decide how the property is to be maintained until the final distribution. He has total authority until the condition is satisfied and the property is then distributed to the named beneficiaries."

"And we don't know who they are? And you're not going to tell us?"

"Correct."

"So we don't even know who will inherit what? We can't even find out the terms of his trust because you say it's a secret?"

"That is correct. You do understand it, after all."

Conor stood up and knocked his chair backward. "That's freakin' nonsense. I demand to know who inherits my father's property. You can't tell me it's left to some blind trust and I'm not entitled to see it."

"Well, I'm afraid I can. Those were your father's wishes."

Riley put his hand on Conor's arm and gestured for him to be seated. He spoke more calmly. "Why do we have to wait to learn who the beneficiaries will be? Even though you say the property must remain in trust, the ultimate division of the property is quite important. Who will inherit my father's farm? Who will inherit his investments? These assets need to be preserved. My father and I had certain investments together. What will become of them?"

"Damn right!" Conor said. "We have a right to know."

"Must I say this again?" O'Neill said in an annoyed monotone. "Because those were your father's wishes." Despite the growing tension in the room, O'Neill stood his ground. "It's all specified in the body of the trust. The trustee will know, as you say, who gets what, and the trustee is charged with the responsibility of preserving those assets for the ultimate beneficiaries."

Conor rose and slammed the table with his open palm. "I don't accept that. Some American we haven't seen in twenty years is going to tell me what will and won't happen with my father's estate? That's horseshit. This can't be legal. I'm going to head straight over to my lawyer. We'll blow this trust to hell."

"Before you go running off, young man, I must tell you that the trust has an *in terrorem* clause."

"And what is that supposed to mean?"

"Whomsoever should contest the provisions of the will or the testamentary trust, will be immediately disinherited, eliminated as a beneficiary, will forfeit his share and will be forever barred from receiving any distributions."

"That's not legal."

Malcolm smugly tilted his head back and raised his pointy nose in the air. "If you wish to test the legality, sir, you do so at considerable risk."

Conor sneered. "Test it? You're damn right we do. Everyone in this room is going to test it and defeat it. We're going to hire a lawyer and we're going to throw this thing out. And you too." He looked around the room. "I'm going to make an appointment with Michael Cooney as soon as I can. He's a tough lawyer. He'll get this bullshit trust thrown out. Who's with me here?" One by one, the relatives turned their heads or lowered their eyes.

"What's the matter with all of you?" Conor said. "Are you all that timid? O'Neill can't write some voodoo trust and turn over all our family's property to an estranged cousin and then keep it all secret. If those were my father's wishes, then maybe he was losing his mind. But I'm going to tell you right now, my lawyer will get this trust nullified and send Liam back where he belongs."

"Let's not be hasty, Conor," Robert said. "If you contest the will or the trust and some court determines that this terrorizing clause is valid, you'll lose your entire inheritance. Do you want to take that chance? Speaking for myself only, I trust Liam to do the right thing. If that's what my brother wanted, we should respect his wishes."

Conor's face was getting red. He looked for support among the other family members but he wasn't getting it. He started to storm out, but then reconsidered, made a U-turn and sat down with a snort. "I just can't believe you're letting this go, Uncle Robert. What if the killer is never found? Did you ever think of that? What if the freakin' police don't want to arrest him or prosecute him? Then what?"

O'Neill nodded. "You raise a valid point, Mr. Taggart. There is an end date. If the conditions do not occur within ten years, there are provisions for distribution of the assets at that time."

"Ten years? Are you kidding me?"

"No, sir. Ten years. And I am not disposed to kidding." O'Neill raised his eyebrows. "If there are no further questions, I have other matters that require my attention. Good day." With that, Solicitor Malcolm O'Neill left the room, followed by Mrs. O'Donohue. When the door was closed, Conor quickly stepped toward me and reached out to take the envelope. I put my hand on it.

"Give me the envelope, Liam. He was my father."

I shook my head. "Can't do it."

He reached for the envelope again and I grabbed his wrist. "Sit down, Conor. I didn't ask to be appointed, I haven't seen the document, I don't know what's in it, and this is a surprise to me as well. But Uncle Fergus trusted me and I'm not going to go against his wishes. Not now, anyway. I'm going to take the envelope back to the hotel, read it and then decide what to do."

Conor didn't move. He was a big guy, but I was pretty sure I could take him. Maybe he thought so too, because he took a step back. Standing over me, he said, "At least open it here and read it. Maybe it gives you permission to tell us more."

Again I shook my head. "I'm going to take this trust document with me and read it in private. Now back off."

Conor was trying to control his rage. He was breathing in and out of his nose like a bull. "Then go back and read it and do it quickly!" He raised his voice to a thundering decibel and slapped the table. "I want a report tomorrow! Understand?" He turned and headed for the door, then stopped. "And you better watch your ass, Liam. You're in my territory now."

After the door slammed, Riley let out a low whistle. "My brother has a low flash point and he can be a tough adversary. I'm sorry my dad put you in this uncomfortable position."

Riley was no sorrier than I. Now it became clear why Fergus didn't appoint Riley. At the very least, he didn't want a war between the brothers. I didn't know what I was ultimately going to do, but I was going to read the trust first. In private.

"Can you let us know something after you've had a chance to go through the document?" Riley added. "Like I said, my dad and I had some investments together. There are decisions that need to be made. I'd kind of like to know what I can do, sooner rather than later."

That was certainly understandable and stated in a civil way. Contrast that with Conor's *"I want a report tomorrow!"* But I had always known Riley to be calm, thoughtful and polite. He was a good friend.

The meeting ended, I took the envelope and walked back to my hotel. This being Conor's territory, I kept a close watch on my ass.

Six

• • •

THE FERGUS TAGGART TESTAMENTARY Trust ran twenty-two pages with numerous arcane and esoteric references, far beyond the comprehension of America's finest private investigator. I was in way over my head and reading through this document was giving me a headache. Besides, it was time to call Catherine anyway.

"What did you get yourself into?" she said.

"Get myself? I didn't volunteer. Uncle Fergus named me as the trustee of his estate. I don't know why he did that."

"It's pretty obvious, Liam."

"He could have just as easily named Aunt Deirdre, she's been his wife, sort of, for the past forty years. Or Riley. Or Uncle Eamon or Uncle Robert. They're all loyal and responsible."

"Somebody killed Fergus or had him killed. What's more, Fergus anticipated his own murder. Maybe he didn't want to involve Deirdre or Riley, or put them at risk, or maybe, heaven forbid, they're not beyond suspicion. What does the instrument provide for distribution to the heirs?"

"I know you're going to think me stupid, but I'm not sure. It's so convoluted, with words like 'hereinbefore' and 'whomsoever.' I need you to come out here and help me."

"Come out there? I can't just pick up, leave my practice and fly to Ireland. Did you forget, Ben is only seven months old? I can't imagine sitting on a plane with him in my lap all the way to Europe."

"I'll buy him a seat. Please."

"If you're going to be there a long time, we'll talk about it. For now, just scan the instrument and email it to me. I'll try to figure it out. Meanwhile, why don't you sit down with Mr. O'Neill and discuss it with him? He can explain all the terms to you. He's certainly in a position to advise you."

"I can't. It's because of Fergus's letter, the one in the wooden box. He told me not to trust anyone."

"Not even his lawyer?"

"He underlined anyone."

"I'm someone."

"In my trustee's discretion, I hereby determine that he didn't mean you. Why don't you come on out here?"

"Stop it. Send me the instrument and I'll give it my once-over."

ALTHOUGH I READ AND reread it, I gave up trying to make sense out of the trust agreement. I would just wait for Catherine's explanation. In the meantime, Janie called and asked that I join her and her boyfriend at Conway's Pub. That sounded like the best idea I'd heard since I arrived in Northern Ireland. I headed right over. I was familiar with Conway's. I had frequented the neighborhood bar on more than one occasion with Annie, back when I was on assignment in the nineties. One could always find a friendly face at Conway's.

Perched on a corner in a residential neighborhood, Conway's was a traditional public house. A huge stone fireplace dominated the long southern wall of the tavern. When I was here in the nineties there were comfortable sitting areas in front of the fireplace where pipes, cigarettes and other smoking materials were indulged along with one's pint of Guinness, which they would refer to as "a pint of Gat." Back then, the air would get quite smoky, enough to irritate your eyes and stink up your clothes. But not anymore. Northern Ireland's pubs were smoke free. On the opposite wall there were several wooden booths, and in the center, a smattering of tables and chairs were set about on the weathered floor. The tarnished brass chandeliers hanging from wooden beams gave a warm glow to the room. At the far end, a raised platform served as a stage where an Irish group was knocking out traditional tunes.

Janie stood and waved her hand wildly when I walked into the room, though she didn't need to wave, her smile was a beacon of light. She was sitting next to a guy who smiled as well and she wasn't wrong about his looks.

"Charles Dalton," he said with a firm handshake. He stood six-three, with broad shoulders, a slender waist and powerful forearms. He appeared to be a few years older than Janie. He had a full head of raven black hair combed back from his forehead and was dressed in expensive casual clothes. To top it off, he had brilliant white teeth. It was easy for a guy to dislike Charles. "And you're Janie's cousin from Chicago, the one she raves about?" he said.

"Be careful," I said. "Janie's given to rash hyperbole."

"Really?" He looked at her and raised his eyebrows. "What does she say about *me*?"

That was a loaded question that could not possibly have a good response. I begged off. "I cannot reveal a confidence."

"Awfully sorry to hear about your uncle," he said. "I was in Istanbul at a marketing conference when Janie called me. I told her I'd fly right back, but . . ." He shrugged.

"I understand you're in the export business."

He smiled with a bit of arrogance. "Oh, that and a wee bit more, I suppose. Northern sells a fair amount of linen to the EU, but I have a large personal portfolio, which I insist on managing myself. I enjoy trading. You know, looking for small inefficiencies in the market where I might make a play for few bucks, as you Yanks would say."

I had the impression that his definition of a few bucks and my definition of a few bucks might vary by more than a few bucks. "I heard you guys met at Robinson's?"

He flashed that broad smile, reached over, put his arm around Janie's shoulder and pulled her close. He was three times her size. "Best bar in the six counties. I go there quite often. It was just a lucky happenstance to meet Janie that night. I was supposed to meet another girl. I waited and waited but she stood me up, and there was Janie, just as cute as she could be." He kissed her on the cheek. "Lucky I was jilted, wasn't I?"

Just then the band finished a number and Janie grabbed my hand and pulled me up to the stage. "C'mon, Liam, I've heard that you sing a mean 'Roddy McCorley.' Get up there!"

I hesitated. "No, no, Janie. Don't do this to me." But she was forceful. "Who told you that? It was Deidre, wasn't it? Janie!"

The bartender ran up with a shot of whiskey and handed it to me. "The stage is yours, Liam. We're waitin'." The fiddle player nodded to his companions who picked up their instruments. "'Roddy McCorley,' gents."

I hadn't done this in years. I downed the shot, looked at Janie and said, "I'll get you for this." She laughed and was joined by others in the bar who smiled and prodded me on. I took a deep breath, grabbed the mic and started slowly.

"O-oh, see the fleet-foot host of men who come with faces wan . . ."

My weak beginning to the anthem brought polite smiles and nods from the gathering at Conway's, but in for a dime, in for a dollar and I plowed ahead.

"From farmstead and from Fisher's cot, along the banks of Ban . . ."

Thank God for the band behind me setting the beat. The crowd started clapping and keeping time with their feet. I got a little louder. And a little bolder.

"They come with vengeance in their eyes, too late, too late are they,
For young Roddy McCorley goes to die on the bridge of Toome today."

I started to hand the mic back to the guitar player, but the banjo picked up the tempo, a man ran up with another shot, and someone shouted, "You can't quit now. On to the second verse. You're doing splendidly."

I shrugged, downed the shot and continued to embarrass myself. While I sang and looked out over the crowd, most of whom had come here, to their local watering hole, to nurse a pint and enjoy a peaceful evening of music and neighborhood camaraderie, it occurred to me that these were my people, my Irish roots, my DNA. For the men and women, especially the older ones, the words to the traditional tunes came to their lips as natural as breathing. And when I got to the third line of the third verse, *"For Antrim town, For Antrim town, he led them to the fray,"* many stood and belted the line boldly, raising their beer glasses in salute.

I finished all four verses to a rousing round of applause for which I bowed deeply. "Another," someone yelled, but I shook my head.

"The honor was all mine, believe me, but I'm not going to press my luck. You've heard enough from me."

"Well done, cousin," Janie said, as I retook my seat at the table. Glasses of beer and shots of whiskey were sent over and for the rest of the night we didn't pay for a drink.

SEVEN

...

THE SUN SLICED THROUGH the hotel curtains and woke me far earlier than I had planned. My cell phone buzzed and I rolled over to pick it up. There was a text message from Catherine. "I'm awake for Ben's midnight feeding. If you're not sleeping, give me a call. Love you." Ireland was six hours ahead of Chicago, so it was indeed midnight back home.

"Hi, Cat. How's my honey and the world's most talented little tyke?"

"We're great, but a little sleepy. Your little tyke still gets hungry in the middle of the night. Liam, have you read this trust agreement?"

"Not really, I spent the night making a fool of myself in a pub."

"That's my Liam!"

"Cat, I started to read it, but it's too damn confusing."

She laughed. "I agree. They still use Old English phrases in their legal documents. But wow, Liam! Your uncle Fergus was certainly a distrustful person."

"With good reason, given the circumstances of his death. What does the trust say?"

"He starts off by appointing you as his trustee. If you refuse or are unable to act, then the Bank of Antrim is next in line as successor trustee. After the payment of his last expenses, he describes how he wants his estate divided. He has this strange condition precedent before the beneficiaries can receive their distributions . . ."

"I know. We have to catch his killer."

"Exactly. His will was what we call a 'pour-over will,' which means that everything Fergus owned poured into his testamentary trust at his death. So really, as trustee, you're in charge of the whole estate. You'll have to manage it as you see fit. And Liam, one of the first provisions of the trust is to immediately establish an account for Ben Taggart in the amount of ten thousand pounds, "for all the good times we had and to make up for all the good times we missed." That's almost fifteen thousand dollars! How did he even know about our child? Did you write to him?"

"No, you know I didn't. I haven't communicated with Uncle Fergus in sixteen years. I don't know how he knew about Ben. I can't believe he did that."

"Well, he did. Additionally, the instrument provides for a salary for the trustee of one thousand pounds per week and reimbursement for all expenses."

I was stunned. I couldn't accept money for something I should do out of love.

"I can't accept that salary, Cat. And I don't think we should accept the gift for Ben either. That's a hefty sum of money that by rights should go to his family. He wasn't all that wealthy."

"Of course, the decision to accept or reject the distribution is entirely up to you. As to the extent of his assets and his wealth, I can't tell from the trust agreement or the will. Some of his property, specifically the farm and his investment in a corporation known as Global Investments, Inc., are listed on an attached Schedule A. His real property included a house, farmlands, fixtures and farm equipment."

"And I'm to be in charge of it all? What am I supposed to do with it? I'm no farmer. How am I to manage a house, a farm and his investments? You know I have a hard enough time managing my little office."

"Well, as far as the house is concerned, the trust provides that Deirdre may stay there as long as she likes. Maybe she's a capable manager. Since Fergus and Deirdre had no children together, the trust dictates that the property is to be sold and the proceeds distributed to Fergus's heirs when Deirdre dies."

"And the rest of it? His bank accounts? His stock?"

"All the rest, the balance of everything Fergus owned, is in your hands as trustee until you distribute to the beneficiaries, which, as you know, is deferred until the murderer is apprehended and brought to justice. Pretty close to the same language that's in your letter."

"So that's the whole thing?"

"Well, there's one other unusual provision that you should know about. Since I don't practice in Northern Ireland, I'm not sure what's commonplace there. In the U.S., when property is left to an heir and the heir dies before the distribution, the property usually passes to the heir's descendants, you know, his children. In Uncle Fergus's trust, if an heir dies before distribution, his share is split up among the other beneficiaries."

"And that's all the details I need to know?"

"Probably, but that's just a summary description. The language is more convoluted. There are several pages that refer to the powers of the trustee, that's you. It says what you can and cannot do with the assets while they are still in trust."

"What am I supposed to do?"

"Well, you can do pretty much anything. It's up to you how the property will be maintained or what expenses will be paid. That's a serious responsibility and that's why there is a thousand-pound payment per week as trustee's compensation."

My thoughts immediately turned to Conor. He's going to blow his top. "My cousin Conor, who is a nasty guy to begin with, is going to go insane over this. Little Ben gets ten thousand pounds, I get a thousand a week and Conor's inheritance stays in purgatory? That's not going to make me a very popular cousin."

"True. But Fergus was no fool. I'm sure he contemplated the dilemma. He made the trust secret, so you don't have to disclose anything about you or Ben at this time."

"Let's suppose we find the bastard or bastards who murdered Fergus. And let's suppose it's some Ulster Volunteer who's been holding a grudge against my uncle for thirty years. What if the guy dies before he can be indicted?"

"That would render the condition satisfied and you could distribute."

"So if he's dead or indicted, even though he's not convicted, I can distribute the assets to the beneficiaries?"

"Yes. The instrument provides that all investments—stocks, bonds, partnership interests—are to be liquidated and reduced to cash. The cash is to be divided into seven equal shares, one each for Deirdre, Conor, Riley, Robert, Eamon, Janie and the Bridget McGregor Trust. The house will be held in trust until Deirdre dies, at which time it will be sold and the proceeds distributed equally to the remaining six beneficiaries."

"What is the Bridget McGregor Trust?"

"I don't know. It's obviously a separate trust or a foundation. Apparently, Uncle Fergus established it to benefit a person named Bridget McGregor. At the time of distribution, a one-seventh share will be added to the existing principal of the Bridget McGregor Trust and paid out to Bridget McGregor as the terms of her trust dictate."

"Do I have a copy of that trust?"

"No. Perhaps Mr. O'Neill has a copy. Presumably you are not the trustee of the Bridget McGregor Trust, but you do have minimal responsibilities."

"What responsibilities? I don't know anything about Bridget McGregor."

"You have a duty to make sure monthly deductions from Fergus's account are sent to a Dublin bank for the account of Bridget McGregor. Did you read through the trust document?"

"Well, sort of. Not really. Who the hell is Bridget McGregor?"

"A child? A charity? A secret love perhaps? We only have the address of a bank in Dublin where the payments are sent. But Liam, the whole thing is very secretive. Fergus directs that no one is to know anything about the terms of his trust or the Bridget McGregor Trust."

"Oh, that's dandy. One more secret trust. So Bridget gets monthly payments?"

"Yes, she does. Or *it* does."

"I don't get it. Why did Fergus want to keep the identity of the beneficiaries or their shares secret? I understand deferring the distributions. You wouldn't want a killer to get a portion of the estate. But why not at least let the beneficiaries know that Fergus left them a share?"

"I can only speculate. There is a murderer out there. It could be an old revenge killing, but it could also be a person who wanted some or all of your uncle's property. Identifying people who are in line to inherit that property might put their lives in danger. And I suppose we should consider the possibility that the killer might be a member of the family. It wouldn't be the first time."

"I hate to think that my uncle was murdered by a member of the family. I hope you're wrong. But I'm sure of one thing—I'm going to get a huge pushback from Conor. He's already threatened to hire a lawyer and contest the validity of the trust."

"If he does, he might find himself disinherited. There's an *in terrorem* clause. That means . . ."

"I know, I know. O'Neill warned us about it. Is that legal?"

"I don't practice in Northern Ireland, but as a general rule, such clauses *are* legal. They serve a valid purpose. Sometimes an heir who thinks she deserves a larger portion of the estate will contest the will and tie up the estate for years. If this were in Illinois, the clause would *not* be enforced because Illinois beneficiaries have a right to know the terms of the trust. But in the UK or Northern Ireland, I don't know. Maybe O'Neill is right. He practices there. Regardless, the *threat* is real and anyone who contests the will or trust will certainly *fear* losing his inheritance."

"Any other provisions I should know about?"

"Not really. But Liam, I want you to think hard whether you should accept the appointment. I know you want to honor your uncle's wishes, but maybe you should turn it over to the Bank of Antrim. Serving as a trustee is an enormous responsibility that may require you to spend a lot of time away from home. As a trustee you'll have a legal duty to take possession of all the accounts and investments and manage them prudently until they are distributed."

"So what am I supposed to do? I don't mind handling it for a little while."

"Well, the trust says you can rely on the advice of Mr. O'Neill or anyone of your choosing. You can hire people to run the farm. You can hire investment counselors. I just want you to think about it. If you decide the responsibility is too much, you should decline." Then in a whisper she said, "I have to go now, Ben's asleep and I'm tired. Good night, my love."

I sat there staring at the phone and wondering what I was getting myself into. Answer a ringing phone and life's direction changes. First I'm going north, now I'm going east. First I'm in a comfort zone, now

I'm in a firestorm. What if I hadn't answered the phone? For years I've been riddled with regret for betraying my uncle and ruining our relationship, but now I know that the relationship wasn't destroyed at all. I hadn't ruined anything. Didn't he set up an account for Ben saying it was for all the good times we missed? Didn't Deirdre say he loved me like no other? Didn't he think enough of me to appoint me as his trustee? I vowed not to let him down.

I dressed and drove off to Fergus's house to meet with Inspector McLaughlin of the Police Service of Northern Ireland in my capacity as trustee of the Fergus Taggart Testamentary Trust.

EIGHT

• • •

THERE WERE THREE POLICE vehicles in Fergus's driveway when I arrived. Two of them bore the distinctive PSNI blue-and-yellow checkerboard designs along the sides of their Skodas. One of them had EVIDENCE TECHNICIAN stenciled on the door. I recognized the third as an aged Tangi Land Rover, a gray armored jeep-like vehicle, formerly used by the Royal Ulster Constabulary for crowd control during the Troubles.

An attractive young police officer, smartly dressed in her PSNI uniform—dark green jacket belted at the waist, creased green trousers, white shirt—stood at the front door, her hands clasped behind her back. Her blond hair was tightly drawn back in a Celtic knot. The name tag over her right pocket read Dooley. "I'm sorry, sir," she said sweetly but firmly, "this residence is secured. There's an investigation in progress."

"I know," I said. "Fergus Taggart was my uncle."

She looked me over with her blue eyes, and then shook her head. "I'm sorry for your loss, sir, but I can't let you in."

I smiled my most engaging smile. "I'm also the appointed trustee of Fergus Taggart's estate. Technically, I own this property right now."

She crossed her arms on her chest. "You'll need to come back at another time to look at your property, Mr. Owner," she said not-so-sweetly. "You're not getting in. Now turn around and be off."

"I want to see Inspector McLaughlin."

"Inspector McLaughlin is busy. And you're becoming a pest. Don't make me remove you from the premises."

I smiled. *"You're* going to remove *me?"*

She started to reach for her belt and I quickly backed up and said, "Look, Officer Dooley, I have a meeting set with Inspector McLaughlin. It's scheduled. Prearranged. He's expecting me. Just ask him. He won't like it if you give me the bum's rush. Would you just tell him that Liam Taggart is here?"

She gave me an exasperated look. "You stand right there. Don't move." I nodded and she left to fetch McLaughlin.

A moment later, a lanky man in civilian dress, tweed sport coat, brown slacks and a checkered wool cap came out and introduced himself. He had a kind face, and while clearly in his late sixties or early seventies, appeared to be strong and fit. I had already informed him by telephone that I was the appointed trustee and that I wanted to be present when he opened the house. After his initial objection, he relented, but only after telling me not to get in the way of his techs.

"Why are you giving my officer a hard time?" he said.

I smiled. "I think she can hold her own."

"We don't get many murders out here anymore," McLaughlin said as we walked inside. "Most of the time we're working on property crimes. Occasional street crime, to be sure, but this one presents quite a conundrum."

"How so?"

"Man shot dead through the heart. No signs of a scuffle. No defensive wounds, no bruises. Happens in broad daylight twenty meters from the side of the house, but there are no witnesses and no murder weapon was found. No apparent motive. We've already questioned half the family. No one knows anything. Everyone tells me he had no enemies, at least not in the last two decades."

"No witnesses and no suspects?"

McLaughlin nodded. "That's correct. Someone drove out to this farmhouse and shot the man. No one heard him drive up. No one heard the gunshot. No one saw or heard anything unusual. No one called the police, not even from the house. The murder happened at ten thirty and we didn't get a call until one thirty, three hours later. And his girlfriend was home all day." He shrugged. "Curious, don't you think?"

"She's an older woman," I said. "She says she didn't know anything until she found him in the field."

"Older? Is she deaf? Blind? She's in her sixties. That's a young woman to me. No, I don't buy that. She's certainly a person of interest."

I shook my head. "You're wrong. Deirdre loved him. They've been together forty years or more. What possible motivation would she have to kill my uncle?"

"You'll excuse me, but I hear that a lot. What motivation? Money? Freedom? Arguments? Another man? Maybe he left his dirty clothes on the floor? You're the trustee, does she stand to inherit from his estate?"

"I can't disclose that information. It's a sealed document."

"It's not sealed to us. We can get it by warrant."

"Then you'll have to do that, but I ask that you keep the information private. It was Fergus Taggart's wish not to reveal the contents of his trust until his murder was solved."

McLaughlin showed surprise and then smiled. "So, you're telling me that he knew he was going to be murdered?"

"Apparently he had some basis to fear it."

"If he thought he was going to be murdered, why didn't he identify his murderer in the trust? Or maybe he did and you're not telling me?"

I shook my head. "No, he didn't. In fact, just the opposite. He doesn't want any disbursements from the trust until his murderer is identified and prosecuted."

"So, he's going to assist me in the investigation of his death by providing financial incentives? That's a new one for me. Well, unless something else develops, I'm going to keep my eyes on the girlfriend."

"I thought *she* called *you* as soon as she found the body?"

"Well, first of all that wouldn't eliminate a suspect, but in fact, no she didn't. And isn't that strange? She says she found the body, but we were contacted by Mr. Taggart's brother, Robert Taggart at 1:32 p.m."

"That's right. I forgot Deirdre said she called Robert right off. She was probably in shock."

"Mm-hmm, no doubt. What's the relationship between the girl-friend and the deceased's brother?"

"Robert and Deirdre? I'm sure they're very close. It's a loving family. If you spent any time talking to her, you'd find it hard to believe she's involved."

"She's convinced you of her innocence, has she?"

"I've known her for years. She wouldn't have to convince me."

"Hmm. I've talked to her. For two hours. And I think she knows more than she says. We understand that the deceased's son Conor and the girlfriend don't get along, what do you know about that?"

I shrugged. "I've heard the same thing. But to be fair, Conor isn't exactly Mr. Warmth."

"The deceased's brother Robert, and the deceased's son Conor, do they also inherit under the will and trust? Or are they disinherited?"

I started to speak, but McLaughlin interrupted and waved me off. "I know, I know, I've got to get a warrant. Well, I'll be doing just that, Liam Taggart. I'll be getting that warrant and then I'll be questioning all your beneficiaries one by one. You know, all these Taggarts have roots in the IRA. Your Taggart family goes way back, deep in the Troubles. No one would describe them as innocent, dyed-in-the-wool pacifists. No, sir, not the Taggart family."

The technicians came out of the house, McLaughlin closed his clipboard and stepped off the porch. He stopped at his car door and said, "If you get any information, you'll be sure to share it with me, won't you?"

"Of course. Will you do the same?"

McLaughlin smiled and got into his car.

WITHIN A FEW HOURS, the police had removed the yellow crime scene tape, removed the padlocks and restored the electrical service. I went in to take stock of what was now in my possession as official trustee of the Fergus Taggart Testamentary Trust. The first thing I noticed was that the bottle of Bushmills and the two tumblers that Deirdre and I had used the other night were gone. Presumably, the police had taken them in for analysis. That would identify me as someone who crossed the DO NOT CROSS tape. If McLaughlin asks me what I saw and what I took, I'll have to turn over the wooden box.

I went from room to room taking pictures with my cell phone and writing notes. In order to make an inventory, I had to search the house, open the cabinets and drawers and look in the closets. It made me feel like an intruder, peeling back the layers of my uncle's privacy, and of course, in many cases I was also violating Deirdre's privacy. I spent considerable time riffling through his office, trying to be alert to anything that might reveal who my uncle thought might be trying to kill him. I was also looking for more information on Bridget McGregor. I didn't find either. There was nothing further in his desk.

What I did encounter were memories in each and every room of the house and I had to stop every so often to dwell in the moment. But there was nothing that implied a death threat and that was disappointing. I was sure there had to be clues. I went into his bedroom and started riffling through the drawers. There, in the top drawer of his bedside bureau, I found a file folder. Nothing was written on the outside and it was held shut by a clasp. I opened it and four pieces of paper fell out. One was a copy of an article written in *The Belfast Telegraph* reporting on a murder outside a Belfast pub in 1999. A young Protestant man was bludgeoned by an unknown assailant. I had no idea why my uncle kept it.

The second piece of paper was a short news article from the *Telegraph* about a murder in the Maghaberry Maximum Security Prison in 2006. An IRA prisoner had been found dead in his jail cell with a *U* painted on his chest, a clear statement that a unionist had killed a republican in jail.

The third was a photograph of an open wooden shipping crate packed with automatic assault rifles. Nothing was written on the back of the photo and there was nothing further to identify it. The fourth was a page from last month's *Irish Times*. A small blurb was circled. It read, "Global Comes under Regulatory Scrutiny for Inflated Financials." I wondered if any of these documents had anything to do with the picture left in Fergus's mailbox. I'd share them all with McLaughlin. Maybe he could tell me if they were connected in some way or if they made any sense in my uncle's homicide investigation.

I thought about McLaughlin. Wise. Experienced. In his cap, he looked like Central Casting's idea of a Scotland Yard investigator. He was also somewhat predictable. I'd have had the same thoughts if I were him. Fergus was shot at close range through the heart. Was it someone who knew him, someone he trusted, someone who could get right up close to him? Family members knew him. Robert, Riley and Conor were all strong enough to force such a confrontation. Not Eamon. Not Deirdre. Not without help, anyway.

McLaughlin brought up the Taggart connection to the IRA and I still believed it made sense to think about ancient adversaries and confederates. Fergus must have made a lot of unionist enemies back in the day. An old vendetta might have been lying in the weeds, waiting to catch up with him. A lot of people were jailed and sentenced during the Troubles and many of them were released after the Good Friday Peace Agreement. Their crimes were deemed politically motivated and they were set free, even some of the most brutal killers, which made no sense then or now. I recalled that the releases were a critical component of the peace agreement and that the agreement wouldn't have been signed without it, but it put a lot of violent people back on the street.

And one can only imagine how twenty years in Crumlin Road Prison would serve to intensify the hate that caused a person to kill in the first place. What's the likelihood that a steadfast unionist would be rehabilitated and full of brotherly love on the day of his release? To my way of thinking, it only put the worst elements back on the street to commit further acts of violence. Did one of them harbor a grudge against my uncle? Could be.

McLaughlin was also correct in another regard—money is a strong motivator. Who coveted Fergus's property so strongly that they would kill him for it? I ran the list of beneficiaries through my mind. His two sons, Conor and Riley, seemed well off, but you never know. Robert and Eamon would never have killed their brother for money. Would they? Janie's a beneficiary but she loved Uncle Fergus. I couldn't imagine Janie as a suspect. Forget about Deirdre. What about Bridget McGregor? Who or what was she? Fergus had demanded that the Bridget McGregor Trust remain secret. Perhaps it was a secret to Bridget McGregor herself. Or itself. Had she been Fergus's girlfriend back in the day? Or now? Was she a daughter that no one knew about?

My phone rang and it was O'Neill calling to tell me he received a call from McLaughlin. A warrant was being issued for a copy of the trust. Fast work, Inspector.

"I'm not about to hand it over so readily," O'Neill said. "No one pushes Malcolm O'Neill around. I'm on my way to the courthouse to file a motion for a protective order. Ultimately, I don't think I will prevail, but the procedure will slow him down and give you more time to investigate before the contents of the trust become public knowledge."

That was something Catherine might do and O'Neill seemed like a hardened trial lawyer to me. "What do you know about Bridget McGregor?" I asked. He took a moment to respond and then said, "Why don't you come over this afternoon and we'll talk."

As I ended the call, a blue Toyota van pulled into the drive. Deirdre stepped out and I met her at the front door.

"Can I come into my house, Mr. Trustee?" she said with a wry smile.

"Of course." I stepped aside. "The electricity's been restored."

She brushed by me, set her purse and car keys on the kitchen table and turned around with an expression that said, *this is bothersome for both of us, isn't it?* "What has my darling Fergus decreed for the disposition of our home?"

Sadly, I shook my head. "I'm sorry. My hands are tied."

She smiled again, this time with a tinge of amusement. "Are you going to evict me?"

"Goodness, no. Until further notice, you can live here just as before. Come and go as you please. We'll change the locks. You and I will each have a key."

"And after further notice?"

"You're pushing me, Aunt Deirdre."

"You bet your ass."

All I could do was shrug. She started busying herself in the kitchen and asked me if I wanted a cup of tea, which I accepted. She brought two cups to the table and sat across from me. "That old rascal," she said, "he made damn sure he wouldn't hand over his property until we knew who murdered him. And that's just fine with me, because there's some of his relatives that don't deserve a damn thing even if they weren't involved."

"And who would that be, Aunt Deirdre?"

"Stick around a while, you'll see."

"What about a holdover from long ago, from the IRA days? What do you think?"

"I think those days are not as long ago as you might believe. Don't underestimate the hate and distrust that still exists on each side of the Peace Wall." She held her cup with both hands, took a sip and raised her eyes. "Fergus was not the peacenik that Robert eulogized. Especially in days of *auld lang syne*. The Taggart boys were rough and ready." She paused and smiled at me. "Back in the day."

I knew that Deirdre possessed a wealth of information behind those cautious eyes and I knew it wouldn't be easy to get her to open up to me. And why should she? Still, I decided to dig a little. "Aunt Deirdre, do you know anyone named Bridget McGregor?"

She shook her head. "Sounds like a Scottish name. Who is she?"

"I don't know. Just a name I've heard." I was immediately sorry I brought it up. That was a mistake. So was my specious answer.

"Just a *name*? You've *heard*? And so you ask *me*? For a private detective, you're a lousy liar. Is this you casting out a fishing line? Or is this you trying to confront me? Am I expected to break into tears and spill the beans? Well, let me tell you, if Fergus was having an affair with a woman named Bridget McGregor, he must have been Houdini. It'd have to be an out-of-body experience because I was with the man all the time." She put down her cup. "As a proper woman, I'd ask you to leave right now, except this is not my home anymore, is it? It's yours more than mine. Until further notice, right, Mr. Trustee?" She got up from the table and walked into the living room. I swallowed. She had surely won that exchange. I trailed her into the living room like a scolded schoolboy.

"Wait, Aunt Deirdre. I didn't suggest that Uncle Fergus was having an affair. Her name did not come up in that context." She gave me an irritated look that told me the conversation was over.

While I stood there trying to think of something more to say, a late model Mercedes pulled into the drive. Through the window I watched Conor exit the car and walk briskly to the door. His expression wasn't any better than Deirdre's. This was bound to be the morning's winning parlay. He threw open the door and walked directly into the living room.

"What are you doing here?" he demanded.

"Good morning, Conor," I replied as politely as I could, given the circumstances. "Was that intended for me or Aunt Deirdre?"

"Take your pick."

"Well, Aunt Deirdre lives here. And me? I'm just the trustee looking after the estate property."

"Don't smart-ass me, Liam. You have no right to be here, either one of you. This house belonged to my father, not to his girlfriend or to some estranged nephew. And my lawyers are going to throw this bogus trust out the window."

I was trying to keep this discourse at a civil level, but I could tell Conor's teakettle was steaming. "If you're right, that will relieve me of a lot of responsibilities that I didn't ask for. But until that day, I'm going to follow your father's wishes and perform my legal duties as trustee."

He pointed a stiff arm in Deirdre's direction. "She's no trustee. She has no business in my father's house."

I shook my head. "*She*, as you so warmly put it, raised you from the time you were in nursery school. She taught you to eat with a fork. It's within my discretion whether or not to let her live here. She's lived here for forty years. I'm going to let her stay."

"I don't want her to stay."

"It's not your choice."

He moved a step closer. "Let's stop the games, Liam. Fergus was my father. Riley and I are his sons, his only heirs at law. She's not an heir; she never married my father. This whole trust business doesn't mean shit to me. Now, you best step aside. I'm going to go through the house and take whatever I want and then I'm going to put the house up for sale. As for Deirdre, she's had a free ride for too long. She's going to pack her things and get out of here so I can clean up the house for sale." He turned to face Deirdre. "Sorry to be so blunt, but that's what's going to happen. Get used to it."

Deirdre started to cry and left the room. I knew this was going to be a bad morning and I wasn't sure I could defuse it. I tried to reason with Conor one more time. "Look, Conor, I'm only doing the job your father asked me to do. The trust was drawn up by your father's attorney to implement his wishes. You may be an heir at law, but there are other interested parties, other beneficiaries. There are other people who stand to inherit from his estate."

He took another step forward. Now he was in my personal space. "What interested parties, what other beneficiaries?" he demanded. "What other people claim an interest in *my* father's property?"

I shook my head. "I can't tell you."

He grabbed my shoulders and started to shake me back and forth. "What beneficiaries?" So much for my attempts to defuse the situation. I shoved him back into the wall. Hard. But he didn't get the message. He rushed me. I stepped to the side and hit him flush with a right cross that put him on his back. With his hand on his jaw, he scrambled to his feet. "You'll pay for this, Liam. You don't know what kind of trouble you just bought."

"Well, I'm already watching my ass. What else should I watch?"

"You smart-ass son of a bitch. You'll find out soon enough."

The door slammed hard as he left.

Now to the second half of the daily double. I went looking for Deirdre. I found her sitting at the kitchen table and staring into her cup of tea, a tissue in her right hand. I pulled up a chair, put my arm around her shoulders and the two of us sat wordlessly for a few minutes. I didn't know how to break the silence. Finally, she spoke without looking up. "It's astonishing how fast a solid foundation can disintegrate beneath your feet. The very ground on which you stand can dissolve in a matter of hours. Providence decrees, and all frames of reference are hereby held for naught. I'll pack my things, but I need at least a week."

"There's no need to do that. You don't ever have to leave this house if you don't want to."

I knew instantly that I shouldn't have said that. I'd broken the code of secrecy, but I felt bad for her and my emotions seized the moment. To be fair, my trustee's skills weren't very good to begin with. Besides, I never applied for this job. She read between the lines, and now she knew that the trust gave her the right to live in the house for the rest of her life. "Thanks," she said softly.

"You're welcome. Keep it to yourself."

"Conor's just like his father, you know? He has a violent streak."

"Uncle Robert said Uncle Fergus was a man of peace."

"Ha! I lived with him for forty years and I loved him every day, but I'll tell you, when the situation presented, you best be out of his way. He could summon the thunder—all those Taggart brothers could. The lot of 'em. Even your father. Especially your father."

"You knew my father?"

She looked away. She didn't want to answer.

I pressed her for the information. There was a gaping hole in my family narrative and I wanted to fill it. As far as I knew, there were no markers, no evidence, no way to prove, other than by the living, breathing existence of yours truly, that Danny Taggart ever roamed the planet Earth. "Tell me about my father," I said.

She firmly shook her head and resumed her stare into her cup of tea.

For all my life, my father was the unspoken topic. The briefest of references. He died in a car crash. Conversation over. I pressed her for the information and then I wished I hadn't. As the song goes, *"Wish I didn't know now what I didn't know then."*

"Tell me, Aunt Deirdre. Tell me about Danny Taggart."

She took a deep breath, nodded, then looked me square in the eyes. "I suppose you have a right, though I hate to be the one bringing it all to you. Danny was a hell of a man. You resemble him in many ways. Good-looking, strong, kind, principled. His death hit us all very hard, and no one harder than Fergus. I had never seen him so enraged."

"Enraged? At whom? My father died in a car accident."

She shook her head. "No son, he was murdered."

Oh, hell. I was floored. *Wish I didn't know now.* "Murdered? I was always told that—"

"Because that's what you'd tell a wee laddie. They weren't about to tell a lad that his father had his throat cut."

I tried to speak, but I had no air. I stood and hung onto the back of the chair for stability. "They told me a car accident and all these years no one told me any different. No one said he'd been murdered. Didn't I have a right to know?"

"It was for your own good."

I sat down and wrapped my head in my hands. "Murdered. Jesus."

"I'm sorry. But that's the God's honest truth."

"Why didn't Fergus tell me when I was here twenty years ago? I wasn't a wee laddie then."

"Because you're a Taggart. When your father was killed, his death ignited a firestorm. The Taggart brothers went out to avenge his death and avenge it they did. Fergus didn't want you to go off half-cocked and stir up another war, so your uncles agreed among themselves not to bring it up."

"Who murdered him, Aunt Deirdre? Tell me."

"Let it lie. Leave it be. It doesn't matter anymore."

"Was it the British soldiers? The UVF? Did he die in prison? You can't just open the door partway."

"Liam, I didn't want to open the door at all."

"But it's open and I'm his son, and I deserve to know."

With her eyes still locked on her tea she said, "I shouldn't have said anything. I should have left the demons locked away." Then she raised her eyes. "Before your government sent you here, did you study up on Northern Ireland and its history?"

"Sure."

"In your studies and your briefings, did you ever come across a unionist bunch known as the Shankill Butchers?"

I shook my head. "I don't think so. They killed my father?"

She hung her head and then nodded. "They were a crazed, murderous gang from the Shankill Road. They were all low-life gunslingers, made up of former Ulster Volunteers, drunks, criminals, rapists. From the early seventies until the early eighties, they were the foulest, most notorious gang of killers in all of Northern Ireland. Late at night, in the shadows and the darkness, they would prowl around the Catholic neighborhoods, the pubs and lodges, and randomly kidnap a man or a woman, beat 'em senseless and carve 'em up. That's why they were called the Butchers. They did their killing with axes, machetes, iron pipes and knives. Their leader was Lenny Murphy, the most heinous of them all. We knew who most of them were and so did the RUC. Because of the way they left their victims, killings were easily attributable to the Shankill Butchers. That was their signature. But they always avoided arrest. The RUC would look the other way and wouldn't do a damn thing about it. Eye for an eye, they'd say. What do you expect when the Provisional IRA bombs a Protestant restaurant and kills innocent women and children, they would say. The butchers aren't doing anything different. 'Tis nuthin' but a street war."

"Why did they kill my father?"

"Well, first of all, there didn't have to be any reason for the Butchers to kill a Catholic."

"And that's what happened? They grabbed my father coming out of a pub?"

She shook her head. "I shouldn't be telling you all this stuff. I can see your temperature rising. You're a hot-blooded Taggart."

"Aunt Deirdre, I need to know. I have a right to know."

"Now do you see why your uncles kept it from you? You've got that Taggart blood boiling in your veins. Back in the nineties, they didn't want young, hotheaded Liam running into the same fate."

"Aunt Deirdre, please."

"Your father wasn't grabbed coming out of a pub, son, he was killed when he went out to seek revenge for Molly."

"My sister?"

Again she nodded. Her eyes glassed over and she stared into the past. "Your sister was his firstborn and your father loved her with all his heart. She had beautiful red hair that your mum would curl into ringlets. Even though none of us had any money, Molly was always dressed in the cutest little dresses with little ribbons in her hair. When they went to church on Sunday, she would skip along in her little patent leather shoes. She was a darling.

"It was a sunny morning in June and we had just returned from church. Your mum was fixing breakfast for the Taggart clan like she usually did. Your dad was in the house changing from his Sunday clothes. Molly was sitting on the front stoop, the sun upon her face, playing with a doll. It was then that Murphy's first lieutenant, Archie Walker, came through the Falls, riding shotgun in Michael Simpson's car, firing wildly out the window. It wasn't the first time he'd done that, but it was the first time anyone got hit.

"Your mother heard the gunshots and quickly ran out to grab Molly but she was too late. Molly caught two of the bullets in her little body. She was still alive, her wounds were turning her white dress red and she looked up at us with her innocent eyes that didn't understand what was happening to her. Danny scooped her up and ran down the street as fast as he could, trying to get her to St. Joseph's Hospital, your mother right behind him screaming like you never heard anybody scream. Wails came from the very bottom of her soul." Deirdre shook her head and swallowed. "They didn't make it in time.

"Danny went insane and nothing we said could calm him down. 'Who was it?' he screamed. 'Who shot my baby?' Finally, one of the neighbors told him that he saw Walker shooting out of Simpson's car.

Your father immediately ran into the house, grabbed his rifle and went out to have his payback against Walker and any Shankill Butcher he could find. Shankill Road wasn't but a few hundred meters away, but it was on the other side of the wall. Danny made his way around the gate and tore through the Shankill screaming for Walker to come out.

"We got word right away to your three uncles. They knew that Danny didn't stand a chance alone in the Shankill. Not against the Butchers and their gang. They grabbed their weapons and chased after him, but they had a hard time getting through the gates. When they finally got in, they went from block to block." Deirdre shook her head and lowered her eyes. "They found Danny lying facedown in the middle of the playground in the back of the Dunberry Primary School. I'm sorry, Liam, but that's the way it happened."

I stood there, dumbstruck. My father and my sister, both killed during the Troubles. On the same day. By the Butchers. No wonder my mother sent me to live in Antrim. But Deirdre wasn't through.

"They waited until after the funeral. Then the Taggart brothers went on a savage rampage. They didn't kill at random, not like the Butchers. They hunted down those responsible. One by one. They set a firebomb to Walker's house and blew it all to hell along with everyone in it. They hunted the gang members and killed seven of them. They laid Simpson's body, riddled with bullets, on the doorstep of the 83rd Loyalist Bar with a note pinned to his chest. 'This is for Danny!' But they didn't find Murphy. He escaped. Of course the RUC blamed the Taggarts for the feud. That's why the whole family moved out to Antrim."

It was hard for me to stand there and take all this in. *Wish I didn't know now.* "I was told the family moved to Antrim to be close to Fergus's farm. I guess I don't really know anything. Was that the end of it?"

Again, Deirdre shook her head. "Not quite. The vendetta wasn't finished until 1982 when Murphy was gunned down in Dublin. The papers all recorded that he was murdered by a Provo, but they never really identified the shooter."

I was drained. I had pressed her for the information and what good did it do me? Was I better off knowing? Her narrative had raised the possibility of other suspects. It took ten years for the Taggarts to close the book on my father's death. Did it take another thirty for the Butchers to close theirs? It seemed doubtful, but what about the newspaper stories, the ones in the folder? Did they have a connection with the ancient feud? Was that why Fergus anticipated his death? It seemed unlikely to me that the Butchers or their descendants would wait thirty years or more to retaliate, but I'd witnessed pent-up anger explode when prisoners were released after the Good Friday Peace Agreement. Many of them sought revenge after twenty years in custody.

"I shouldn't have told you," Deirdre said. "I can see what's going through your mind, don't think I can't, and you can just put those thoughts away. This feud is over. Done. You have a life in America. If you were smart you'd get on the next plane back."

"Who knew, Aunt Deirdre? Who knew about my father and didn't tell me?"

"Well, we all knew, but I know what you're asking."

I nodded. "Did she know? Did Annie know?"

Deirdre hung her head again and answered me in a whisper. "Aye, that she did."

This was all too much for me. Annie, my betrothed, the woman who shared my innermost thoughts, knew all about my father and my sister and kept it from me. I started to leave and then stopped. "One more thing, Aunt Deirdre. What ever happened to Fergus's first wife, Margaret Taggart?"

"His *only* wife?" Deirdre waved her hand back and forth. "She was dead before the Shankill Butcher feud. She died before I met Fergus. I don't know the details, but they say she was killed on her way home from the store. Eamon knows more. Of course, Fergus knew, but he never told me. Maybe there's lots of things he didn't tell me. Now, like Fergus, they're buried away."

I took my teacup to the sink. While I washed it, dried it and put it in the cupboard I thought there must be a lot more they didn't tell me as well. When I returned to the table, Deirdre was weeping.

"Tell me, Liam, why am I left here without my Fergus? What am I supposed to do now? Forty years. How do I go on without him?"

I put my arm around her. "You and Uncle Fergus had forty wonderful years. You should cherish the memories."

She wiped her tears. "Memories? Shall I look at the pictures? Shall

I walk around the house and look at our things, our mementoes? They're nothing but reminders of what I've lost. Pictures of people who no longer share my life. Mementoes to remind me of the grand times that are gone and will never be mine again. People tell me that Fergus still lives in my heart. Maybe he does, but I can't talk to him. I can't hold him."

What could I say? She was right.

She looked at me and a sad smile appeared on her face. "Have I suitably depressed you? I'm sorry to be so maudlin. I'll get over it." She touched the side of my face. "Thank you for being here. I know you have an appointment to keep. You better be on your way."

I looked at my watch. It was already one o'clock and I had a meeting scheduled with O'Neill. I thanked Deirdre for the tea and told her to order a locksmith and a security system for the house. As I got up, she grabbed my hand and held it tightly. "Find him, Liam. Find the rotten bastard who took my Fergus from me."

I kissed her on the forehead and got into my car for the drive back to Antrim town center, still shaky from the revelations.

NINE

...

S OLICITOR O'NEILL HAS BEEN expecting you for the last
twenty-five minutes," Mrs. O'Donohue said curtly when I entered the reception area. She rose from behind her desk and com-
manded me to follow.

"And a good afternoon to you as well, Mrs. O'Donohue," I said,
trying to brighten the mood. After all, I'd had a pretty sobering day. But
she would have no part of it. Pleasant banter was not in her repertoire.
She raised her left eyebrow and opened the door to O'Neill's office.

"Please be seated, Mr. Taggart," he said. "Would you care for a cup
of tea? Or coffee?"

"You have real coffee?"

"I have K-cups. We're not a third world country, you know."

"Then coffee, thank you. A little cream, a little sugar." Mrs. O'Donohue
left to fill the order.

"So, you spoke to Inspector McLaughlin?" I said, settling onto my
uncomfortable wooden chair.

He nodded. "Of course. I know Farrell for many years. As I told
you on the phone, I prepared a motion to quash the anticipated warrant, but it won't succeed. At the most, I can keep the trust out of
Farrell's hands for a couple weeks. Perhaps in that time there will be
progress in your investigation. Farrell told me that you and he had a
conversation at the house. He asked me to confirm that you have been
officially appointed by the court as trustee of Fergus Taggart's trust. I
assured him it was so."

"I had a run-in with Conor this morning," I said. "He bolted through the door and ordered Deirdre and me to leave the home, and when we refused, he became belligerent. I expect you'll be hearing from his attorneys. He said he was going to challenge the trust."

Our conversation was interrupted by Mrs. O'Donohue, who brought in coffee service on a silver tray. She laid a white linen doily down on the desk in front of me, then carefully set a cloth napkin, a spoon, a small pitcher of cream, two cubes of sugar and a white china cup and saucer. She poured the coffee into the cup from a silver pitcher and left the room. All without a word.

"Conor can be an annoyance," O'Neill said, "but I don't think he'll contest the will."

"I almost wish he would. I'm not qualified to be a trustee, and frankly, I need to get back home."

O'Neill leaned over and I saw a look of concern. "Mr. Taggart, I strongly urge you not to decline the appointment. Fergus and I discussed this matter for days on end. You are the only one suited to serve."

"But I don't know how to manage his investments or his farm and the family doesn't trust me. The bank is the successor, why don't we let the bank take over?"

That suggestion was instantly rejected. "Absolutely not! We must do everything in our power to prevent that occurrence. I cautioned Fergus against naming the bank all throughout our discussions. They will manage the estate impersonally and without regard to the needs of the heirs, especially Deirdre. They will assign a team of professional bean counters that will each bill for their services and they will grind through all of the estate assets leaving nothing for the heirs. The farm will have to be sold to pay expenses and taxes. Deirdre will lose her life estate. And all of that is decidedly against your uncle's desires."

"Then why did he name the bank? Why not Conor, or Riley, or one of his brothers?"

"I'm afraid I can't answer that."

"But I can't live here until the homicide is solved. That could take months, years. Isn't there a provision to decline in favor of another family member, perhaps Janie?"

O'Neill pursed his lips in a show of exasperation. Hadn't he just explained to me that Fergus and he had discussed this for days on end? Hadn't they come to the conclusion that I was the *only* one suited to the appointment? Wasn't I even listening?

He drew a deep breath through his nostrils and said, "Janie is not suitable. For one thing she is young. For another, there is the matter of her boyfriend. Fergus didn't care for the man."

That was also my impression when I met him. I don't know why. It was just a feeling. He was a little too full of himself. Perhaps, as I like to tease Catherine, 'twas me Irish intuition.

"Nothing requires you to stay in Northern Ireland until the investigation is over, Mr. Taggart. It is only necessary that you be present during court hearings."

"What court hearings?"

"Well, none are currently scheduled, but if one of the heirs were to raise a challenge to the will or the trust, a hearing would be set. So far, no one has come forward, and they only have two more weeks. Even so, when we successfully defeat a challenge, or the time expires without a challenge, you are free to return to America. Most of our business can be conducted through email."

"Let's suppose one of the family members does raise a challenge. How long would the court's consideration take?"

O'Neill shrugged. "Hard to say. Maybe a few weeks."

"Conor's threatened to do just that."

"It would be quite a bold and risky move for him, with an *in terrorem* clause staring him in the face. I don't know whether anyone else might be motivated to challenge the trust. Eventually, I'll have to turn the trust document over to McLaughlin and the terms are bound to leak out. There may be disappointed heirs, relatives who think they should receive a greater share—again, I'm thinking of Conor or Riley. It's not unusual for an heir to contest a trust or its provisions. Or even the will itself. That's precisely why we inserted the *in terrorem* clause." He leaned forward and whispered, "But between you and me, I don't think the court will enforce it."

He stood. "Accept the appointment, Mr. Taggart, and I'll support you one hundred percent. It was your uncle's final wish. We don't want the bank to be the trustee under any circumstances."

I nodded. What choice did I have? Since O'Neill and I were now on the same team, it was time for me to ask the jackpot question. "How did Uncle Fergus know he was going to be murdered? Who did he suspect? He must have discussed it with you."

O'Neill shook his head. "Not a word. It was not a matter he chose to reveal to me."

"You prepared a will and trust that contemplated your client's homicide. Are you telling me you never asked him about it?"

"I should tell you that such a discussion falls within the purview of the lawyer-client privilege, but in fact, I asked him several times and he refused to answer."

"No clues? An old vendetta, a relic of the Troubles? A family member?"

O'Neill shook his head. "Sorry. He only made it clear that there was an imminent danger. He had seen the signs."

"What signs?"

"He wouldn't say."

I started to leave and then remembered what prompted me to come over here in the first place. "Who is Bridget McGregor?"

"There is a trust, established long ago by Fergus, entitled 'the Bridget McGregor Trust.' That's all I'm permitted to tell you."

"That's a little too clandestine for me, Malcolm."

"Again, I'm sorry. As you have no doubt come to realize, your uncle could be quite secretive. Part of your duties as trustee is to make sure a given sum is withdrawn every month from Fergus's general account and transferred to a bank in Dublin for the account of the Bridget McGregor Trust. That's pretty much it. In fact, it's done automatically by electronic funds transfer. Just make sure the account maintains sufficient funds for the transfer at the end of the month. Otherwise, you needn't be concerned with Bridget McGregor, at least for the time being."

"Well, I am concerned because the Bridget McGregor Trust is a one-seventh beneficiary and I am the trustee. I need to know more, otherwise I can't do my job."

"Your job? I just finished telling you that all you had to do was make sure the general account maintains sufficient funds. That's your job. It's also your job to honor your uncle's wishes and directions. The Bridget McGregor Trust is to remain secret."

I turned for the door when O'Neill said, "Liam, quite earnestly, thank you for your service. I can see that Fergus was right about you." Then he added, "But be careful. There is a murderer out there. Stay alert for signs of danger."

I walked out of the door and stopped short in my tracks. I didn't have to stay alert for long. Two of the tires on my Audi had been slashed.

TEN

· · ·

I T TOOK THE GARAGE an hour and a half to replace two tires on my rental car. Leaning his back against the door of his truck and wiping his blackened hands on a cloth, the mechanic said, "It never seems to stop, does it? The petty crime out here?" He held up a long sharp awl. "I found this on the ground. It's them teenagers, the ones that hang around the mall with nothing to do but be about their mischief. You can bet yourself that's what it is. Yep. It's them teenagers, you best believe it."

"Would you mind if I keep the awl and may I have your cloth as well, please?" I said.

He looked at me inquisitively. "There's nothing special about a six-inch scratch awl. Sure as hell, you can buy one of these in any hardware store." He shrugged. Then he smiled. "Oh, I get it. You want to show it to the police. Smart. Well, here you are." He handed the instrument to me wrapped in his cloth. Of course, my hope was that McLaughlin could lift a print.

My day of staying alert wasn't over. When I finally returned to my hotel room, a corner room on the fourth floor, the door was wide open. The lock had been jimmied. It was an old hotel and I'm sure the lock gave in easily, probably with a strong push of a screwdriver. The room was in shambles. Drawers lay open and my clothes were spread around in rumpled heaps. Flattening my tires would have given them plenty of time to ransack my room. But who knew I would be parking my car at O'Neill's? The only people who knew where I was going were Deirdre and O'Neill himself. I suppose I could have been followed, but I didn't see anyone. Maybe I was careless.

And why tear up my room and throw my clothes all over? Was I going to hide the trust document in a pair of boxers? The conclusion was obvious. Whoever did this knew I wouldn't be dumb enough to leave a copy of the sealed trust in an unsecured hotel room. They were sending a message.

A survey of the disarray confirmed my thoughts. A note lay in the middle of the bed. "Get your arse back to Chicago where you can look after what's yours. You're not wanted here!" No handwriting, just a printed note. Again, I hoped McLaughlin could get a fingerprint. I'd give him a call.

M CLAUGHLIN PUT THE AWL and rag in a plastic bag and shook his head as he surveyed the mess in my room. His tech was busy dusting for prints, but this was a hotel room and there were hundreds of prints. Maybe one would match the awl. "Doubt it," he said.

When his crew had finished, McLaughlin turned to me and tapped me on the shoulder. "I'm in the mood for a spot of tea. Will you join me? There's a café across the street."

The café was a pastry shop with a dozen small tables. McLaughlin hung his jacket on the back of his chair, picked out two caramel pastries and ordered Twinings Irish Breakfast Tea, which was served with a spoonful of leaves and an infuser. It looked good to me. I had the same.

"Does all this frighten you, Liam? I mean the acts directed against you—the slashed tires, the note and the burglary?" I started to brush off the remark, but he held his hand up and interrupted me. "Because it should. You've received a threat. I know you think you're a tough guy, you can take care of yourself, but your uncle was a tough guy too."

"Whoever's doing this, why are they trying to get me out of here?"

"Well, the logical reason is that you are the appointed trustee and you stand between them and whatever assets your uncle owned when he died. He stood in the way before and now he's dead. Now you're in the way."

I shook my head. "No, I don't buy that. If I went home, another trustee would take my place as a successor. Someone would always be in the way. Ultimately, a court could step in and make all the distributions."

McLaughlin smiled and pointed his finger at me. "But you're an imposing figure, someone who won't be bullied. Maybe a weaker person could be persuaded to step outside the lines. Make certain decisions. To the extent there are discretionary withdrawals allowed, or trust assets handled in a certain way . . . you get the idea."

I did. Catherine told me I could basically do anything I wanted while I was in charge.

"Besides," McLaughlin added, "you're a private investigator. Maybe the killer doesn't want you snooping around, like you snooped the other night at Fergus's farmhouse. That's another good reason to get you out of town."

So, he ran the prints on the Bushmills and knew I snuck into the house when it was cordoned off. Pretty sharp. He swirled the spoon in his teacup, putting in a precise amount of sugar and milk. I copied him. Twinings was a bold tea that held up well. I could get used to drinking it. Or maybe not. Maybe it would just taste good in a little pastry shop in Northern Ireland.

"Why don't you let me in on the secret?" he said. "What assets are held by the trust? Where's the gold, Liam?"

"I haven't had a chance to make an inventory yet, but I don't think there's any gold. He was comfortable. He had some money, some investments, his farm, but why kill him over that?"

"Why indeed? You've seen the provisions—who gets disinherited? Who gets shorted? Who doesn't get as much as he thinks he should? In my forty-six years, I have developed a tried-and-true principle of homicide investigation in cases where there's no apparent suspect. I call it McLaughlin's first theory of relativity—it means: the first thing you do is look at the relatives. Who's pissed off enough to kill Fergus? Who needs money bad enough to accelerate his inheritance rights? Why don't you let me in on it? Maybe we can keep an eye out together."

I was getting the feeling that McLaughlin could be an ally. If I shared some of the details with him, maybe he'd share some of his information with me. Maybe we could work together. He was going to find out sooner or later anyway. I decided to abrogate my trustee's duties once again, but only partway. I took my uncle's letter out of my pocket and slid it across the table. McLaughlin read it slowly without showing any emotion.

Finally, he set it down and looked up at me. "That's what you told me before. He knew he was going to be killed."

"That's not all. I found a few newspaper articles and a picture. They were in a folder in a drawer beside Fergus's bed. One article reported an attack at a Belfast pub and the other a jailhouse killing. They don't mean much to me. There was also a photograph of a wooden crate filled with assault rifles and a page from the financial section of the *Irish Times* referencing a governmental investigation of Global Investments for financial fraud. Finally, Deirdre found a picture of a fire-ravaged house in an envelope in Fergus's mailbox the day he was killed."

McLaughlin nodded. "Get me the originals. I'll look into the stories and the pictures. As to the box of guns, unless there's identifying marks in the picture, it wouldn't distinguish that box from the thousands of boxes we've confiscated over the years." He pursed his lips. "A box of guns is nothing unusual in Northern Ireland. Even a box of assault rifles. Hell, all they do is kill people. The Good Lord knows that arms like that were shipped in every day." McLaughlin tapped his pencil and shook his head. "Why would Global be important to Fergus?"

I know I shouldn't have said anything, but I did. "Fergus owned shares in the company. They're part of his estate. Do you know anything about this company?"

"Not yet, but I will. What does Deirdre know?"

"For all I know, she hasn't seen the folder or the papers inside. If she has, she hasn't mentioned them. I never discussed Global with her. You know . . ."

"I know. It's a secret. Why does she think Fergus feared for his life?"

"She says she doesn't know, he didn't discuss it with her. She says he was on edge lately but she didn't know anything about any death threats."

"Hmmph. I find that hard to believe. She was his wife for forty years and he wouldn't discuss something as important as that?"

"She wasn't his wife."

"Well, then she was a girlfriend, what's the difference?" He paused and gave me a wry smile. "Never mind. I know what the difference is. Does she inherit under the trust?"

I shook my head. "Sorry. It's sealed. And I have a hard time believing that the murder has anything to do with the rights of inheritance. I don't think it's an inheritance issue at all, despite your theory of relativity."

"Then why postpone the distributions? Why tell the heirs that they get nothing until the murder is solved? It makes no sense unless Fergus suspected a member of the family. Who gets the lion's share, Liam? Who gets disinherited?"

I shook my head again. I knew that there were no disproportionate distributions, and that the heirs all took equally. "I really think you're barking up the wrong tree. His trust is sealed. No one has seen the trust, so nobody would know who gets a lion's share or who gets disinherited unless Fergus said so before he died. The funny thing is, the trust is very generous. No one is disinherited and no one gets a disproportionate share."

He looked up at me and smiled. "Generous, huh? Does the girlfriend get a share?"

I nodded. "She has rights. I don't want to go into details, but she benefits as well as others. Why are you so focused on the family? Why on my aunt Deirdre of all people? Why couldn't the killer come from my uncle's past? One of the Shankill Butchers maybe."

He laughed hard. "The Butchers! Haven't heard that name in a while. What a lovely bunch they were. You know, I was working in Belfast district back then, when those bastards were running wild. Why do you bring them up?"

"I heard that my family had run-ins with the Butchers."

"Well, they weren't alone. So I guess it could be."

"Then you're not discounting a vendetta, a revenge killing?"

"I'm not discounting anyone or anything. This is Northern Ireland, after all. Revenge of the Butchers, is that what you think?"

"I don't know. Hell, there's a lot I don't know. I didn't know how my father died until Deirdre told me this morning. They kept it from me all these years. Even when I came back here during the nineties." I paused. That was a slipup. I didn't mean to open that door. He probably didn't know I was back here, and certainly didn't know I was working for the Agency. For a guy who was a covert spy for the Central Intelligence Agency, I sure had loose lips. So I quickly added, "The U.S. Department of State assigned me to do an agrarian research project here in 1994 and I stayed until 1999. I spent a lot of time with my family, but no one told me about the war between the Taggarts and the Butchers."

McLaughlin gave me an all-knowing look. "The State Department, eh? Agrarian research?"

"Right. 'Ninety-four to 'ninety-nine."

Then McLaughlin broke into another hearty laugh.

"What's so funny?" I said. "I was here for six years. Mostly brokering grain."

"Stop, Liam. I know all about you. You reported to Jim Westerfield."

I was shocked. Again. How the hell did McLaughlin know Westerfield was my station chief?

McLaughlin rose from his seat, picked up the check, took some coins out of his pocket and laid them on the table. He stretched his long arms and put his jacket on. "Are you going to let me see the trust? I'm going to get it sooner or later."

"Let's hold off for the time being. I don't want to violate my trustee's oath any more than I already have. I'm sure you'll get it sooner or later, but take my word for it, it won't help you solve this crime."

He shrugged. "My gut tells me there's gold somewhere and that this is a family affair. I could be wrong, but maybe someone wants more than his fair share. Maybe one of the relatives had a bone to pick. Fergus had a reputation. He was a tough old bird. Maybe he rubbed one of his brothers the wrong way. Or his kids." McLaughlin popped me on the chest with his index finger. "First theory of relativity. Fergus must have suspected that the killer would come from the family, otherwise why postpone the family distributions until the killer is found?"

I had to concede that was logical. "Those were my initial thoughts as well, but my wife came up with an alternate theory. Maybe Fergus deferred disclosure because he was *protecting* his heirs, because he didn't want the killer to know who was next in line to inherit the property."

"Hmm. Smart woman, your wife."

"You have no idea."

"Still, I want to talk to your uncles, but they won't talk to me."

"That's understandable. They've been at odds with the likes of you all their lives."

"The war is over, Liam."

"It may be for some people. Maybe not for my uncles. Maybe not for the Butchers. And maybe it wasn't for my poor Uncle Fergus. I'm not going to cross the Troubles off my list. Not yet."

McLaughlin smiled. "You're right. Some grudges don't go away. The smart money's on a member of the family, but the Taggarts did make a lot of enemies during the Troubles. See if you can get his brothers to talk to me. And drop by the station tomorrow. There's someone I want you to meet."

ELEVEN

• • •

MY MORNING RUN TOOK me south along the banks of the river and into the countryside. The weather was clear, the sky was Cubbie blue and the hills were emerald green, just as advertised. The morning dew added a little moisture to the air and the fragrance was sweet. It was surprising to me how much of the land was devoted to farming and how little commercial development surrounded Antrim. What a contrast to my morning run along Chicago's lakefront.

It wasn't hard to develop an abiding love for these enchanting green hills and valleys. In former times, hadn't I been bewitched myself? Not that Annie didn't play a prominent role in that regard during the year we spent together. She and this mystical island cast a spell on me, nothing less, and I was intoxicated by the prospect of spending the rest of my life in Ireland. She laughed and blamed it on the leprechauns. And what a beguiling laugh she had. As they say, the lilt of Irish laughter. I wonder what my life would have been like if I didn't have that falling out with Uncle Fergus. If I'd never met Seamus McManus. But those were not constructive thoughts for a man with a loving wife and a baby. I put them out of my mind and continued with my run.

Riley had called me late last night and asked if I'd meet him for lunch. I was looking forward to it. He was low-keyed and easygoing. The exact opposite of his mercurial brother. As youngsters, we spent many an afternoon kicking a soccer ball in the pasture. I had nothing but affection for Riley.

He suggested a place west of Antrim, famous for its grilled trout. The restaurant, Harbor House, turned out to be on the western shore of Lough Neagh, and right on the water's edge. I rightfully assumed that the trout was freshly caught.

Riley was already seated when I arrived and was enjoying a bottle of Harp and some chips. His greeting was warm. He had a smile on his face. The first thing he did was to ask about Catherine and Ben. Riley took out his phone to show me pictures of his daughters. Humble though I may be, I couldn't resist showing off my handsome boy.

The food was fresh and the beer was good, though not as cold as I prefer. As it was bound to, the conversation finally circled around to the trust. What was I going to do?

"I suppose I have to wait for the condition to occur," I answered. "I can't do anything until your father's murder is solved."

Riley leaned forward and spoke softly. "I have a problem, Liam. I need your help. My dad and I bought some shares in the company I work for, Global Investments, Inc. It was a stock offering to employees at the company, but it was pricey and most of my fellow employees couldn't swing it. I asked my dad if he would loan me the money to buy some of the shares and he asked me if it was a good investment. You know, I'm not exactly objective, but I really thought this would be a fabulous opportunity for us. So my dad said we could buy the lot and he would put up the money. We could own them jointly."

"How much were the shares?"

Riley grimaced a bit, then quietly said, "Eighty thousand pounds."

I let out a low whistle. "That's a lot of money."

"I know, but they'll be worth a lot more when Global gets past this financial mess."

"Uncle Fergus put up all the money?"

Riley nodded. "Since he put up the money and wire transferred the purchase price from his account through the underwriter, the stock was issued in the name of Fergus Taggart, but it was our joint investment. Really my investment, but he put up the money."

Uh-oh, I thought. This is heading in a dangerous direction. "Is there anything in writing that shows it was your *joint* investment?"

Riley shook his head. "I don't think my dad wanted Deirdre to know he invested so much money for me in the stock of my company.

The money came from their savings. At the time it was a great investment. Since then, we've run into problems with the regulators. That's why I need better control over the stock and that's why I need your help."

"What do you want me to do?"

"Does the trust say anything about the stock?"

"You know I can't discuss the terms."

"Liam, come on."

I shook my head. I probably shouldn't have taken the discussion any further but I wanted to see if I could help Riley. "It's an asset of the trust. A substantial one. I'm not sure my authority permits me to do this, Riley, and I would need some legal advice, but are you in a position to buy the stock from the trust for a fair market value, if the trust permits it?"

"Not at this time. Not yet. But you've read the trust and you know what it says. Does he leave the stock to me? It's really mine anyway."

What I knew was that all assets were to be held until the murderer was found. Then the assets were to be sold and the cash split seven ways, but I couldn't tell him that. "You know I really can't discuss it. The trust has to remain secret for now."

"Well, the way I figure it, Liam, the stock properly belongs to me. It was, at the very least, a joint investment, so why wouldn't it pass to me automatically on the death of my dad?"

"I think we're going to have to leave that issue for a later time, Riley. You know I can't do anything until the murder is solved."

Riley started to become agitated. "Liam, it's *my* company. It's *my* stock. Global's president, Ross Penters, offered it to *me*. There are things going on at the company that require flexibility and affirmative action by the shareholders. You have no right to withhold it."

"I'm sorry, Riley."

He became increasingly anxious and I saw little sweat beads forming on his forehead. This was a Riley I had never seen before. "Liam, maybe you don't fully appreciate the situation. It's a closely held company. The stock was offered to *me* because I'm a trusted insider. Mr. Penters isn't going to like anyone else holding stock in his company. It can't go to my brother or Deirdre or anyone else. Don't you understand? It has to go to me."

Now the issue was becoming more complicated. If Penters wouldn't like another Taggart family member owning shares in his company, he certainly wouldn't want me to sell the stock to the public in order to liquidate the asset. But I had my instructions. My hands were tied.

"Again, Riley, I'm sorry. There's nothing I can do at this time."

With that, he stood, looked down at me and shook his head. "I'm really disappointed in you, Liam. Really. This is totally unfair."

I tried to repeat that I was sorry, but he flipped his napkin on the table and walked out of the door. I was sure this was only the beginning. Make way for a parade of problems, including the fact that he stuck me with the check.

It was time to call Catherine, so I returned to the hotel.

R ECONNECTING WITH MY WIFE was the highlight of my day. My loving, brilliant wife who, unfortunately, was three thousand six hundred miles away. I described the documents I found in the folder, the articles and the pictures. I recounted my discussions with McLaughlin and his opinions. I also told her what Deirdre revealed about the tragedies that befell my family forty years ago. It was painful but the telling was a catharsis. Catherine was such a good listener. It seemed like I'd been away for months, rather than days.

"I can't believe it," she said, "your father and your sister were both murdered on the same day during the Troubles? And your family kept it from you?"

"I'm afraid so. Every day things get more complicated. I might have bitten off more than I can chew on this one, Cat. Now Riley wants me to give him the stock that sits in Fergus's name."

"You can't do that. You'd be breaching your fiduciary duty as a trustee. You could end up liable to the other beneficiaries who are entitled to a portion of the value of that stock. Although, I suppose it would be all right if Riley deposited the fair market value of the stock in exchange for the shares."

"I suggested it, but he doesn't have the money. He wants the stock outright."

"You can't do it. Sorry you're in a fix, but it's not your fault. The trust controls. It dictates what you can and cannot do. Your job is to follow the instructions laid out in the trust. Your relatives should understand that. It was your uncle that set it all up, not you. You're only doing what he wanted done with his estate."

"Right. Tell that to Conor, tell that to Riley and tell that to whoever else is going to complain once the terms become known. How did I get in the middle of this mess? I think it was you that said I should come here and pay my respects. Make amends."

"Oh, I'm to blame, am I?"

"Of course. And now you need to come here and help me with it. I'm not sure when I can get back to Chicago."

There was a pause, then, "Liam, I've been getting some crank telephone calls."

"From who?"

"I don't know. The caller ID reads 'Caller Unknown.'"

"What does the caller say?"

"Well, it's all in a whisper. Someone breathes into the phone and then hangs up."

I froze. The note in my hotel room—"Get your arse back to Chicago where you can look after what's yours." This was no coincidence. My nervous condition immediately shot up to the level of DEFCON 3—Military on Standby.

"Cat, this is no crank. Get on a plane and get over here right now."

"Honey, I miss you too, but I can't do that, I have—"

"Listen to me. Those telephone calls aren't directed at you. They are messages for me, warnings, telling me to get out of Northern Ireland and go home. I didn't want to upset you, but my tires were slashed and my room was ransacked and a note was left on the bed telling me to go to Chicago and look after what's mine. That means you and Ben. Whoever it is doesn't want me to stay here as a trustee. Until I can leave, you need to be where I can keep an eye on you. I need to know you and Ben are safe."

"I'm sorry, Liam, but do you know how ridiculous that is? You're just a functionary, an appointed trustee in a testamentary trust who has to follow the trust instructions. If you left, someone else would have to follow those same instructions. Anyone would know that."

"McLaughlin thinks there are reasons someone is trying to scare me out of Antrim. He said I'm an imposing figure who won't be bullied.

Besides I'm a private investigator. There is someone who wants me out of Northern Ireland."

"Do you honestly believe that someone in Northern Ireland is foolish enough to think that Liam Taggart is going to quit because of crank calls? Seriously? That's juvenile. I'm not scared. I shouldn't have said anything. I'll be fine, don't worry. I'll even be extra careful."

"Cat, don't make light of this. I wish you'd just come here and then I could keep you safe."

"That's sweet. But these are just annoying pranks. I'll keep a good lookout. Here, your son wants to talk to you."

I heard some gurgles and then, "Ook, ah, ughoo." More squealing noises and Catherine laughing in the background. I sure missed those two. I'm not going to stop worrying until I get home.

N O SOONER HAD I finished the call and set the phone down, than it rang. It was O'Neill. "Well, Conor's gone ahead and hired a solicitor," he said. "Sure surprised me. I never thought he'd have the guts to do it. He's hired Michael Cooney, a young colt and a bit of a smart-ass. Cooney called to let me know that he's going to file a lawsuit first thing tomorrow morning to declare the will and trust null and void. He said he was going to schedule an emergency hearing as soon as he could get on the docket."

I wanted to say, "That's the best news I've had all day, now somebody else can sit in the dunk tank," but I kept it to myself. I said, more properly, "What is your advice?"

"Cooney asked that we convene a meeting at his office of all parties with rights under the trust agreement. I assume that means all of the trust beneficiaries."

"How does he know who the beneficiaries are?"

"I don't think he does, but he's a very good fisherman, and this is his way of forcing us to identify who the beneficiaries are."

"What's the Irish equivalent of 'Piss off'?"

"Piss off."

"Then tell him your client said 'Piss off.'"

"I would happily comply, but for the fact that the case will be assigned to Judge McNulty. She'll insist that the parties meet and confer at the earliest opportunity, and in all events, prior to any hearing. So even if I said piss off, Judge McNulty would instruct us to meet."

"Then I ask you again, what is your advice?"

"I say we throw the meeting open to anyone who would like to come. Any interested party. That way, we're not tipping our hand. We don't identify anyone as a beneficiary."

"Okay. When and where?"

"I'll suggest tomorrow at his office."

"By the way, Malcolm, on what basis do Conor and his lawyer seek to invalidate the will and trust?"

"Why, lunacy of course. No sane person would write a will in anticipation of being assassinated without involving the police or, at a minimum, exposing the would-be assassin."

That thought had occurred to me as well.

A FORMIDABLE BURGUNDY BRICK structure houses the Antrim PSNI station. I can understand that an architect isn't inclined to make a jail warm and fuzzy, but this one borders on medieval. I went through a security gate, entered the building and asked for Inspector McLaughlin. Inside, the station didn't differ from those I'd come to know in Chicago. The officers, women and men alike, were neatly dressed with pressed uniforms, white shirts, neckties and hats placed squarely on their heads. But not Inspector McLaughlin. Even though it was August, he was in a dark green and plum wool plaid sport coat over a tan shirt and dark brown slacks. He nodded when he saw me and gestured for me to follow him back into his office.

"Have a seat," he said. "As I told you, I'm running into a brick wall with your Taggart family. They won't work with me. They won't even talk to me."

"I can ask them to cooperate, but there's an ingrained animosity where the Royal Ulster Constabulary is concerned."

"We're not the RUC any more, Liam. PSNI. Police Service of Northern Ireland. Since 2001. Supported by all political parties, left and right." He tapped an engraved plaque that sat on the corner of his desk. It read THE ACHIEVEMENT OF A PEACEFUL AND JUST SOCIETY WOULD BE THE TRUE MEMORIAL TO THE VICTIMS OF THE VIOLENCE.

"That's straight out of the Good Friday Peace Agreement, and I believe in it."

"I'm sure that's true, but as far as my uncles are concerned, before this department was called the PSNI, it was the RUC, which they regard as a bunch of unionist jaw breakers, you'll pardon the expression. It reminds me of Abraham Lincoln's parable: 'If you call a tail a leg, how many legs does a dog have?' It's four of course, because it doesn't matter what you call it, it's still a tail. Northern Ireland may have reorganized its force and renamed it, but to my uncles, it's still a tail."

McLaughlin nodded. "That's why I asked you to come here today. They'll all open up to you, Liam. People will talk to you. You can go places I can't and get information unavailable to me. You can find the hidden pieces to this puzzle. And besides, you know what you're doing. You did it all in the nineties."

I couldn't believe that he was asking me to snoop on my family again. I was just starting to earn their confidence after deceiving them twenty years ago. I answered immediately, "No. Don't ask me to be dishonest again. I conned them before, I used them, I betrayed them and I'll never do that again."

"For Chrissake, Liam, I'm not asking you to be dishonest. I'm asking you to help me run an investigation. Do it right out in the open, and don't limit it to your family, but I do need their help."

I was doubtful. It's not that I didn't trust McLaughlin, which I didn't entirely, but how effective could I be? "How can I do that?" I answered. "I have no authority in Northern Ireland. I'm not licensed here. I don't even have a gun permit."

"Well, I'm not asking you to shoot anyone. As for your investigator's license, that's a mere technicality. Just ask and I'll get you whatever authority you need, and I'll assign one of my top officers to work with you full-time." He pressed a button on his phone and said, "Send in Sergeant Dooley."

"Wait a minute. Dooley? Blond? A hundred and twenty pounds? The one who stood like a pit bull at my uncle's front door? You want me to partner up with her?"

McLaughlin laughed. "She's one of my best."

Sgt. Dooley knocked politely on the door and entered. Crisply dressed, she stood at ease in front of McLaughlin's desk. She gave me a sideways glance and had to stifle a smile.

"This is Liam Taggart, Sergeant. Do you two know each other?" McLaughlin asked.

"Yes, sir," she said. "I believe he claims to be the owner of the property at 68 Long Road."

"Trustee," I said.

Another whimsical look from her. Askance. "Pretty sure you said *owner.*"

"Maybe I did."

McLaughlin interrupted. "Sergeant, I'm assigning you to assist Mr. Taggart, who has generously agreed to help us investigate Fergus Taggart's homicide. He knows his way around; the CIA stationed him here in the nineties. He's also a valuable resource to us because of his close relationship to his family. I'd like you to be available to him at all times and make sure he gets whatever he needs."

"Yes, sir."

Just as McLaughlin finished his instructions, my cell phone buzzed. Janie's message read, "Would you please come out to the house? Eamon and Robert are here with Deirdre. Problem."

I showed the text to McLaughlin. "Ah, a family get-together. Why don't the two of you take a ride out there," he said. "It'll be a fine opportunity for Sgt. Dooley to get acquainted."

I cringed. "If she goes out there in a uniform, my family will shut us both out. I think she should go in plainclothes and I don't think she should volunteer that she's a police officer."

McLaughlin nodded. "You're right." He shooed her out with a brush of his hand. She saluted, turned with a snap and left to change.

"You'll like working with her. She's very smart and tireless. Not to mention very skilled. She's an Olympic sharpshooter."

"What?"

"Seriously, it's true. Megan Dooley captained the UK women's sharpshooting team in the London Olympics and just missed medaling. Your family will like her even if they find out she's a police officer."

I shook my head. "You don't know my family. They all cut their teeth in the Lower Falls. There's resentment that'll never go away. Even now they're convinced the murder is a leftover vendetta from the Troubles."

McLaughlin put his feet up on his desk and leaned back in his chair. "You think I don't know the likes of the Taggart clan? Citizens of the Lower Falls? I was there, Liam. As a young officer in the RUC, I was assigned to West Belfast. My unit, a bunch of raw recruits, rolled into the Falls every other day looking for guns. No matter what anyone says—Catholics, Protestants, republicans, loyalists—it was the endless supply of armaments that kept that sectarian war going. Forget the class struggle, the religious differences, the civil rights marches, it could have all been resolved peacefully if it weren't for the endless supply of weapons.

"They were coming in from every direction, Liam. From liberal do-gooders in California, to arms merchants in Eastern Europe, to Colonel Ghadaffi himself. You can't keep a bonfire going unless you keep tossing in more wood. Same with the Troubles.

"Shit, we'd assemble in the morning, roll down Divis, onto Falls Road, Leeson Street, Ross Road. We were nothing but a bunch of scared twenty-year-olds with flak jackets and rifles. Find those IRA guns, they told us. Find the explosives. We'd go door-to-door. Kids would throw rocks at us. Snipers would take potshots at us. And you know what? We'd find 'em. Sure as hell. Stashes of armaments in basements and closets and back bedrooms. It's true we'd rough people up, but we'd find the goddamn guns. We'd confiscate 'em and the next day there'd be another shipment coming in. You think we were fighting the Catholics? Hell no. We were fighting the arms merchants.

"It was big money, Liam. Millions and millions in weapons all paid for by foreign money, Hollywood types, folk singers, do-gooders, and fund-raisers thinking they were donating money to help the poor oppressed Catholics, but what they were really doing was putting that money in the pockets of the arms dealers. You think the RUC was there to oppress the Catholics? I couldn't have given a shit about the Catholics. Sorry. We weren't there to oppress anyone. We were trying to take the goddamn weapons away. Look at all your recent conflicts—Bosnia, Somalia, Syria or even the streets of your hometown Chicago—it's all a money game for the arms merchants. The gun dealers cause more damage to society than any plague ever did."

I shared his opinion on the arms merchants, but not on the RUC. There was no disputing the pervasive oppression of the Catholic minority during the Troubles. I changed the subject. "Were you able to get any prints off the papers from the folder or the photographs?"

He shook his head. "Nope. Just yours. Your uncle's."

Just then Megan Dooley walked back into the room. She was sharply dressed in a dark blue suit, midlength skirt, lavender blouse and contrasting scarf. Best-looking policeman I'd ever seen.

TWELVE

• • •

A S IT TURNED OUT, it was not a fine opportunity to get acquainted. I was taking her to meet my uncles and I thought
the family would be thrilled that I brought in someone local
to help me with the investigation. I thought they'd be as charmed by
Megan Dooley as I was. I was dead wrong. I should have better appreciated the depth of my uncles' distrust of anyone who wasn't a Taggart.
Especially Uncle Eamon. That was conveyed to me the moment we
walked in and Uncle Eamon said, "What is *she* doing here?"

"Her name is Megan Dooley and she's here to help me. From the
minute I got here, you have all asked me to investigate and there's only
so much I can do as an unlicensed PI. Megan's experienced and fully
licensed. All of us have the same goal in mind—finding Uncle Fergus's
killer."

"I don't like airing family laundry with outsiders," Eamon said, ges-
turing with his thumb in Megan's direction. "Is she a Protestant?"

"I didn't ask. And I won't. Don't insult her. I'm sure you'll appreciate her help."

"We don't need her help, Liam. Back in the nineties, while you
were out snooping, this one here was skipping rope at some fancy Protestant girls' school in Whitehead. What can she do for us?"

I started to speak, but Megan stepped forward. "I grew up in Derry,
not Whitehead, five of us in a two-bedroom apartment. My father was
a mail carrier. No one in my family ever fought in the Troubles. I
earned the highest marks in criminal justice at Queen's University. I

captained the UK Olympic sharpshooting team. I'm fully licensed. I can get Liam into places he can't go. And I'm a damn good rope skipper."

Eamon looked at his brother and the two of them shrugged. "I didn't mean nothing personal," Eamon said quietly.

Janie laughed. "If that wasn't personal, what is?"

Megan brushed it off. "It's okay. If I were in your shoes with your history, I might feel the same way."

Nice move, I thought. "Let's get to the text message. What's the problem? Why are we all together?"

Eamon handed a letter-sized envelope to me. Inside were two pictures. One was a duplicate of the picture Deirdre had handed to me, the redbrick house, ravaged by a fire and reduced to rubble. But on the back of Eamon's picture, in block printing, a note read, "PAYBACK TIME TAGGARTS."

"It was in my mailbox this morning," Eamon said. "That picture," he pointed to the rubble that was once a residence, "do you recognize it?"

I shrugged and then shook my head.

"Well, I do. That was Archie Walker's house, or what was left of it after the fire."

"They've come back to exact their vengeance," Robert said quietly. "Marked for death."

"But it's been forty years," I said. "It doesn't make sense. Why would they wait this long? Why now? And what does that mean, 'Marked for death'?"

"Tit for tat, son. Back in the day," Eamon said, "when someone found a note or a picture like this in his mailbox, people said he was marked for death. It's a calling card, Liam. Fergus was marked for death and now me. Maybe the Walker boys have been away, maybe they've been in prison and now they got out. But it's them. And isn't it just like a Walker to boast about a murder and let you know the Butchers are back in business. They want us to know that they exacted their revenge on Fergus and now I'm next in line."

I looked carefully at the other picture. It appeared to be taken at a wake. It was obviously in a funeral home, and a unionist one at that. A folded Union Jack hung over the foot of the closed coffin. "What do you make of this?" I said.

"Why don't you take a close look at the sign behind the door on the right," Eamon said. "It's Archie Walker's wake. Look at it. Got his name on the sign. The Walkers—they want us to know it's payback time."

I put the pictures back in the envelope and handed it to Megan. "What type of security do you have where you live?" she said.

"I live on the other side of Antrim, fifteen miles up," Eamon said. "My security is a locked door, a disagreeable dog and a loaded carbine. I'll be ready for the Walkers, you can bet your ass."

I didn't like the odds of my frail, old uncle shooting it out at the O.K. Corral. "What about moving in with one of your nephews for a while?" I said.

"Couldn't and wouldn't. I won't be putting them in danger."

"You're welcome to move in here," Deirdre said. "There's plenty of room and I've got the security company installing a system tomorrow."

"Bah. Not necessary. I can take care of myself."

I raised my hand like a stop sign. "Hold on, Uncle Eamon, it's a good idea. Deirdre's closer to town and I can keep an eye on you."

"I will, as well," Megan said. She took two blank cards and a pen from her pocket, wrote on the cards and handed one to Eamon and one to Robert. "That's my cell phone number on the card. If you can't reach Liam, you can call me anytime." They nodded and smiled. My initial thoughts were correct, Megan radiates competence. She took out a notepad, sat on the edge of the couch and said, "What can you tell me about the Walker family?"

"The Walkers was just Ulster trash," Eamon said. "They were part of the Shankill Butchers. Archie was a first lieutenant to Lenny Murphy, as I recall." He looked directly at Megan and emphasized his points with his index finger. "He was nothing but a dirty bastard who killed in cold blood. He shot my innocent little niece, Molly, her being six years old, and he was responsible for the death of me brother Danny."

"This was during the Troubles?"

Eamon nodded. "Aye. In 1974. Afterward, we heard tell that some righteous Catholics firebombed his house." Eamon shot a sideways glance at Robert. "Don't really know who was in it at the time. Heard that Archie had a wife and three kids. He also had three brothers: Thomas, Geoffrey and Edward. One of them was killed by the IRA in

1977. I also heard that one of the Walker boys died in 1982, about the time that Lenny Murphy was killed."

"Edward Walker died alongside his partner Lenny Murphy in Dublin," Megan said. "They never caught the shooter."

"And they never will."

"What about the third brother, Thomas?"

"Don't know. Far as I know, he's alive somewhere."

"Uncle Eamon, I'm going to leave now, but I want you to call me or call Megan if you see anything that doesn't look right or if you receive any more threats."

I walked Megan out to the car. She smiled at me. "Was that your uncle taking credit for Murphy and Walker?"

"I didn't hear anything."

"Right. He's like so many of his generation, they'll never let it go. To them, these ancient feuds are like smoldering embers. They never quite go out, and then a wind comes along and ignites a brushfire. Do you think it was one of the Walker clan that killed your uncle?"

"I didn't at first, but somebody planted that picture in Fergus's mailbox before he died and now Eamon's found two in his mailbox. Marked for death. Sure points to the Butchers."

She shook her head. "Not to me. That would be too easy."

Megan and I took the pictures back to the station to see whether any useful prints could be identified, but I knew there wouldn't be. On the way back, I received a call from O'Neill telling me that he confirmed a meeting at Michael Cooney's office. "Be prepared for a showboat and some fireworks."

A S MCLAUGHLIN STUDIED THE photos, I filled him in on my telephone call with O'Neill. "Michael Cooney wants to have a meeting. He hasn't seen the trust and he doesn't know who the beneficiaries are, so O'Neill opened it up to anyone who wants to appear. All interested parties. I expect the meeting to be noisy and contentious."

"Good. If the killer is a related party, he or she will be there and might make a mistake."

I was convinced that the killer wasn't a family member, no matter what McLaughlin thought. I knew the family and no one was that coldhearted. My instincts were pushing me in the direction of a Walker revenge killing, or maybe some other ancient vendetta that I didn't know about. "What makes you think it's not a holdover from the Troubles?" I said.

McLaughlin tilted his chair back and crossed his fingers on his stomach. "I don't know. I hope to hell it's not. The last thing we need is the reemergence of another sectarian skirmish. I'm going to work real hard to make sure that doesn't happen, but I'm not going to eliminate the current cast of characters. Not yet. I'd like to see what happens at the gathering of *all interested parties.*"

"Do you want to be there? You're an interested party."

"Interested, yes. Party, no. No one would open their mouth if I was sitting in the room. Take Dooley. She has a keen mind. I told you she's one of my best."

I shook McLaughlin's hand and left to grab a quick dinner before returning to the hotel. By then it would be time to call Catherine.

B AD NEWS, CAT. CONOR'S filing a lawsuit and there'll be a hearing soon. Mr. O'Neill insists I have to stay here and testify at the hearing."

"I know you blame me for all this. What is it you say, 'pick up the telephone and your train goes off the track'?"

"Something like that."

"Well, don't worry. Ben and I will get along just fine. Don't let those wigged barristers intimidate you."

I laughed at that. I saw visions of me sitting in the dock at Old Bailey and a robed barrister leveling accusations at me, accosting me in thunderous tones.

"I don't think there'll be any barristers, Cat. The lawyers in the lower courts are solicitors. Just like your colleagues in Chicago. So how are things going at home? Any more of those phone calls?"

"Yes. Four more. I'm changing the number on the house phone and I'll keep it unlisted. Call me on my cell until I give you the new number. But don't worry, we're fine here."

More calls and she says don't worry? Her indifference only serves to increase my worry. "Cat, it's so obvious. The calls are coming from

Northern Ireland. They want to frighten both of us so that I'll come home. If you don't want to come here, then go stay at your sister's for a while. You'll feel safer and I need to make sure you're safe."

"These are just prank calls. Even if they are from Northern Ireland, they're ineffectual. They're not dangerous."

"You don't know that. They're clearly a warning. Warnings, if not heeded, can become unwanted consequences. There's no doubt they're part of a continuing effort to get me to leave Northern Ireland."

"But they're just phone calls. And they don't scare me. They're having more effect on you than me. I can't leave just yet. I have a petition to present next week. I'm knee-deep in a very contentious case and I can't run out on clients who have been paying me to litigate their cases. Maybe when this month's hearings are finished, I'll go out to Carol's or come to see you. In the meantime, I need to stay here. I'll be extra careful."

"I don't like it, Cat. Double-lock the doors. Be careful going to and from the car."

"Yes, sir."

"Love you, Cat."

"Love you too."

I HAD BARELY HUNG up with Catherine when there was a knock on my hotel room door. The first thought that came to mind: I wish I had my gun. I walked quietly to the door and looked through the peephole. It was Janie and she didn't look good.

"I hope I'm not intruding," she said. "I . . . I mean on your privacy." Her bottom lip was quivering and her eyes were watery.

I shook my head. "Of course not, don't be silly." I swung back the door to let her in. "What's wrong?"

"Oh, nothing really." Her voice was strained. "I just wondered if maybe . . . you weren't doing anything important and wanted . . . wanted to get a beer or something." Then she broke into tears. I held her while she buried her head in my chest and cried for an uncomfortably long period of time. Finally she backed up, wiped her eyes and sniffled. Her pretty little face was flushed. "I'm so sorry," she said between gasps. "I'm making a fool of myself, I need to go."

"No, no. Why don't you tell me what's wrong?"

"It's nothing. It's just been a bad day. This evening was pretty tough."

"Charles?"

She hesitated, then nodded. "But it's not like this all the time. He's really a good guy. It's only when there's been a crisis in his business and the stress gets too hard for him." She forced a smile. "He doesn't handle stress very well."

"He didn't hurt you, did he?"

She shook her head. "Not physically. Not really." She wiped her eyes and blew her nose. "I should know better. I should know to get out of the house when one of his deals is in trouble. Today, he was having an argument with some shipping company. He couldn't get the containers loaded on time. He was shouting at the phone and then, then he couldn't find his briefcase and he said it was all my fault and I . . . I just felt like I needed to see a friendly face, that's all."

I took her around the corner to a pub where we each ordered a beer. I could tell she felt embarrassed by all this. "Do you think you should stay apart for a while? Give things a chance to cool down? Think this thing through?"

She shook her head. "No, I'll go home and he'll be fine. He'll apologize like he always does and things will be great again. Really, he treats me very well."

What do I say to someone who's caught in a relationship like that? I'm a PI, not a therapist, but two thoughts came to mind: Janie needs to get out of this abusive relationship or I need to go have a serious discussion with this punk. Maybe both. "It doesn't sound like he treated you very well tonight."

"No, not tonight."

"Why don't you get a room at the hotel for a day or two," I said. "I think there's a lot of empty rooms."

She thought for a moment and then nodded. "Yeah, you're right, maybe I will. Maybe that will show him that he shouldn't treat me so harshly." She took a sip of beer and then changed the subject. "Are you going to the meeting at Solicitor Cooney's office tomorrow?"

"I am. I'm an interested party. More than that. I'm the bull's-eye in the center of Conor's target."

"Ah yes, the unwilling volunteer. I'm sorry I got you into this. It was my phone call that dragged you out here, wasn't it?"

"Nope. It was my uncle's will and trust that drafted me into service." Then a lightbulb went off in my head. "Come to think of it, when you called and told me to come to Antrim, you said 'The family needs you, Uncle Fergus needs you.'"

"That I did."

"You knew, didn't you? You knew that my uncle had prepared a will and trust that appointed me as trustee!"

"Yes, I did."

"What else did you know, Janie?"

"Well, quite a bit, actually. Uncle Fergus and I were very close. I knew he was going to put all his property in a trust and appoint someone he could rely on. That was you. He told me that he didn't want to appoint me as trustee, that he thought there might be trouble and he knew he could depend on you. Deirdre was there when he told me. We both knew that you were going to be appointed trustee, but I don't think either of us has seen the trust. Not me anyway. Other than Deirdre and me, I don't think anyone else even knew there was a trust."

"Did he tell you he feared someone was trying to kill him?"

"No. Just what I told you. He also didn't tell me anything about the terms of the trust or who the beneficiaries would be and it wasn't my place to ask."

"Do you know anyone named Bridget McGregor?"

She shrugged her shoulders and shook her head. "No, should I?"

"I guess not."

We shared a couple more beers and I paid the bill. As we walked to the door, Janie gave me a kiss on the cheek and said, "Thanks for being here for me. I'm going to head home."

"Are you sure?"

She nodded. "It'll be fine."

"Do you want me to go with you? Maybe have a little talk with Charles?"

She smiled and shook her pretty head.

I went back to the bar, ordered another beer and sat there thinking about Deirdre. She knew about the will and trust. She knew I was the appointed trustee. She knew Fergus was on edge. What else did she know? I was sure she knew a lot more than she was letting on. If so, why wouldn't she open up to me? I know there was a sixteen-year lapse in communications and that I should have called, but I didn't feel she was holding it against me. I was confident we had reconnected, reestablished our close relationship. Maybe we never lost it. For six very important years of my boyhood we forged a strong bond—like mother and son. We still had it; I could see it in her eyes.

THIRTEEN

• • •

THE OFFICES OF SOLICITOR Michael Cooney, Esq., were space-age compared to Malcolm O'Neill's Elizabethan suite. Everything was new and high-tech—ergonomic furniture and desk chairs, tables with minimalistic lines and brightly colored occasional pieces. His conference room was larger than O'Neill's, and that turned out to be a bonus given the number of interested parties that showed up. Sitting around the long rectangular glass-and-steel table, the participants positioned themselves according to their dispositions— older and calmer on one side, younger and combative on the other. To my left were Conor, Riley and Conor's two sons: Sean and Harry—the aggressive bunch. To the right were Deirdre, Robert and Eamon. I sat next to O'Neill at one end alongside Megan, who arrived looking very corporate—a gray suit, powder blue blouse and contrasting paisley scarf. Me? Jeans and a Chicago Cubs sweatshirt. Okay, I was making a statement. I wasn't going to fancy-up for Solicitor Michael Cooney, Esq., who was trying to fire me. Besides, it was one of my dressier sweatshirts. There was an empty chair next to Conor, which I assumed would be occupied by Cooney whenever he decided to make his grand entrance.

Janie was missing and her absence worried me. I shouldn't have let her go home last night. The least I could have done was to check up on her, but I fell asleep. The more the seconds ticked, the more anxious I became and just as I made up my mind to step out into the hall and place the call, Janie and Charles waltzed into the room.

"Sorry that we're late," she said, as bouncy and cheerful as ever, as if last night had never occurred. She wore a sparkly gold necklace. I wondered if that was Charles's peace offering. Charles was his gregarious self, flashing his Colgate smile and warmly shaking everybody's hand. They took their seats beside Robert on the congenial side of the table, and small talk occupied the air for a few minutes until Cooney entered.

Considerably younger than O'Neill, Cooney breezed in, set his papers on the table next to Conor and walked around introducing himself and thanking everyone for coming to the meeting on such short notice. When he got to Megan, he said, "I don't think I know who you are. I'm Mike Cooney."

"Megan Dooley."

"May I know the purpose of your presence here?"

I interrupted and answered for her. "She's assisting me in looking into the death of my uncle."

"In what capacity?"

"Investigator," she replied. "I'm acting at the direction of Liam Taggart."

Cooney put on a patronizing smile. "Well isn't that nice, but this is a gathering of Fergus Taggart's family, so is it really appropriate for you to be here today?"

"It is if you want *me* here," I said.

"I see, so you want to put this on a contentious platform from the very beginning? I had hopes that we could all work together. Peacefully. I believe it's necessary that we try very hard to come together and have this matter straightened out at the earliest possible time," he said, looking to O'Neill for concurrence. "That benefits all of us, don't you agree, Malcolm?"

"It's your show, Michael," O'Neill said. "Why did you bring us here?"

"Yes, well, we all know why. Conor has filed a lawsuit to end this farce. The reason we have gathered in my office this morning is to comply with court rules that require us to meet and confer in advance of our initial court appearance." He leaned in my direction. "Mr. Taggart, did you bring the trust agreement with you today?"

I nodded. "Yes, I did."

"Excellent. May I see it, please?"

"No, I'm afraid not. I brought it for reference purposes only. It's confidential."

"Pardon me?"

"I said no."

"Mr. Taggart, I don't think you fully understand the nature of our proceedings here in Northern Ireland. Judge McNulty will ask us if we have met and conferred prior to the first court appearance. That means to share information. You and I both know that ultimately we will see a copy of the trust. In fact, beneficiaries have a *right* to see the trust. Therefore, I *insist* on seeing the document right now." He tapped his finger on the table.

"Oh, you insist? Well then, when you put it that way, the answer is still no."

Turning to O'Neill, he said, "Malcolm, I appeal to you. The laws of this realm give my client an absolute right to a copy of that trust. I don't think there's any argument on that point, is there? We all agree, don't we?"

"Michael, let's stop the games," O'Neill said. "The trust is sealed until the testator's killer is found. What we all agree on is that Liam is the named trustee and he is only following Fergus's instructions. You knew that would be our position. Please tell me you didn't gather us all here this morning just to hear that in person."

"Excuse me, Malcolm, but apparently not everyone agrees. Fergus Taggart's two children do not agree. His grandchildren Sean Taggart and Harry Taggart do not agree. So it seems as though Fergus Taggart's lineal heirs are rightfully contesting the total control that is being exerted by an estranged American nephew. They are justifiably concerned that some trickery is afoot to deny them their inheritance rights."

O'Neill bounced to his feet. "Trickery, is it? Fergus Taggart possessed the right to bequest his property to whomsoever he chose in whatever manner he chose. I drafted the documents. *Me*, Michael. You can be damn well sure they're valid and enforceable. You've seen the will. The will was witnessed and is unquestionably valid."

Cooney stood as well. They faced each other in defiance, like prize-fighters ready for the bell. I considered the possibility that we might have a little bare knuckles going on.

"Afraid not," Cooney said. "The validity is questioned. Fergus Taggart's mental state is questioned. Once we're allowed to see it, I'm sure the bizarre terms of his trust will also be brought into question. There will be questions galore. We are *contesting* the will. We'll let the judge decide the validity of the instruments." Then surprisingly, he waved his hand from side to side, as though dispensing with everything that had been said. "But, but, but. That is not the only reason I have asked you all to join me this morning."

Cooney gestured toward his client. "Conor has a proposal. Let's all discuss it here like gentlemen and ladies and come to a reasonable accommodation. Otherwise I will present my emergency motion to the court and we'll do it the hard way. Conor?"

Conor looked around the room, but avoided making eye contact with me. "Yeah, as Mr. Cooney says, I have a proposal. It's like I said before, I propose that we all hire a professional investigator licensed in Northern Ireland to find the bastard that killed my father. We all know the PSNI won't do shit. We also know that the reason my father put that weird language in the will was to make sure we'd catch the guy who was threatening him. You know, it was his way of motivating us. He didn't intend to disinherit his own kids. So I propose we carry out my father's intent, be properly motivated and appoint a qualified private detective."

Then Conor turned his attention to me. "Liam's an American, he doesn't know anything about our customs or our way of life. He's never worked here and he's not even licensed here. Let's turn it over to a *real* professional, one who will find the killer, no matter who he is. And once we turn it over, that should be sufficient. My father's last wishes will have achieved their purpose. We will have been motivated. Once it's out of our hands and in the hands of the independent investigator, then we've done all we can and we should all get our copies of the trust so that we can protect our rights. No more secrets."

Now it was O'Neill's turn. "You may be right, Conor, that the appointment of an independent investigator might serve your father's subjective intent, but none of us sitting here really know what Fergus's subjective intent was, do we? We are left only with the written word. The killer has to be found before any of you get to see the document. Those were his words. Take them at their plain meaning.

"As to the qualifications of an investigator, Conor, Ms. Dooley is fully licensed and authorized in Northern Ireland. She's working closely with Liam and she knows all about Irish customs and ways of life. Inspector McLaughlin is an experienced police officer and he is also independent and he's working hard as well. Finally, as attorney for the trustee, I cannot recommend spending any trust money to hire another investigator, which I consider unnecessary and superfluous."

Conor looked over at Megan with a sneer. "Dooley? How experienced is she? Did she finish high school yet?"

"That's enough, Conor," I said.

His mercury was rising. "Look, Liam, it's not just her, it's *you*. I don't want you poking around my father's property. You're nothing but a bloody snoop. You've been that way for twenty years. You turned your back on your family. You turned your back on your uncle who raised you. You even turned your back on Annie. You coulda had her if you weren't a slimy rat. She dumped you because you turned out to be a dishonest asshole. I don't like your intrusion, Liam. I don't like your attitude. In fact, I don't like *you* at all. I want you to stay the hell out of my family's house. I grew up in that house. That's my house. That's Riley's house. Maybe Deirdre would argue it's her house, but it's sure as hell ain't *your* house. So stay the hell out. In fact, get your ass out of Antrim, the sooner the better."

O'Neill rose to his feet again. So did I. Bare knuckles were sounding better and better. And bringing Annie into this discussion was way out of line.

"Are we done here, Mr. Cooney?" O'Neill said. "Is this your idea of a good faith attempt at compromise? Unless and until the court decrees otherwise, Mr. Liam Taggart is the duly appointed trustee of all of the assets belonging to the late Fergus Taggart. So, Conor, you're wrong. It *is* his house, at least for the time being. And he will conduct whatever investigations he deems prudent to the circumstances."

With that, Cooney reached into his stack of papers and handed a document to O'Neill. "Not so fast, Malcolm. This is a copy of my emergency motion to turn over copies of the trust, which I have set for tomorrow morning in Judge McNulty's courtroom. It's what I warned you about. We will represent to her that we held our good faith conference and despite our best efforts, we could not come to an agreement. I will ask the judge to order the turnover of the trust and the removal of Liam Taggart as trustee. We will dissolve this nonsensical trust. I have a client to represent and I will do so vigorously, no matter what the remainder of this dysfunctional family wants."

I looked to my right. Robert had his head down, sadly shaking it from side to side. Eamon's lips were pressed together and his eyes were glaring. Deirdre was sobbing. Tears rolled down her cheeks and fell on the table. "Vultures," she said, her voice rising. "Ravens, grackles. All picking at Fergus's remains. Carrion eaters!" She rose from her chair and left the room.

Eamon glared at Cooney. "You better watch your mouth, sonny."

"You knew that Conor's ridiculous proposal was a sham," O'Neill said. "You brought us here so you could falsely represent to Judge McNulty that we had a *good faith* meeting, but there was nothing good faith about it. File your motion, solicitor. We'll be there."

Cooney shrugged. "As you see fit. Call it what you will, I think it was in good faith. But I have another good faith suggestion. Seeing as the family is all here and most of them agree with me, why don't we vote on Conor's proposal?"

"A vote?" barked O'Neill, with as much sarcasm as he could muster, which in all fairness was quite a bit. "By all means, let's vote. After all, this is a democracy, isn't it? Oh, wait. No, it's not. This is a will and trust, which contain a testator's specific instructions. The majority voice of these people is totally irrelevant. The documents control. Liam is the duly appointed trustee and is acting wholly within his authority."

"How would we know he's acting within his authority, Malcolm?" said Cooney with a smug smile. "The trust is sealed. We've never seen it."

"Indeed it is. Good day."

"One minute," I said. "I need to clear the air on a very troublesome problem. Someone has been making phone calls to my home, to my wife. Calling at all hours and then hanging up. I don't know where they're coming from. Yet. But if I find they're coming from someone in this room, I'm going to make damn sure that person will have a hard time ever dialing a telephone in the future. And I want to let you all know, I'm not leaving. Threaten all you want, I'm staying. It's one thing to slash my tires, another to mess up my room, but when you threaten my wife, you've crossed my line."

"No one in here is phoning your damn house, Liam," Conor said. "Get off your horse. But maybe if you went home where you belong, the calls would stop."

That was enough. It was close enough to an admission. I started around the corner of the table, but O'Neill grabbed my arm. "Not the time or the place. Let's go."

"Adios until tomorrow," Cooney said and winked at Conor.

O'Neill, Megan and I left the room. Deirdre and Eamon were walking slowly down the hall, their arms around each other. Two old warriors. They did not deserve the disrespect.

"C'mon, I'll drive you home." They nodded and we started walking toward the car.

"Liam," Charles called. "Do you have a moment?"

I opened the car for Deirdre and Eamon, and walked over to talk to Charles.

"Janie told me about those pictures," he said. "The ones of the Walker house. What do you make of that?"

"I don't really know, Charles. It seems as though someone wants us to think that Fergus's death was a revenge killing, doesn't it?"

"It does indeed. Eamon said he got one in his mailbox. Just like Fergus. You know, during the Troubles these kinds of photos were a murderer's calling card. It meant the recipient was marked for death."

"I've heard that, but this isn't the Troubles anymore and I don't buy into that crap. What sense does it make? If it's revenge, why not just kill him and be done with it? Like Uncle Eamon says, tit for tat. Why warn him and alert him to the threat?"

"Because serial killers take a ghoulish pleasure in announcing their plans, torturing their victims with fear before they kill them. Eamon thinks he's marked for death and I do too. His life is in danger and I'd like to help if I can. I know a number of security companies. I can talk to them about placing a guard at the house."

"I'll let Deirdre and Eamon know."

"I'll help in any way I can," he said.

I nodded. "I'm sure that would be gratefully appreciated. I'll tell Inspector McLaughlin."

"I'd just as soon work with you, Liam."

"Sure," I said. "Let me know if you learn anything." I shook his hand and got into the car.

N OTHING MUCH WAS SAID between the three of us on the fifteen-minute ride to Deirdre's house. We stood at the door for a moment while she fumbled for her key.

"Will you be okay?" I said.

She nodded. Her face was flushed, her eyes were red. I felt so badly for her. "Talk to me, Aunt Deirdre."

She swallowed hard. "It's all hanging by a thread, Liam."

"Do you want me to come in for a while?"

She shook her head. "Eamon's here. And Fergus is always waiting for me. I need to be with him."

I didn't like that answer. "Aunt Deirdre, I know right now your grief seems overwhelming, but Uncle Fergus would want you to be strong. He wouldn't want you to do anything crazy. He'd want you to carry on."

She waived me off. "I'm not going to kill myself, Liam. I'm going to go inside, mix up a little tea and have my conversations with Fergus, like I always do, because he's there for me. He's sitting in every room in this house. He's everywhere I look. Now leave me be. Give me my time to grieve."

I smiled and gave her a strong hug. I loved that woman. "I'm sorry, I'm just worried about you."

She smiled back. "Back at that slimy lawyer's office, sitting in that room, all anyone cared about was how much they were going to get and how quickly they could get it. They're just a bunch of bloody harpies. All I could think about was my man was gone and I'll never see him again. I don't give a damn about any property. I just want my Fergus back. But I'll get through it. Don't worry about me."

I gave her another hug. Truth was, I could have stood there hugging her for an hour, and I'd have been the better for it. "You take care," I said. "Call me anytime."

I started to leave when she said, "What Conor said about Annie? It's not true, not one word of it. I know for a fact."

"It doesn't matter, Aunt Deirdre. It's ancient history, from another lifetime."

FOURTEEN

• • •

AFTER I LEFT DEIRDRE, I got a call from Megan. She said she had a couple of matters that demanded her attention, but she wanted to get together later. I told her I'd come by after lunch. The morning's turmoil had unsettled me and I needed to take a long run to clear my head. I slipped on my shorts and shoes and headed north from Antrim through familiar territory—little country hamlets, old churches, cute little homes with thatched roofs and well-tended flower gardens—the Northern Irish countryside. The afternoon was warm and I felt like I was sweating my tensions away.

As I passed Chapeltown Road, I saw the Hillside Primary School and I had to stop. I wondered if she still worked there. Classes were in session, I could see through the windows. If I entered the school and turned down the left hallway, would I see her in Room 112 and would she be standing at the blackboard? If I peeked in the door, would she wink at me and give me the sign to wait until her lesson was finished? I shook those memories from my consciousness. I didn't need to know. It took me many months to erase those feelings after I left in 1999. Ancient history, from another lifetime. The book is closed. I resumed my run.

Five miles out and five miles back and I felt like a new man. Of course, it was only a temporary reprieve. Upon my return to the hotel, my cell phone buzzed.

"Where have you been all day?" Megan asked.

"Taking in the pleasantries. Or as you locals like to say, 'Out for a constitutional.'"

"I thought you were going to come over? We've uncovered some interesting information."

"I need to shower first," I said, still breathing hard.

"We thank you for that."

I FOUND MEGAN SITTING with McLaughlin in the inspector's office. "What's up?" I said.

"Dooley's been looking into your vendetta theory," McLaughlin said. "Reemergence of the Troubles. Truthfully, I never gave much credence to it, but it's starting to grow on me. I'll let her tell you."

She opened her notebook to show me a chart she had drawn. It looked like a family tree. "Archie Walker, the alleged shooter of little Molly Taggart, lived at 45 Spiers Place in Belfast's Lower Shankill neighborhood. The redbrick house, the one in the picture found in Fergus's and Eamon's mailboxes, still has the number forty-five on the front façade. It was home to Archie, his wife and three children. Archie also had three brothers: Thomas, Edward and Geoffrey."

"That's what Eamon told us."

"And Eamon was correct, as far as he went. So I've spent a little time this afternoon looking into the Walker family. News archives confirm that Walker's house was firebombed. The story is that Archie, his wife and three children were killed in the explosion. It was the middle of a school day, but Mrs. Walker and the children were unexpectedly at home. There are five death certificates issued by the Belfast coroner's office.

"Now on to his three brothers. Like Archie, they were all affiliated one way or another with the Shankill Butchers. As Eamon told you, Geoffrey was killed in 1977 by the IRA. Edward was killed in 1982 and we won't bother going into the circumstances. Eamon pretty much told us all we need to know. After the bloody battle between the Walkers and the Taggarts in 1974, the third brother, Thomas, disappeared. He didn't resurface until 1978 when he was identified as one of the Shankill Butchers involved in a massacre at a Belfast social club. It was a tit-for-tat raid. The shooters came in, separated the

Catholics from the Protestants, lined the Catholics up against the wall and shot them all dead. It was one of the most grisly crimes of the era.

"Later that year, the RUC rounded up Thomas and the eight other Butchers responsible for that massacre. Each one was given twelve life sentences, one for each of the twelve victims. Naturally, there was huge publicity surrounding the trials, not only because of the ghastly nature of the massacre, but also because of a general feeling that the RUC had been covering up for the gang for too long."

I nodded my understanding. "Deirdre told me how the RUC was covering for the Butchers."

Megan nodded. "Getting back to the Walkers, Thomas Walker was given twelve life sentences, but two years ago . . ."

"You're going to tell me he was paroled? Doesn't a life sentence mean anything in Northern Ireland? How about twelve life sentences?"

"The GFA would not have passed in 1998 without a substantial early release program. The Provisional IRA, the UVF and the UDA all demanded it. Over five hundred prisoners have been released. Walker was paroled to an address in Belfast in 2013, but he's no longer there."

"I suppose we have Thomas's prints on file?" I said.

"We do."

"Any matches from Fergus's house, my hotel room or the tool used to puncture my tires?"

Megan shook her head. "The scratch awl was too smeared to get a print or even a partial. Unfortunately, there were no matches to any of the prints we collected from your room or your uncle's house. And as you know, there were no prints on any of the papers or the pictures."

"So, with all this are you any more serious about the vendetta theory than you were before?"

McLaughlin tilted his head this way and that. "Listen, you talk to historians and half of them will tell you that the Troubles, the whole sectarian war, was fueled by tit-for-tat killings. So, of course I'm willing to consider it. It's as good a theory as any we have right now, but I'm not jumping on it." McLaughlin leaned forward and pointed his finger. "I'm not abandoning my first theory of relativity. It's worked for me for many years. I told Dooley to take a hard look at Fergus's kids,

Riley and Conor. My guess is that they're going to inherit his estate, am I right?"

I grimaced.

"I know. You can't tell me, but we'll find out soon enough. I want Dooley to see if either one of them is in financial trouble, or in a situation where he'd need his father's money to bail him out. Maybe they're gamblers? Maybe they owe back taxes? Maybe they've got addictions?"

"I sat in that conference room today," Megan said. "Conor screamed that he wanted Liam out of his business. Out of Northern Ireland altogether. He all but confessed to rifling the hotel room and slashing the tires. I wouldn't be surprised if he made the prank calls to Liam's house in Chicago. He's paying good money to a solicitor to file an emergency motion to get the trust unsealed and throw Liam out."

Hard to argue with her reasoning, but something in my bones told me that Thomas Walker was a more likely suspect than either of my cousins. Conor's an irritant, for sure. But patricide? If I were complicit in a murder, I sure wouldn't be drawing attention to myself in such a blatant, open manner. And Riley has always been as gentle and as timid as a mouse. I doubt that he had the courage or the strength to scuffle with or even confront his father. I knew Fergus, and I didn't see Riley standing up to him. I didn't think that either Conor or Riley needed money badly enough to commit such a horrific act. I was leaning hard toward Walker and the Butchers.

I stood to leave, and turned to Megan. "As long as you're doing all these background checks, could you look at Charles Dalton?"

"Janie's boyfriend? Mr. Gladhand?"

"Right. And also his company, Northern Exports."

"How do they enter the picture?" McLaughlin said. "Is he mentioned in the Trust?"

"I shouldn't but . . . no, he's not mentioned. Janie is."

"Do you think he has some involvement in the homicide?"

"Oh, no. There's no reason to think he had anything to do with Fergus's death or the photos. I like Janie a lot and I think she might be over her head with this guy. He treats her a little too roughly for me. I'd just like to know more about him. Also, would you please look into Global Investments, the company where Riley works? Fergus has a large stock holding in Global and we have that newspaper blurb that Fergus circled."

Megan nodded. "Okay, I'll get on it."

I stopped at the door. "I've told you much more than I should have. I'm a lousy trustee. Please keep it confidential until you're able to legally get a copy of the trust."

"I'd like to learn a little more about the ongoing feud between the Taggarts and the Butchers," Megan said, "and we think Eamon knows more than he gave us."

"So you want me to see what I can get from my uncle?"

"We do."

"Okay," I said, "I'll work on it. I'm going to get some dinner and turn in early. I have to face her honor Judge McNulty at nine tomorrow morning. Are you coming for the show?"

"Wouldn't miss it," Megan said.

I COULDN'T STOP THINKING about the Walkers and the whole Butcher gang. Archie Walker was the man who shot my sister. The man responsible for the death of my father. Archie Walker's violent brother was released from prison two years ago and no one knows where he is? Is he now carrying the banner for the Walker family? It sure lends credence to the vendetta theory.

I also started worrying about Deirdre. She was so depressed when I left her. She seemed so frail to me. Here was a woman who forty years ago broke the curfew at the Falls. She marched down Leeson Street, defying armed soldiers, tanks and barricades to bring food into the Falls. She stepped in and raised Fergus's two rowdy boys, one of whom now wants to throw her out on the street. She raised me for six formative years and I was thoughtless enough to ignore her for the last sixteen, but it didn't diminish her love for me one bit. She's still as warm and loving as she ever was. She doesn't deserve the treatment she's getting, especially now at the toughest time of her life. I vowed to give her the love and support that she gave to me when I needed it.

I also needed to talk to Eamon and he was staying with Deirdre for the time being. It was a good excuse to drive out there and check up on those two.

Deirdre swung open the door and gave me a warm hug. "Come on in and sit for a spell while I go wet some tea," she said.

"Don't put yourself to any bother. Really, I came by for a few minutes to talk to Uncle Eamon."

"Well, you just missed him. He got a telephone call and ran out of here like a bat out of hell. And don't tell me it's a bother. It's never a bother to have tea with my Liam."

FIFTEEN

• • •

T HE ANTRIM COURTHOUSE, ON Castle Way, was a short
walk from my hotel. The building housed several different
courtrooms, including the magistrate courts, the county courts
and the crown courts. Judge McNulty presided in a county court on
the third floor. Megan was waiting for me in the hall outside the courtroom.

"Ready for the fireworks?" she said.

"I suppose. I wish I didn't have to be. I called Deirdre this morning
and offered to bring her and Eamon to the hearing, but she told me it
wasn't necessary and she added that Eamon hadn't returned from the
night before. I'm worried about them."

"They're both here. I saw them enter a few minutes ago. The courtroom is full of Taggarts." She opened the door. "Shall we?"

With a smack of her gavel, Judge McNulty convened the hearing.
She was younger than I had imagined. I knew she wouldn't be wearing
a powdered wig, but I had envisioned a craggy, gray-haired woman.
Why? I don't know. To the contrary, she was attractive, had dark brown
hair and was no older than Catherine. A stack of papers from the Taggart Estate file, including Conor's motion to dissolve the trust and
send me packing, sat before her. She commenced the hearing by calling
the two lawyers to the bench.

"Mr. Cooney, I have read your petition. Do you have anything to
add?"

Cooney looked hard in my direction and then said, "Your Honor, I set this matter on your emergency call because there is not a moment to lose. Every minute this valuable estate remains in limbo and unsupervised exposes it to the likelihood that everything will be lost. This estate, this valuable collection of real and personal assets, sits in the hands of a person without any connection to this country, a person who is responsible to absolutely no one for his conduct. We haven't been allowed to see the trust agreement, so not one of us even knows what Liam Taggart is supposed to do with the estate. How can we hold him to his duties if we don't even know what they are?

"Your Honor, even a cursory reading of Fergus Taggart's will clearly shows that the man had taken leave of his senses. How bizarre is it to anticipate one's own murder and not even alert the police? I would be disposed to suggest that he did himself in, but for the fact that there was no gun found at the crime scene. Even then, it is not beyond our contemplation that he hired another to end his life for him."

"You monster!" screamed Deirdre. "What a vile thing to say. You have not a shred of proof to make such a foul, irresponsible claim."

"I couldn't have said it better myself," O'Neill said.

Judge McNulty slammed her gavel. "There will be no more outbursts, madam, or I will have you removed from my court. And as for you, Solicitor Cooney, this is neither the time nor the place for wild speculation."

"My apologies, Your Honor. I was merely pointing out one of the bewildering elements of this peculiar estate. We have a testator who knows he will be murdered, yet does nothing about it, but then proceeds to place his entire estate into the hands of an estranged nephew from Chicago. In America."

"We all know where Chicago is, solicitor."

"And then he seals his trust agreement from the very people he intends to benefit, so that no one can read it. Who does that? What sane person would ever do such a thing? How can the beneficiaries protect their inheritance rights when they are prohibited from knowing what their rights are? Your Honor has no choice but to void this ridiculous trust and distribute the decedent's assets to Mr. Taggart's two rightful heirs, his sons Conor and Riley, in equal shares."

Cooney finished his argument, looked at Conor and smiled. "That is all, Your Honor. We seek to declare Fergus Taggart's Last Will and

Testament and his trust null and void and relieve Liam Taggart of all authority and responsibilities."

Judge McNulty turned her attention to O'Neill. "What say you, Solicitor O'Neill?"

"May it please the court, Your Honor. I myself drafted the will and the trust. The will bears the certification of three competent witnesses who affirm that Mr. Taggart was of sound mind and memory and knew the objects of his bounty on the date he signed the documents. After considerable thought, it was his decision to place his assets into a trust. I saw him sign the instrument of his own free will and judgment, as did the witnesses. In fact, we videotaped the signing ceremony. I daresay, Fergus Taggart was no more of a lunatic than Solicitor Cooney, though I harbor doubts as to the latter."

Chuckles skittered through the courtroom and Judge McNulty slammed her gavel again. "That's enough, though I concede he had it coming."

O'Neill continued. "It is an unspeakable tragedy that Fergus Taggart lived in fear of his own homicide. But he had a right to bequest his assets in any way he saw fit and there is nothing illegal about inserting a condition for future distribution. It's done every day."

Judge McNulty interrupted. "That is so, however, absent the most extraordinary circumstances, beneficiaries have a right to know that a trust estate has been established for their benefit and what the terms are. Here, Mr. Taggart has prevented the beneficiaries from knowing either. I'd like you to address that issue, Mr. O'Neill. How do you overcome the holding in the case of *In re: McGovern*?"

"I maintain the case is distinguishable from ours because McGovern did not fear for his life. Nor did he anticipate that his murderer might benefit from his estate. Quite a different factual scenario."

"I'm not so sure that matters," said the judge. "Beneficiaries have a right to see their trust in Northern Ireland. Have you brought the trust instrument to court today?"

O'Neill looked at me. I nodded.

"We have, Your Honor."

"May I see it please? I wish to examine it *in camera*."

O'Neill nodded at me. I walked up to the bench and handed the envelope to the judge. She gave me a warm and friendly smile and said,

"Welcome to Northern Ireland, Mr. Taggart. I'm going to take this document back into chambers and read it. The court will recess for one hour."

All the "interested parties," as we had come to refer to ourselves, adjourned to the hallway. Conor had a grin from ear to ear. On his way out the door he said, "Safe travels, Liam."

I walked out into the hall with Megan. O'Neill looked at her and said, "My apologies, Miss Dooley, but I don't think you're a private investigator. I've seen you before. Where was it?"

"Probably at Henry's Alehouse. I think you bought me a drink."

O'Neill laughed hard, and I'd never even seen him smile. That Megan was a charmer. He raised his eyebrows. "PSNI? Do you work for McLaughlin?"

"Guilty as charged."

O'Neill gave me a look. "You might have told me, Liam. I am your lawyer, you know."

"It's supposed to be a secret, at least for the time being. My family's not inclined to trust the police. I didn't know what your attitude would be."

"Well, I'm pleased to have the assistance of Officer Dooley."

"What's your best guess on Judge McNulty's ruling?" I asked.

He twisted his lips back and forth, and said, "I'm quite certain she'll release the trust. The law is fairly settled. I told Fergus this might happen, but we thought the *in terrorem* clause would discourage a challenge. Most likely we'll return to court, the terms will be revealed, including the generous gift to your son and your weekly stipend, and I suspect that—"

"I know. Any moment now, all hell's gonna break loose."

"Precisely."

"So, I guess either Conor will be appointed or the trust will be administered by the bank. I can't say I'll be heartbroken. I just regret I let my uncle down."

"Don't give up yet. McNulty's a pretty sharp jurist."

The clerk called us back into the courtroom and Judge McNulty returned to the bench. She brought out a stack of stapled papers, which she handed to her clerk. No doubt, copies of the trust agreement. She smiled, stretched out her arms and waved for us all to be seated.

"I've read the agreement. Well drafted, Mr. O'Neill. It's not complicated, confusing or in any way irrational. It's a clear disposition of Mr. Taggart's estate. However, the law in Northern Ireland is also clear. Beneficiaries have a right to a copy of the trust instrument. Therefore, we've made copies and I will distribute them at the conclusion of the hearing."

"All right!" Conor said, with a fist pump. "See ya, Liam."

Judge McNulty slammed her gavel. "While I intend to unseal the trust, I see no reason to tamper with any of its provisions at this time. The only issues before me this morning are whether the instrument is valid on its face and whether it should remain sealed. I have heard no evidence of Fergus Taggart's lack of competence, nor any evidence that would disqualify Liam Taggart as a trustee. He has not been accused of any wrongdoing or breach of his duties. There are no allegations that he is incapable of carrying out his duties. The fact that he resides in America or was estranged from the testator are not disqualifying factors. Perhaps at some later time we will revisit those matters, but they are not before me today. The only ruling this morning is that the trust shall be unsealed and available to all beneficiaries. That will be the order."

I turned to Conor and shot him a wink. I couldn't help it. It's not that I wanted to remain as trustee, I didn't, but it just felt good. At least for the moment. Wait till he sees that the estate is divided seven ways. And wait till he reads that Uncle Fergus provided for a generous gift to Ben and weekly compensation for me. That's the "all hell" part.

It broke loose about ten minutes after the copies had been passed around. "What is this?" Conor yelled in the hallway. "Deirdre gets an equal share? Janie Taggart gets the same share as Riley and me? Who the hell is Bridget McGregor? And this part about ten grand to Ben Taggart? Over my dead body." He grabbed Solicitor Cooney by the lapels. "Mike, you better get this goddamn thing thrown out! Null and void. Do you hear me?"

"Get your hands off me," Cooney said. "And calm down. We'll get it thrown out. You heard the judge, those issues were not before her this morning. This was just an emergency hearing to get our copies of the trust agreement and I prevailed. We won. You now have the agreement. One thing at a time, Conor."

"No, we didn't win, Mike, because goddamn Liam is still in charge. I want him out of here!"

"All in good time, Conor."

"The time is now. If you can't do it, I'll do it myself."

And with that last remark, Conor shot an angry look in my direction. He pointed at me, said, "Your days are numbered," and stormed out of the building.

Megan leaned over and whispered, "Do you want me to bring him in? He threatened you."

I shook my head. "He only threatened to remove me as trustee. There's nothing illegal in that."

She shrugged her shoulders. "We could give him a hard time at the station. He might admit to the phone calls. We could let him know we're watching."

"Thanks, but no thanks. Let him cool down and we'll see what happens. Catherine had the phone number changed and I can take care of myself. But I wouldn't mind if you could get me a gun permit and a Smith and Wesson nine millimeter."

"I'll look into it."

I walked over to Eamon who was standing off to the side with Deirdre. Thank God they had each other during these stressful times. "Is everything all right, Uncle Eamon?" I asked. "I heard that you left the house suddenly and did not return."

He smiled. "Are you going to campus me?"

"I'm just worried about you."

He shrugged. "I got a call from a neighbor that someone was snooping around my house and I had to check it out. I didn't see anyone when I got there, so I spent the night."

"Did the neighbor tell you what he meant by 'snooping around the house'?" I said.

"Peeking in the windows. Walking around the back. But I checked all the windows and everything's okay. No worries."

"Why don't you both come for dinner tonight?" Deirdre said. "I'll make a nice stew for us."

Eamon and I nodded. "Sounds great."

Sixteen

• • •

ONOR'S TIRADE NOT ONLY ramped up the tension among the family members, but it gave me further concern for Catherine's safety. I called her before going to dinner.

"Conor was out of control in court today. I have no proof that he had anything to do with the phone calls," I said, "but I'm glad you changed the number."

"The calls have stopped, thank God. But Liam, the most curious thing happened. I received a FedEx envelope this morning from an address in Belfast: 45 Spiers Place. I was sure it was a love note from you."

"I didn't send you anything. Don't open it."

"But I already did. It was a photograph."

"Don't tell me. Was it the remains of a redbrick house that had burned down?"

"Yes, how did you know? And there was writing on the back that just said, 'The Taggarts.' What is this, Liam?"

"You've got to get out of the house, Cat. Right now. Either come here or take Ben and go stay with your sister."

"I can't right now. You know I'm in the middle of a hearing. But why is this dangerous? Even if you consider it a threat, it's just another childish prank to get you to leave Ireland. Today you went to court and the judge held the trust was valid and that you were properly appointed. I expect these amateur pranks—phone calls and pictures—will stop. I'm sure of it. I find it hard to believe that Conor would continue to harass us when he's hired a lawyer and the matter is in court."

"You don't know this guy. He's a real control freak. Let me hire Chick Chaikin to keep an eye out for you until I can get home. Just to be on the safe side."

"Chick Chaikin with the broken nose?"

"He's a tough guy, Cat, and a good man. He'll sit in his car with a cup of coffee and make sure nothing happens."

"Liam, this is going a little too far. We're fine here. We don't need Chick Chaikin or anyone else. All we need is for you to come home when you can. Our neighborhood is safe. We're careful. I've alerted the police about the phone calls. Quit worrying."

"I don't like it, Cat. I got a bad feeling about this."

"I know. Blame your Irish intuition."

"It's not funny. I'm going to finish setting up this trust and come home as soon as I can. In the meantime, please let me call Chick to watch the house."

"No, and that's final. I'm not going to have someone sitting out front spying on me. I have to go now. Love you. Bye."

I hung up and immediately dialed Chick. I hired him to watch the house every day from six at night until eight the next morning. His partner would keep a lookout during the day when Catherine left for work. Nobody screws with Chick. I could depend on him. I told him it would probably be just a matter of days until I could get home. I told him about the pictures—marked for death. Now my family has been served with a calling card. He chuckled and told me that was a wacky theory. Not to worry. Catherine was in good hands.

DINNER AT AUNT DEIRDRE'S. An island of comfort amidst the sea of tumult. I stood in the foyer and breathed deeply. The bouquet of Deirdre's Irish stew instantly transported me back twenty years. I closed my eyes and let the aromas carry me back. For one moment it was 1975 and Riley and I were scrambling in from the front yard to wash up for dinner. For another moment it was 1994 or 1999 or any year in between. Maybe it would be that June night in 1998. All I'd have to do is walk into the kitchen and time would revert. Aunt Deirdre would be working her magic on the stove. Maybe Uncle Fergus, Uncle Robert and Uncle Eamon would be expounding on the world's problems. Maybe Aunt Nora had brought along a pretty girl for me to meet. She'd pull me aside and whisper, "Isn't she adorable?" Maybe this night it would be Annie.

I remember well that first night I met Annie. I was a late arrival. I apologized to everyone, blaming it all on an imaginary grain contract I was supposedly negotiating. In truth, I'd been with Westerfield all afternoon analyzing wiretaps. When I arrived everyone was already seated and dinner had begun, but a chair was left empty for me right next to this pretty young girl with sparkling green eyes and fine auburn hair. She looked at me, nodded and smiled.

"I'm Liam," I said, settling into my seat and reaching for the bread tray.

"Annie Grossman," she said, and offered me her hand. It was smooth and petite, gentle and delicate, like Annie herself. There was a twinkle in her eye and the hint of a smile that told me that she knew and I knew that Aunt Nora had orchestrated this meeting. Maybe it was for just that reason that for the balance of the evening Annie was engaged in lively conversation with everyone but me. Too bad, I thought. She had a keen intellect; she was cute and totally enchanting. She had all of the dinner guests in the palm of her hand. Myself? I spent a good portion of the evening staring, covertly of course, at the gentle curves of her facial profile, the way her lips formed her words and broke into a smile, the way she casually brushed her hair away from her forehead with the backs of her fingers. But, sadly, it was patently clear she had no interest in me.

At the end of the evening, I was standing in the driveway talking with Uncle Robert when Annie walked out of the house. As she passed, she handed a piece of paper to me and whispered, "Call me." That was the start of my year with Annie.

I waited three days before calling her. I didn't want to appear too eager. Truth be told, I was hesitant about asking her out on a date. I wasn't normally apprehensive around women, I was a pretty confident twenty-seven-year-old. And hell, I was a CIA operative. But I had a feeling about this woman. She had unsettled me, charmed me, and I put off calling her for a few days while I worked up the nerve and practiced my urbane dialogue. The Antrim Summer Solstice Festival was Saturday night at the Antrim Castle Gardens and everyone was going. I asked her if I could come by and take her to the festival. She hesitated for an uncomfortably long moment and then told me she'd meet me in the gardens.

We ended up in a group of six, a busy bunch of single young professionals, all of us twentysomething, self-confident and full of energy. We meandered about the gardens, stopping here and there for an ice-cream cone or to listen to music. There was a lot going on that night, but I really didn't notice much of anything but Annie. It was hard to divert my attention even if I wanted to, which I didn't. Annie was twenty-four, five-foot-three, with the most engaging smile I'd ever known. There was a bounce in her step. She was joyful, animated and expressive, and she wore her emotions on her sleeve in a delightfully transparent way. Head over heels didn't begin to describe the effect she had on me that magical night.

Toward the end of the evening, we broke away from the group and walked slowly through the paths along the riverfront. These were the things I learned about her that night: she was a primary school teacher, she lived with a roommate in a home just outside Antrim in Greenvale Park, and she was Jewish, one of only six hundred in Northern Ireland. Her mother died when she was young and her father raised her without any help. He tried his best, but he set rules that she thought were far too strict. Still, she loved her father very much and held him in high regard. She'd dated a man for two years, but they separated last winter. Her father was disappointed; he liked the boyfriend. The breakup was hard on her and she wasn't sure she wanted to get involved again for a while. I felt I could move her off that last point, given time and me Irish charm.

The June night was warm and the sun didn't set until after ten o'clock. As the festival closed, several couples took to wandering by the old castle ruins, through the winding tree-lined gardens and down to the riverbank.

"These gardens are haunted, you know," Annie said with a wistful smile. "By the White Lady. She died in the castle hundreds of years ago and she appears at midnight searching for her faithless lover. There have been many sightings."

I checked my watch. It was 10:45. "Should we wait?"

"Heavens, no! I've never been in this park at midnight and besides, I think I'd have a heart attack if I saw a ghost."

"I'll protect you."

"Against a ghost?"

"You have a point. Would you rather get a beer?"

"Sounds perfect."

We ended up at Conway's, trading stories and sharing laughs. She was enchanting. I was enchanted. She was charming and I was charmed. The pub closed at two and I offered to drive her home. She suggested we walk. We strolled along the two miles to Greenvale Park, her hand in mine. When we stopped at her door, she leaned over and kissed me good night, just a quick, gentle good night kiss on the cheek. Then she smiled, turned and went inside, leaving me standing on the stoop wondering if I did something wrong. Maybe I shouldn't have been so reserved. Maybe I let an opportunity get away. Maybe my consternation was her strategy because I second-guessed myself for several days.

That was twenty years ago, but the memories are strong and this night at Deirdre's they came flooding back, along with the pain I suffered twelve months later. I shook the memories from my head as best I could and walked into the kitchen. Tonight, there would be no Annie, no Nora and no Fergus. Just Deirdre, Eamon and me. The room seemed large and the table seemed empty with only three of us. I'm sure it must have felt that way to Deirdre as well. Eamon was a quiet man, so whatever conversations came to pass were generated mainly by Deirdre and me. Shortly after we'd cleared the table, Eamon stood to leave, and I walked him to the door.

"I think I'll stick around and help Aunt Deirdre with the dishes," I said.

"You're a good boy, Liam, I've always thought so," he said, "and it warms my heart to see you. I've missed you all these years." I would remember those words long afterward.

I returned to the kitchen and busied myself with a dish towel. Almost immediately I heard a slam of metal, a screech of tires and the continuous blare of a horn. I rushed outside to see Eamon's car leaning sideways against a tree, totally smashed on the driver's side. I yelled for

Deirdre to call an ambulance and I ran to the car. Eamon was lying inside, his head was bleeding and he didn't appear to be conscious. Whoever rammed into him was long gone.

Try as I might, I couldn't open the door. I ran to the shed and grabbed a shovel and a tire iron. I was working frantically on the door when the paramedics arrived. They managed to free him from the car and lay him gently on a stretcher. He was unconscious, in bad shape, but still alive. As they lifted him into the ambulance, Deirdre and I stood by watching, helpless, in a state of total disbelief. Was this a consequence of the calling card?

We followed the ambulance to Trinity Hospital. Deirdre sat beside me staring straight ahead. A dull sense of resignation had settled over her, as though she were a wobbly boxer, dazed and defenseless, taking punches, one after another, with the certainty that she would soon be knocked to the canvas. Dead to the world. Lights out.

Eamon was rushed into surgery and we paced the waiting area in silence until a portly policeman with a notepad confronted us. What had we seen? Did we have a description of the other car? Did we have any explanation for the accident?

"This was no accident," I said.

"I beg your pardon, sir?"

"I mean that someone intentionally collided with my uncle and pushed him into a tree. He was marked for death. This was an attempted murder."

"Well, you have no proof of that, do you now? That seems like a bloody poor excuse for an old man who backed into oncoming traffic."

That infuriated me and I quickly got up into his face. "You stupid son of a bitch, he was targeted," I yelled. "Don't you get it, someone tried to kill him!"

He yelled, "Back off," and his hand went for his baton when I heard, "I'll take it from here, patrolman." It was Megan. She put her arm around my shoulders and led me to the bank of chairs along the wall.

"I'm so sorry, Liam," she said. "Did anyone get a look at the other car?"

I hung my head. "No. From the look of Uncle Eamon's Toyota, he was hammered by something a lot bigger than a car."

"Hopefully, your uncle will be able to give us a description."

I nodded, but I had my doubts. He was in bad shape when they took him out of the car. All of his vitals were weak. And he was no spring chicken. Even if he fully recovered, there's no assurance that he'd remember. The human mind often blocks memories of sudden trauma. But to be frank, I didn't know when or if he'd ever be cognizant enough to talk about it.

"Why Eamon, Liam? Why would someone want to kill Eamon?" Deirdre said.

"I wish I knew, Aunt Deirdre. I wish I could have prevented it."

Megan looked at me and whispered, "The picture—payback time—is that what you're thinking?"

I nodded. "The Walker calling card was in his mailbox. Just like Fergus. If Fergus was killed because of the vendetta, then Eamon was targeted because he's one of the Taggart brothers who retaliated against the Walkers. On the other hand, if you believe Fergus was killed for his property, Eamon stands to inherit as an equal beneficiary. He has a one-seventh share. With him out of the way, everyone else's share increases."

"What if there's another theory, one we haven't articulated?" Megan said.

"What would that be?"

"I don't know. I just don't buy into the certainty that there are only two motives, only two valid theories. McLaughlin's got his relativity theory and you seem locked into a remnant of the Troubles, but both of those theories are simple solutions and life is complicated. I don't know why there can't be another reason."

"Why don't you believe that Fergus and Eamon were targets of a Shankill gang? The Taggart boys went on a rampage after my father was killed. I've been told that some of these sectarian vendettas lay dormant for years and then explode."

"Liam's right," Deirdre said. "Eye for an eye. Tit for tat. It's the law of Northern Ireland."

"It was also forty years ago, Deirdre," Megan said. "Northern Ireland has changed. All those combatants are dead and buried. Just like the Troubles."

"I don't think you believe that any more than I do," I said. "Otherwise, why are the peace walls still standing almost twenty years after the peace agreement?"

The door to the waiting room opened and a doctor walked in, still in his green scrubs, his surgical mask loosely hanging around his neck. We rushed over. His eyes looked down and his face bore the signs of exhaustion and disappointment. We could tell in an instant that the news was bad.

"We did all we could," he said quietly. "His injuries were too severe. I'm sorry."

Deirdre dropped to her knees and buried her face in her hands. Her wails tore at my heart. We helped her back to her seat. I didn't know how much more this poor lady could take. Once upon a time there were five Taggart siblings and now there were just two.

SEVENTEEN

...

Cat, I have terrible news. Uncle Eamon died tonight.
He had just got into his car after dinner and . . ."

"Oh, how awful. I'm so sorry. How did the accident happen?"

"It was no accident, Cat. Uncle Eamon was murdered, just as sure as if someone had shot him dead. His car was intentionally rammed from the side."

"Oh, my God. Who hit him? Did they catch the guy?"

"Nope. Hit and run. Long gone. Somewhere out here there are people who are trying to kill off the Taggarts one by one. I'm certain of it, and I believe it's an old vendetta from the Troubles."

"Is that what the police think as well?"

"No. McLaughlin believes it has something to do with my uncle's estate. We don't agree. However, what we both know is that Fergus and Eamon were each marked for death. They had pictures of Walker's house in their mailboxes."

"And now I have one as well, is that what you're saying?"

"Yes. It sure is. I need you to come here right now where I can protect you."

"Liam, it's such a bad time, but if you really want me to come to Antrim, give me a couple of days to continue my court hearings and I'll come. I'll have to bring Ben."

I sighed. She didn't want to come. Was I going overboard? She was three thousand miles away and I had hired around-the-clock protection.

And I would be home soon. She had her practice and her clients to consider. Neither of us wanted to drag Ben on this trip. Besides, if there are killers running around Antrim, I didn't want Catherine and Ben anywhere near the crossfire. They were much safer in Chicago. Chick Chaikin was reporting that everything was quiet on our block.

"No," I said with a sigh. "I don't really want you to come. It's too dangerous. I'm sure I'll be home in a few days, and I don't want to screw up your practice. But we think so well together and I bet if you were here, we'd figure this thing out."

"I've been giving this matter a lot of thought as well, Liam. One question stands out as foundational: what was it that prompted Uncle Fergus to fear for his life? Why did he believe that someone would try to kill him? It wasn't because he was 'marked for death.' The picture was still in the mailbox when he was killed. Whatever clues he saw were developed over time, while he was preparing his will and trust with O'Neill. Remember the letter he wrote to you? It said, 'Over the past several weeks, I have become alarmed over certain things that I have heard and seen.' What had he heard and seen over the past several weeks? Whether he thought it was some leftover vendetta from the Troubles, or something to do with his property, it was frightening enough to threaten everything he valued."

"I know," I said, "'the entire treasure of a man's life.' So, why wouldn't he identify the danger or his suspect? Why would he write me a note that forecast his assassination without naming his assassin?"

"I admit it's puzzling, but he also said he could be wrong. I'm sure he didn't want to carelessly accuse someone. Or, maybe Uncle Fergus was on to something and he knew who it was but he thought he could talk him out of it, or work it out? I'm siding with Inspector McLaughlin and his theory of relativity. I think it might be someone very close to Uncle Fergus, not some stranger or enemy from bygone years. There was a reason he deferred all distributions until the killer was identified. The only people who are getting distributions are family members."

It was hard to argue with Catherine's logic. "There are only six beneficiaries left, and one of them is the Bridget McGregor Trust."

"It's a puzzle, Liam. No doubt about it. But you're the best. I'm sure you'll come across the answer soon enough. I've been thinking about that box, the newspaper articles and the picture of the guns. They're there for a reason."

"I agree. I've studied the newspaper clippings and the picture, and I've even given them to McLaughlin, but we haven't come up with anything. Especially with that picture. It's just a box of guns."

"Is there something hidden in that picture?"

"Oh, come on, Cat, this isn't a video game."

"I know you, Liam, you're a great investigator. Something will come up, it always does."

"This is a tough one, Cat. The picture of the Walker house, doesn't it stand to reason that the Walker gang is picking off the Taggarts and claiming credit? That's what I'm focusing on right now."

"Well, you've got the bloodhound's nose. For me, it's too obvious."

"Bloodhound's nose? Is that what you think?" I checked my reflection in the mirror. "I think it's a damn fine nose."

Catherine laughed. "It's just an okay nose, nothing special." I wished she were here with me. But then she added, almost as an afterthought, "Why couldn't the Walker picture be a misdirection? I mean if someone wanted to divert suspicion, shift attention, that's a pretty clever way to do it."

"I can't fault your logic," I said. "It would be a masterful misdirection. Still, if you were out here with this family, you'd find it hard to believe that one of them is a murderer."

"Even Conor? Aren't you the one who says he was responsible for the phone calls, the slashed tires and the note in your room? You said he was out of control."

"Out of control, yes. Violent, to be sure. A whack job, I'm certain. But a man who would kill his father and his uncle? I don't see it."

"Be careful, Liam. If you're right, and if this is clan warfare, they're not exactly a neutral observer. You're a Taggart."

"I know. But I can take of myself. You and Ben are the ones that need to be careful. You're Taggarts as well."

"Is that why Mr. Bent Nose is sitting out front? Did you think I wouldn't notice?"

"Let him be, Cat. It's for your own good. He's there to protect you twenty-four/seven until I get home. It lets me sleep at night."

"All right, you win. I'll let him enjoy his coffee. I'll even bring him a donut. Now I gotta go. I love you, take care."

I hung up the phone and retrieved the walnut box from the trunk of my car. I laid the documents out on the bed and examined them for yet another time. I saw bank statements with no unusual withdrawals in recent months. I saw deeds that were forty years old. I saw grain contracts and machinery invoices. I saw the Global Investments stock certificate in the name of Fergus Taggart. I saw several printed proxy forms and notices of Global meetings of shareholders. Then I looked at the handwritten letter again. Was there a clue? Is there something imbedded? I read every word, considered every implication. Nothing.

W HEN I ARRIVED AT Deirdre's later that evening, the family had once again gathered to mourn a loved one. Robert, Harry, Sean, Riley, Janie and Charles were already there. Megan was seated quietly in the foyer. Deirdre was in the living room and when I entered she came over and put her arms around me. Her face was flushed, her eyes were red and her bearing was a bit unsteady. Since Fergus's death, Eamon and Deidre had grown closer. They had leaned on one another. She blew her nose into a handkerchief and sniffled. "I'm really going to miss that old curmudgeon. You know, he had a heart of gold."

"I do know that."

"You were special to him."

Memories of Eamon flipped like flashcards and materialized in my mind. The nights I spent at his house playing matchstick poker. His "famous" breakfast of eggs, rashers and brown bread for soakage. The way he'd look at me out of the corner of his eye with a knowing smile that challenged me to confess the mischief I was up to.

"He was special to me too," I said.

"What am I supposed to do, Liam? I'm scared. Are they coming for me next? Or will it be Robert? Look around. Look at us, Liam. We're all scared to death." She grabbed my hand. "Please help us, Liam. Find the man who killed Fergus and Eamon and take him off the face of the earth."

I assured her that she'd be all right, that we were all looking out for her, but she was right to be afraid. I'm sure that everyone had the same fears and they'd all sleep with one eye open. Shocked, saddened and scared to death. Whoever was doing this was terrorizing my family.

I made my way back to the foyer where I pulled up a chair next to Megan. "You were right about the size of the vehicle," she said. "We see tire tracks from a heavy-duty pickup. Eamon was T-boned and pinned against the tree. There are grille impressions on Eamon's car consistent with a GMC Sierra and there are silver paint marks on the door. We've put out an alert for a silver Sierra. There can't be that many of them in this area."

"Deirdre's worried. They all are. They're terror-stricken."

"With good reason. We've assigned a patrolman to watch her house around the clock. We offered a guard to Robert as well, but he says he feels safe. He lives in a sixth-floor apartment in the Titanic Quarter and there's security in the lobby."

I shook my head. "He's not safe. Robert's not going to stay inside all the time. Eamon was killed in his car."

"I know. Belfast division has been alerted. They'll keep an eye out. There's not a lot more I can do. Inspector McLaughlin is still looking into the Walker family and the documents you gave him. We're trying to follow every lead."

Charles and Janie walked toward the front door. They were ready to leave when Charles walked over. "I'm so sorry," he said. "Eamon was always very nice to me."

After they left, I asked Megan, "Did you come across anything on Northern Exports or Charles Dalton?"

"Very little. Northern is a privately held company that operates out of a warehouse near the harbor. It's gated and well secured."

"Gated and secured?"

She nodded. "There's a guard in a gatehouse that controls entry in and out."

"Don't you think that's unusual for a linen distributor?"

"Yes, but it's not illegal."

"How about Riley's company, Global Investments?"

"Not much more than the newspapers disclose. The company seems to be in trouble with the financial regulators. You saw the paragraph in the *Financial Times*."

"Seems to be? Nothing more specific than that? The financial regulators are part of your government. Come on, you must know more than you're telling me. Don't they talk to you?"

She smiled. "Not really. Their activities are top secret."

"Come on."

"The EU requires each member to operate an Egmont Financial Intelligence Unit, called that because directors of each FIU meet at the Egmont Arenberg Palace in Brussels to discuss and monitor money laundering and potential terrorist financial transactions. Here in Northern Ireland, the National Crime Agency operates the FIU. NCA tells us that both Northern Export and Global Investments have open files in Egmont. But that's all they'll say. Neither has been prosecuted, but there is ongoing analysis. NCA requires top-security clearance, which I don't have. That's as much as I can tell you."

Just then, Conor arrived, threw open the door and burst into the hallway with all the subtlety of McNamara's Band. He gave me a dismissive look and headed into the living room. I turned to Megan. "Hurricane Conor just made landfall."

"That's bound to raise the tension level."

"No doubt. Still, I don't think he has a killer's profile, do you?"

"He wouldn't be my first choice," she said. "But I also wouldn't cross him off the list."

"Who would be your first choice?"

She shrugged her shoulders, shook her head, reached into her purse for her car keys and said, "I don't have one. Inspector McLaughlin would like you to come by the station in the morning. Can you make it?"

"I'll be there," I answered. No sooner had Megan left the house than her prediction came true. Tension levels climbed rapidly. Loud pronouncements bounced off the walls of the living room. Conor was exercising his pipes.

"To hell with the PSNI, to hell with Liam," he bellowed. "There's not a one of them can find their ass in the dark. I say we hire a team of investigators to find these Walker bastards and we'll take care of them ourselves."

"I'm with my dad," Sean said. "Are we going to stand by and let them pick us off one by one?"

Robert, characteristically quiet, sat on the couch and nodded his head. "I hate to say it, but I agree with Conor. There's no doubt in my mind that this is the work of the Butchers. It has their stink all over it. Blindside an eighty-year-old man with a truck. Next thing you know it's a firebomb through one of our windows."

"I tell you right now, every one of you best have a loaded gun sitting by your bed," Conor said. "The war is on. When the time comes, there'll be—"

"Uncle Eamon had a loaded gun," I said, interrupting this vigilante talk. "What good did it do him against a half-ton pickup? How many of you ever fired a gun? You think you're John Wayne, you can pull your six-gun out of your holster and hit a bull's-eye at a hundred yards? This foolish talk will end up getting you killed."

"This is no time to be a coward, Liam," Sean said. "It's time to finish the Walkers for what they've done to our family."

"You're going to go hunting some Walker descendant who could be totally innocent? What do you want to do, rekindle the Troubles? Restart the war? Do you have a burning desire to go to prison? Leave the police work to the police. I know firsthand that they're working on it."

"Well, if you'll excuse me, Mr. Chicago Private Investigator, you got your nose where it don't belong," Conor said and looked around the room for concurrence. "Don't be coming here and telling us what we should be doing."

Robert stood. "Conor, there's no call for disrespect. He's done nothing to warrant it. You may not agree with him, but he's your cousin and he's only trying to do his best. However, you and your son raise a valid point. We can't depend on the PSNI to stop the killings or chase down the Walker gang. They're Protestants, we're Catholics. They're loyalists and we're nationalists. All the old allegiances have reared their ugly heads and here we go again. It's the UVF and the IRA. The Butchers and the Taggarts. Just because they put fancy lipstick on Belfast doesn't mean the old neighborhoods are gone. The Walker gang has emerged like the locusts from the ground and it's time for us to take matters into our own hands."

That was enough for me. "What Walker gang? We don't have any proof that any Walker descendant still walks the earth. Look, I want to catch the killer as badly as you do. He sent one of those pictures to my house in Chicago. I had to hire armed guards to sit outside my house around the clock. I want him just as bad, but I'm not walking into the Shankill with six-guns blazing. This ain't the Wild West."

"Then you're a coward," Conor said.

Robert got his coat and started for the door. "I'm going to head over to Eamon's and pick up old Wicklow. Someone's got to care for that dog now that my brother is gone." He wiped a tear. "No one will mourn Eamon's passing harder than that old shaggy Lab." The room was silent as Robert left. Then the Rambo talk picked up and continued for an hour or more, until the last of the visitors had gone. Deirdre quietly joined me in the kitchen.

"They're not all wrong to talk that way, you know," she said. "They're frightened. I'm frightened. You should be too."

"A war between the Taggarts and the Butchers? Is that the answer, Aunt Deirdre?"

"Fergus wouldn't back away from it. He'd get his revenge."

"Revenge against whom? We don't have any proof that any of the former Butchers are responsible. At this stage, we have no evidence who the killers are. The pictures could be a hoax." Then it occurred to me that I was sounding like Catherine, Megan and McLaughlin.

"What more evidence do you need? It has Butcher written all over it. They put pictures in mailboxes the night before they kill. You were smart to hire guards." She put her cup in the sink, leaned over and gave me a kiss on the cheek. "I'm tired and I'm going to bed. You're welcome to stay here tonight. If you're hungry, there's good corned beef in the icebox. I boiled it this morning." She tapped me on the top of my head like I was eight years old and shuffled off to bed.

I looked at my watch. It was three thirty. The sun would be up in a couple of hours. I decided to accept her offer and sleep on the couch. Goodness knows, I spent many a night on that couch. And I was also well practiced in raiding her icebox. I made a corned beef sandwich on black bread, opened a Harp and sat reminiscing in the still of the early morning.

As it was bound to, sitting in the kitchen and savoring Deirdre's boiled corned beef brought back memories of Annie. Deirdre served corned beef to Annie and me our third time together right at this table. A few days after the festival, I had telephoned to ask Annie out. I told her I had a great time and she said she did too. The conversation stumbled along for a while and I said, "I'd love to have dinner together, just the two of us without the crowd."

"What do you have in mind?" she said.

Loaded question, I thought. "Actually, I make a fabulous lamb ragout," I said, which was a total lie. I'd never made a ragout anything.

She hesitated for an uncomfortable moment. I broke in, "Or we could go to Aunt Deirdre's for Sunday dinner."

"I like that idea," she said.

This dinner with Annie was different. We came as a couple. We talked as a couple. We looked at each other like a couple. Aunt Nora smiled at us. She was clearly putting us in the success column in her matchmaking notebook.

When I drove Annie home, we sat in the car for an hour. Finally, in a justifiable state of anticipation, I walked her to the door and took her in my arms. The softness of her kiss, her arms around my neck and the feeling of my hand in the small of her back are imprinted in my memory. I can feel them still. But she said a quick good night, turned and closed the door, leaving me once again standing on the stoop, bewildered. And come to think of it, bewitched and bothered as well. I chose to attribute the abrupt ending to the hurtful residue of her previous breakup and her fear of a subsequent entanglement. Or perhaps it could have been due to a romantic stumble on my part, though I chose to reject that theory.

After that dinner we began to date more frequently—lengthy dinners, walks through the park, tickets to whatever theater group we could find. We delighted in exploring how much we shared in common. I was infatuated by her wit, her playfulness, the depth of her reasoning and her luminous femininity. I was treading in deep water.

My attempts to take our relationship to the next level were met with cautious resistance which, again, I chose to attribute to Annie's recent breakup. But, after a few awkward starts and stops, the inevitable night arrived when we threw Annie's caution to the wind. Both of us had known it was coming and it was altogether pleasing and comfortable. Our bodies seemed to fold together, a perfect fit. As Annie would remark, we were made for each other, as though we had placed the orders directly with the manufacturer. From then on, a sexual nightcap to an evening out was as natural as an after-dinner cordial. It became our routine, but it was never routine. And never at her place.

I took a bite of my corned beef sandwich and told myself those were thoughts of Annie and life a hundred years ago. I needed to get my mind back to Chicago, back to reality. I already felt like I had been away too long. I was tired of getting into cold sheets. I wanted my Catherine. I wanted to give Ben his evening bottle. I needed to go home. Darn you, Fergus. I curled up on the couch and fell asleep.

EIGHTEEN

• • •

"Y<small>OU LOOK TROUBLED, MY</small> boy." Fergus sat in the wingback chair facing the couch, his legs crossed, his elbow resting on the arm of the chair, a familiar pose. He had a concerned look on his face, but he smiled paternalistically.

"I *am* troubled, Uncle Fergus, can you blame me?"

"You're mad at me, aren't you, Liam, for dragging your sorry self back here?"

"Not just for bringing me back to Ireland, but for throwing me in the middle of a firestorm. Everyone's looking to me for answers and I don't have any. Why did you pull me into this?"

"Because I trust you like no other."

"Then help me out. Give me some answers. Point me in the right direction. At least give me a clue."

"That's not my role."

"Oh, excuse me. What is your role?"

"I guess you'd say I'm out and about on my heavenly pursuits."

"What pursuits? You're dead."

"Why, the evolution of my soul, dear boy. The better place. The life beyond. The next world. I'm hanging with my heavenly hosts."

"And I suppose you're too busy? Maybe saving the life of another Taggart interferes with your having a pint with a heavenly hostess?"

"Watch yourself now, son, disrespect'll get you nowhere."

"Then help me."

Fergus pondered the question, twisted his lips, and finally said,

"Use your good judgment, it's never failed you in the past. And pay attention to your wife."

"Are you chiding me for thinking about Annie? Is that it? Well, hell, it's not my fault, you brought me back here and I keep running into memories all over the place. You know how much I loved her and how crushed I was when we broke up. But I assure you, I've put that all in the past. You needn't worry; Annie is a closed subject. It's all behind me now."

Fergus raised his eyebrows and pointed his finger at me. "All behind you now? All in the past, is it? No thoughts of your nights together? No feelings for her? No desires? Don't fib to your uncle Fergus, Liam. I can see right through you."

"It was another time, another life. I have a wife and a child. I'm devoted to them and I wish I was with them."

Fergus just sat there with a concerned look on his face. "You asked me to help you. The best answer I can give you is to pay attention to your wife." His voice came across in a distant echo.

"Okay, I won't think about Annie. Is that it?"

Fergus shook his head.

"I don't get it. What do you mean pay attention to my wife? If not Annie, then what? Are Catherine's *theories* correct? Should I pay attention to those? Does she have the answers?"

Fergus stood and brushed off his slacks. He shook his head again.

"It's not about Catherine's theories? It's not about Annie? Then what?"

Fergus raised his eyebrows and continued to shake his head. His appearance was starting to fade.

Then I thought about Catherine, the phone calls and the FedEx'd picture, marked for death, and I started to panic. "Wait, Uncle Fergus. Is her life in danger? Is that it? Is that why you keep telling me to pay attention to her? Is something going to happen to Catherine? Is she marked for death? Answer me!"

Silence. I looked around the room. Fergus was gone. "Wait a minute, you can't leave. Come back here. What do you mean pay attention to my wife?"

"Uncle Fergus!" I shouted. I woke up in a sweat, jumped off the couch and looked around the living room. Dawn was breaking.

"I'd like to pay attention to my wife," I said to the empty room, "but she's three thousand six hundred miles away."

MEGAN AND MCLAUGHLIN WERE waiting for me when I arrived at the station. McLaughlin extended his condolences on the death of Uncle Eamon. I thanked him for that.

"Do you now concede that this is the work of the Shankill Butchers, or what remains of them?" I said. "They've killed my sister, my father, my uncle Fergus and now my uncle Eamon."

"I'm sorry, Liam, truly I am. And I do concede that your theory has merit, certainly it's the strongest theory we have, but I'm not closing the book on other causes and other persons. Do you know what question keeps recurring? Who stands to benefit the most from the deaths of Fergus and Eamon? To my way of thinking it may very well be the remaining beneficiaries. I keep wondering what Fergus possessed that was so damn valuable. Would we be so off-base to focus on another member of the family?"

"Megan, you've met them all," I said. "Riley, Conor, Janie, Deirdre and Robert. Do any of them seem capable of committing or arranging for these murders? Do any of them impress you as needing a greater share of my uncle's estate, enough to murder two people?"

She shook her head. "No, not from what I've seen, but we don't know them well enough."

"I happen to know that the two of you have been digging into each one of their lives."

"Guilty," McLaughlin said, "but nothing stands out. Robert seems comfortable in his retirement. He lives in the Titanic Quarter. Credit report is good, but he's on retirement income and his apartment is pricey. Could he be in over his head? Conor's divorced and that's always a financial disaster, but he has an insurance business that seems to be on solid footing and he doesn't have any sizable debt. Deirdre shared a bank account with Fergus that went to her as a survivor. It had a decent balance. The trust gives her a life estate in the farm. She's comfortable enough, but does she think she's entitled to more because she's a surviving spouse? Riley's a highly compensated officer at Global, but Global is being investigated and it's on shaky footing. It may crater.

He's got a wife and kids and lives in an upscale development. Is he try-ing to move up the distribution chain? Then there's this McGregor trust. Maybe the recipient is desperate for money? I'd like to know more, but there are levels of security to clear before we can open that trust and we haven't been able to do that yet. And then there's Janie."

"What about her?"

"She has an apartment here in Antrim, but she dates Charles Dal-ton and stays at his condo most of the time," Megan said. "He's a high roller."

"Listen, I'm not crazy about the guy, but having a lot of money doesn't make you a criminal or even a suspect. What's wrong with Charles Dalton?"

"As far as we can tell, he doesn't exist."

"I shook the man's hand. I can positively affirm that he exists."

McLaughlin leaned forward. "There are no birth records for Charles Dalton, no court orders changing somebody's name to Charles Dalton, and prior to eight years ago, there are no Dalton records whatsoever. No social security, no tax records, no bank records, no titles to property. He just appears out of nowhere in 2008."

"Janie told me he graduated from Princeton."

"He did. With honors."

I sat back and shrugged my shoulders. "Well, those are records."

"True. When he applied to Princeton, he submitted a high school transcript from St. Patrick High School. Straight As. Played football."

"And?"

"St. Patrick has no record of a student named Charles Dalton."

"There must be some explanation. He's been living and working here for years. He's a real person. Presumably he pays taxes."

"IDs are easy to forge," Megan said.

"Forged documents don't make him a killer."

"Makes him dishonest," McLaughlin said.

"Not necessarily. There could be an explanation."

"Add to that the mystery of his company, Northern Exports. Sup-posedly he buys and sells linen and ships it to the continent, to a warehouse in Bosnia. From there it's a dead-end."

I shrugged. "What's mysterious about that? Irish linen is a quality product."

"Indeed it is, but these days it's a small boutique industry. In fact, there's really only one traditional linen weaver left in all of Northern Ireland: Thomas Ferguson & Co. in County Down. It's the only one I know of. The rest of the linen industry took the last boat out many years ago. There's no fortune to be made there anymore."

"And Charles Dalton lives large."

"Yes, he certainly does. And so does his company. His warehouse is far larger than it needs to be."

"What's in it?"

McLaughlin shrugged his shoulders. "I'll wager it's more than linen."

I spread my hands. "He says he's also a successful investor who plays the markets for a 'few dollars.'" I put the phrase in quotes. "Can't you get into the warehouse with a warrant?"

"I could. I don't have probable cause to get a warrant at this time and I don't know if I want to play that card at this stage. I may not want Mr. Dalton to know I'm curious. And another thing, Liam," McLaughlin said with his finger in the air, "I find it highly unlikely that your aunt Deirdre is as clueless as she professes. She couldn't have lived with Fergus for all these years and been deaf and blind to what was going on. I think she knows a lot, but doesn't want to say. I'll wager she also knows more than you think about Global Investments and this Bridget McGregor Trust."

I shook my head. "She seemed surprised, even offended when I brought up the McGregor trust. My uncle could be very secretive when he wanted to."

"Hmm. Maybe she doesn't know what she knows. Maybe she's overheard conversations and didn't place significance in them. Why don't you see if she remembers anything about Global?"

McLaughlin reached into a drawer and pulled out a gun. "You asked Megan for a Smith and Wesson and a permit. I'll give you one of ours: standard-issue Glock 17. Please be careful."

I signed the paperwork and left the station. I had a lot on my mind, and a lot had gone down in the past few days, but thoughts of Catherine and her welfare dominated my thinking. My dream conversation with Uncle Fergus was doing a number on my nerves. I called Chick Chaikin to get a little reassurance that everything was all right, but that made it worse.

"I didn't want to alarm you until I was more certain," Chick said, "but I'm keeping my eyes open and the safety off my Walther."

"Chick, what the hell are you talking about?"

"Just a feeling I got. Didn't want to get you all jumpy. I'm not even sure I'm right, but I think I've seen the same car drive by the house off and on for the past few days, usually about two in the morning. A green Camry. The guy drives slow, stares at the houses, then speeds up at the end of the block and drives away. I mean, maybe the guy's got a girlfriend in the neighborhood, but I don't like it. It smells. I ran the plate and the Camry came up stolen. I phoned it into CPD a few days ago, but earlier this morning I seen the car again. This time with a different plate. Same deal. Slows down, speeds up, drives away. I think if he comes by tonight, me and him are going to have a little conversation."

"Is there only one person?"

"The lighting ain't great, but I think it's only one guy. White dude, baseball cap, needs a shave."

"You haven't talked to Catherine about this, have you?"

"No way. You know, she brings me coffee and pastries. You got a real special lady there."

"I'm aware. This all makes me very uneasy, Chick. I'm going to get this damn trust account set up, finish my business and come home."

"Don't worry, boss. I'll take care of everything till you get here."

Nineteen

...

Eamon's wake was a quiet and somber affair. No matter what they say about Irish wakes, this one was chilling and foreboding. Everyone was still in shock, and if you spoke at all, you spoke in a whisper. Most people sat in quiet meditation. Deirdre and Janie had assembled groupings of pictures of Eamon's life and they displayed them on poster boards.

Looking at the pictures was a nostalgic roller coaster for me. Happy times, sad times, frightened times. There were photographs of the Taggart brothers, photographs of my father as a young man, and even a photo of my mother and father as a young couple, one I had never seen before. My father had a full head of black hair and was shown wearing a white shirt, open at the neck, sleeves rolled up to his biceps. My mother was a diminutive, curly haired girl and shown in a knee-length cotton skirt. She was biting her bottom lip in a distinctly flirtatious pose. I don't ever remember her smiling like that. In my memories, she is frequently sullen and depressed, especially so in the months before she died. The more time I spend in Northern Ireland, the more I understand the reasons for her depression.

I came across a photo of Eamon and Annie, taken on Fergus's front porch after a Sunday dinner. I remembered that night. Uncle Eamon was out on the porch smoking a cigarette and he had pulled me aside.

"Deirdre tells me that this is the third time Annie's been back to the house for a Sunday dinner," Eamon said. "That's a new record for you, isn't it?"

I smiled. "I know. She's different from the others."

"Well, go fetch her, Liam, I want to give her the Taggart once-over."

"Uncle Eamon."

"Go."

"Please don't mess this up now, Uncle Eamon. I like her." He laughed and I went inside to bring her out to the porch.

"My uncle Eamon wants to talk to you," I said to her. "Don't believe a word he says."

She gave me the eye. "So I'm finally going to get the truth?"

"No." I shook my head. "He's a rascal. A solid troublemaker. And he's bound to give you the third degree. Remember you have a right to have an attorney present during all questioning."

She laughed and said, "I can handle myself. No worries."

We walked out onto the porch and I quickly said, "I'm warning you now, Uncle Eamon."

He waved me off and talked directly to Annie. "You know, it's not like Liam to invite a girl back here. He's taking a big chance exposing a young lassie to this grizzly lot more than once."

I protested, "Uncle Eamon, come on."

But Annie gave me a look. "I can handle it."

"Did you come here of your own accord, or did Liam have to pay you?"

She nodded. "He gave me twenty pounds."

"Figures. No way a pretty girl like you would willingly associate with the likes of me nephew."

"I really came for the food," she said.

Eamon smiled. She was holding her own. "Are you Catholic or Protestant?" he put to her. Oh Christ, I thought. Pleasantries over.

"I'm a Jew," she said.

He pondered that response and took a drag on his cigarette. "Well, are you a Catholic Jew or a Protestant Jew?" I laughed hard at the question, but I wasn't sure he meant it as a joke. That's how people thought in those days.

Annie squinted her eyes and wrinkled her nose, a delightfully cute mannerism of hers. "What does that mean? I'm just a Jew."

Eamon shook his head. "No, you gotta be one or the other if you live in the North."

"Nope. Not Catholic. Not Protestant. Just a Jew. We've been here in Northern Ireland for a hundred and fifty years."

Eamon smiled. "Then you must have been hiding all those years."

Annie put her hands on her hips in a decidedly pugnacious manner. "Oh, it's to be like that, is it? I'll have you know that it was a substantial Jewish immigration that organized and promoted your Irish linen industry in the 1860s. A Jew, Sir Otto Jaffe, was twice the Lord Mayor of Belfast. I attend services at the Belfast Hebrew Congregation where Isaac Herzog served as rabbi and he later became the chief rabbi of Israel. His son, Chaim Herzog, born right here in Belfast, was elected president of Israel in 1983."

Eamon turned his head in my direction and gave me a wink. "There's not much left to the linen industry, you know. Can't be too many Jews working there."

"I know," she said. "Our community is shrinking. It's just a few hundred now. In fact, there are only eighty members left in our synagogue. A small community. But as Shakespeare wrote, 'Though she be but little, she is fierce.'"

That drew a laugh from Eamon. "What does your father do?" he asked her.

"He works for Social Security. At the Carvaghy Road clinic. And he volunteers for troubled teens."

"And you, pretty young colleen, what do you do?"

"Uncle Eamon," I interrupted, "give her a break. This isn't a job interview."

"Maybe 'tis, maybe 'tisn't," he replied with a twinkle in his eye.

"I'm a teacher in the primary school," she said. "On Roseleigh Street."

My uncle nodded. "Would that be Holy Family?"

Annie smiled and shook her head. "No, I teach at Mary Conover. It's a public school with a multiethnic enrollment."

"In Northern Ireland? And they get along?"

Annie chuckled. "They're little children. They don't know any better. It will take them a few years before they develop and refine their skills of bigotry and distrust."

My uncle was taken aback and sat up straight with a startled look on his face. Then he broke into a spirited laugh from deep in his belly. He pointed his finger directly at Annie and said, "You picked a good one here, Liam. I like her wit. She's a feisty one. Spit and vinegar. She may be a Jew, but to my way of thinking, she's a solid Catholic Jew, from the right side of Divis Street."

I worried how Annie would take that, but she smiled, shook his hand and said, "Then I will accept that designation in the spirit in which it is given." And from then on she was Eamon's Catholic Jew.

While I lingered in that memory, Deirdre walked up behind me and pointed at the picture. "He always thought you and Annie were a good pair, that you'd tie the knot."

"So did I, until the end of summer."

"I remember," she said. "All too well."

I shook my head. "No regrets, Aunt Deirdre. It's all ancient history. It doesn't even seem like the same lifetime. All behind me. When I left here I was an emotional wreck. Annie and I were bound together so tightly it was inconceivable that anything would ever separate us. I had no future plans that didn't include her. When she suddenly broke it off, I returned to Chicago in a state of shock. It took a long time to work through all those feelings of anger and resentment, but I did. I vowed never to let myself be that vulnerable again."

Deirdre smiled. "You have a wife and a baby."

"That's true because the heart is a tough little muscle. Just when you think it's down for the count, and the referee is standing over you going 'six, seven, eight,' it bounces back up for another round. It took a while, but two years ago I reconnected with Catherine, a girl I idolized in high school but never had the courage to date, and now I'm as happy as can be. All my successes, my present circumstances, my emotional well-being, it's all because of Catherine. But since I've returned to Antrim, I find myself running into all these old memories and it's uncomfortable. I need to go home."

"So that's why you were hollering in your sleep last night? You yelled out Fergus's name."

I nodded. "I had a bad dream. Uncle Fergus was sitting in his chair just as real as could be. He asked me if I was mad at him for bringing me back to Antrim. I scolded him for putting me in this situation and I asked for his help. He told me that wasn't his role and he was out and about on his heavenly pursuits. And I accused him of consorting with a heavenly hostess."

Deirdre put her hands on her hips. "If he's up there consorting with some other woman, he better run like hell when I get there."

That made me laugh. "Toward the end of the dream he told me to pay attention to my wife and that upset me. That's when I yelled and woke up."

"I know it's hard for you, Liam. It hasn't been easy for any of us."

I turned away from the pictures to see Megan and McLaughlin enter the chapel to pay their respects. They even stayed during Father Sweeney's prayer vigil. I was thanking them for their condolences when Riley came bursting into the chapel with an envelope in his hand. He went straight to McLaughlin and shook it in the air.

"I stopped by my house on the way here and guess what was stuck in my mailbox," he said. "This! This goddam picture. Just like Uncle Eamon." He had sweat on his brow, his face was flushed, and his jaw was quivering. He pulled out the photograph and handed it to McLaughlin. "Walker's house. Read the words on the back."

McLaughlin read them out loud. "'Two down. How many to go? As many as it takes! Up the Union. Down the murdering Taggarts.'"

If this was to be a call to arms, nowhere did it resonate any louder than it did with Conor. "Over my dead body, you Walker bastards," he shouted. Then he turned to McLaughlin. "What are you going to do about this? You and the PSNI? Are you going to arrest Walker or is this just tossed aside with all the other Catholic victims?"

McLaughlin, to his credit, remained calm and just nodded. "We'll give it our highest attention, Mr. Taggart. You can be assured that we're not brushing you aside."

"Horseshit," Conor said and stormed out of the chapel.

I looked at Megan. "Still not convinced that the Walkers or their confederates are behind this?" I said.

"No, I'm not. It seems all too obvious, too brazen."

"You think it's a diversionary tactic?"

"I do. It's a hall of mirrors," she whispered.

"Who's behind it then? Riley? He seems genuinely upset to me. Same with Conor."

Megan nodded. "They do. Maybe it's not them. Maybe it's someone else. Whoever it is wants us to think it's the Walkers."

TWENTY

• • •

THE SKIES WERE DARK and dismal on the morning of Uncle Eamon's funeral, a clear reflection of our mood. Beneath our black umbrellas, we all filed into the church vestibule. Hadn't we just been here at St. Michael's? Didn't we just eulogize a loving uncle? Once again, we stood behind a casket and followed it inside to the disconsolate strains.

> Oh Danny boy, the pipes, the pipes are calling
> From glen to glen, and down the mountainside
> The summer's gone, and all the flowers are dying
> 'Tis you, 'tis you must go and I must bide.

Once again, Uncle Robert took to the pulpit. This time he was physically and emotionally drained. His voice was barely audible. His hands shook as they held his notes. He delivered his eulogy with a mixture of sorrow and anger. "We are fighting a specter in the dark," he said. "Come forth! Confront us in the daylight."

He wiped his eyes. "My brother Eamon was a gentle soul. At eighty-two he was a threat to no one. Brutally struck down and taken from us by a cowardly murderer. One that will pay, I promise you."

"Hear, hear."

"Still, let us not focus on despair. Let us join in affirming Eamon's life. The happier times. His wisdom. His warmth. His crooked smile and the way he'd stare you down through the corners of his eyes. He was my older brother, my mentor, my protector. Woe be to any bully who picked on me in the schoolyard, for he'd have to answer to Eamon Taggart." At that, he choked up and his legs were unsteady. "I'll miss him so dearly." Uncle Robert couldn't go on and Janie rushed up to help him back to his seat. He sobbed loudly and his profound sadness touched us all.

We listened to a few more eulogies before the priest resumed the service. I leaned over and whispered to Janie, "Where's Charles?"

She nodded. "Last-minute trip to the continent. He offered to stay, but I told him to go."

I saw what appeared to be a bruise beside her right eye, covered with a thin mask of makeup. "Are you okay?" I said.

"Me? Sure. You mean between Charles and me, is everything okay? Is that what you're asking?"

I nodded.

"We're fine. No problems." She leaned over and gave me a peck on the cheek. "Don't be a worrier."

During communion Janie tapped me on the arm and said, "Do you see her?"

I looked at her quizzically. "See who?"

"Annie. She's here, sitting in the back. I didn't notice where she was until her row went up for communion. She stayed seated. You know, Jewish and all."

I turned and our eyes locked for a moment. Her lips formed a sweet smile in recognition, then the communicants filed back into their seats and blocked my vision.

"I didn't see her at Uncle Fergus's funeral," I said to Janie.

"She was there. She has remained close to your uncles throughout the years, but I don't think she wanted to be noticed at the funeral."

The mass was finished. The priest gave his benediction and the congregants stood to file out of the church and down to the graveyard. Annie was waiting for me outside the church doors. She gave me a cordial kiss on the cheek, one reserved for greeting acquaintances. It felt uncomfortable.

"Hello, Liam. It's nice to see you again. I'm sorry it took these tragedies to bring you back."

I nodded. "Me too." We turned to join the crowd walking down the hillside.

"You're looking great," she said. "How is life in America?"

I shrugged and smiled. "It's good, Annie. I'm married and we have a ten-month-old boy. His name is Ben."

"I know. I'm very happy for you." Annie was still beautiful, still enchanting. Sixteen years had passed since she was twenty-four, since she told me good-bye. She was now more elegant than cute, but either way, there was no denying her allure.

"Thanks. And you? How is it going?"

She smiled demurely. "Same old Annie. Still teaching. Still volunteering. I took over some of my father's charities and a small foundation. He died in 2000, less than a year after you left."

Her father, Jacob Grossman, was a powerful man who turned out to be the insurmountable impediment to the prospective union of Liam and Annie Taggart. Had he died before 1999, she'd no doubt be my wife, but that's a scenario long ago discarded. "I'm sorry, Annie, he was an imposing figure and a prominent civic leader."

"Yes, he was. Thank you for that."

A steady mist began to fall and we stood at the graveside, each of us with a black umbrella. It brought to mind Gustave Caillebotte's, *Paris Street; Rainy Day,* one of Catherine's favorite paintings and it made me homesick for Chicago. I missed Catherine. I missed Ben. I didn't want to be standing here with Annie. I'd had more than enough of Northern Ireland and memories of what was and what might have been. My prayers at the gravesite included a wish for a swift end to this assignment and a prompt return home. I am not an Irishman anymore.

As we walked back up the hill, Annie said, "We should really get together and catch up one day while you're here." She wrote her number on a piece of paper and handed it to me, just like she did seventeen years ago.

I nodded. "That would be nice," I said, though I was pretty sure I would never do so.

In the parking lot, Megan told me that a silver GMC had been found abandoned in a quarry not far from Coleraine. The interior had been badly torched and no identifiable prints were obtained. There were traces of Eamon's red Toyota on the bumper. The car was registered to Damon Gladley, who had reported it stolen ten days ago. Gladley was a sheep farmer with no police history, and as far as they could tell, he had no connection to the Butchers or any other paramilitary organization.

The post-funeral plans included a lunch at Bailey's and that's where everyone was headed. I wanted to call Catherine, but I had forgotten my cell phone back at the house and I told the group I'd catch up with them. As I approached Deirdre's driveway, I caught sight of a motorcycle pushed deep into the bushes. I left the car at the end of the driveway and quietly approached the house from the north side.

A stout man in a tattered jeans jacket and checkered woolen cap was eyeing the front door, a canvas gym bag in his hand. He looked from side to side and stood on his tiptoes to stare in the window. The rain had intensified, which silenced my approach from behind. I saw him reach into his bag and extract a half-filled soda bottle and a torch. I watched him prepare to light the wick and I stuck the barrel of my Glock on the back of his neck.

"Drop the cocktail," I said in his ear, "or I'll blow a hole through your head."

He opened his hands and the bottle dropped to the dirt.

"Who sent you?" I said.

No answer.

I spun him around and put the gun to his face. "Look at me. I'm not a cop. I have no ethics or professional responsibilities. You're a trespasser, and not just an ordinary trespasser, but a low-life son of a bitch who wants to firebomb my aunt's house. And given some shitty circumstances, I am now in charge of this house. So I'm in a real foul mood and I'd just as soon shoot you. Can you tell?"

Silence.

"Can you tell?" I shouted. "Who sent you?"

"I don't know. Really, I don't know anything."

"Just out for a good time burning houses? A joyriding arsonist, is that it? Wouldn't that just be my luck to stumble across the only random arsonist in County Antrim?" I pushed him hard against the stone wall. "Last time. Who sent you?"

"I'm serious. I don't know. I got a call asking me to do the job and promising to pay a thousand quid."

"You'd pitch a firebomb into someone's house for a thousand pounds without even knowing who they were or who asked you to do it?"

"It's me business, gov'nor. Man's gotta eat."

I thought about that extraordinary answer for a second, and then I flattened him with a right cross that I'm sure broke his jaw. I dragged him into the barn and tied his arms and legs. Then I retrieved my cell phone and called McLaughlin.

An hour later, I was back at PSNI sitting in McLaughlin's office. I was pissed. "I thought you were posting a man at the house? Where the hell was the protection?"

"Take it easy, Liam. He was at the funeral looking after your family."

"The funeral was over, Farrell. Deirdre could have been in that house. She'd have been killed along with anyone who was with her. Hell, I was there. I could have been killed."

"All the members of your family were at Bailey's. My guy was stationed outside the restaurant. I can't have people everywhere, I don't have the staff." McLaughlin slid an envelope across his desk. "We found this in your aunt's mailbox when we picked up your prisoner."

It was the same picture. The Walker house. Deirdre had been marked for death, and the arsonist was there to carry out the sentence.

Just then, Megan entered the room. "His name is Rory Devlin. He's just a punk with a long record of minor felonies and several outstanding warrants. We're glad you caught him for us, Liam. He says he doesn't know who hired him and I'm pretty sure he's telling the truth. He was hired with a phone call. He says he gets his assignments that way and picks up his money in an envelope at Flannigan's bar. We have his cell phone. He got the call last night. The caller ID showed 'Unknown Caller.' I contacted the carrier and we'll try to locate the caller, but I'm pretty sure that's a dead-end as well. We talked to Flannigan. He said an envelope was dropped off by a neighborhood kid."

These explanations weren't good enough for me. "I want to interrogate Devlin. I'll find out who's responsible. And I want round-the-clock protection for all of the Taggarts."

McLaughlin rocked back in his desk chair. "I can't do that. I don't have the manpower. I'll post a patrolman at Deirdre's, but I can't put people in Belfast high-rises, and I can't assign seven patrol officers to round-the-clock protection for each of the Taggart beneficiaries. You'll have to hire private security. Be reasonable."

I was furious. "Reasonable? Either the Walkers or some loyalist group is gunning for my family one by one. Fergus, then Eamon and now Deirdre. We're entitled to police protection. I hate to say it, but maybe Conor's right, maybe this is still the RUC and we're still Catholics and we're second-class citizens."

"You're out of line, Liam. Way out of line. I'll cut you some slack because you're upset, but you have no call to doubt my concern. Or Dooley's. Or our professionalism."

I was sorry I accused McLaughlin, but I wasn't through. "What would you like me to tell the remaining beneficiaries? The Police Service of Northern Ireland knows that each of you is targeted for assassination, but it can't spare a policeman from his traffic duties? Do you think that will calm them down? Or do you think that hotheads like Conor are going to go straight into the Lower Shankill, armed to the teeth and looking for Walker?"

"We don't think it's the Walkers, Liam. I know someone's leaving a Walker calling card, but it doesn't make sense to us. Why would they give a damn about Deirdre? She wasn't one of the Taggart siblings. I'm convinced this is all about the will and trust."

"How much more proof do you need? Aren't the pictures enough? You know the history of the Butchers and the Taggarts. And to the whole world, Deirdre is a Taggart wife. I always thought she was."

"But why now? The history book was closed forty years ago."

"Why are you so quick to say it's *not* the Walkers? Why wouldn't they have hired Devlin to firebomb the house?" I said. "That's their M.O."

"First of all, they wouldn't have hired an outsider. If there is a Walker involved, and I don't even know if one is alive, he wouldn't bother with a punk like Devlin. The Walkers would have done it themselves. *That's* their M.O. Second of all, their M.O. is to firebomb a house when people are *in* the house, not when there's no one home."

"Devlin didn't know whether anyone was in the house. And I assure you he didn't care."

"Look, you might be right. Maybe a dirtbag like Devlin wouldn't give a damn whether or not people died, but don't discount Dooley's theory: that all this Walker crap is just a diversion, meant to distract our attention from the real killer. I'm liking that explanation better every day."

"Only because it fits with your relativity theory. Whoever it is, we need protection. Whether it's Walker or anyone else, someone is after my family. Please see what you can do, at least here in Antrim. I'll try to get Robert, Riley and Conor to come out and stay in the house until this is over."

"What about your cousin Janie? Isn't she living with Mr. Fancypants in Belfast?"

"I think so, but he's wealthy enough to hire protection."

"Well, for the rest of them, I can do more in Antrim than I can in Belfast."

I nodded. "Why don't you let me have a private talk with Devlin? I can be more persuasive than Megan. I guarantee he'll open up to me."

McLaughlin smiled and shook his head. "You already broke his jaw. I want to keep my job. We'll keep questioning him, but I don't think anything will come of it. We'll let you know."

"I'd just as soon we not tell Deirdre about the picture or Devlin," I said. "She's an emotional wreck as it is."

"We're not going to tell anyone, Liam. We're going to see if one of your relatives reacts. The house didn't burn down. Someone may call Devlin's phone and ask why. Picking off beneficiaries one by one doesn't sound like a Walker to me. It sounds like a greedy beneficiary."

I DROVE BACK TO my hotel. I was exhausted and depressed. I lay down on the bed and finally nodded off.

My sleep was restless and once again filed with bizarre dreams. There I was, back at the Orange Order's Drumcree parade. July 1998. Hundreds of Protestants with banners and signs, proudly singing provocative songs, brazenly marching down Garvaghy Road through the staunchly Catholic neighborhood of Portadown. The streets are lined with Catholic protestors intent on stopping the parade, and dozens of them are lying down in the middle of the street. RUC patrolmen in their riot helmets are pulling men, women and children from the street, pounding them with their billy clubs. Rioters are everywhere. Bulldozers and gasoline trucks block the side streets. Suddenly rocks and firebombs are flying through the air in all directions. Flames are shooting out of the windows of buildings and people are running wildly, trampling anyone in their way. I panic. I have to find Annie and protect her. Finally I see her, holding the hands of screaming schoolchildren and fleeing from the rioting. I try to catch up to her, but people are in my way. Suddenly her father, Jacob Grossman, appears out of nowhere and stands right in front of me. "Get out of my way, Mr. Grossman, I have to get to Annie." He plants himself directly in my path in a defiant posture, stern and imperious, and he wags his finger back and forth denying me passage. "I need to save her," I yell. "Don't you see what's going on?" But he shakes his head. Despite the chaos all around, there is only Jacob and me, and he refuses to let me by. I plead with him but he stands steadfast and orders me to turn around. Over his shoulder I see Annie running into the crowd, away from me, and I scream for her. "Annie, Annie." I try to run but he grabs my arms and holds me back. "Annie!"

Finally, I woke up and shook my head. What a ghastly nightmare. What a macabre contrivance. Except the Drumcree marches were real, they were no dream. And Jacob Grossman was as formidable a barrier as any brick wall ever was.

TWENTY-ONE

• • •

I DECIDED TO FOLLOW McLaughlin's instincts and seek a more in-depth dialogue with Deirdre. McLaughlin had a point. It did seem odd that Fergus would have feared for his life, collected newspaper clippings, prepared a bizarre will and trust, written a letter to me to be opened after his death, and that Deidre, his lifelong companion, would be totally oblivious. She had to know something. Maybe she really didn't know what she knew. I didn't think she was lying to me, so I intended to prod her subconscious. I invited her out for breakfast but she would have none of it. She insisted I come over. "I was just getting ready to stir up some eggs," she said, "and I'll put on a little pudding."

I was relieved to see the green-and-white patrol car when I arrived at her house half an hour later. The PSNI officer asked for my ID at the door. "Everything quiet, Officer?" I asked. He nodded with a smile. Pretty cushy assignment, I thought, and I bet there was a bonus every few hours: a plate of Deirdre's yummy cooking.

"You'd think I was the prime minister," Deirdre said, as she opened the door. "They have a guard outside my house all day long. It's just like 10 Downing Street."

"It's for your protection, Aunt Deirdre, until this whole thing is over."

"You mean until they catch that Walker boy?"

I nodded. "If he's the one. What do *you* think?"

She shrugged and spread her palms. "I'm just a simple homemaker, I leave the detective work to you and the police."

That brought a chuckle; there was nothing simple about Deirdre. "Go on, Aunt Deirdre, you can't pull the wool over my eyes. What do you know about the Walkers?"

Deirdre brought two plates to the table and poured two cups of tea. "I know the night the Taggart boys went out to settle the score. I didn't think they'd be coming back. Getting into the Shankill in the middle of the night was one thing, getting back after doing their business was another. But they did, and it ended up forcing us out of the Falls and into the country. Those were the tit-for-tat murder days and we knew that someday they'd be coming for us."

"But why now? Why forty years later? The war is long over."

"Who says? When a person's been fighting the war since the cradle, it's never over. It's in his bones. There's not a day goes by that a person carrying that grudge doesn't plan to get even. If it sits with him in the Crumlin Road Prison, it festers. It becomes his reason for being. Let him out and what's the first thing he's going to do? He's going to seek that revenge. Why forty years, you ask? Who knows what the killer's been thinking and planning for the last forty years?"

"So you think it's a paroled prisoner?"

"Could be, but it doesn't have to be. Maybe he's new to the streets or maybe he's a child avenging his father."

"What did Uncle Fergus think? What did he say to you?"

She shook her head. "He wasn't one to share such thoughts. He wouldn't have wanted to worry me. He always said he could handle anything, but I know this time it was different. He was getting up in the middle of the night and sitting in the front room by the window."

"And you never asked him why he couldn't sleep, or what was on his mind?"

Deirdre hesitated again. "That I did. I asked him what was going on. All he would say is that he got some troubling news and he would take care of it."

I took out the newspaper clippings and the picture of the guns and laid them on the table. "Where did you get these?" she said.

"They were in a folder in Uncle Fergus's bedside bureau. Did you know they were there? Have you seen them before?"

She looked at each of them and shook her head. "No. I don't know what these are all about. He never showed them to me." She pointed to the article about the murder in 1999. "Wasn't that about the time you left?"

I nodded. "I left a couple of months later."

Deirdre sighed. "That was one of the saddest times in Fergus's life. The most upset I can ever remember."

Tears formed in my eyes and I brushed them away. "You can't know how sorry I was that I betrayed him. I've carried that with me all these years, Aunt Deirdre. The last thing I ever wanted to do was to disappoint my uncle."

She smiled that warm, maternal smile of hers and placed her gentle hands on mine. "You can let it go, son. His disappointment was only momentary. He was proud of you every day of his life. Carry that with you instead of a misplaced guilt."

Her words coursed through my veins like waters of absolution. No amends were ever required. I never needed to search for the right words to open a discourse. All I had to do was pick up the phone. My uncle was proud of me. Was it now okay to be proud of myself as well?

Our conversation was interrupted by a knock on the door. Riley was standing on the stoop with an envelope in his hand. He tilted his head in the direction of the PSNI patrol car. "You finally got our mum a police guard," he said. "Thanks."

Deirdre embraced him and set about making him breakfast. He sat next to me at the table, just like when we were kids. Deirdre served our eggs and pudding as she had forty years ago. Two of her three boys. She even told Riley to go wash his hands. When we had finished and cleared our plates, Riley whispered to me, "Can I talk to you in private?"

I asked Deirdre to excuse us for a few minutes and we went into the living room.

"What's on your mind, Riley?"

He opened the envelope and took out an unsigned printed document. As I feared, it was a stock transfer agreement prepared to convey ownership of the shares of Global Investments, Inc., from the Fergus Taggart Trust to Riley Taggart.

"My boss has demanded that I get the shares back in my name," Riley said. "He's trying real hard to nail down a refinance and he's obtained a conditional approval. All he needs is the outstanding shares. I don't know if you've looked into us at all, but Global is under investigation for financial irregularities. We're being accused of cooking the books, overstating our earnings, and understating our liabilities. There are questions about promises made to investors that may not have been totally accurate. We need the loan to survive. I really need your help here, Liam."

I had a sick feeling in my stomach. I didn't want to turn him down again but there was no way I could sign his paper. "You've read the trust, Riley. You know what I can do and what I cannot do. I'm bound to the terms of the trust. My hands are tied. The Global stock is part of Uncle Fergus's assets. It wasn't left to you alone. Until the day the trust distributes, I can't do anything at all."

"Please, Liam. It's really *my* stock. No other family member has any rights to this stock. It should have been owned jointly."

"Maybe so, but it wasn't, and your father didn't leave it to you alone. I'm sorry."

Riley's frustrations were bubbling over. "Damn you, Liam. Conor was right, you have no business here in Northern Ireland. My father must have been out of his mind when he drew up this crazy trust and appointed you as trustee. It's sheer madness. You're going to ruin my company and I'll be out of a job. Maybe worse than that. If we can't get the financing to bail us out, I could go to jail. You've got to do something! Please!"

"You know I would do whatever I could. I'll make a call to Solicitor O'Neill and get his advice. That's the best I can do." I stepped outside and called O'Neill. I ran the whole scenario by him.

"Is there any way I can legally do what he asks?"

"Transfer the shares into Riley's name? I'm afraid not."

"What if I kept the shares in Fergus's name but allowed the company to use the stock as collateral?"

"My advice would be the same. The stock would be all tied up in the refinance. It would no longer be liquid. The trust would lose control of the stock for an indeterminate period of time. Maybe forever. No, I'm afraid such an encumbrance would violate the terms of the trust."

I returned to Riley and sadly shook my head. "I wish I could help, but I can't."

Riley was trying hard to control himself. "I have another suggestion. What if you stepped down and let Conor be the trustee? If you said you had to go home to America, then Conor could become the trustee. Someone is calling your wife, maybe she's in danger. You should go home to her. People would understand if you left. I know Conor would help me out and you wouldn't be responsible."

"That's not the way it works. If I declined, then the Bank of Antrim would be the successor trustee and they'd be a lot tougher to deal with."

He put his hands on my shoulders. "Listen, Liam, please." He was shaking like a leaf. "We all know who the killer is. It's Thomas Walker. We've identified the killer, just like the trust says. It's what my father wanted. But who knows if Walker will ever be caught. No one would blame you if you declared the condition satisfied and distributed the assets now. Then you could finish your job and go home. You could be with your wife and child. It would all work out if you'd only be reasonable and go along. Who would be harmed?"

"Are you making those phone calls, Riley? Are you the one calling my house?"

He shook his head. "No, but someone is. If I were you, I'd go home."

"Look, the conditions aren't satisfied. We don't have proof that Walker is responsible. That's only a theory. And he hasn't been apprehended or even located. And to be honest, we don't know if Thomas Walker is even alive. You heard the judge. She said there was nothing wrong with the way the trust was written. I have my instructions and I have to follow them. Those were your father's wishes and I have a judge looking over my shoulder."

Riley snatched up the paper from the table. "You're shitting on your family again, Liam," he screamed. "Conor is right about you! And he's right about what we have to do. We're going to get the judge to declare the trust condition satisfied and kick you the hell out of Northern Ireland."

He slammed the door hard when he left, so hard that the patrolman grabbed him by the arm and brought him back into the house.

"Has he caused you any trouble?" the patrolman asked Deirdre and me.

"No," I said. "It's okay."

When Riley left, I returned to the kitchen. There were tears in Deirdre's eyes. "Just like before," she said.

"Before what?"

"Riley and Fergus had fierce arguments."

"When, Aunt Deirdre? When did they argue?"

"Well, they argued a lot in the last few years, but just recently they've been arguing over that damn stock. I told Fergus to just give him the stock, it's not worth it, but Fergus said he had a lot of money tied up in it. Besides, he was worried that Riley was doing something he shouldn't."

"So that's why Fergus circled the newspaper blurb on Global. Did Fergus fear for his life because of that stock?"

Deirdre shrugged. "I don't know."

"Did someone besides Riley threaten Uncle Fergus about that stock?"

Again she shrugged.

I showed her the picture of the guns again. She squinted, held the picture close to her eyes and then shook her head. "What am I supposed to see here?" she said.

"I don't know. I was hoping you might know. Did Fergus ever say anything about shipments of guns?"

"No. These look like machine guns. Fergus never had a gun like that. Not that I know of. I don't think that was a box of guns that Fergus owned."

I nodded. "They are assault rifles. I'm not saying he owned them, but this picture was in the folder with the newspaper clippings."

"I have no idea where that picture came from, or what it is."

"The last article, Aunt Deirdre, the one about the man killed in prison in 2008, does that bring anything to mind?"

She read the article and placed it back down. "I'm sorry, I have no idea why he would have saved that article. Some IRA prisoner killed in jail by unionists? There must have been a thousand of those murders. But in April 2008 there was nothing in particular going on in our lives."

She poured another cup of tea for me and said, "I saw you talking to Annie at the funeral."

I nodded. I wished she wouldn't have brought that up.

"You know, she never married," she said.

I smiled and took out my cell phone. "Aunt Deirdre, I want to show you something." I clicked on my photos. "This is my wife, Catherine, and my son, Ben. I don't want to think about Annie anymore. It was nice to see her yesterday but that book is closed."

"You're taking it the wrong way," she said. "I know you've moved on. I only bring it up because over the years Fergus and I have stayed close to Annie. You know, Annie always felt a bond with Fergus and even after the breakup, she came around quite often. She spent many an evening crying on your uncle's shoulders."

"I did not know that."

"She made Fergus promise not to tell you."

"It took me a while but I got over her, I moved on. Now I'm happy and fulfilled. If Annie's not, I'm sorry for her, but that was a decision she made a long time ago and she needs to move on as well."

"That's not why I brought it up. No one wants to plan a pity party for Annie, least of all Annie. I brought it up because she and Fergus spent a lot of time talking about personal matters. There were times when I thought Fergus was more open with Annie than he was with me. You're asking me whether I had any hint of what was going on in Fergus's life over the last few months. I've told you what I know. I'm only suggesting that Annie may know a lot more than I do."

I saw where this was heading and I didn't like it. "I suppose you think I should call up Annie and find out what she knows?"

"No, I think you should go *see* Annie and find out what she knows."

"That would not be easy for me. Why don't you talk to her for me?"

"It's not my place. If Fergus told her things he didn't want me to know, then I don't think it's fair to use me as a go-between. Besides, she probably won't open up to me."

I shook my head. "I'll think about it."

"Just as a final word, Liam, we came to know Annie as a very good and kind person, and I feel bad that you carry such hard feelings. The breakup wasn't really her fault. It was her father . . ."

"Aunt Deirdre, I don't carry hard feelings. In truth, I haven't thought about Annie at all in years. And I know all about her father. So let's close the subject. Thanks for the breakfast."

I gave her a kiss, nodded to the patrolman on my way out and got into my car for the drive back to Antrim.

MY PEACEFUL RIDE THROUGH the countryside was interrupted by the ring of my cell phone. I wasn't in the mood to talk to anyone, but the caller ID said it was Janie.

"Hi, Janie. Everything okay? Are you all right?"

"Of course. Charles and I would like to take you to dinner tonight. Are you busy?"

Charles? The elusive Charles, the man who doesn't exist, who is always out of the country or off on business and unable to attend funerals, but he wants to make time to take me to dinner? It would surely be a chance to fill in some blanks. How could I turn that down?

"I'd love to," I said. "Where shall I meet you?"

"Charles said he'd send a car for you. We'll be eating at Charles's golf club, Royal Portrush on the Antrim coast. If you'd like to play a quick round, he'll send the car at two o'clock. Otherwise, if you're busy this afternoon, the car will be at your hotel at six. Do you play golf?"

I was an average weekend golfer, and normally I'd say no and save the embarrassment, but I certainly couldn't turn down an afternoon probing into the life of the man who doesn't exist.

"I'd love to play a round. Tell Charles I'll need shoes and clubs."

"That'll be no problem. Be ready at two."

Twenty-two

• • •

A BLACK MERCEDES S550 was waiting at the curb when I walked out of the hotel. A large, uniformed driver stood next to the open passenger door. "Good afternoon, Mr. Taggart," he said stiffly. "Mr. Dalton sends his greetings." He gestured to the center console. "For your indulgence on the journey, Mr. Dalton has supplied the car with Bushmills single malt and Taittinger on ice. Please help yourself. The ride will take about forty-five minutes. My name is Starkman." Apt appellation, I thought.

Starkman handed me a white golf cap and a folded navy blue Peter Millar golf shirt, both bearing the emblem of the Royal Portrush Golf Club, Dunluce Links. "Mr. Dalton's compliments," he said. "There is a golf course guide in the seat pocket. Fair warning." He smiled. "Dunluce is a formidable challenge."

The ride north through County Antrim was idyllic. Rolling hills and fields were ripe with the summer's bounty. True to Starkman's prediction we reached Royal Portrush at 2:45 p.m. It was nothing short of breathtaking. Built along the Antrim coast, it sat proudly on a rocky bluff high above the North Atlantic Ocean. To the west lay the resort town of Portstewart, its beaches and the North Channel. To the east were white cliffs, the Dunluce Castle and the Giant's Causeway. It was hard to imagine a more picturesque layout for a golf course.

Starkman directed me to the locker room where a chipper attendant welcomed me and ushered me to a walnut locker with my name on it. He brought a pair of golf shoes and filled me in on the celebrity of the club. "We've recently been ranked the number one British course by *Golf Digest* and we'll be hosting the 2019 Open Championship. All the greats have played here—Watson, Palmer, Nicklaus, Faldo—and it's one of Rory's favorites, you know." I nodded, duly respectful. He handed me two dozen golf balls, compliments of Mr. Dalton, who would meet me in the cocktail lounge when I was settled. I put on my shoes, my new polo shirt and hat, and went to greet the man who did not exist in any database.

Dalton was sitting in the lounge holding a martini glass, chatting with the bartender. He was wearing white Bermuda shorts with calf-high argyle socks. He stood and greeted me with a firm handshake. "Liam, my good man, welcome to the club. I trust the ride up was not too strenuous."

"Not at all, quite comfortable, Charles, thank you for your kind invitation."

"My pleasure. Well, let's not waste any time. Janie won't like it if we're late for dinner." He slapped me on the back and chuckled. "Would you care for a refreshment to take along?"

I politely declined and he led me out to the first tee where caddies were waiting. The first hole at Royal Portrush was an intimidating four-hundred-yard undulating straightaway with the wind in our face and the ocean on our right.

"Should we make a game of it?" Dalton said. "A friendly hundred-pound Nassau, just to keep it sporting? I'll give you three a side." I knew that he was hustling me, that a hundred-pound Nassau would mean a hundred pounds for the front nine, a hundred pounds for the back nine and a hundred pounds for the round. And it was only a hundred pounds to begin with. Either of us had the right to press the bet at any time, which would have the effect of doubling the stakes. There would be no limit to the amount of times the bets could be pressed. It could get very pricey. Nevertheless, in for a pound, in for a shilling, or something like that. "You're on," I said, and Charles smiled. Definitely a smug, *gotcha* smile.

Charles hit his drive straight down the middle. Position A. I wound up and sliced mine into the water. "Hard luck, old boy," he said, with a smile. He took the first hole by three strokes. There went my front-side handicap.

It didn't take long for Dalton to bring the conversation around to the investigation. As we approached the third tee, he said, "It's so unsettling, this Walker business. I've hired a full-time security guard for Janie. How is the investigation coming along? Have you zeroed in on his whereabouts?"

"I believe that question is more aptly directed to Inspector McLaughlin," I said. "He's in charge of the investigation. As far as I know, there hasn't been any progress locating anybody named Walker."

"Oh, but I've heard rumors, you know, and Janie fills me in. It seems as though this Walker fellow keeps dropping his calling card."

"Really? Have you received one?"

"Me? Heavens, no. Why would I?"

I shrugged. "You're dating a Taggart. That might be reason enough for a Walker." I smiled and hit a high six iron onto the green on the par three third. "But I understand that the PSNI is still looking seriously into several others." Dalton pulled his five iron into the greenside bunker. I took the hole. He pressed the bet.

"What others?" he said as we approached the fourth.

I shrugged. "I really don't know. My plate is full just managing the trust."

"Oh, come on, you must know more than that. Who are they looking at besides Walker?"

I didn't care for his fascination with the serial crimes. He should keep his nose out of it. "Anyone and everyone. Maybe even you, Charles."

He smiled broadly, but his teeth were clenched. "Not funny, Liam."

I burst into a hearty laugh. "Not even a little?"

We were all square going into the fifth, a signature hole, named White Rocks because the green lay against the seashore. Dalton was getting tense and he hooked his drive. I was sure he was deep in the fescue far off the fairway, but his caddie miraculously found his ball sitting up nicely on the short cut grass. Okay, so he was a cheater. It would be that kind of a day. Nevertheless he launched his shot over the green and onto the beach, and slammed his club hard onto the ground. I took the hole by two strokes. He pressed the bet again, and that wouldn't be the last time. This man had all the money in the world, but he couldn't stand to lose. Especially today.

I knew that if Charles continued to lose, he would become even more tense and would clam up. There would be no friendly conversation and I wouldn't learn a thing about him. But if he were ahead and thrashing me in the Nassau, he'd bend over backward to be gracious. I planned to miss a few shots and let him pull ahead, and truthfully, it wasn't all that hard to do. The course was demanding and the more relaxed Charles became, the better he shot. The round was costing me money, but I was hunting for information. I wondered whether I could charge the trust for my gambling losses—are they considered proper trust expenses?

I asked him about his linen business and he shrugged. "It's been successful, Liam, a family business for three generations. We're really the only distributor in Northern Ireland. We ship to nine countries."

"I thought Janie said you shipped to a warehouse in Bosnia?"

He curled his lips. "Janie said that? Well, she really wouldn't know. We do have a warehouse in Bosnia, and from there the products are sent to other countries."

I knew his Princeton application said he played football at St. Patrick, so I said, "I heard that you that you were a football player. Did you play in high school?"

He shook his head. "I play Gaelic football not American football, but I didn't pick it up until after I returned from college. At Princeton I played rugby. They didn't have football."

"Princeton has soccer and American football, aren't they like Gaelic football?"

"No. They're not! They didn't interest me. Gaelic football was really my game. At Princeton, I settled for rugby, which has some similarity to Gaelic football."

"So Gaelic football was really your game and you had to settle for rugby?"

"That's right. That's what I said."

"But I thought you said you didn't play Gaelic football until you returned after college?"

I caught the glimmer of a sneer, but just for a moment. He was very good at controlling his anger. At least with me. "Yes, that's right. I didn't play until after college. Now I play for the Belfast Club. When I was young I just fooled around with playground football. Why do you keep asking me about this?"

"Obviously because Janie says you're quite an accomplished player. I'm just wondering how come you didn't play at St. Patrick? I bet you would have been a high school star. Didn't St. Patrick have a team?"

"Janie said that, huh? Well, I don't really recall whether St. Patrick did or didn't have a team. It was a small school. The bottom line is I didn't play sports in high school. I was concentrating on my academics. After all, I did get into Princeton. Let's play golf. You're up, I believe."

A few holes later, I dug again. I don't know why I was so interested in Dalton, but I was. Maybe because I was protective of Janie, maybe because of his mysterious past, or maybe because there was something so arrogantly phony about him. "How come you went all the way to New Jersey for college when you could have gone to prestigious colleges right here in the UK? I mean Queens College, Trinity, Oxford, Cambridge, and some of them would have had Gaelic football."

"Gaelic football again? Football was not my primary focus, it was academics. And why are you so damn interested in my sports activities?"

"You needn't take offense, Charles, I'm just trying to get to know you better. You know, casual conversation."

"Really? Where did you go to college, Liam, and did you play football?"

I smiled. "Thank you for asking. I went to the University of Illinois. The Fightin' Illini, you know? I played football till I blew out my knee. Let me ask you, did you grow up in West Belfast where St. Patrick is?"

"I grew up in Belfast, okay? But that's enough about my childhood."

I shrugged and started to say, "I'm only trying—" But he quickly interrupted me, putting his hand on my shoulder, and said, "Look. Let me say this to you, Liam. You better be very careful."

"Really? How so?"

He looked at me sternly and then broke into laughter. "Because we're coming up on the fourteenth hole, the toughest hole on the course. Beware. It's named Calamity and for good reason." He smiled and slapped me on the back. Hard. "One of the most famous golf holes in the world. Be very careful."

I figured that was enough probing for a little while, so I left any further questions on the table. And he was right about the fourteenth hole. Calamity for sure. It was an expensive hole for me. At the end of the round, I was forty-eight hundred pounds in the red and Charles was deliriously cheerful. With his arm around my shoulder he led me to the bar.

"Hard luck, old man," he said as we ordered martinis. "I'm afraid old Dunluce got the better of you today."

I nodded. "It was humbling."

T HE PORTRUSH DINING HALL was stunning, with a picturesque overlook of the rugged seashore. Janie had arrived soon after we finished our round. I couldn't help but notice the large ruby ring on her right hand. She did say that Charles was very good to her. We had a couple of cocktails and took our seats at a table by the windows where we enjoyed a superbly cooked meal of freshly caught salmon and summer vegetables. Charles ordered a bottle of ridiculous white burgundy. Out of the blue, he said, "As I was trying to mention on the course, before you became so interested in my childhood, I think I might be able to help you find Thomas Walker. I have a lot of contacts."

"Really?"

He lifted his eyebrows and nodded. "There are some in the business community who might have some answers. I told you, I'd like to be hands-on in the investigation and help find the bastard who killed Janie's uncles. He's causing quite a measure of alarm in Janie's family and disruption in my life."

Janie looked at him and smiled proudly. "My protector."

"Like I told you on the golf course," I said, "I'm not heading up this investigation. I can put you in touch with Inspector McLaughlin. You could work with him and share your many contacts."

He shook his head. "I need to stay in the background. I don't want to be seen working with the police. A lot of my business contacts are strong nationalists, ex-IRA guys. I can't be seen working alongside all these former RUC lads. Hell, McLaughlin himself was an Ulster copper swinging his baton in the Lower Falls. I'd just as soon be doing investigation on the private side, like you. You and I, Liam, we could be a team, share information."

"I'm not a very good team player, Charles, and I don't think I will be staying here very much longer. You should really work with Inspector McLaughlin. I'm sure he'd be discreet."

Charles nodded and tipped his glass in my direction. "Well, it's all quite disconcerting. We know that Walker is responsible for Fergus and Eamon. Marked for death, they were. And now he's served his death notice on Riley. We need to find him and bring him in before anyone else is hurt."

"I don't think that Inspector McLaughlin shares your certainty. He's not convinced that it's Walker."

"That's patently derelict. What could be more palpable?" Charles took a sip of his wine. "This arsonist fellow, the one you caught, what's he been telling the police? Did he confess that Walker paid him to torch Deirdre's house?"

"Not that I'm aware of."

"He might have received his orders over the phone from some untraceable source. That's how they do those things, you know."

I shrugged. I wondered how Charles had arrived at that conclusion. I wondered if one of Charles's many contacts worked for the PSNI. Given the way Charles throws money around, it wouldn't be unheard of to have a policeman on his payroll.

"Anyway," Charles said as he emptied the wine bottle, "I'd like to work with you and help you in your investigation, as long as you're here. You know, study at the feet of the master. It would be most enjoyable and I do have my connections."

"That's very kind of you, and I'll keep it in mind. I will gratefully accept any information you can pass along."

Tea and chocolates were served and we wrapped up our conversation. Charles phoned Starkman to bring the car around. "He'll take you back to your hotel. I'll drive home with Janie. And Liam, don't worry about the Nassau. I wouldn't feel right taking your money. The Dunluce eighteen can be pretty rough, especially on first-timers."

Were I more of a man, I would have insisted that the debt was due and payment was the honorable thing to do. Instead, I said, "Thank you, Charles. Very sporting of you."

TWENTY-THREE

• • •

I T WAS RAINING WHEN I went out for my early morning run, one of those Irish mists they talk about—foggy, little visibility and slippery streets. Still, it felt good to get my heart pumping and prepare me for whatever misadventure was sure to develop later in my day. It didn't take long. As I was getting out of the shower, I got a call from O'Neill.

"Liam, we've just been served with another emergency motion. This one was filed jointly by Conor and Riley."

"Let me guess. They want to distribute the assets immediately and send me packing to Chicago."

"How did you know?"

"Riley. He threatened it. When is it scheduled to be heard?"

"This morning at eleven."

"Does the motion have something to do with the Global Investments stock? Is that the emergency?"

"Partially. They ask the judge to declare that Fergus's intent—that of preventing a murderer from profiting from his death—has been satisfied. They reason that Thomas Walker is the presumptive suspect, not a relative, and that there is no evidence of any complicity by any trust beneficiary."

"How is that any different than what they brought up last week when the judge shot them down?"

"Technically, identifying a suspect was not on the judge's docket last week. It wasn't a part of the motion. Today's motion also alleges that you are stalling the investigation and the ultimate distributions in order to collect your weekly stipend of one thousand pounds. Finally, as you anticipated, the motion alleges that the trust assets are endangered by your mismanagement, citing your refusal to pledge the Global stock."

Collect my stipend? That infuriated me. I had never taken a cent. I didn't ask for this assignment or the stipend. Half of me hoped the judge would grant the motion and let me go home and back to my wife as soon as possible. The other half wanted the judge to send Riley and Conor, those two whiny children, to bed without any supper. "What is your strategy?" I asked.

"I called Inspector McLaughlin and asked him to come to court this morning to testify that the PSNI does not have a primary suspect and has not eliminated any person. He has agreed to say that it is an open, ongoing investigation."

"Shall I notify Deirdre, Robert and Janie?"

"You may if you like, but there's no need at this time. I don't believe their testimony would be persuasive one way or the other. If they want to appear, that is certainly their right."

I told O'Neill that I'd meet him in the courtroom and that I'd inform the others. I called Deirdre and Janie, and both of them said they might show up. I couldn't reach Robert. I wanted to call Catherine and check up on her, but it was the middle of the night in Chicago. I'd call her later.

I DIDN'T EXPECT TO see you all back here so soon," Judge McNulty said with a smile as she took the bench. For an emergency motion set on very short notice, the hearing was well-attended. Conor and Riley were there, of course, each one throwing an evil eye in my direction. Deirdre sat quietly in a back row. Although I wasn't the one who notified him, Robert was also present. Perhaps he had chosen to side with Conor and Riley. Janie was there in the second row with Charles seated right beside her.

Conor's lawyer, Michael Cooney, began his oratory by reminding the judge that I was not a resident of Northern Ireland, that I had been estranged from the family for decades, that I was unconcerned with the preservation of the assets, and that I was insensitive to the needs of the beneficiaries, Riley in particular. I was in it for my own monetary gain. "I'm sure everyone will agree," he said, "that paying a trustee a thousand pounds per week is an outrageous figure, considering the fact that he does nothing."

Finally, he assured the judge that there was no need to keep this charade going when it was clear that the murder was a revenge killing by Thomas Walker, a member of a Shankill gang.

"Are you prepared to submit proof to this court on each of those premises this morning?" Judge McNulty said.

"Of course," Cooney answered, "although it's self-evident that Liam Taggart lives in America and that he had a falling out with his family in 1999. I don't believe that needs further evidence. Just the other day he refused to pledge or transfer the Global stock, which could save the company and protect Riley Taggart's job. I don't think anyone will dispute that. The trust authorizes an obscene stipend. That's in black-and-white. I believe the trust is picking up his hotel room and I assume all of his meals as well, so he's living like the Prince of Wales off the trust's limited assets. To my mind, the only matter requiring any proof at all is the undeniable conclusion that Thomas Walker committed the murders and not any of Fergus Taggart's loving family members, and we're prepared to meet that burden."

I looked to my right and Riley and Conor were vigorously nodding their heads in unison, as though they were two bobblehead dolls. When Cooney sat down, Judge McNulty turned her attention to O'Neill. "Do you wish to make an opening statement as well, Solicitor O'Neill?"

O'Neill rose from his chair. "May it please this honorable court, Your Honor. My rejoinder is simple. It's all poppycock! Pure conjecture! Mr. Cooney could not possibly have evidence that Thomas Walker is the murderer. Pictures of the remains of a house are hardly sufficient to convict a man of murder and Inspector McLaughlin is here to tell you that." And he sat down. Short and sweet. I liked the way this guy worked.

Judge McNulty looked at us with a kind expression, but she seemed a little annoyed. "I have to tell you," she said, "I am not concerned that Liam Taggart resides in America. I told you that last time and there isn't any need to bring that up again. I consider the comments relative to his previous estrangement, his living conditions in Antrim, his hotel room, his meals and his weekly stipend, to be nothing but embittered rhetoric. But I do have a concern about the Global stock and the accusations regarding Mr. Walker and their effect on distribution of the trust assets. I will hear evidence on those issues. You may begin, Solicitor Cooney."

Cooney called Riley as his first witness. "Your Honor, by rights that stock belongs to me," Riley said. "My father bought it for me. It's my company. Recently, Global has faced a need to raise capital. Refinancing of our line of credit is available but only if one hundred percent of the stock is pledged. I told Liam how badly we needed to obtain refinancing." Riley glared at me angrily. "That's why we're here. Without the loan, Global will not survive, it's as simple as that. And unless Global can secure refinancing, the stock will be worthless to the trust or anyone else. I told Liam that as well and he just doesn't care. He said his hands are tied."

Riley was desperate and I suspected it had more to do with his fear of being swept up in a criminal prosecution for financial fraud than his devotion to his company. Nevertheless I felt bad. I always liked Riley. Still, I didn't see how I could transfer the shares to him without violating the trust agreement. Besides, I was acting on advice from O'Neill.

As expected, I was called as the next witness. Cooney asked me if Riley had requested my approval to pledge the shares and I said yes. And wasn't it true that I told him that I would not transfer or encumber the shares? Again, I said yes.

"I would have been happy to help Riley if I could," I said. "But transferring the shares into Riley's name or pledging them would have been a violation of my fiduciary duty. The trust requires all the assets to be liquidated, reduced to cash and distributed to *all* the beneficiaries at the appropriate time. I knew that and Riley knew that. He's had a copy of the trust since the first time we were in court."

Cooney then turned his attention to evidence that Walker was the presumptive killer. This was tricky for Cooney. He could hardly put one of my relatives on the stand to testify that the Taggart brothers were guilty of firebombing Walker's house. Cooney called Robert to the stand. He danced around the historical basis for the feud between the Taggarts and the Walkers referring obliquely to events in the early 1970s. "It was well-known that Walker was a member of the notorious Shankill Butchers," Robert said. "They were archenemies of the Taggarts, then and now. Cooney showed him the picture of Walker's house. "Have you seen that picture before?"

Robert nodded sharply. "The murderer left that picture in me brother Eamon's mailbox right before me brother was killed," he said with a catch in his throat. "And it was found in Fergus's and Riley's mailboxes as well."

"And in yours as well?"

"No."

"Do you know to your own knowledge whose house is shown in that picture?"

Robert nodded again. "It was Archie Walker's house."

"Do you know who was in that house at the time it was set on fire?" Cooney said.

"I wasn't there. According to the newspaper, the entire Walker family was killed in the fire."

"And you know all of this because there was a feud between the Taggart family and the Walker family during the Troubles?"

Robert nodded. "Not just the Taggart family. The Walker family was feuding with every Catholic family in the Lower Falls. Since the Taggarts were Catholic, I suppose you'd have to say that."

"If the entire family was killed in the house fire, who is left to carry on the feud between the Taggarts and the Walkers?"

Robert shrugged. "I hear it's one of Archie's brothers."

"Which one would that be?"

"I hear tell that Thomas was released from prison and is living somewhere, I don't know exactly where. If I knew, you better believe I'd . . . well, I don't know where."

Then Cooney called Riley to identify the picture he'd found in his mailbox. Of course, Riley couldn't say for certain who put it there.

"The circumstantial evidence is very compelling in this case," Cooney said in his wrap-up. "It should be obvious to all that the horrific murders of Fergus and Eamon Taggart were remnants of the Troubles. They were revenge killings by a relative of Archie Walker. They were certainly not committed by any beneficiaries. There is not a shred of evidence that any family member participated in the homicides of either Fergus Taggart or Eamon Taggart. Therefore, Fergus Taggart's expressed fear of distributing assets to a homicidal relative, as bizarre as that might seem, has been completely eliminated and there should be no further impediment to the immediate distribution of the trust assets to the rightful beneficiaries. We ask that Liam Taggart be relieved of his position as trustee and that the court oversee the immediate distribution of the trust assets." Cooney nodded to Conor and Riley and sat down.

O'Neill rose. "As our first witness, Your Honor, we respectfully call Inspector Farrell McLaughlin of the Antrim District of the Police Service of Northern Ireland." McLaughlin stood.

Judge McNulty shook her head. "It's not necessary. I'm prepared to rule on the motion. You may be seated, Inspector. First, with regard to the Global stock and the request for transfer or encumbrance. The stock sits in the name of the decedent, Fergus Taggart, and it belongs to his trust estate. It does not belong to Riley Taggart or the Global Investment Company. Pledging the stock to secure a loan to the company, based on Riley's speculation that its value might be adversely affected if the company did not get the loan it was seeking, would have the result of removing the stock from the estate assets. Such a transaction would be in direct conflict with the terms of the trust, which require liquidation and distribution to seven beneficiaries. I find in favor of the trustee's decision not to transfer or encumber the stock.

"As to the request for immediate distribution of all of the trust assets and removal of the trustee because—how do I phrase this?—*the presumptive killer* is a member of the family of Archie Walker and not a Taggart family member? I find that to be pure conjecture without any evidentiary support. I deny this emergency motion in all respects. Court is adjourned."

Conor and Riley were livid. Conor turned to Cooney and shot out a pointed finger. "You are totally useless. You've lost two hearings in a row."

Cooney shook his head and held out his arms. "I did what I could. She ruled against us. I told you the case was weak. You need evidence, more evidence of this Thomas Walker or whoever the hell the killer is. There was nothing more I could have done."

"You are discharged, fired, relieved of your duties."

"That suits me fine. You'll have my bill for services this afternoon."

Then it was my turn to be the target. Conor and Riley stormed over to me and got right up in my face. "You think you won something this morning, Liam? You won nothing. This ain't over. We don't want you here, don't you get it? If you're smart, you'll get out of Antrim this afternoon. Do you understand me, Liam?"

"Go home, Conor. We're done for today."

On his way out, Robert looked at me with disappointment in his eyes and shook his head. "This is a family matter, Liam. Since you've arrived there's been quite a bit of dissension. Conor's right, you should go home. Go home to your family, go home to your life in America."

It was pretty obvious I didn't have many friends left in this room, but when I glanced over at Charles, he was nodding to me. I wouldn't put him in the friend category, but he was clearly contented with the ruling. So were Janie and Deirdre. Me, I felt sad at the way the family was falling apart. So much discord. I only wished for peace and there wasn't much of that to be found.

Janie and Charles asked me to join them for lunch. I declined. I wanted to take a walk. Alone. I needed a friendly voice. I checked my watch, but it was still too early to call Catherine.

As I was leaving the courthouse, McLaughlin told me he had a line on Thomas Walker. "I put out a bulletin asking if anyone knew Walker's whereabouts. One of my officers told me he saw him in Belfast recently. He was called upon to quiet a disturbance in a west side pub, and he saw Walker acting loud and obnoxious with his cohorts, singing the old Ulster marching songs, but not breaking any laws. My officer knew him from the seventies and was shocked to learn that he was out of prison and back on the streets."

That was also disturbing news to me. It was confirmation that a Walker was out on the loose, raising hell and theoretically capable of committing the murders. "Your officer, he didn't bring him in?"

"For what? Singing while under the influence?"

"Walker must live in the Shankill area."

McLaughlin nodded. "That's what I think. I'll get the name of the bar and give you a call. I'd like to go out there tomorrow and see what I can find out."

Twenty-four

· · ·

I ROSE EARLY AND TOOK a long run around the northern shore of Lough Neagh, along the road to Toome. As I neared the city, the traditional Irish song I sang at Conway's played out in my mind—young Roddy McCorley, the hemp rope 'round his neck, fated to die on the Bridge of Toome.

There was never a one of all your dead, more bravely died in fray, then he who marches to his death in Toomebridge town today.

That was too grim an omen to start my day. I'm not normally given to superstitions, but I made a U-turn and headed back to Antrim. I didn't want to push my luck.

As a private investigator, I was a flop. Try as I might, I could not come up with a plan for solving these murders or preventing the next one. Every solution seemed to raise more questions than answers. The most likely theory, that of a latent vendetta, made the most sense but I was hesitant where Thomas Walker was concerned. If Walker was avenging his family's murders, why wouldn't he seek to replicate the crime? What is the point of dropping warnings like bread crumbs and picking off Taggarts one by one? Uncle Fergus was shot at very close range. There were powder stains on his shirt. Fergus wasn't weak and he wasn't stupid. Why would he let a guy like Thomas Walker get that close?

If it wasn't Walker, then who? Was it someone related to the newspaper clippings? Why did Fergus save two articles about crimes fifteen years and eight years ago? Why did he have a picture of a box of guns? Fergus wasn't killed with an assault rifle.

I kept thinking about the Bridget McGregor Trust. McLaughlin said his investigation was blocked by a bunch of red tape. McLaughlin had no jurisdiction in Dublin and had to work through the Dublin police. That required something akin to an international warrant. And of course, the jackpot question, ladies and gentlemen: why did Fergus defer distribution of his estate until the killer was caught? Was it because he suspected involvement of a family member, or was it to protect the beneficiaries? These questions all needed answers and I didn't have them.

McLaughlin had called me late last night and said, "There's a unionist bar called Willy's Pub, where my officer spotted Walker. It's always been a UVF and LVF haunt and probably a watering hole for a bunch of former gang members as well, like your Butchers. I'm going to pay the bar a visit tomorrow. Come along if you like."

When I finished my run, I had just enough time for a shower and a quick breakfast before heading over to the station. McLaughlin wanted to hit the bar at the lunch hour. Physically, I felt fine. Mentally, I was frustrated, confused and exhausted, and to make it worse, I hadn't spoken with Catherine for two days. The six-hour time difference made connections difficult. I had intended to call her last night, but I was so tired I fell asleep.

Just after eleven o'clock, I took a seat in McLaughlin's unmarked Skoda and the two of us headed off for West Belfast. Willy's Pub was a block or two off Shankill Road in a staunchly unionist neighborhood. Lampposts were painted red, white and blue and Union Jacks flew from houses, stores and street signs, reminding you, just in case you forgot, that you were in the UK and this was solid loyalist territory.

Willy's Pub sat directly across the street from a huge mural painted on the side of a three-story brick building. It depicted a young King William III sitting high upon his rearing white horse, gleaming sword in hand, with the date 1690 prominently displayed behind him. That was the year that Protestant William III, Prince of Orange, defeated Catholic King James at the Battle of the Boyne. Protestants 1, Catholics 0.

It was almost noon and there was a smattering of customers in the dimly lit bar. Pictures of Reverend Ian Paisley and assorted Protestant political leaders hung on the walls. Colorful shields of the UDA, UVF,

UDR and other paramilitary brigades were hanging over the bar. Ominously, the largest poster on the back wall depicted a paramilitary fighter dressed in black with a balaclava covering his head, under a banner reading: ULSTER OR DIE. Other plaques in the room cheerily declared, AN ULSTERMAN HAS THE RIGHT TO DEFEND HIMSELF, FOR GOD AND ULSTER and the ever-popular MY ULSTER BLOOD IS MY MOST PRECIOUS HERITAGE.

Behind the bar was a middle-aged man in a blue T-shirt. Tall, thin, ruddy-faced and clearly suspicious of two people he didn't know, he looked us over and said, "Gents, what'll it be?"

"Two pints of Gat," McLaughlin said and slid onto a stool. I sat down next to him.

The bartender looked at us like a cautious dog might eye an offering of meat from a stranger. He pulled the draught lever over a pint glass and said, "I don't know you two, do I?"

McLaughlin shook his head. "Probably not. It's been a long time since I worked in this neighborhood. I'm trying to catch up with Thomas Walker. I heard he was in here a couple days ago."

"Wouldn't know him." The bartender finished his pour, let the foam settle and placed the two pint glasses of Guinness in front of us. "That be all? Four pound forty."

McLaughlin placed a five on the bar. "We need to talk to Walker."

"I told you, I don't know him. Who are you anyway? This isn't the kind of place where people ask a lot of questions. Folks around here don't take to outsiders asking questions. I knew I didn't like you two when you walked into my bar. Finish your beer and be off."

McLaughlin flipped open his wallet to show his PSNI star. "I should have figured," the bartender said with a sneer. "Well, I don't have to like you, I don't have to serve you and I don't have to give you any information. I don't know anybody named Walker."

"You'd be doing Mr. Walker a favor. He's violating his parole. His home address is no longer valid. I could throw him back into the yard, but all I want to do is talk to him. I need a current address and a current report, so why don't you help me out? Where does he live?"

"I don't know. That's a fact. I don't know."

"When does he usually come in?"

The bartender shrugged. "Sometimes in the evening. He was here a couple of days ago. He's not a regular, just comes in from time to time when he gets some money. He's not a troublemaker. Oh, he gets a little juiced, makes a little noise, him and some fellows get to singing some old marching songs, telling stories about the Troubles and cursing the Catholics, but there's nothing against the law there. Why the hell are you chasing him? He's an old man, white hair, walks with a limp and a cane. Why is the parole board hassling the man? They should just let him be, he couldn't be a problem to nobody."

"Limp or not, he's going back to the prison for VOP unless I talk to him."

The bartender gave us a sour look. "If I see him again, I'll be sure to tell him to go by his parole officer and update his info."

"No, I want to see him personally."

"You ain't no different from any other police stiff. He can see anybody he wants. Now you guys drink up and get out of here."

McLaughlin took out his card and placed it on the bar. He took a sip of his beer and patted me on the back. "Liam, when do you suppose was the last time the health department went through this rattrap?" He looked around. "Do you think they'd find a violation or two?"

"Oh, I bet they'd find a hundred or more, starting with that bolted back door. It's a flat-out fire trap. Then there's the cracked window, the mouse hole in that wall and I haven't even seen the toilets. I figure the health department would shut this place down in an instant."

"I agree. Probably cost the owner a pretty penny to correct all the violations before he could reopen. Might take weeks, even months."

"I'd guess the fines alone would cause this joint to shut down," I said. "Probably lose its license as well. I know one thing—when the Department of Health gets through with this place it will definitely improve the neighborhood."

"Do you want to know something interesting, Liam? The new Minister of Health is a republican, imagine that. Yep, she's a member of Sinn Fein and a good Catholic woman. I wonder what she'd think of this rat's ass bar and all these hateful loyalist slogans hanging on the walls?"

The bartender pocketed the card. "All right, you made your point."

"Good. When you see Walker, you give me a call and I'll come out.

If you run a trick on me, if you tip him off, Willy's will be a shelter for battered and abused women next week."

He wiped his hands on a towel and said, "I'll give you a call when I see him, but that's as far as I go."

We left the bar to some very unfriendly stares and headed back to Antrim. Once in the car, I took out my cell phone. I hadn't spoken to Catherine since the day before yesterday. It was only six in the morning, but she might be awake. I texted her to call me.

"Why did we come out here, Farrell? You don't think Walker's the killer."

"I'm just following up a lead. He's not my first choice, but I've been wrong before. We might as well keep tabs on Walker. He might know why those pictures are being circulated."

I had to admit, doubts were creeping into my mind as well. Even before our visit to Willy's. I still believed that Walker was a prime suspect. He met all the qualifications. He was a living remnant of the Taggart/Walker feud and his brother's murder could provide the motivation. The picture of the Walker house, the wake, the warnings, they all pointed to a Walker. But standing in that low-life bar, my instincts were telling me to look elsewhere. How is an impoverished old guy with a limp, hanging in ratty bars, going to coordinate a series of murders in Antrim? Is he going to show up at my uncle's farm, limp up to him with his cane, take out his gun and shoot him at close range? Is he going to steal and drive a sixty-thousand-dollar truck? Is he going to figure out where I live and FedEx a calling card to my house in Chicago? None of those scenarios made any sense for a guy like Walker.

"Walker's got to be in his late sixties, early seventies, right?" I said. "He's an old man now, locked up in prison for almost forty years, probably just a tired old guff. I'm growing doubtful."

"Old man? He's younger than I am. Am I a tired old guff? Don't answer that. But now you're doubtful? Are you coming around to my way of thinking? It seems to me that you're backing off your vendetta theory and that puts you smack in the middle of relativity."

"Maybe. To tell you the truth, I don't know what to think. It could be an old vendetta. It doesn't have to be Walker. It could be some other unionist from the past who carries a grudge against the Taggarts, maybe even a former Shankill Butcher who knew about the Walkers. A vendetta makes as much sense as anything else. But going into that bar, seeing the trash that's hanging out there, I find it hard to believe that a washout like Walker is behind it all."

"We'll get the guy, Liam. Sooner or later, something will break. Whoever he is, it's obvious he's not finished yet, that's for sure."

I nodded my understanding. Not exactly encouraging, but true. The killer was still out there and he wasn't finished. I checked my phone. Nothing from Catherine. Wake up, Cat, I thought. Return the text. Give me a call. I need some encouragement.

I NSPECTOR, I'D LIKE TO follow up on some loose ends," I said when we arrived back at the station. "Specifically, the two newspaper articles in Fergus's folder."

McLaughlin went into his file cabinet and pulled out his Taggart file, which was getting thicker every day. "We've looked into them, Liam, and we didn't see any connections. The first article concerned the murder of a Protestant aid worker on June 23, 1999. The worker's name was Vernon Bishop. He was coming out of an Antrim restaurant with his wife when he was beaten to death by a single assailant with a lead pipe. The perpetrator was apprehended later that night and held in jail, right here in this building, until his trial. Bishop's wife ID'd the perp, there were two other witnesses, he had blood on his clothes and he had no alibi. His conviction was never in doubt. The trial was short and he was given a life sentence. As far as I can tell, it had nothing to do with the Taggarts."

"Who was he?"

"An IRA bomb maker named Seamus McManus. Real bad sort. Very skilled at his craft. We always believed he was a central figure in several IRA bombings. He was arrested and convicted in 1977 for setting off the bomb at the Belfast Arms Hotel. He served twenty-two years and was paroled in 1999 because of the GFA's early prisoner release program. No sooner does he get out of the can than he clubs an innocent aid worker."

I was floored. Seamus McManus was the main reason I had to leave Northern Ireland. "I know that guy," I said. "I played him for information when he was arrested in 1999. We heard that McManus was back in the bomb-making business and was in the middle of a plot to blow up an Orange parade."

"How did you learn that? From your uncles?"

I nodded. "They said that a splinter group called the Real IRA was intending to plant a car bomb alongside the Orange parade route. There were bound to be multiple deaths and injuries. McManus was arrested for killing that aid worker, and his apartment had a stash of explosives and maps of the parade route. My station chief knew that McManus could finger the rest of the RIRA brigade, but McManus wouldn't say a word. Westerfield came up with the idea of planting someone in the cell with McManus, pretending to be another IRA street fighter, and maybe he'd open up. I volunteered.

"McManus was told that I was arrested for trying to shoot up a Protestant church. McManus said he was proud of me. We sat there cursing the RUC, the UVF, the queen and the prime minister and by the end of the day, I had the names and locations of all of his co-conspirators. I found out what was going down in Portadown. If we hadn't stopped it, it would have been a bloodbath. Lives lost, people injured. That attack could have been a major setback to the peace process.

"I was able to give eight names to Westerfield, who passed them along to the RUC. The RUC arrested them all, confiscated bombs and assault rifles and threw them all into prison."

"Seriously? That was you? I remember the sweep. You did a great job."

I nodded. "But it was bittersweet. That operation was the main reason I had to leave Antrim. My uncles discovered I was an operative, my cover was blown and the CIA sent me back to Chicago. I suppose that's why Fergus saved the article. I know I should be proud of the job I did, but it's a sad memory for me. It destroyed the relationship I had with my uncles."

"Well, I'm sorry it affected your relationship, but you put a lot of bad guys away."

"I assumed they all went to prison for a long time. What happened to McManus?"

"He went back to prison in 1999 and that's where his story ended.

You might say it was jailhouse justice. His throat was slashed and he was found stripped naked in the yard with a rat painted on his chest. So your uncles ended up blaming you? They weren't RIRA, were they?"

"No, no way. They were staunch nationalists, they were members of the IRA, but they were politicians, not street fighters. By 1999 they were working hard for peace. But to their way of thinking, I was disloyal. I had betrayed my people. They felt I could have handled things differently without spying on Catholics and turning them into the RUC. It was a bad ending."

McLaughlin put his hand on my shoulder and looked at me sympathetically. "You did the right thing, Liam."

"I don't think so. I lied to my family. I deceived them and conned them and abused their confidence. I could no longer be trusted. That's never the right thing to do. Fergus sent me away, told me we had nothing more to say to each other. I was devastated. Since I've returned I've learned that he was sorry about the whole thing as well. I'm pretty sure that's why he saved the article. Maybe he meant to call me and reconnect and the article was a reminder. I doubt it had something to do with recent death threats. Does it raise suspicion in your mind?"

"I'm quite sure that recent death threats aren't coming from Seamus McManus. He's dead and buried."

"But maybe one of McManus's kin? Isn't that the reason we're chasing Thomas Walker? A pissed-off relative who wants to settle the score?"

"There's a big difference between Walker and McManus. There was a prominent feud between the Taggarts and the Walkers. The other night your uncle Robert practically confessed to firebombing Walker's house and killing everyone inside. What connection could there be between the Taggarts and McManus?"

"He was killed for being a rat, for giving up the names of the RIRA. Suppose someone in his family found out that I was the one who pumped him for the names and got him killed?"

"How would anyone know it was you? McManus didn't know you personally, did he? You didn't give him your real name, did you?"

"Of course not. I was Danny Foy. McManus didn't know who I was and he only saw me for two days. But there were other people involved. Prison authorities, agency staff. My uncles were able to find out."

He shook his head and twisted his lips. "It's a long shot. Not impossible, but highly unlikely."

"What about the other newspaper article, the one about the murder in 2008 at the Maghaberry Prison?"

McLaughlin pulled out the clipping. "Sean Lefferty. IRA gun runner. Killed by other inmates in Maghaberry, probably loyalists. He was found with a knife in his back. Lefferty was a major prong in the IRA's gun smuggling network and was responsible for bringing in tons of weapons during the seventies and eighties. He was on our radar for years. He actually traveled to Libya and connected with Ghadaffi. Lefferty was a huge arrest for us—"

I stopped him. "You don't have to go any further, Inspector. He was arrested in 1999 because I fingered him. Me! Lefferty was one of the names given to me by McManus. He also gave me Lefferty's address where the weapons were stashed. Not only did the RUC grab Lefferty, but they seized a huge cache of RIRA weapons. The question is why did my uncle save these particular clippings? Could it be that somehow these guys had resurfaced and were threatening my uncle? Is that why he feared for his life?"

McLaughlin chuckled. "Unless their name is also Lazarus, they have not resurfaced. They are both underground for good."

"Not funny. You know what I mean. Maybe there's a member of the family carrying the torch, gunning for my uncles. Or me!"

McLaughlin shook his head. "No, I reject that theory. Even if Lefferty has a surviving member of his family, how would that person know about you? Or the Walkers? How could he possibly connect the dots? How could he circle back to you or to your uncles sixteen years later? Nah. It's someone who knows about the Walkers and the Taggarts and you can't eliminate a family member. Relativity theory. I like it more every day, especially since I saw the anger in the courtroom yesterday."

"Then why would my uncle keep those clippings in a folder? Isn't it possible that they had something to do with his murder?"

"Why don't you ask your aunt Deirdre?"

I shook my head. "I think she's given me everything she knows. Fergus didn't want to worry her and didn't open up to her about these matters."

A thought came to mind. Deirdre said that Annie was close to Fergus and he discussed personal matters with her. That disturbed me on several levels. I didn't like the idea of Annie knowing all about this and I certainly didn't want to reopen communication channels with Annie to find out. It was uncomfortable enough seeing her at the church. I didn't want to go sleuthing with her.

"If you think the documents in the folder are all related, then the picture of the box of guns makes more sense," McLaughlin said. "It might have been a picture of the guns seized from Lefferty in 1999."

I nodded. "So, you agree that my suspicions might have merit? Why else would my uncle put that photo in the folder?"

"Maybe, but let's not jump to conclusions."

I stood up to leave. I was anxious to get back to Deirdre and ask her about McManus and Lefferty and if she knew anything more about them. Besides, I had to call Catherine. Why hadn't she called me back? I'd texted her hours ago.

I grabbed a sandwich from Flaherty's and ate it in the car. The more I tried to make sense of the killings, the more frustrated I became. It was now one o'clock and time to call Catherine. I placed the call but reached her voice mail. Half an hour later, I got the voice mail message again. Where the hell was she at seven thirty in the morning when I needed to talk to her? She couldn't have been sleeping. I left another message for her to call me and proceeded down A26 toward Deirdre.

As I neared the farm, I placed another call. Voice mail: "Sorry I can't come to the phone right now, please leave a message." I tried all her numbers. No answer at home, no answer on her cell and no answer at the office. I was getting nervous. I called Chick Chaikin. Voice mail. Now I was sure something was wrong. I could feel it. I was practically crawling out of my skin when my phone rang. Caller ID said it was Gladys Jimenez, Catherine's secretary. Thank God, Cat's office was calling me back.

"Hey Gladys," I teased, "how many paper clips did Catherine use this week?"

There was no joy in her voice. "They're all okay, Liam. I mean, I'm sure they'll all *be* okay."

"Who's okay? What's okay? What are you talking about, Gladys?"

"There was a fire. At your house. A man threw a bottle of gasoline through your front window. It exploded and caused a big fire. They're all at the hospital now. Ben, Cat and Mr. Chaikin. It happened early this morning."

"Gladys, what's their condition? Cat and the baby, how are they?"

Gladys started to cry. "Cat got burned real bad on her leg and her hip. Ben had smoke in his lungs. He couldn't breathe. They're both in the hospital, but they're alive. Doctor says they're gonna be okay. Mr. Chaikin was shot bad and he's in surgery."

"What about the man who threw the bottle? Where is he?"

"The man who threw the bottle is dead. Mr. Chaikin shot him and it was a good thing because the man had a gun and he would have . . ." Gladys was crying harder and couldn't finish her sentence. She took a breath.

"What, Gladys? Tell me."

"He was ready to shoot Cat and the baby when they came outside."

Son of a bitch. Son of a bitch. I was going out of my mind. "Gladys, I'm coming right back, I'll catch the next plane."

"Cat says no, you need to stay and finish your job."

"Tell her I'll be there as soon as possible." She was sobbing heavily into the phone. "Gladys, listen to me, is there a policeman guarding Catherine's room? Is there anyone watching out for her? Gladys?"

"No, I don't think so. I don't see a policeman."

"Are you anywhere near Catherine? Can I speak to her?"

"I'm at the hospital, outside her room. They gave her medicine for the pain and she's sleeping."

"Can you stay with her for a while?"

"*Sí,*"

"Gladys, I'm going to try to get a policeman to watch over them, but in the meantime, if you see anything, anything at all, I want you to shout for help at the top of your lungs, okay?"

Gladys was sobbing, breathing in gasps. "Why did they do this, Liam? Who would do such a thing? My Catherine! And the little baby! *Oh Dios mio. El pequeño bebé! Por qué? Por qué? Que haria esta cosa?*"

"Gladys, Gladys, listen to me. You must guard her until the police come. Shout for help."

"I will. I will."

"You said Mr. Chaikin was in surgery. What happened to him?"

"He tried to stop the man from throwing the gasoline. He jumped out of his car, but the man saw him, turned and shot him in the stomach. *Pero Senor Chaikin lo mato. Gracias a Dios.* Lying in the street, Mr. Chaikin, he shot the man dead."

"Gladys, stay with Cat. Guard her. Don't leave her. Call me if anything at all happens. Anything. Do you follow me?"

"Liam, I'm going crazy, but I'm not scared and I'm not stupid. Don't you worry; No one's coming near my Catherine or the baby. No one's getting by this Puerto Rican woman. And I'll call you when I know about Mr. Chaikin."

"Thanks, Gladys, I love you. I'll be there soon."

I made a quick U-turn and headed for the Dublin airport. Even though my route took me by Belfast International I knew there were no direct flights to Chicago. A cell phone check with Aer Lingus informed me that there was a four o'clock out of Dublin. If I stepped on it, I might make it.

Next I called McLaughlin. "Farrell, the bastards attacked my family. They firebombed my house. I'm headed back to Chicago."

"What?"

"Just like the one I stopped at Deirdre's. Same deal. A Molotov was tossed through the window in the middle of the night. The guy was armed and Catherine's secretary thought he intended to shoot my wife and baby if they came out of the door. I had hired a friend of mine, a private guy, to sit outside the house and thank God he was there. He killed the shooter, but not before the bomb was tossed through the window. My wife's been injured and she's in the hospital. So's my little boy. I'm headed home."

"Jesus, Mary and Joseph, I'm so sorry, Liam. How bad are the injuries?"

"I don't know. Gladys says they're bad. My friend Chick is in surgery. He may not make it."

"Who's looking out for your wife right now? She could still be a target, even in the hospital."

"I don't know if the guy who threw the bomb was working alone, or if there were others, but I agree with you and I'd feel a lot better with police protection. Catherine's secretary is with her right now and she's one tough woman, a real pit bull. She'll do what she can, but Farrell, I need a favor. Can you contact the Chicago police? See if they'll post a guard outside Catherine's hospital room? At least until I get there? I don't know if they'd do it for me, but if the call came from you, it might make a difference."

"Consider it done. Where is your wife?"

"Northwestern Memorial. Listen Farrell, I don't think this is Walker's doing. A lowlife like Walker would not have the funds or the wherewithal to get this done three thousand miles away. I believe you've been right from the beginning: the killer's a relative, and I'm betting it's one of my two cousins. I'd like to know where Conor and Riley are right now and what they've been doing for the past two days. Maybe you can get their phone records and find out if there are any calls to the States."

"I understand. I'll do my best to track them down. When you get back to Chicago, try to get an ID on the arsonist. Find out if he has any travel records. Get his cell phone. Where are you right now?"

"On the A26 heading toward Antrim from Deirdre's, I'm trying to catch a four o'clock out of Dublin."

"Four o'clock out of Dublin, are you kidding? It's two thirty. Are you anywhere near Belfast International? I've got a chopper there."

"Just passed it."

"Go back. I'll get you to Dublin. I don't want you getting killed on my highways. You'll make the flight on time, I'll take care of it."

"Thanks, Farrell. I owe you."

I pulled into the lot at Belfast International and waited for McLaughlin. I had never endured anything like the pure panic I was feeling. I paced around my car waiting for Farrell.

My phone rang again and I slipped into the car to take the call. It was Gladys. "You told me to tell you when Mr. Chaikin was out of surgery. They've taken him down to ICU. His doctor says his condition is critical, but he's got a chance. Cat woke up and she wants to talk to you."

Chills ran up my spine. I had almost lost her. Thank God I could talk to my wife.

"Hi, honey," she said in a weak, breathy voice. "How are you?"

"How am I? Oh my God, sweetheart, how are *you* and Ben?"

"We're going to be okay. I got burned on my leg from the fire and . . ." Cat didn't finish her sentence and even though she tried to muffle the phone, I could tell she was crying. I was so upset. Here I was in Northern Ireland and my family, my responsibility, my whole life was in Chicago fighting for their lives. I clenched my fists. I could have ripped the steering wheel off the post. I should have been there. I should have been in Chicago protecting them ever since the threats started coming. What was I doing playing trustee, trying to protect money and stock certificates from being prematurely distributed, when my wife and my son had received a death threat? I'm going home and I'm never coming back. Damn the Fergus Taggart Trust!

"Liam," Catherine said, sniffling. "I love you."

"Cat, I love you so much. I'm coming home, sweetheart. Take care of little Benny and I'll see you soon."

"Ben's fine. He's right next to me. I guess you were right about the phone calls. I should have listened." She started crying again.

"I'll be there before you know it. Just be real careful and alert to anyone in the area. Gladys said she'll stay with you until I get there."

"I know. She's so sweet." Catherine was slurring her words. I assumed she was heavily medicated. "When I didn't show up at the office this morning, Gladys called the police and tracked me down. She's been sitting here ever since. She won't leave. I tried to send her home."

"Don't send her away, Cat. Not unless a policeman comes. I'll be there tonight."

"Okay," she said weakly. "Liam, I just want to go home. I don't know when the doctors will let us go home, but I want to go home. Would you tell them to let us go home?" Her words were all melting together and she was hard to understand. I was sure the medicine was making her goofy.

"Go home? Honey, we had a fire. Wasn't the house destroyed?"

"Oh, how silly. I forgot. Yes, it was. The fire was real bad. I'm tired, Liam, I'm sorry."

"Cat, just be careful, get well, watch Benny and I'll be there soon."

Just then the PSNI patrol car pulled into the lot. "Get in," Megan yelled, and with lights flashing she drove out onto the tarmac where a helicopter was waiting. The flight took about thirty minutes. We didn't get to Dublin International until 4:15, but Megan ushered me through security and down to the gate where Aer Lingus was holding the plane for me. Nice job, Farrell.

Twenty-five

• • •

THE MINUTE I STEPPED out of the elevator onto the sixth floor at Northwestern Memorial I could sense the heightened security. I was required to stop at the nurses' station, empty my pockets and show my ID. A uniformed police officer was sitting on a chair outside Catherine's room.

"Liam Taggart?" he said. I nodded and showed him my ID. "You've got friends in high places. It's not often we set up in a hospital. When I got the assignment, I thought it was a government informant in witpro. Then they told me about the gasoline bomb. Real sorry, man. It was front page in the *Trib*. You had some enemy out there. I think your family's doing okay, though. Mrs. Taggart's sleeping right now."

I slowly opened the door. The room was dark and Cat was sleeping. Ben was in a crib next to the bed. He looked so beautiful, so innocent, lying there all curled up. I pulled up a chair and sat beside my family. Tears were rolling down my cheeks. I clenched my fists. Whatever happened to them, whatever could have happened to them, was all my fault. If this was an outcrop of the Troubles, if it was because the Taggarts were targets of the Walkers or some other Butcher gang, it was my lineage and it was all my fault. If my CIA activities in Northern Ireland, or the deaths of McManus or Lefferty or anyone else brought this on, then it was all my fault. If it was because I accepted an appointment as trustee and Conor or Riley or any family member wanted me out of the way, it was all my fault. No matter how you looked at it, it was *all my fault*. I felt like I had personally put Catherine in this bed and endangered the life of my little boy. I could not have felt any worse. One thing I knew for sure, sooner or later I was going to get the guy behind this.

There was a text message on my phone from McLaughlin. "No word on Walker. Bartender hasn't seen him. Saw Riley at his house. Gave me his phone. Nothing. He was sorry re: fire. Not able to find Conor. Be careful."

Farrell had proven himself to be a great friend. So had Megan. I hated to leave them with the whole matter unresolved, but I did not intend to return to Antrim. To be honest, I didn't know how much I was adding to the investigative process anyway. Truth be told, I had no level of confidence in any suspect. My instincts had totally failed me. The one certainty was my resolve not to abandon Catherine and Ben ever again.

I walked out to the nurses' station. I wanted to find out about Chick Chaikin. Although he was a professional and he knew the score, I was the one who put him in the line of fire and I felt responsible. Again, all my fault. The nurse told me that the surgery went as well as it could, but it was a serious gunshot wound. They would know more in a day or two.

"You know, he saved the lives of my wife and my son," I said.

She smiled. "I know. It's all over the papers. He's a hero. If you want to see him, he's in ICU, but he's not conscious."

The door to his room was open. He was wired and tubed. The monitors were flashing and beeping. I stood at the foot of his bed. His eyes were shut and his breathing was shallow.

"I owe you, Chick. You're a hell of a man," I said to his unconscious body. I blinked the tears out of my eyes and held his hand. "I'm sorry I put you and my family in harm's way. The blame is all mine. I should have stayed in Chicago where I belong. Safe at home in Chicago." I smiled at that irony. "When you get out of here, Chick, I'll buy you a case of Canadian Club and a box of those ten-dollar cigars you love. We'll take in a Cubs game and . . ." My emotions wouldn't let me finish. I shook my head and returned to Catherine.

I sat in the dark for two or three hours, dozing off now and then, when I heard Ben stir and make some chattering noises. I leaned over the rails on his crib and started to reach down for him when Catherine said, "Hi honey, when did you get here?"

"A little while ago." She threw her arm around my neck, pulled me down hard to the pillow and hugged me tightly. We both cried.

"I think he's hungry," she said. "Would you hand him to me? I'm not supposed to walk very much. I have to keep my leg elevated."

I sat beside her while she gave Ben his bottle. I didn't want to ask her about the incident. I didn't want her to relive the terror. I was so damn thankful just to be sitting in the company of my wife and child. Everybody alive. Everybody safe. My focus was on tomorrow and the day after. Yesterday, Northern Ireland, the Walkers, the trust, the death threats—as far as I was concerned, they never got on the plane. They did not come with me to Chicago.

In a little while the nurse came in to change Catherine's bandages. She pulled back the covers. Catherine's left leg was wrapped in white from her hip to her ankle. She grimaced and clenched her teeth as her bandage was removed. I consider myself a tough guy, but when I saw my wife's leg, my stomach turned in twisted knots and I almost lost it. She saw my reaction.

"My robe was burning, but I had the baby in my arms and there wasn't anything I could do about it until I made it outside."

The nurse looked at me. "She's very brave, your wife. She didn't hesitate. She knew what she had to do. She held that baby and brought him to safety even though her leg was on fire."

"How bad is it?" I said.

"Mostly second-degree. Some a little worse. We'll treat it with antibiotics and ointment. She might need some grafting, but she'll recover. She's very brave."

"And Ben's okay?"

She nodded. "He got a little smoke in his lungs, that's all. He didn't get burned."

"I was sleeping. Liam. It was the middle of the night. I heard a crash and the first thing I thought was that someone threw a rock through our window. Maybe the man who was making the phone calls or whoever sent that picture decided to do something more serious. I dialed 911 and I was waiting for the operator when I smelled the smoke and the smoke alarm went off. I dropped the phone, ran and got the baby, but when I reached the staircase . . ." Her words got caught in her throat.

"It's okay, Cat. Let's leave it for now. Someday you'll tell me all about it."

She shook her head. "When I reached the staircase I saw the flames at the bottom. They were so bright and red and yellow and orange. And the heat, Liam, you could feel it from the second floor. The fire was in the living room and had spread to the foyer and was starting to burn the stairs. I knew that if I didn't get out right then, I'd be trapped. I wet the baby's blanket, wrapped him up tight and ran down the stairs. My robe caught fire, and it was sticking to my body but I had to protect the baby, and I ran, and running made the flames worse and . . ."

"That's enough, Cat. I understand."

"I made it to the walkway where I could lie on the grass and put out the flames. There was a man's body on the sidewalk. There was a gun in his hand but he was dead. Mr. Chaikin was lying in the street. Then I heard the sirens and the fire truck and then the paramedics were there and they put us in the ambulance. That's when I realized my leg was really hurting me. Ben was coughing. He was having trouble breathing and the paramedics put an oxygen mask on him. Oh, Liam . . ."

I put my arms around Catherine and she cried onto my shoulder for several minutes.

The nurse finished replacing the bandages, gave Catherine more medicine and closed the door.

Catherine sniffled, looked at me with sad eyes, pushed out her lower lip and said, "They told me I'm going to have a scar, Liam. A big one. My leg won't be pretty anymore."

"You'll still be the most beautiful woman in Chicago."

I hugged her, so happy that it wasn't any worse. I shuddered to think of what might have been.

"How is Mr. Chaikin?" she said.

"He's recovering. They tell me the surgery went well and his vitals are good. He's a tough old bird. We'll pray for him."

After a few minutes, Catherine said, "I'm scared, Liam. When you go back, what should I do?"

"I'm not going back. I'm going to resign as trustee and let the Bank of Antrim and O'Neill finish up the estate. McLaughlin will work on the criminal case. My place is here."

"No, Liam. You have to go back. You have to finish. You're not a quitter."

I shook my head. "This is not a matter open for discussion. It's my decision."

Six days later, I moved Catherine and Ben into a two-bedroom condominium I rented on north Lake Shore Drive. We didn't have a final report on the fire damage yet and we didn't know how much of the house could be salvaged. Assuming it was repairable, it would be months until the work could be completed. The insurance policy provided for alternative housing and I opted for a unit in a thirty-story building with a doorman and good security.

During the remaining days at the hospital, we did not discuss Antrim, the murders, the investigation or the fire. Because it was the eight-hundred-pound gorilla in the room, there were many hours that passed in silence. But that was okay with me. Silence was better than rehashing the fire or arguing whether or not I should return to Northern Ireland. I didn't want to talk about the murders or the investigation. I really wanted to put the whole thing behind me and close the door on Northern Ireland.

Catherine needed skin grafts on her leg—what they called split-level thickness grafts. It was a deep burn in places and the recovery was painful for her. She really needed restful sleep but the pain in her leg and her recurrent nightmares kept her from anything but short naps. Me? I came to a better appreciation of the dark emotions that stir revenge and retribution. All I wanted to do was catch the son of a bitch and have ten minutes with him before the police arrived. And I was lucky. I didn't lose my wife or my child. I vowed there would come a time, you could be damn sure, that I would have my revenge. I would settle the score.

Our new apartment was comfortable, the view was nice, the kitchen was modern, but it wasn't our home. It didn't have any of our furniture, our precious mementoes, our pictures, or the special things we'd saved to mark the days of our lives. What little was salvageable was in storage. The condo was temporary, it was someone else's home and it felt that way.

The attack on Catherine had taken a toll on all of us. How casually we throw around terminology in everyday conversations. We say "terrorist" so casually, but in fact, Cat and I had been terrorized. Nothing would ever be the same. Could we ever feel totally safe again? Deirdre was terrorized. Robert was terrorized. The Taggart family had fallen victim to terrorism.

I didn't want to let Catherine and the baby out of my sight and that was driving Cat crazy. If we needed groceries, I wouldn't leave to go to the store. There were delivery services. I could call them. If we needed medicine from the pharmacy, I paid for delivery.

Catherine was homebound until her leg healed and I think she would have gone stir crazy but for her law practice. Thank God for the Law Offices of Catherine Lockhart. Gladys shuttled Catherine's work papers and mail back and forth. When Cat wasn't on the phone, she was on her computer. I was happy just to be her nursemaid. Her movement was limited and she wasn't allowed to walk very far. I assisted her with her bandages and her ointment. Otherwise I sat and read a book. I was present. I was there. Nobody was going to hurt my wife ever again.

Back when Uncle Fergus died and I returned to Antrim for the funeral, I placed my PI practice on hold. I told my client base that I was taking a short leave and I'd contact them on my return. Of course, I had no way of anticipating the series of disasters that would unfold. Now that I was back, I told my clients I couldn't accept any assignments for the time being, but I hoped things would normalize in a few weeks.

As the days wore on, it became obvious that my service as Cat's constant guardian angel was becoming an irritation. The condo was a small two-bedroom unit and it felt cramped. The first bedroom was ours, with a twin bed and a bulky hospital bed. We used the second bedroom as Ben's nursery. Catherine had commandeered the living room for an office. That pretty much accounted for all the square footage in the unit. There wasn't much more room left. I'd sit in the kitchen and read or watch the Cubs on a small TV with headphones. Sometimes it felt like the walls were closing in.

"Will you go take a walk?" Catherine would say, and I'd say, "No."

"I'm getting better, Liam. I can manage by myself for a few hours.

I'm allowed to walk around the condo. I don't need you sitting here looking at me all day."

"I'm catching up on my reading," I'd say. "I'm becoming steeped in the humanities."

"I don't buy it."

"Well, why don't we just pretend we're having a three-foot snowfall, and we can't go outside for a few days and we have to hunker down?"

"They call that cabin fever, Liam, and it makes people go bananas. And it's not snowing. Go run an errand or take a run in the park or something. Liam, we can't live like this forever."

"It's not forever. In a little while, you'll be up and around and then we can all go out . . . you know, a family outing."

That proffered solution did not carry the day, but truth be told, even if she was 100 percent better, I would still worry for her safety and I wouldn't feel comfortable leaving them alone. There was still a maniac out there.

Throughout the travail, Catherine had kept her nanny on salary, even though she wasn't needed. Sarah felt guilty about taking our money and not providing nanny services. She insisted that she be allowed to come over to the condo to watch Ben or to take him for a walk or to do anything to help out. Catherine finally decided that Sarah should come for six hours a day. Now there were four of us in the little apartment. After a few days of that, I decided that short breaks in furtherance of saving my marriage were worth the risk. And the risk was slight. It was unlikely that anyone in Northern Ireland would know our new address and it certainly wouldn't be easy to firebomb the twenty-first floor of a residential high-rise.

So, with that in mind, I went to visit Chick Chaikin. He had been moved to a regular room and his condition had been lowered to "guarded." I repeated my deep appreciation and my promise to give him a case of Canadian Club, which I had initially offered to him when he was unconscious.

"I think I must have heard you," he said, "because I keep asking the nurse for a cocktail glass and some ice."

"I owe you big time, my friend. You saved their lives."

He waved it off. "No big deal," he said, shrugging his shoulders, which was a typical Chaikin response.

"I nailed that asshole, didn't I?" he said. "What do they know about him?"

"Not much. He had no identification. He didn't have a cell phone. CPD found his Toyota a block away. The plate came up stolen. They took his prints and they'll let me know if there are any matches. CPD is working on it out of Belmont station. What do they say about you, old man?"

He lifted his bedsheet and showed me the wound in the middle of his generous paunch. "I took one in the gut. It didn't get very far, so you see, it pays to have ample padding. All those beers, people thought I was getting fat, but I was building an impenetrable barrier—that's what they call preventative medicine."

I had to smile. "How long will you be here?"

"They tell me a few more days. Then I'll collect on the CC and those cigars."

I RETURNED TO OUR Lake Shore Drive address and nodded to the doorman before heading to the elevators. It was comforting to have that level of security.

"Back so soon?" Catherine said.

"Love you too, dear."

My phone rang. It was McLaughlin. God bless him. He had called every few days. I filled him in on everyone's condition and thanked him again for arranging for the helicopter and the police protection.

"You don't need to keep thanking me, Liam. I was glad to do it and it's good to hear that everyone is recovering."

"What about Conor? Were you able to locate him and did you find any connection with the fire? I'm sure that he's in the middle of this somehow."

"I wouldn't be so sure of that, Liam. He walked into my office, on his own. Unannounced. 'I heard you were looking for me,' he said. 'I was up north, vacationing with the family.' He verified his story with a hotel receipt from Castlerock Beach and pictures of his kids playing in the sand. I ran his phone through the carrier and there were no calls to the U.S. He said he was shocked and sorry about your family and offered to help in any way he could."

"You believe him?"

"Do I believe he had an alibi? Yes. Do I believe he was shocked and sorry? Maybe. He seemed genuine."

"Why are you so quick to cross Conor off the list? You're the one with the relativity theory."

"Well, I didn't say I was crossing him off. Hell, he could have been involved for all I know. But when he stood in my office and I told him everything that happened, he was visibly shaken. He confronted me. He said, 'Because I threatened Liam, you think I had something to do with this, am I right?'

"I shrugged and I said, 'Well, did you?' My question pissed him off and ignited that famous Conor temper. 'I'd never do that,' he snapped. 'Oh sure, I wanted Liam to leave. I told him to get the hell out of Antrim. More than once. I resented him sticking his Chicago nose into my father's estate. I cursed him, I even shoved him, but I would never do harm to him or his family and you can go to hell for thinking that.'"

"And you believe him, Farrell?"

"I don't know. Maybe. You should have seen his face. He looked sincere. Maybe he's able to fool me like Deirdre fools you?" McLaughlin chuckled.

"Where does that leave us? It certainly couldn't have been Walker."

"Well, don't cross Walker off your list just yet. Our friend the bartender called and told me that Walker had stopped by Willy's and tried to cash a three-hundred-fifty-pound check. Apparently, he's a master pipefitter and he gets assignments from time to time. The check was drawn on a Gladstone Heating company account. Willy's wouldn't cash it."

"So now you're thinking that he has enough money to get something done in Chicago, and the firebomb of my house mirrors what happened to his brother Archie, is that it? Payback time?"

"Look, I don't know if the payments came from Walker or from some unknown guy. Who knows where the arsonist got his money? Does Walker have enough money to hire someone in the U.S.? Just add that to all the things we don't know."

"That's disturbing."

"Yes it is. Any second thoughts on returning?"

"To Antrim? Nope. I'm not returning. I'm resigning my appointment as trustee. O'Neill and the Bank of Antrim can take over."

"We'll miss you, Liam, but that's probably a smart decision. Just don't let your guard down in Chicago, not until we catch the guy."

TWENTY-SIX

• • •

CATHERINE WAS GETTING STRONGER every day and her leg was healing nicely. Sarah was coming to the condo each morning to take care of Ben during the day while Catherine did her legal work. She had also taken over the job of helping Catherine with her bandages. So I decided I would go to my office for a few hours every day. I let my clients know that I was able to accept some investigations, as long as they weren't surveillance assignments or jobs that would take me out of town. I had a very loyal client base and most were happy to give me work.

I told myself I had washed my hands of Northern Ireland—I guess I had become my mother's son—but I often wondered how Farrell and Megan were faring with the investigation. It was more than curiosity; I was emotionally invested in the case. I didn't want to pester them, but every so often I'd call one of them. Farrell told me that the investigation was active, but he was disappointed that so little progress was being made. Efforts to find Walker were thus far unsuccessful. Because of the newspaper clippings, he and Megan were looking into whether McManus or Lefferty had surviving relatives. Otherwise, he and the PSNI were keeping an eye on the Taggart clan. No more photographs had been found in any mailboxes.

I also called Deirdre at least twice a week. I promised to not shut her out again. I'd failed to stay in touch with her for sixteen years and that hurt her deeply. So now I would call, if for no other reason than to tell her I loved her and I was thinking of her.

I called O'Neill to tell him that I wasn't coming back. I asked him to contact the Bank of Antrim to arrange for an orderly transfer of authority and to send whatever documents he needed me to sign in order to resign my trusteeship.

"Please don't do that," he said. "You know how I feel about an institutional trustee. It will not be in the best interests of the beneficiaries and the bank officials will eat away the assets. You can continue to serve as trustee from your office in Chicago. I will represent your interests here."

I discussed it with Catherine and she sided with O'Neill. Most of the trustee's duties could be managed by email but I was resistant. I had a bad taste in my mouth and I didn't want to stay involved with the trust. If I remained as trustee, something was bound to come up and drag me back and I did not intend to return. It had almost cost me my family. From the very beginning, from the time that someone rifled my hotel room and slashed my tires, there were people that wanted me out of the picture. Maybe these were the same people that firebombed my house. Why would I ever consider returning there and putting my family at risk?

"Because your uncle trusted you, that's why," Catherine said. "He knew that something evil was afoot. He saw the future. I'm sorry I never met your uncle, but I feel like I know him from your stories. It's true he feared for his *own* life, he said so in his letter, but he also feared for his family. He said that too. And in the midst of all this, the only one he felt he could trust was you, Liam."

Catherine sat with me and put her hand on my shoulder. "Please don't take this the wrong way. I know the past few weeks have been very hard on you. I can't imagine what you must have gone through in Northern Ireland when you found out about Ben and me. But you can't let it change who you are. You're Liam Taggart. You can't sit here, hang around this condo and babysit me forever. The Liam I know would never back away from a responsibility. He is not a quitter. I'm sorry, Liam, but I do not want to be the reason that Liam Taggart turns into somebody else."

She might as well have hit me with a two-by-four. She was right, of course. I was changing. I was becoming an isolationist. I was living on an island. But everything that mattered to me was living there too and

I intended to defend my island at all costs. To my way of thinking, that was the right move. As long as there was a killer on the loose, Liam Taggart would be whoever I needed him to be. If that was isolationism, I had no regrets. Still, Catherine hit a nerve when she accused me of shirking a responsibility or betraying the trust my uncle had placed in me. I did not want to let my uncle down again. If I could handle the trustee's duties from my office in Chicago without traveling back to Antrim, then I would continue to serve.

I called O'Neill back and told him that I would not resign yet. I would try to manage the best I could from afar. But if it became too much of a problem, if it required me to be present in Northern Ireland, then I would resign at that time.

"Excellent," he said. "I am delighted. Actually, the bank will be pleased as well. When I discussed the possibility of your resignation with the bank president last week, he told me that the bank would prefer not to take the trust in-house. There's far too much controversy associated with the Taggart Trust. It would be bad banking business."

"What would happen if the bank declined an appointment as a successor trustee?"

"I expect that Judge McNulty would have to appoint a trustee."

"Could it be a family member? Could it be one of the beneficiaries?"

"There's no law against it. But if the family members could not agree or there were objections, then she'd have to select an independent attorney, probably a solicitor who practices in her courtroom. On the other hand, if the beneficiaries all came to a consensus, then I don't see why Judge McNulty would refuse to adopt it."

"That's just what Uncle Fergus wanted to avoid."

"Precisely. But since you've decided to stay, it's a moot point. As your first duty as trustee-in-exile, I should tell you that Riley's been calling me. Quite frequently. He has issues with his company's stock."

"Great. I'm already having second thoughts. What are the issues this time?"

"He wants to own the stock, or at the very least control the stock, so that it may be pledged to secure a loan."

"The court has already rejected his request. Judge McNulty upheld my decision."

"She did. But since you left, he has been lobbying the other beneficiaries. He reasons that if he can get consent from the others—Conor, Robert, Deirdre and Janie—the judge will go along with him. Especially since you aren't here to object. Apparently Conor will agree. Riley is using Conor's attorney, Mike Cooney."

"I thought Conor fired Cooney."

"It certainly seemed that way in court, but Cooney is still of record in the case."

"Do Robert, Deirdre and Janie go along with Riley?"

"From what I can tell, Deirdre is cloistered. She has round-the-clock police protection and she prefers to stay in her home and shy away from controversy. I don't think she agrees with Riley, but she will not come to court to object. Janie is living with a very wealthy man and doesn't seem to care if the stock is taken out of the trust estate. Robert wants the trust to remain as it is until a new trustee is appointed. Since he believes you have resigned and that a successor will be appointed, he prefers to wait and listen to the opinion of the new trustee. Now that you have decided not to resign, I suppose Robert would want to know what your position will be."

"It hasn't changed. I don't think the Global stock should be transferred or encumbered. Judge McNulty ruled on that issue. She said it would violate the terms of the trust. I'm not going to go against the judge. And besides, we're forgetting something: there is another beneficiary, the Bridget McGregor Trust."

"Indeed. But Cooney hasn't forgotten. He asserts that the Bridget McGregor Trust must go along with the others because it is not represented in the court case and won't formally object."

"Is he right?"

"No," O'Neill said sharply. "The Bridget McGregor Trust is represented by Liam Taggart, the duly appointed trustee and Malcolm O'Neill, the attorney of record."

"But you're not the attorney if I withdraw, right?"

"You can assume that if Conor becomes the trustee he will not retain my services."

"So as of now, Riley must get my permission or he won't have a consensus?"

"Right."

"Well, he's not getting it."

"I will inform Mr. Cooney. I'm glad you've decided to stay involved, Liam. It's what your uncle wanted. You've shown yourself to be the person that Fergus Taggart thought you were."

I hung up with O'Neill and sat there thinking about Deirdre. I worried about her. I could see her sitting by herself in her tufted chair in the dark corner of the living room with a glass of Bushmills. I missed her and I wished I could comfort her. She'd comforted me when I needed it and I still thought of her as my second mother. She had always been a strong woman and a perfect pairing for Uncle Fergus but now she was depressed, alone and frightened for her life. I called her.

"What's for dinner?" I said.

"Roast and potatoes. I have company tonight."

"Terrific. Who's the lucky guest?"

She paused. "Annie. She's been coming over every few days, checking up on me, keeping me company."

Annie had been close to Fergus and Deirdre for all these years and now she was looking after Deirdre. I was grateful for that. I wondered how much Annie really knew. How much did Fergus confide in her? Deirdre seemed to think it was quite a bit. "I'm glad she's not afraid to come over to the house," I said.

"There's a police car sitting in my driveway, Liam. Day and night. It's the safest place in County Antrim."

"What does Annie think about all this? I know that Uncle Fergus and she talked a lot before he died."

"Aye, that they did. But Annie and I do not talk about murders or fires or crimes. We talk about movies and art and TV shows and cooking and anything we can think of except what's going on. If you want to know what Annie knows, you should talk to her directly and not pump me for information. Annie spent a lot of time talking to your uncle. Whatever he knew, whatever he feared, he understood it would frighten me and he spared me from the worry. When he wanted to talk to someone, it was usually Annie."

I knew that I couldn't telephone Annie and question her for any number of reasons, not to mention the emotional awkwardness. She had cut me out of her life sixteen years ago and other than the few words exchanged at the funeral, we hadn't talked since. I doubted she knew who the killer was or she would have gone straight to McLaughlin.

Still, she was privy to my uncle's thinking. It's likely she would possess bits of information that could be helpful in the investigation. If I was in Antrim, and if I talked to her in person, maybe I could get that information. I didn't think I was up to discussing it with her on the phone.

I gave Deirdre my love, told her I would call next week and told her to say hello to Annie.

IT WASN'T VERY LONG afterward that I received the inevitable call from Riley. I was sitting in my office and the phone rang. The caller ID gave me a Northern Ireland area code. Déjà vu. The telephone rings and life's direction changes. Wasn't that how the whole damn thing started? I knew I shouldn't pick it up, but I did. Riley's tone was anything but friendly.

"Look, Liam, I know that you and I don't see eye to eye on this, but I'm asking you to give me a couple of minutes of your time to try to reach a compromise on my Global stock. If it weren't a life-or-death situation, I wouldn't be calling you. Mr. Cooney says you are still the trustee until he can remove you and that might take a while."

"Go ahead, Riley."

"Thank you. I won't repeat the fact that my company faces foreclosure if we can't get our financing or that the stock without the financing will be worthless to you and everyone else. Even if you don't believe that, even if you think the company will survive anyway, you must know that Mr. Penters considers me to be the sole reason that Global can't get a new loan. I will be fired and that will be the least of my problems. He's an arrogant, powerful man and he scares the shit out of me. I'd be fired already but for the fact that he needs my father's shares and he doesn't want to alienate me. Look, I've got kids in school, I've got a wife who doesn't work, I have a mortgage on my house. I have to find a way to make this work."

"I know all that, Riley, and I do believe you. I'm not unsympathetic. I feel for you and for your situation. As it stands today, the stock is one of the largest assets in the trust. There are other beneficiaries that have rights that I cannot ignore. I can't take an eighty-thousand-pound asset and give it away or encumber it. You heard the judge: I'd be violating the terms of the trust. But you said you want to talk about a compromise solution. I'm open to that if it works. What do you have in mind?"

"All right, here's the deal. I will personally sign a six-month promissory note to the trust equal to the value of the stock when my father purchased it, even though today, given the current financial crisis, the stock is worth less. There will be no risk to the trust. The trust won't lose a shilling."

"Can I ask you, Riley, do you have the funds to pay the note if it came due today?"

"Not today."

"I hate to question you like a banker, but I have a duty to act as a careful trustee. What will change in six months so that you will have the funds?"

"Well, a lot of things can happen. First, the killer should be found by then and the trust will be distributed. My share would be more than enough to pay the note. Otherwise, I'll have six months to save up the money."

I knew there was no way he could get that kind of money together in six months. If the financial regulators have their way, both Riley and his boss will be in trouble. If the trust does not distribute within six months, Riley's promissory note will be worthless. I also knew that if the regulators took over the company, they would endeavor to preserve the company for the benefit of the stockholders. It wasn't necessarily true that the stock would be worthless. Likely, but not necessarily.

"Okay," I said, "here's what I can do. I'll discuss your proposal with Mr. O'Neill, the attorney for the trust, and if he says it's okay, he'll draw up the note. But if he says it's too uncertain, then you'll have to think of something else."

"What if I had someone guarantee my note? Someone with money, like Conor or Uncle Robert?"

"I think that might make a difference. Have either of them offered to guarantee your loan?"

"Not yet, I haven't asked them, but what if they would?"

"Again, I'd have to run it by Mr. O'Neill, but I think that might make a big difference. Of course, they'd probably have to put up some security."

"Right. I get it. Thanks, Liam. Thanks a lot. I mean it. Please talk to Mr. O'Neill and get back to me as soon as possible."

"I will. Riley, are you being cautious for yourself and your family? You received one of those photos in your mailbox. Look what happened to me. I don't want you to get hurt."

"Thanks, Liam. I appreciate it. I'm being real careful. I have a shotgun in the house and I keep it loaded. The PSNI car goes through my neighborhood several times a day and frequently stops by to check up on us. We're okay. By the way, Janie got one of those pictures as well. It was left at her house in Antrim. As you know, she spends most of her time in Belfast with Charles, but last weekend she came home and found the envelope in her mailbox. She didn't know how long it had been there. She gave it to Inspector McLaughlin."

That sent shivers up my spine. "Is she okay? Is she a nervous wreck?"

"A little. Charles hired a bodyguard at his house but she's nervous. Not quite her happy-go-lucky self."

TWENTY-SEVEN

• • •

FOUR DAYS AFTER RILEY'S call, while I was sitting in front of the TV with Catherine and Ben, enjoying a deep-dish pizza, my cell phone rang and once again it displayed a Northern Ireland number. I showed it to Catherine and asked, "Should I send this directly to voice mail?"

"Don't, Liam. It's two o'clock in the morning there, it must be important." I nodded and answered the call.

"Liam, it's Janie. I'm at the hospital." She was crying. "My father, he's been shot."

My heart sank. Uncle Robert, so warm and smiling, that Irish face I loved. I felt so hollow. The killer had struck again and taken another piece of my life.

"When is the funeral?"

"He's not dead, Liam. They tried to kill him but he survived. He's alive but in bad shape."

"What happened?"

"He was alone in his apartment. You know, he lives in the Waterfront Apartments on the sixth floor. And he was being real careful because last week he got a calling card. He was standing by the window and he dropped his book. As he bent down to pick it up, a bullet came through the window, hit him in the shoulder and knocked him backward. Liam, if he hadn't bent over just at that moment, my father would be dead. As it is, his left shoulder is shattered."

"But he's all right now?"

"No, he's not all right, his shoulder was blown away. He's in terrible pain. They had to knock him out."

"Does Inspector McLaughlin know about this?"

"The Belfast police called McLaughlin. He's here at the hospital. Liam, can you come back? I'm scared."

"I know, I'm sorry. But the police will protect you. And Riley told me that Charles has hired a bodyguard."

"The bodyguard doesn't follow me around, he's just at the house. When I have to go out, I'm on my own. And you can't depend on the PSNI. They didn't protect my father. They can't protect everyone all the time. There's a crazy killer out here and he's trying to kill our whole family. Please come back. You have to find this man."

"Who else is at the hospital with you?"

"Charles and Conor."

"Where is Deirdre?"

"She's at home. She never goes anywhere. She's scared to death, just like me. I told her I would come out as soon as I could."

"And Riley, where is he?"

"No one knows. My father said that Riley came by three days ago and they had a terrible argument. Something about guaranteeing a loan. Why can't you come back until the killer is found? Just for a little while?"

"I wish I could, but I can't come back to Antrim right now. My family needs me in Chicago. I'm concerned for their safety as well and Catherine is still recovering from her injuries."

Catherine poked me in the ribs and whispered, "You can go, I'll be fine. Don't use me for an excuse." I shook my head and put my finger on my lips.

"Janie, would you tell Inspector McLaughlin to call me when he gets a chance?"

"He's standing a few feet away. I'll hand him the phone. . . .'"

"Hello, Liam."

"Farrell, what happened? What do you know?"

"Not much. We think the shot came from the Clarendon Dock Area across the channel. Hell of a shot. High-powered rifle with a scope, had to be an M24 with a thirty-aught-six shell. It took a skilled marksman to make that shot. A real pro."

"As I recall, Robert lived in the center building overlooking the harbor. Someone would have to shoot over the channel and the harbor into a darkened apartment window."

"Right. A distance of three hundred meters. As I said, it took a hell of a sharpshooter. But the apartment wasn't dark. Mr. Taggart had not yet retired. He remembers it occurring at eleven this evening. He had just taken his dog for a walk and returned to the apartment. We believe the shot was fired from one of the higher floor units in a building directly across the channel. There are only a few buildings that are tall enough to give him a clear shot. We have officers searching the units right now."

"None of the people we suspect are skilled enough to pull that off," I said. "We're either overlooking a suspect or someone on our list has enough money and contacts to hire a sniper."

"I agree. No one stands out, Liam. Hell of a shot. There aren't many PSNI shooters who could pull that off. Dooley could, but I don't know many others. The M24 has a range of eight hundred meters, but it's a tough shot and you only get one chance. Your uncle is lucky; he's going to make it. He'll need a new shoulder, but he's going to live. I'm assigning an officer here in the hospital, and Deirdre's got her patrolman. But add Conor, Riley and Janie to the mix and it's almost impossible to prevent the next assault. Maybe you'd like to come back and help me?"

"I'm not coming back, Farrell. I can't leave my family."

"I understand. Take care, my friend."

I KNOW I ONLY caught half the conversation," Catherine said, "but I can't believe what I just heard."

"This is the toughest case I've ever worked. Another one of my family down and I can't even develop a theory that holds true for more than a week. Initially, I was sure the murders were retaliatory, left over from the Troubles. McLaughlin believed the killer was an heir, a relative. Then, with all the court cases and the vicious arguments, I came around to McLaughlin's way of thinking: it could very well be somebody in the family. Then, after I spent time with the family, I discarded those thoughts. The killer had to come from the outside. The pictures of Walker's house and his wake led me to believe it was Walker, but seeing his neighborhood and learning about his circumstances, I came to doubt it. When they attacked you, I was certain that it was Conor or Riley, because both of them had threatened me, wanted me out of Ireland and had the money to get it done. Now a professional sniper pops up and fires a scoped shot three hundred meters into Uncle Robert's apartment. Would Conor or Riley hire a sniper to kill their uncle? I don't know what the hell to think anymore."

"They want you to come back, don't they?"

I nodded. "It's not going to happen. Seriously, what can I add? What can I do that McLaughlin and the PSNI can't? They have the same information I do, probably much more. Farrell is an experienced investigator. He's got fifty years with the force. He doesn't need me."

"But he wants you."

"I'm staying here. I'm not leaving you and Ben. Discussion closed."

"I don't like it when people tell me 'discussion closed.' It's closed when I have nothing more to say. Farrell may be an experienced investigator, but he wants you to help him. He knows what I know, that Liam Taggart is an extraordinarily gifted man with remarkable instincts. Why don't you go back for a little while and help him solve the crime?"

"Cat, would you concede that it's my decision? Whether I leave or stay, whether I perform my services here or abroad, that's my decision, isn't it?"

"Yes."

"Then please respect my decision. Let's close the subject."

THE SUBJECT WAS CLOSED for less than twenty-four hours. O'Neill called me the next morning.

"Well, we should have known it was coming, Liam."

"Cooney filed another petition?"

"Good guess. It's scheduled to be heard the day after tomorrow. I don't suppose you'd like to appear at the hearing."

"Not a chance."

"I surmised so."

"What does Cooney allege this time?"

"That you have permanently left the jurisdiction and do not intend to pay attention to the details of running the farm and managing the assets. He states, 'How can the court possibly condone an absentee trustee?' He also cites your failure to compromise on the sale of the Global stock placing the asset in jeopardy. Then he decries the extraordinary injustice of taking weekly withdrawals from the trust estate for your trustee's exorbitant salary when you don't live here and you don't intend to serve. Finally he asserts that there is a consensus among the beneficiaries to remove you as trustee."

"Is that true? Is there a consensus?"

"I don't think so. Robert is in the hospital and under heavy sedation. I don't believe Deirdre consents, but I also don't think she'll come to court to object. I'm not sure about Janie."

"You know I haven't taken a single salary payment. I haven't even reimbursed myself for my costs."

"I understand. That's foolish, but I understand."

"Can you handle this motion without me?"

"Technically yes, but it would be better with you. There is no law requiring a trustee to be present in Northern Ireland at all times. Riley's offer to sign a note was financially unsound and without a guarantor, and rightly rejected by you. I'll inform Her Honor that you haven't taken any money, even though you are entitled to it, especially to cover your costs."

"Thanks, Malcolm. Please call me after the hearing."

THE CALL CAME TWO days later as we were sitting down to breakfast.

"It didn't go well, Liam. Cooney ranted and raved and accused you of abandoning your post. He claimed that Deirdre was an emotional wreck, afraid to leave the house and incapable of managing the farm or the house. I really couldn't argue with that—from all I've heard she's quite distraught, a bundle of nerves. She didn't show up in court. Cooney said that any responsible trustee would remove Deirdre from the house immediately and rent it to a farmer who could properly manage the property and who didn't need police protection. In fact, Conor offered to move in himself until a renter could be found. Cooney told the judge that he has not received an objection from any beneficiary."

"Is that true? No one has objected?"

"Well, Janie wasn't in court. Robert, of course, is still in the hospital. As I said, Deirdre won't leave the house. So who was in court to object? I told the judge that you were properly administering the trust from your office in Chicago and doing whatever is necessary to perform your duties, but Judge McNulty seemed very concerned about the welfare of the farm and the house. She seemed open to having a tenant move in, maybe even Conor."

"Conor wants to toss his mother on the street? What a guy. You know she has essentially been his mother since he was a toddler. That has to be breaking her heart."

"That's what I hear."

"Well, what happened? Did the judge remove me as trustee? Did she appoint the bank?"

"Well, that's another problem. With the attack on Robert and all that's going on, the bank will not accept an appointment as successor trustee. You can imagine, the bank wants no part of this private war. With the bank out of the picture, and no one to object, I believe Cooney will ask the judge to appoint Conor as successor trustee. Again, I doubt there will be anyone in court to object. Sorry, I did the best I could."

"I'm sure you did. What did the judge do?"

"Well, she didn't do anything yet. She continued the hearing until Friday, primarily to give you an opportunity to appear and convince her that you should remain as trustee."

"I'm not coming back, Malcolm. You'll have go to the hearing and win without me."

"Oh my. Well, I'm not so sure I can do that."

"I'll try to reach Janie and maybe she'll bring Deirdre with her to court. Robert might be able to give you an affidavit from his hospital bed. Let's see if we can defeat the motion without me."

Catherine was sitting at the breakfast table feeding Ben his cereal and listening to my side of the conversation. When I hung up she said, "You have to go back for the hearing."

"Let's not start this again, Cat. I'm not going to leave you."

"You and I both know that O'Neill can't win this motion without you sitting in the courtroom. Deirdre will be put out of her house. Where will she go?"

I shook my head and tried not to let my frustrations get the best of me, but they did. I raised my voice. "Don't you think I know all this? Do you think I want my aunt Deirdre on the street? I love that woman. Do you think I want Conor and Riley taking over this trust? Damn it, Cat."

"Take it easy, honey, I'm not your enemy. I want to help. I know you fear for Ben and me, I know you blame yourself for what happened to us and I know you won't go back to Northern Ireland and leave us in Chicago. But you have no choice. So . . . you'll go back and we'll go with you."

"Out of the question and I don't care what you say, that book is closed."

She smiled. "Don't you put your foot down on me, Mr. Irishman. It's not closed as long as I have something more to say. Here's my proposal: we'll go back with you and stay at Deirdre's, under police protection. You'll go to court and convince Judge McNulty that you can handle the management of the trust estate. If you appear in her courtroom, then she'll know you haven't left permanently. Then you can take care of what needs to be done."

"It's too dangerous. In case I need to remind you, Uncle Robert was shot by a professional sniper from three hundred meters away. Uncle Eamon was killed right out in the open, rammed by a maniac in a GMC truck. Uncle Fergus was shot on his own property, evidently by someone he knew. And by sheer luck, I happened to stop a man from throwing a firebomb into Deirdre's house. It's a field of war and I can't take you there."

"Neither Uncle Robert, Uncle Eamon nor Uncle Fergus had police protection or even Liam Taggart's protection. In case I need to remind *you*, it's not so safe for us in Chicago either. I hope you don't think I'm going to be cloistered in this condo for the rest of my life. I'm going back to work and I work in a law office and in a courthouse and in other lawyers' offices. I don't have police protection in Chicago and you're not going to be by my side every minute of every day. Ugh. What a thought!"

"It's more dangerous in Antrim, and Deirdre lives on a farm, not even in the city."

"She has police protection on the premises. And we'll be very careful. I'll always be under the protection of you or the Antrim police. I promise not to go out alone."

I shook my head. "Do you know what you're asking me? You're asking me to put my family at risk so that I can go back and defend my appointment as trustee over Uncle Fergus's assets. *Assets*, Catherine. Money. Stocks. Property. As he said in his letter, everything of *value*. His *treasures*. Well, to my way of thinking, people are a lot more important than property and treasures. I'm not going to take my family into a battlefield to preserve Uncle Fergus's treasures."

Catherine gave me that look, the one that told me that she understood the situation a lot better than I did. "It's not about property, Liam. You're wrong. You misread the letter. He said there was 'a danger that threatens everything I value, the entire treasure of a man's life.' He meant his *family*, Liam, not his property. He meant his children and his brothers and above all he meant Deirdre. Those were the treasures of his life, and that's what he valued. He knew how vulnerable Deirdre and Eamon and Robert would be and he appointed *you* to protect those treasures. He relied on *you*, the only one he could trust.

"Think about it. It's all so clear to me. Why would Uncle Fergus defer distributions until the killer is caught? It's not because he was so concerned about his property, or that a killer might inherit some of it and profit by his death. It was all about you! You were the reason he deferred the distribution. He needed Liam Taggart to stay in control until the end, to protect his loved ones, his treasures until the killer was caught. Don't you see, you're not relieved of your responsibilities until the trust dissolves and the trust doesn't dissolve until the killer is caught. Liam Taggart has to be there until the end. And I'm pretty sure that's why he had the trust pay you a thousand pounds a week. He was pretty clever, your uncle."

I never thought of it that way, but the more she talked the clearer it became.

"Liam, what if the whole reason he set up the trust was to protect the family from whatever danger he feared? He knew there was a killer out there, and he wrote in his letter that he intended to find out if his suspicions were correct and stop it in its tracks. He wrote, 'God help this family if I fail.' Don't you see, he knew he could fail and he knew you were the only one who could finish the job, who could stop it in its tracks. You Liam. You were the ex-marine, the ex-CIA agent, the man who makes a living investigating crimes and protecting people. You were appointed trustee because you were the only person he could trust to protect his family. He knew you for the man you are—strong, solid, dependable. Who could flush out the killer? Only you, Liam.

"If you don't return, Conor and Riley will evict Deirdre from her home, the home Fergus promised to her, the home she's lived in all her life. She'd be left on the streets with no one to protect her. And what about the rest of them? Robert narrowly escaped assassination, Janie is scared to death, begging you to come back, and Riley and Conor are out of control. And Liam, the truth is I'm scared too. I'm afraid every day for Ben and me. Do you think I want to go to Northern Ireland? I don't want to be anywhere near that place, but I know that Ben and I will never be safe until you find and stop this murderer. And, just like your uncle, you are the only one I can trust."

I sat there in a daze. I didn't want Catherine and Ben anywhere near Northern Ireland either, but what if she was right on point? I didn't know if I could flush the killer out or catch him, but I would do the best I could. At the very least, I could help protect Deirdre and the family. I owed it to her and Uncle Fergus. I owed it to my wife and my son. I was not about to let them down. I nodded. "We'll go back, the three of us."

I MADE MY TELEPHONE calls that afternoon. My decision to re- turn made a lot of people happy. O'Neill for one. "I hate to confess my vulnerabilities, Liam, but I do not think I could have carried the day. Your appearance will make all the difference. I think Judge Mc- Nulty likes you, and if you're there it'll convince her that you will duti- fully manage the trust property."

Deirdre was also relieved when I called. "I raised Conor and Riley from the time they were in short pants. I don't know why they would turn on me and want me out of my own house. I know Fergus wouldn't put up with it. I'm glad you're coming back, son. I'm glad you're pro- tecting me."

"Me too," I said. "I'm looking forward to introducing you to Cath- erine and my baby boy."

That seemed to lift her spirits. "It's going to be so busy in my house again," she said with some joy in her voice. "I can't wait to see the wee baby. I'll start planning my menus right now."

McLaughlin said he knew all along that I'd come back. "An old bloodhound like you can't stay away while there's still a fresh trail." He chuckled. "Dooley and I have uncovered some interesting information and we'll share it with you when you get here."

"Farrell, I'm bringing my wife and child with me. I don't have to tell you how nervous I am about their safety. They'll be staying at Deirdre's and I need to know that the round-the-clock protection will be in place the entire time. And I'll need my gun and permit back."

"I already have men stationed at Deirdre's. Twenty-four/seven. And, thanks to Deirdre, they're getting fat. They'll be there until this case is solved. As to the gun, I'll have it for you when you get off the plane. In fact, I'll meet you at the plane and bring you out to Antrim."

"Thank you. That's very generous. I'll gladly accept."

Janie was also happy to hear that I was returning and bringing the family. She was eager to meet Catherine. I asked her about the others: Robert, Riley and Conor.

"My father is still at Belfast General awaiting shoulder replacement surgery. They're going to give him a brand-new shoulder but they want to get him a little stronger first. He's been carrying a low-grade fever. He's also an emotional basket case. You know my dad, he's always the jolly one, joking, laughing and smiling. It's going to take some time before we'll see that again."

"What about Riley and Conor?"

"I don't know where Riley is. He hasn't been to the hospital. I don't think anyone has seen him in a few days. I know that Mr. Cooney has been looking for him, because he called me and asked me to come to court for a hearing. Charles told me not to go. Then Mr. Cooney asked me how to reach Riley. I gave him the cell number, but he said he had tried it several times with no answer. So, no one knows where Riley is."

"Why did Charles tell you not to go to court?"

"Maybe he didn't want me to take sides, I don't know. I think he doesn't want me mixed up in all of Riley's problems. He cares about me and he tries to protect me. He's sweet that way."

"What about Conor?"

"Well, you know Conor. You wouldn't call him Mr. Calm-and-Steady. This whole business has him rattled and now he's paranoid. He carries a pistol in his belt. But he's been to the hospital every day and stays for hours. He's been a godsend for my dad."

"Janie, did Conor get one of those Walker pictures in his mailbox?"

"Not that I know of."

TWENTY-EIGHT

• • •

W E HAD NEVER TRAVELED as a family before, so I didn't know what I was in for—a stroller, baby seat, diaper bags, fold-up crib, changing kits, jars of food, play mats, a whole suitcase full of baby clothes and an extra paid seat in Economy Plus. Catherine's suitcase alone was over the limit, which she attributed to the weight of several pairs of shoes.

We took the overnight flight and Ben slept most of the way. What a trooper. Neither Cat nor I could sleep. We both knew what the dangers were and there was no way to minimize it. The serial killer, whoever he was, had served us with his calling card, we were marked for death and we were flying into his territory.

As we neared the end of the flight, Cat tried to lighten the mood by asking me questions about Northern Ireland.

"I wish we were going as tourists and not under a death threat," I said. "I'd love to just take you around and show you the sights. The rugged Antrim coast, the rich, pastoral countryside. It's quaint and charming in an old world way. Belfast is a booming, modern city. The city center is also charming, with brick pedestrian walkways lined with cafés, coffee houses and pubs. Developers sunk over half a billion dollars into Victoria Square, a domed shopping mall. There's Queens College, the botanic gardens, the Ulster Museum, the *Titanic* Museum, so many things for tourists to visit. Still has its problems, though."

"Catholics versus Protestants?"

I nodded. "Unionists versus nationalists. The separation walls still stand."

"Hard to fathom isn't it? Catholics versus Protestants—both Christian denominations with practically the same beliefs."

"It's not a religious dispute, Cat. It's not about their religious practices. Hell, many of these people don't ever set foot in a church. There are churches closing in West Belfast because of a lack of attendance. It's about culture. It's about group identity. To whom do you belong? By virtue of your membership, who are you obliged to dislike and distrust? And it self-perpetuates. Parents generally don't send their children to mixed schools. Kids grow up with their own kind. And it's hard to shake that prejudice."

"Is that why you think that a unionist may be responsible for the attacks on your family? Is that why you blame the Troubles?"

"It could be the reason, especially if Walker is the guilty party. But my uncle saved newspaper articles that concerned IRA members Seamus McManus and Sean Lefferty. They were Catholics, not Protestants."

"But you told me that McManus and Lefferty are both dead."

"They are, but maybe they have relatives who seek revenge, although neither family knew I was responsible for the arrests. I didn't reveal my identity to McManus at the jail and I wasn't personally involved in arresting or prosecuting Lefferty. McLaughlin still believes it's a relative, but that would mean Conor or Riley."

"You don't believe that's possible?"

"Oh, it's possible. Conor is a loose cannon and the only one who didn't receive a calling card. I grew up with Riley. We were close. I would never suspect him of a violent act, but I've never seen him so desperate. And now he's gone missing. Still, I just don't see either of them killing their father or Uncle Eamon."

"And trying to kill Uncle Robert?"

"And that's not all."

"I know. Ben and me."

"Right. Whoever he is, he better hope the PSNI gets to him before I do."

. . .

FARRELL MET US IN the baggage area of Dublin International. He surveyed everything we brought with us and shook his head. "Jesus, Liam, I didn't know you were moving here. It's a good thing I brought the Land Rover."

Catherine and Farrell hit it off right away. She was curious about Northern Ireland and Farrell was only too happy to be her tour guide. He had a wealth of knowledge about the country he had lovingly served for so many years and he wore his pride for all to see. As we drove, he pointed out several locations of historical or cultural significance.

When we stopped at a rest area to change the baby, Farrell pulled me aside and said that he still hadn't come across Walker and that he and Megan had been looking into McManus and Lefferty as well.

"We can't locate any McManus relative," he said. "As you know, he entered the prison system when he was young and right after he was released, he was rearrested. As far as we know, he didn't have any children. We can't locate any members of his family. So we think there's no McManus left to carry a sword on his behalf. Sean Lefferty, on the other hand, was married and had two sons. One of them lives in America, and the other one is dead. You may recall, when we arrested Sean Lefferty he was running one of the biggest arms smuggling operations in Northern Ireland."

"One lives in America?"

"Right, New Jersey. His name is Denny Lefferty and he owns a cartage company in North Bergen. He's a naturalized U.S. citizen. He's lived there for the past twenty years. He moved there with his mother when Sean Lefferty was sent to prison. According to U.S. Customs and Border Protection, his passport hasn't been used for several years. He hasn't left the country."

"He could have been the guy who threw the cocktail into my house."

McLaughlin shook his head. "CPD identified the attacker as Vincent Bertucci. Last known address in Queens."

"That's awfully close to New Jersey."

"I know, but he wasn't a Lefferty. Besides, how would Lefferty's kid know anything about you? You weren't connected with his father's arrest. You gave Lefferty's name to Westerfield who gave his name to the police. There's no way he would know that it was Liam Taggart who disclosed his father's name."

"How did the other son die?"

"We don't have that information. His name was Michael Lefferty. Vital records show he is buried in the St. Francis Cemetery in north Belfast. He was eighteen."

"Did you find out anything about the sniper?"

McLaughlin shook his head and snorted. "Nah. He's a pro and he's long gone. We scanned the area and all the warehouses and apartment units that he might have used to make the shot, but we came up empty. Robert is still in the hospital and Belfast PSNI has a man stationed there. Your cousin Riley, on the other hand, has not been seen since the shooting."

"Maybe he's on vacation. Did you check with his family?"

"His wife hasn't heard from him and doesn't know where he is. She's going to file a missing person's report. Conspicuous absence, don't you think? To my way of thinking, it makes him either complicit or another victim. I heard he had a serious argument with Robert."

I sure hoped he wasn't either another victim or complicit. I hoped there were other explanations. "He may have asked Robert to guarantee a loan to buy some stock from Fergus's trust. He told me he was going to do that. Robert may have refused. That could have been the cause of the argument. Did you ask Robert?"

"He's recuperating at Belfast General. We haven't interviewed him yet. I told you about Conor, that he seemed genuinely upset to learn your house was firebombed. He's been to the hospital several times to visit his uncle. If he's the killer, he's got me fooled. That's about all we have on the suspects, except for one."

"Janie?"

"Nah. The Dublin trust, the one called the Bridget McGregor Trust. It's become a pain in the ass for me to get information on that trust. Through channels, I sent a request to the Garda Síochána, Dublin Metropolitan Region, to issue a warrant for the trust documents, but it's all tied up in red tape. The trustee, whoever he is, doesn't want to provide the information. I am being told that I have to come up with 'compelling reasons' to break the confidentiality of the trust."

"Well, the murder of the man who set up the trust would seem pretty compelling."

"Seems that way to me too, but not to the powers that be. Any help you can provide will be appreciated. Maybe, as trustee of Fergus's trust, you can influence the trustee of the Bridget McGregor Trust."

I didn't know who the trustee was. I didn't know who Bridget McGregor was. All I knew was that money was deducted and sent to a trust account in a Dublin bank. Deirdre didn't seem to know anything about Bridget McGregor either, or if she did, she wasn't telling me. I had a feeling that Annie knew and would give me the information if I asked her. I don't know why, but I felt that Annie had a lot of answers. She hadn't come forward, but maybe she didn't know she had answers. The thought of having to spend an afternoon probing Annie's memory was very unsettling.

W E ARRIVED AT THE farm a little after noon and unloaded the Land Rover. The medical community should be informed immediately that the best antidepressant for a great-aunt is to show up with a little baby. All signs of depression and sullenness will immediately vanish. Deirdre was full of joy.

"Let me hold that wee laddie," she squealed. She got no argument from Catherine who had been holding Ben for nine hours.

Deirdre had prepared a bountiful lunch of roasted chicken, scalloped potatoes and fresh baked bread. She insisted that McLaughlin stay and she took a plate to the officer who stood watch outside on the front porch. "I can see why Frank is gaining weight," McLaughlin said.

"Robert may be released from the hospital Friday," Deirdre said. "He'll be moving into our back bedroom for the time being. I'm planning a dinner for Sunday night. Just like old times. You may come as well, Inspector."

McLaughlin smiled. "I may just do that. I've been hearing a lot about your cooking skills and now I know for a fact that they're true."

McLaughlin's phone buzzed and he stepped outside to take the call. It was nice to see flashes of the old Deirdre returning. I hadn't seen that look on her face since I was here in the nineties. It was solid evidence that the laugh of a baby can blow away all symptoms of melancholia. Catherine made herself right at home and was helping with the dishes when McLaughlin hurried back into the house. "Liam, that was the bartender at Willy's. Walker's there right now."

Catherine and I looked at each other. "There's an armed policeman sitting on the front porch," she said. "Go with Inspector McLaughlin. We're fine here." I told her I wouldn't be long and I jumped into McLaughlin's car. "Please be careful," she said as we left.

Twenty-nine

• • •

THOUGH THE NOONDAY SUN was bright, not much of it made it to the inside of Willy's Pub. There were a couple dozen men scattered here and there, downing beers in the dimly lit, staunchly unionist watering hole. Sometimes people say they can feel tension when they walk into a room, but at Willy's it was embitterment. It was instantly apparent to me that these men perceived themselves as disenfranchised. They exuded resentment for being marginalized by a society run by the damn politicians and Catholics, who were all combining to keep them off of easy street where they most assuredly belonged.

The bartender saw us come in and tilted his head toward the end of the bar where two white-haired men were arguing over the upcoming Mayo/Tyrone football match. We didn't have a picture of Walker, so we didn't know right off who was who. We slid down to their end of the bar and ordered a couple of pints of Guinness. The two men looked at us in an unfriendly way. We were intruders. Worse than that, we were strangers. The entire bar was open, why the hell would we choose to stand right next to them and horn in on their football conversation?

McLaughlin butted right in. "Mayo's Simon is a far superior midfielder. Rusten doesn't have the lateral movement. Any fool knows that, and that is why Tyrone cannot beat Mayo."

As little as I knew about Gaelic football, I was smart enough to know that favoring the Republic of Ireland's Mayo over Northern Ireland's beloved Tyrone in a championship match was a social faux pas in Willy's Pub, certain to raise the hair on the back of the necks of these two barflies.

"Aye," the smaller of the two men said, "and you have shit for brains as well, but I agree that Rusten is a stiff. Still, we'll bury the Mayo ballers and that is a fact."

McLaughlin raised his mug and saluted him. "The name's Farrell," he said, and he stuck out his right hand. "And this here is me partner, Liam."

"Tom," he said taking McLaughlin's hand. "And he's Lloyd. And what are you exactly meaning by 'partner'?" He put a sly grin on his face, snickered and winked to his companion.

McLaughlin tightened his grip on Walker's hand and pulled him up close, showing him his badge with his other hand. "I mean you and I need to go outside without making any trouble in this fine establishment." He clipped the cuffs on Walker's wrists as quickly and as smoothly as I'd ever seen anybody do it. If this was the son of a bitch who'd fire-bombed my home, he was either going to have the worst day of his life or the last day of his life.

"What did I do? You got no cause to pinch me."

McLaughlin held his left arm and slowly walked him forward. "Come along now, Thomas, and I'll tell you all about it."

As we walked out of the pub, the other patrons gave us the eye, and I was thankful that no one took a step in our direction. Still, I had my hand on my Glock. McLaughlin put Walker in the back of the PSNI Land Rover, where he cursed and complained the entire thirty minutes it took to drive to Antrim. "Where's the warrant? I didn't see no warrant. I wasn't committin' no crime, there wasn't no complainant, wasn't nobody dead, why the foock am I being kidnapped? This is bullshit."

"He sure sounds put out, doesn't he, Liam?"

"That he does, Farrell."

McLAUGHLIN TOOK MUG SHOTS and fingerprinted Walker. Then he put him in an interrogation room and let him cool off for a couple of hours before we returned to question him. He stopped me at the door. "I know how you feel, Liam, but you've got to let the police do their work here. I can't let you in the room if you're planning on giving Walker his due."

"I'll behave. I promise."

McLaughlin brought in copies of the photographs and laid them on the table. He pointed to the burned-out remains of the Walker residence. "Do you recognize this house, Tom?"

Walker nodded and pursed his lips. "I should say I do. That's me brother Archie's house, burned up by the foockin' Taggarts forty years ago. Why you showin' me that now? You think I burned my brother's house down? He was kilt with his wife and his kids inside by the mutherfoockin' Taggarts. Did you catch 'em, is that it? You want me to be a witness?"

"Are you a witness, Tom? Did you see anyone firebomb this house?"

"Nah. I was livin' in Derry, but everyone knows it was them Taggart boys."

"How are things going for you these days, Tom?"

"I'm a master pipefitter, when I can get the work. Work is tough to get. I ain't livin' in no boomin' economy.

"Where are you living?"

"Why the foock do you care?"

"Well, you're out on parole and your address is invalid. You don't live on Brookmount Street anymore."

"Landlord gave me the boot. So what?"

"So where are you living? You're violating parole unless we have a valid address."

"I'm staying with a lady on Bootle Street. Number 14 Bootle."

McLaughlin looked at me and raised his eyebrows. "He's got a lady."

"She's eighty-two and I'm renting a bedroom. What's it to you? What's that got to do with me brother's house?"

"This picture was found in the mailbox of a man who was murdered. Kind of makes us wonder."

"Foock," he said under his breath. "I shoulda told the guy to get lost." Walker closed his eyes and nodded his head. "I sold that picture. A man bought it off me for a hundred quid. I also sold the picture of me brother's wake, the other one right here on the table. My prints are probably on both those pictures."

"There are no prints on the pictures. They've been wiped clean. And these are copies. Who did you sell these pictures to?"

"I don't know his name. Tall guy. Taller than me. Shows up at my place on Bootle and asks if I have any pictures of me brother Archie. I got a few, I say. What's it to you? I'll buy 'em, he says. Hundred quid apiece. Why you want 'em, I say, and he just shakes his head. I had three in a footlocker. I ask him if he wants pictures of me mother, I got those too. He says no, just Archie. I ask again why he wants Archie's pictures, but he just smiles. Do I want to sell them or not? Foock yeah, I'll sell 'em. He goes into his pocket, pulls out a wad and hands me three hundred."

"What name did he give you?"

Walker shook his head and smiled. "He didn't give me no name and I didn't ask."

"I need a better description, Tom."

"Look, he was tall, taller than me, that's all I remember."

"Where were you on Monday, August first, Tom, just a few weeks ago?"

"How am I supposed to know? Probably drunk at Willy's. That was about the time I got the three hundred."

"What about August sixth?"

"I was in Derry at me son's house. At a birthday party for me grand-daughter. You can check."

McLaughlin nodded to me and we stood to leave the room. "Wait a minute," Walker said. "You can't leave me in here. I didn't do nothin'. There's no law against selling pictures, is there?"

"I need better cooperation, Tom. A more detailed description of the man who gave you the money would help. I'm going to give you time to think. All the time you need. I have plenty of beds here."

"Hey wait, no, wait. Foock. Foock both of yourselfs."

We shut the door and walked down to McLaughlin's office. "I have to cut him loose. I've got nothing to hold him on, Liam."

"It couldn't have been Walker, anyway," I said. "It would take money and connections to run this string of crimes. He's a part-time pipefit-ter. He's been evicted from his apartment. I don't see how an impover-ished old man like this could get close enough to my Uncle Fergus to shoot him in the chest, or to drive a stolen truck into my Uncle Eamon, or to hire an arsonist in the U.S. or a sniper in Belfast. Does he harbor resentment and hatred for the Taggarts? No question. But I think he's telling the truth."

McLaughlin nodded. "Me too. Someone's using Walker's identity to divert our attention. Someone who knows the Taggart family history. Before I let him go I'm going to see if I can get a better description of the guy who bought the pictures."

"Do you want to go back there now?"

McLaughlin shook his head. "No, let's let him steam for a while. In the meantime, I want to talk to you about your cousin Riley. I was told that he had an argument with Robert three days before the sniper. What can you tell me about Riley?"

That was a disturbing question. I'd been thinking a lot about Riley and Conor. They seemed to be the only viable suspects left. I was already cooling on Walker before we brought him in, but now I was certain he had nothing to do with any of the crimes. Conor was a wild man but was he the sort of guy who would murder his own father and uncle? I didn't think so. Would he murder me? Well, that's a different story, but I didn't think he'd murder my wife. Riley had always been the quiet type. He and I were fast buddies in the seventies. I always liked him, but now the doubts were seeping in. He was in a jam. Could he be desperate enough to commit these murders?

"I think we should look at Riley," I said. "This Global stock may be more important than I realize."

McLaughlin nodded. He knew what I was talking about. No doubt he and Megan had done their homework.

"Riley's employed by Global as an investment counselor," McLaughlin said. "He's been there for eight years. The word is that indictments are coming down soon, not only against the company but all of its top executives."

"Riley wanted me to transfer the Global stock to him. The judge told me I couldn't do it. Then, while I was in Chicago, he called and proposed furnishing a promissory note in the amount of the stock's market value. Although that sounded reasonable, he told me he has no way of repaying the note. So I had to decline. Then he proposed having Uncle Robert guarantee the note. I thought that was fair and O'Neill told me it would be okay. I'm sure he went to Uncle Robert afterward to ask for the guarantee.

"Janie told me that Riley visited Robert a couple days later. She said they had a terrible argument. I can only imagine. Robert is a conservative man and he lives very frugally. He probably declined. Riley has a temper. Things could have gone south quickly."

"It wasn't a crime of passion, Liam. It didn't happen in a moment of anger. Someone hired a professional. This was a carefully planned attempt at cold-blooded murder."

"What good would it do Riley to kill his uncle? Robert was Riley's only hope at getting a guarantor. I would think that Riley would keep trying to convince him."

McLaughlin spread his hands. "Maybe he felt that he could never convince Robert and he needed the stock. In a hurry. Like I said, indictments are coming down. With Robert dead, there's one less beneficiary standing in the way of Riley getting full ownership of the stock. Theory of relativity, Liam."

"But now Riley's gone missing. What do you make of that?"

"An innocent man doesn't run. Flight creates an inference of guilt. But he could also be a victim. Let's go see if Walker's memory is any better."

Walker's hands were chained to the desk and he rattled the chains as Farrell and I walked in. "Either charge me or let me go," he yelled. "You can't keep me tied to this table."

McLaughlin smiled. "Did I hear him correctly, Liam? He wants to be charged with two murders, arson and an attempted murder. That sounds very much like a confession, doesn't it?"

"Sounds that way to me, Farrell."

"Go foock yourselfs."

"Such a potty mouth. If you want to get out of here, Tommy, give me a better description of the man who bought the pictures. Was he as tall as I am?"

McLaughlin was every bit of six feet. Walker nodded. "Maybe a little taller." Riley wasn't that tall. Neither was Conor.

"Did he have brown hair, black hair, gray hair? What color was his hair, Tom?"

Walker shook his head. "He wore a cap what covered his hair."

"What kind of cap?"

"I don't know, just a cap, like a sport cap. A white cap."

"How was he dressed?"

"I don't remember, truly I don't. Wasn't blue jeans. Regular pants."

"Any marks, scars, anything special you remember?"

"No. Can I go?"

McLaughlin thought about it, shook his head and surprisingly said, "I don't think so, Tom. VOP. You violated parole. The address thing, you know?"

"C'mon guv'nor. It was an oversight. I didn't bloody remember. I promise not to move again without telling you. I won't leave Belfast. You know I didn't kill no one."

"I'll tell you what. I'll forget about VOP and let your sorry ass go, but I want to know if this photo buff ever comes back."

"I promise, I'll call you. Can I take his money first?"

McLaughlin uncuffed him and handed him a card. "You can go, Tommy, but if you see this man again, you call me immediately. Catch his license plate. And keep me advised of your address. You change your address again and don't tell me within the hour, you'll be back here for good."

"Right you are." Walker quickly headed for the exit in case McLaughlin changed his mind. When he had gone, McLaughlin said, "I've got a tail on him. If he goes back to the guy who paid him, we'll pick them both up."

Thirty

• • •

WHEN I RETURNED TO the house, it was evening. I nodded to the patrolman sitting comfortably on a rocker on the front porch of what I had come to call "Fortress Deirdre." Old Wicklow was sleeping next to the rocker. He greeted me with a sweep of his tail. In the living room my aunt was sitting in the middle of the floor, cross-legged on a quilt with Ben. Several toys were strewn about and Ben was loving every minute of it. When she saw me she tilted her head toward the kitchen.

Catherine was standing at the sink drying dishes. She looked cute in her striped apron. I hugged her from behind and kissed her on the neck. "I know, it's way past his bedtime," she said with a smile, "but you saw the two of them. How could I break it up?" She took a plate out of the warmer and set it on the table. She was still walking gingerly, favoring her left leg, and every time I saw her wince, my anger rose and my muscles tensed.

"We saved some dinner for you," she said. "It's really good. Deirdre can sure teach me a thing or two." She poured two glasses of white wine and sat next to me. "Except for Ben's nap, Great-Aunt Deirdre has been with him every minute since we arrived. I wonder if we can take her back to Chicago with us."

"She might not mind that at all. What have you two been up to this afternoon?"

"It's been a very interesting day. I've been treated to an illustrated odyssey through the Taggart family historical museum."

"What does that mean?"

"Deirdre and I pored through her photo albums. It was a learning experience."

"Uh-oh."

Catherine smiled. "Nope, it's all good."

"Phew."

Then she stared at me with that cat-that-ate-the-canary look of hers. "There were more than a few pictures of you and a certain young lady named Annie. So, how come you never told me about her?"

Oh brother, I thought. I knew it was a mistake to leave those two alone. "She's an old girlfriend, Cat. Do you tell me all about all your old boyfriends? I was through with that relationship five years before we got together. I believe you were married to Mr. Stock Exchange at the same time I was dating Annie."

"There's no reason to get defensive, but she wasn't just an old girl-friend. You were engaged to her."

"Well, it isn't the kind of thing that makes for pleasant dinner conversation for you and me. Certainly not for me. Just what did my lovely aunt Deirdre tell you?"

"Never mind, then."

"Oh no you don't. You opened the door. What is it you lawyers say, 'The hand once set to the task, may not withdraw it with impunity'? What did she tell you? I might have to correct some glaring inaccuracies. What did she say about me and Annie?"

"She said that the two of you dated for a year, that it was serious and that you were planning to get married. You told Uncle Fergus that you were going to marry her. You even bought her a ring. Deirdre saw the ring. Everyone thought you were going to get married and it was a shock when you two broke up."

"Thanks, Deirdre."

Catherine took a sip of her wine and smiled. "Liam, neither one of us were kids when we got together. I didn't think you had been celibate. In fact, you were dating Donna Talcott at the time. I'm not disturbed by anything Deirdre told me or that you loved somebody before me. We have each other now. I'm not worried."

"I assume you asked Deirdre why we broke up?"

Catherine rolled her eyes. "Well, maybe. Come on, you can't blame me for being curious. But Deirdre wouldn't tell me. She just said you broke up with Annie at the same time you and your uncles had a falling-out. I'm sure she knows more, but I felt I was being nosey enough. I didn't push her."

I wasn't sure how much more my aunt knew. I'd never discussed it with her. But Annie might have. Deirdre told me she's stayed close to Annie over the years, so I imagine my aunt knows it all. I respect her for not telling Catherine. If anybody is going to reveal the intimacies of my life to my wife, it should be me. "So because you're curious, you think I should tell you about it."

"Not necessarily. Not unless you want to."

"Well, I think you do, or you wouldn't have brought it up."

Catherine's expressions are so revealing. She raised her eyebrows and tilted her head to the side, which I knew was prefatory to confronting me with a prior inconsistent statement. That's one of the inconvenient aspects of being married to a trial attorney. They remember everything you say. "Well, Liam . . . just a few weeks ago, when you told me about Deirdre's Sunday dinners and the 'darling girls' that Aunt Nora introduced you to, I believe you said 'nothing ever came of the darling girls.' So, that wasn't exactly true, was it? When Deirdre told me that Aunt Nora fixed you up with Annie and you planned to marry her, it came as a surprise. Do you blame me for wondering why you didn't marry her?"

Catherine and I prided ourselves in having an honest relationship, so I had to clear the air. "You're right, I wasn't truthful. I apologize. It's not that I wanted to keep secrets, it's really about my aversion to discussing my relationship with Annie. That happened to be a very unpleasant time in my life that I don't like to think about, let alone discuss with anyone. When I left Ireland, I closed the door and locked those memories away, just like my mother did."

"I'm sorry, honey, I didn't mean to open Pandora's box. It was just idle curiosity, really. It doesn't matter to me."

"Well, it does matter or you wouldn't have brought it up. And I shouldn't have lied to you. Annie and I didn't get married because *she* broke it off. I wanted to marry her, but at the last minute, she didn't want to go through with it. It wasn't due to my uncles and it wasn't due to my service with the CIA. And it wasn't because I got cold feet. She ended it. That's the truth.

"Annie and I dated for a year and Aunt Deirdre was right, it was serious, almost from the beginning. Then 1999 came along. I was living in Northern Ireland and working for the Agency. Annie was teaching. At the time there was no reason for either of us to think that anything would change. I thought I'd be here for years. Then the Good Friday Peace Agreement brought an end to the sectarian warfare. At least on paper. With the Troubles over, the CIA began winding down its operations. There were just a few of us left by the summer of '99, but there were no plans to close the station. I had no reason to believe that I would be reassigned. Annie and I started to talk about getting married and having a family. We knew there would be problems with Annie's father but we figured we could work them out when the time came.

"Annie's father was a prominent member of his community, a selfless man who always devoted himself to helping others. He worked for social services and administered generously, no matter who the recipient was: Catholic, Protestant, Jewish or no faith at all. He was all-embracing. *But,* where his daughter was concerned, it was a different story.

"Jacob was a deeply religious man. He was second generation in Northern Ireland; his Jewish grandparents had emigrated from Germany with traditions they brought over from their Orthodox communities. Jacob and his Belfast Jewish community were very observant, steeped in the old ways. They chose to live by conventions, rules and customs. For example, the men all dressed alike—black coats, white shirts, black shoes. They did so to identify themselves as members of their community. No one would want to wear a blue shirt or a striped shirt. After all, if you were truly devoted to your community, why would you want to dress differently? It was all about a sense of belonging.

"With Annie, he set stern rules. He was rigid. Intolerant. In their community, a daughter obeyed her father without question. And when it came to marriage, she did not marry outside the community. No exceptions."

"Annie must have realized that before she got involved with you."

"When she and I started dating, she was hesitant with me and I didn't know why. I thought she was being cautious because she had been hurt by a previous relationship. But really, she was stepping outside of her father's boundaries, she knew it and she was nervous. Truth be told, Annie was always a bit rebellious."

"How old was she at the time?" Catherine said. "I'm getting the impression she must have been very young."

"What's very young? We were both in our midtwenties."

"That sounds young to me now, Liam."

"You're right. Young and impulsive and foolish. I offered to meet with her father, but Annie said no. She told me that her father would not approve of her dating a Catholic man. She was keeping our relationship from him. It wasn't that he didn't like Catholics; it was all about the cohesion of his community.

"He would also lecture her about assimilation. According to Annie's father, outside of the observant Orthodox communities, in the more liberal Jewish communities, three out of four Jewish children were entering into interfaith marriages, and the resulting union often became secular. Jacob couldn't conceive of his daughter not carrying on the customs of his ancestors, or that his grandchildren might grow up in a secular home. 'Intermarriage weakens our community,' he would tell her. 'Assimilated Jews move away, they don't observe our laws and customs, they don't teach the faith to their children. We must not dilute our community by interfaith marriage.'"

"Yet, she continued to date you," Catherine said. "She disobeyed her father."

"As I said, she was rebellious. We punted the problem downfield. We knew there would come a time. We would address it then. Her father didn't know about us, so he didn't forbid her from seeing me, and so she wasn't really disobeying, but . . . of course she was.

"Jacob was getting up in years, he was not particularly healthy, and in the spring of 1999 he had a crippling heart attack that left him homebound and needing a lot of help. Annie took a leave of absence for a while and devoted her days to assisting him. When the leave ended, she hired a nurse, but Annie continued to spend most of her nonworking hours with him. We'd get together late at night. She'd ask me to be patient and understanding, and somehow she'd work it out. Annie's mother had died when she was young and Jacob devoted his life to raising Annie, so Annie felt that it was her duty to reciprocate.

"Still, we'd talk about our life together. We discussed braiding our two religions many times and we were comfortable we could work it out. We would each be respectful of our personal convictions. Knowing that a secular home could forever separate Jacob from our family, I agreed to raise our children Jewish and I was comfortable with that. It wasn't so great a sacrifice for me. I didn't have any community pressures and I wasn't nearly as devout as Annie. And to tell you the truth, as far as I'm concerned, Jews and Catholics have a lot in common. We're both built on the same foundation.

"While all this was going on, everything started to unravel for me. That was the time my uncles discovered I had been lying to them and my cover was blown. The Agency concluded I was of no further use in Northern Ireland and they decided to repost me back to Washington. My visa was up. I had been reassigned. I couldn't continue to live in Northern Ireland.

"That brought the whole thing to a head. I bought a ring and asked Annie to marry me and live with me in Washington. I never expected her to say no, or even to say she had to think about it. It was a given. We were devoted to each other. And she said yes. We would leave for Washington in a few weeks and plan a wedding.

"There were matters that needed attention before we could go. First, there was Jacob's continuing nursing care. Annie had to be sure he would be well cared for. Then there was this Catholic/Jewish thing. We knew we'd get a big pushback from Jacob, but Annie said she just needed a little time. She was confident. It would all work out. I'm afraid we were naïve.

"A few days later, after her father had gone to sleep, she met me at my apartment. She said she had arranged for Jacob's nursing care. All she needed to do was work out the religious issue. She had tried to broach the subject, she told her father she was dating a man outside their community."

Catherine caught the ambiguity. "A Catholic man?"

I shook my head. "Not yet. Even so, Jacob had waved her off. He would hear none of it. Now, in my apartment, she told me she was going to be firm. Her father would have to understand. After all, he loved her and would want what's best for her. Above all, he would want her to be happy. That night we broke out a bottle of Champagne, called the airlines and bought our plane tickets. Oh, how clueless we were.

"As the date approached, both of us were busy making final arrangements. We weren't able to see each other very much, but we'd talk on the phone several times a day. I started to hear something in her voice, something that wasn't right. I kept asking her what's wrong and she'd say nothing. I asked her how the talks with her father were going and she'd change the subject. I knew she was having a rough time. I suppose I should have seen the writing on the wall.

"Finally, it was the day of our departure. Everything was in order. All my belongings were boxed, packed and ready for shipping. Annie showed up at the apartment. She didn't have a suitcase or any of her things. She just stood in the doorway crying. She wouldn't even come into the room. 'I can't leave,' she said. 'He won't be able to deal with it.'

"'It's not his life,' I said.

"'I don't expect you to understand this,' she said, 'but my father devoted his life to me. I owe him so much. Now he's sick and he's dying. He's lying there in his bed and he needs me. If the situation were reversed, he'd never run out on me. How can I do that to him? I know you're upset because you think you betrayed your uncles. Imagine what I'm going through. I am not able to turn my back on my father. I just can't do it. I have to stay.'

"I knew that if she ran out on her father, she'd never forgive herself. She was that kind of person. 'I do understand,' I said. 'And I respect you for what you're doing. I have to leave, I have no choice, but I'll get a place for us in D.C. and I'll wait for you. You'll come to me when he no longer needs you.'

"She shook her head. Now the tears were really flowing. 'No, Liam, I can't. I had to tell him the truth about us. I couldn't leave Northern Ireland without telling him everything. Liam, it hurt him so badly. He cried, he begged me. Liam, a man like my father, he could never understand. And now he's so sick and he knows he's dying.' She hung her head and spoke in a whisper. 'He said it was a dying father's last request. He held my hands and he begged me. You say you have no choice;

I had no choice either. I made a vow. I gave him my word that I wouldn't marry you. I'm so sorry.'

"I was floored. How could she do that? She couldn't be serious. I pleaded with her to reconsider. 'To hell with these old world customs. We're not living in a shtetl. This isn't the eighteen hundreds. It's 1999 and it's our lives. He knows he's dying, we all know he's dying. Stay with him, and when he passes, you'll be released from your vow. Then you'll come to me.'

" 'No,' she said, 'I gave him my word. I promised. It wasn't a promise that lasted only as long as he was alive. It was a solemn vow that I would not marry a man outside our community. I gave my word to my dying father. I cannot break my vow.' Then she held out her hand, gave me back my ring, turned, and walked out of my life."

Just then we heard Ben fussing from the living room. Catherine stood. She had tears in her eyes. "I have to get the baby. I'll be right back."

I didn't think it was necessary to tell Catherine the rest—how devastated I was and what a mess it made of my life. At first, I was sure Annie would change her mind. A few hours would pass, the pressure of the moment would fade and she'd come to her senses. She'd get her priorities right. I couldn't accept such a sudden finale and I didn't see how she could either. I put the ring in my pocket and left for the airport fully expecting her to show up, running down the concourse at the last moment, like in a movie. I stood there like a fool, watching and waiting at the gate. Finally, the gate agent told me I'd have to board if I was going to Washington; they were shutting the doors.

For weeks afterward, I fully expected to get a phone call. She'd apologize. She'd beg me to forgive her. Maybe she'd just show up at my apartment door. But I never heard another word. She didn't write and neither did I. I returned to a desk job at the CIA, but my heart wasn't in it. I'd go about my day-to-day activities and carry on as best I could, but I avoided the social scene entirely. Big, tough Liam on the outside; a dishrag on the inside. I came to believe that my entire frame of reference, everything I took for granted, was illusory. As time passed, my sadness turned into anger. I hated Annie for walking out on our plans. I hated her for being so weak. I hated her for being manipulated.

I hated Jacob for his selfishness. I was getting more bitter by the day and I didn't like myself. I needed to change my life.

I resigned from the Agency and returned to Chicago where I got a PI license and opened a small investigation office. I was determined to make a clean break and put all Northern Ireland memories into a locked chamber never to be opened again. And I did for all these years. Until my uncle died.

Catherine returned to the kitchen with Ben and set him in his high chair. She still had tears in her eyes. She leaned over and gave me a kiss.

"All that happened sixteen years ago, Cat, and it's ancient history to me now. It was rough for a while, but I'm over it. I saw Annie for the first time last month at the funeral. There was no love, no anger, no resentment. No feelings at all. I was uncomfortable talking to her. Actually, I felt sorry for her. Apparently she's never moved on. But that's it. You can believe me."

"There was never a question whether I would believe you, Liam. I brought it up out of curiosity. In the entire time we've been together, I've never felt the least bit threatened and now I fear that I've become the prying wife. Shame on me."

"Why are you crying?"

"Partly because I'm ashamed of myself, partly because it's a sad story. You know me, I always cry at sad romantic stories. I love you and it made me sad. Is that silly?"

I had to smile. She's that kind of girl. "Seriously, Cat, I harbor no regrets. It was another lifetime and the one I have now fits me perfectly."

"The subject is closed, Liam. I'm not worried. Deirdre told me that Annie stayed close to your uncle throughout the years. I guess you didn't know that."

"No, there was no way for me to know. I didn't speak to anyone here for sixteen years. But it doesn't matter. I knew Uncle Fergus and Annie were close before I left, and Deirdre said they stayed close afterward."

"Do you suppose Uncle Fergus told Annie things he didn't tell Deirdre? Do you suppose that Annie has pieces of information that would help you in the investigation?"

"I do think that's possible. Uncle Fergus wouldn't want to alarm

Deirdre. He would have confided in Annie. I've been considering the awkward likelihood that I would have to sit down with Annie and find out what she knows."

Catherine stood and gave me a kiss. "Well, don't worry about me. I have no uncertainties where you are concerned." She smiled and started mixing cereal for Ben.

Sitting there thinking about Annie, I remembered that she gave me her phone number at Eamon's funeral. *"We should catch up sometime,"* she said. Was that just a meaningless platitude or did she really have important things to tell me? Did she mean to tell me that Fergus shared ideas with her that I should know about? I looked at the paper. Funny. Her number hadn't changed since 1999. I took out my cell phone, stared at it, thought about it, took a deep breath and dialed.

"Hello, this is Annie." *Déjà vu.*

"Hi, Annie."

"Hi, Liam. How is your family? I was shocked when I heard about the fire and the attack on your wife and baby. Are they okay?"

"Catherine suffered pretty serious burns on her leg, but she's on the mend. Thanks for asking. They're here with me in Antrim. I couldn't leave them at home."

"I know."

"Really? How do you know?"

She uttered a soft chuckle. "You're not the only one with spies. I'm still in touch with Deirdre and Janie. Actually, Janie and I are best friends."

"I've been told you stayed close to the family and that's really the main reason I'm bothering you. I was wondering if Uncle Fergus might have shared some of his thoughts and fears with you in the months before he died. We're reaching for straws, Annie, and any bit of information might help."

"I visited with Fergus quite often after you left. He was a great comfort for me when my father died. But over the past few months, he did seem distracted and some of the things he said were strange, out of context. They really had no meaning for me. I can't be sure if I remember them all. I don't know how much help I'd be."

"Every little bit helps, Annie. Do you think you can spare me an hour or so?"

"'Spare me an hour'? That's a rather impersonal way of putting it, don't you think?"

"I'm sorry it came out impersonally. I didn't intend it that way. If you're too uncomfortable, maybe we can just talk on the phone."

"I'm not uncomfortable. It's only uncomfortable talking about whether I'm uncomfortable." Then she started to laugh. I did too. "I'm not teaching Friday afternoon and I work in Antrim. I could stop by at around two if that's convenient."

I said, "Sure. Great. See you then," before it occurred to me that she meant to stop by the house and Catherine would be here. Now *that* could be uncomfortable. Oh well.

T HE NEXT MORNING I went out for a short five-miler. My first full day back and it was going to be busy. I needed to go to Belfast General and visit Uncle Robert. I also wanted to touch base with McLaughlin and see if we couldn't move the investigation forward. I had returned to protect my family. I intended to flush out the murderer.

On my way back to the house, out of habit, I stopped at the mailbox. And there it was—a blank white envelope. Inside was the Walker calling card and on the back, in printed letters, it read, "WELCOME BACK." I had been in Northern Ireland for less than twenty-four hours and now I was marked for death. Who knew I was returning? Clearly not Walker, or any vengeful unionist. It certainly strengthened the view that the killer was intimately connected to the family. Maybe it wouldn't be as difficult as I thought to flush out the killer. Apparently he intended to come to me. Given the heightened state of apprehension in Fortress Deirdre, I decided not to say anything about the photo to anyone at the house.

W HEN I ARRIVED AT the hospital, Uncle Robert was on the surgical floor with a uniformed officer sitting outside his room. Though he had been through hell, he had a broad smile on his face. He'd survived an attempted murder, but still showed signs of his jovial old self, sitting up in his bed in a chipper mood. He could look death in the face and keep on dancing. That's my uncle Robert. Such an attitude adjustment was hard for me to fathom, but then I hadn't lived through thirty years of the Troubles.

He gave me a strong hug with his right arm. His left arm was tightly bound to his body. "It's always a grand day when I get to see my nephew," he said. "I hear you brought your bride and your son along for the ride this time."

"That I did and I can't wait for you to meet them. When will they let you out of this jail?"

"Tomorrow if I'm a good boy. I'm going out to stay with Deirdre for a while. From what I understand, it'll be a busy little house."

"Busy is an understatement, but there's round-the-clock protection and lots of good food. In fact, I understand that Aunt Deirdre is planning one of her special Sunday dinners."

He nodded and then his face became serious. "I hope everyone will be there. Have you heard from Riley?"

I shook my head. "No one seems to know where he went. I'm hoping he just wanted to get away for a bit to assess his situation and decide on the best course forward."

"I guess you heard that we had a fierce argument a couple of nights before I was shot. He wanted me to guarantee a loan for eighty thousand pounds and put up security. I don't have that kind of money, or property to secure the loan. He promised me that I would never have to pay anything, that he could raise the money, but I told him I couldn't risk it. Riley drives around in a BMW, has a fancy house and his kids are in private school. He's always lived on the edge. Maybe he could raise the money, but I'm on retirement income now and I can't take the chance. I don't want to end up in the poorhouse."

"I think you made a wise decision."

"Liam, he was as angry as I'd ever seen him. For the first time in his life, he cursed at me, and then he stormed out of my apartment. I wish I had the money to help him out, but I don't. And now I suppose he's taken off. I hope I wasn't the cause."

I nodded. Uncle Robert looked down at his bandaged arm. "You don't think he was desperate enough to . . ." He shook his head in the middle of his sentence. "Shame on myself for thinking something so devilish."

"Someone hired that sniper, Uncle Robert."

"Aye, and it's a safe bet it's Thomas Walker, not my nephew Riley. I sure couldn't guarantee a note if I was dead."

I shrugged. "It could be Walker, it could be anyone. That's why we're going to keep you safe until this mess is over."

The door swung open and I turned to see Conor step into the room. "Hello, Liam. I heard you were coming back."

"Did you now? Well, it wasn't for a holiday jaunt, Conor. I believe you and your lawyer accused me of being irresponsible and scheduled a court hearing to remove me from office. It seems that all your efforts to keep me out of Antrim were counterproductive, weren't they? I returned to defend myself and finish my job. But let's not have an argument in Uncle Robert's hospital room, okay?"

"I didn't come here to argue. I came to visit my uncle. I come every day."

"That's right," Robert said. "Conor's been grand company. Every day."

Conor smiled, an expression I rarely encountered from him. He grabbed a chair, pulled it over to the side of the bed, set it right next to me and stuck out his hand. "Peace, Liam. I'm never going to get rid of you anyway, am I?"

I took his hand. "That's right, Conor, no matter how hard you try."

"For your information, Liam, I didn't ask Cooney to file this latest petition. I didn't want to drag you back here, especially after the fire and the injury to your wife. You had enough to deal with. You should know that all of us were shocked by it. Everyone is now on edge. I know my son had double locks installed on all his doors and I keep a shotgun by my bed."

"The petition has your name on it, Conor."

"Yeah, but I didn't ask Cooney to do it. It was Riley. The hearing that Cooney set for tomorrow, the petition to remove you, it was all Riley's doing. I told you, I think you've had enough to deal with without suffering attacks from your own family. Riley told Cooney he had to have that stock and asked him to do whatever it takes to get it."

"Did you go along with it?"

Conor shrugged and then nodded. "Look, he's my brother. I told Cooney I'd go along with it. Riley's in a bad way. He's afraid he's going to jail. Why don't you give the stock to him? No one cares. It might help to bail him out of his jam."

"If that's what the judge orders, then I'll give it to him, but I don't have the authority to do it on my own. Don't you think that if your father wanted him to have the stock, he would have given it to him while he was still alive? Deirdre told me they had fierce arguments about it."

"It's true, they did. Riley has been trying to get that stock for months. His company's in big trouble. The regulators believe that his group was running something akin to a Ponzi scheme. They claim that Global had been appropriating client deposits and investing them in risky financial products, hoping for a quick return to cover the misappropriations. Global needs to borrow a lot of money and it needs to pledge all the stock to get that kind of financing. Why not give it him? None of the rest of us would object."

"Judge McNulty told me I can't do it; it violates my fiduciary duty. I'll do whatever the judge orders, but you can be damn sure I'll not be intimidated by Riley or you or anyone else."

"Hold on, Liam. Who's intimidating you? We're having a civil conversation."

Now my blood was starting to boil and I was sorry that we were having this argument in front of my uncle. Truth be told, I wouldn't have come to the hospital if I knew Conor would be here. He was right at the top of possible suspects. And he was the only one who hadn't received a calling card. I should have calmed down and shut up, but I didn't.

"It's not so goddamn civil when my house is bombed and my wife and son are almost killed, is it?" I snapped. "It's not so damn civil when you tear up my hotel room and slash my tires. It's not so civil when you make threatening phone calls to my wife. But, you know what? A reckoning is coming. I'm here and I'm not going away and everyone should know that."

Conor furrowed his brows. "Jesus, Liam, I hope to hell you're not accusing me of any of that shit. I know we had bad words. Even a shoving match or two. But come on, I would never do anything like that. I didn't break into your hotel room or slash any tires or make any calls to your house and I sure as shit didn't have anything to do with the fire at your house. How could you think that was me?"

"Maybe because you said you hated me and wanted me the hell out of Antrim. Maybe because you told me to watch my ass. Maybe because you told me that I didn't know how much trouble I just bought. Maybe because you want to throw Aunt Deirdre out on the street? Am I talking to the same Conor Taggart?"

"So I get a little hotheaded. I say some bad shit. Jesus, Liam, you had just knocked me on my ass. But give me a break. My father dies and instead of leaving the family home and his estate to his two sons, like every other Irish father would, he leaves it to a blind trust and appoints an estranged nephew, one who betrayed the whole family twenty years ago, as a trustee. Then he postpones all distributions until we find the unionist fuck who killed him. And even then, he leaves his estate to seven different beneficiaries and gives the farm to his girl-friend, who is a basket case and can't take care of the farm or herself. I wouldn't have thrown her on the street, Liam. I would have rented her an apartment. But she should get out of the house. She can't take care of it and I don't want to see my father's farm go to hell. And you can't see why I'm pissed?"

"No, I can't. It's not your property to begin with, and if he wants to leave it all to Mother Teresa, then that's his right. And it was his *girlfriend,* as you put it, who raised you, you prick."

Finally Robert had had enough. He raised his right arm like a stop sign. "Hold on, fellows. I let this go on so you could both have your say and get it off your chests. Now that's enough. Let's quit this. We're a family and we can't be blaming each other. I've known Conor since he was a baby, and I would bet my soul he didn't do anything other than holler a lot and hire that loudmouth lawyer. There's no doubt in my mind that all this evil is due to the Walkers trying to get their revenge. They killed my two brothers and they tried to kill me. I don't doubt they bombed your house as well, Liam. That's their style."

I shook my head. "It wasn't the Walkers. It would take money and connections and intelligence and Thomas Walker is short on all three."

"Then who? Who is dealing the Walker death cards?"

I just shook my head. "Why don't you ask Conor? He's the only Taggart that didn't get one."

"Oh really?" Conor said as he got out of his chair. "What's this?"

He pulled a folded picture from his back pocket and held it out for me to see. "I found this a week ago." On the back of the photo was written, "A tisket, a tasket, a Taggart in a casket."

"It ain't Conor," Robert said. "I'd bet my lot on it."

Much as I didn't like Conor, I was starting to agree with my uncle. Conor had nothing to gain. He didn't need the money and didn't have a bone to pick with Fergus or Eamon. The circle of suspects was shrinking, and no clear answer was emerging. The same could not be said for Riley. He had a cause. Desperate people will do desperate things. I hung around the hospital room for a few more minutes, told Conor I'd see him in court tomorrow, said good-bye to Uncle Robert and headed back to Fortress Deirdre.

Thirty-one

• • •

J UDGE MCNULTY'S COURTROOM WAS practically empty. Other than the two lawyers, only Conor and I were present. Deirdre and Robert were at the house with Catherine and the baby. Janie called to say that Charles was at a golf outing, that neither she nor he would appear, and that anything I decided would be okay with her. Riley was not in attendance, which was puzzling because according to Conor, it was Riley who instructed Cooney to file the petition. If he had decided to go into hiding because of the Global Investment scandal, why would he tell Cooney to set a petition? Of course, the unarticulated alternative was obvious, and all of us now feared the worst.

Precisely at eleven, the judge took the bench, looked down at the four of us, shook her head and said, "Well, it seems as though we are going to rehash the same old arguments this morning. Is that right, Mr. Cooney?"

He bounced to his feet. "Not entirely, Your Honor. Similar issues to be sure, but there are recent changes in circumstances. Liam Taggart, the sole trustee, went back to living in America and although he has returned for this morning's hearing, he has given clear indications that he will not be residing in Northern Ireland to manage and oversee the estate. That's why, at this time, we are justified in seeking his removal."

"Isn't Liam Taggart sitting right here in my courtroom?"

"Yes, Your Honor, but he only returned to defend the petition."

"Is he not here on trust business? Can we agree that your petition concerns trust business? Didn't he return to Antrim because it was necessary to exercise his authority as a trustee, Mr. Cooney?"

"I'm afraid you miss my point, Your Honor. He's not here on a day-to-day basis. He only comes in for the sole purpose of defending his appointment. He hasn't been here the last few weeks and no one has been looking after the property or the best interests of the estate. We are very concerned that the farm and the house are rapidly falling into disrepair. Inevitably, there will be a significant decrease in crop production that will cost the estate substantial money. Deirdre Kerrigan is not capable of managing the property."

"Isn't the farmland leased to a tenant farmer? I mean, you don't expect Deirdre Kerrigan to drive a tractor, do you?"

"No, of course not. But someone has to oversee the operation of the farm, the finances, the tenant farmer. We want you to order Ms. Kerrigan to vacate the home. We are requesting that you appoint a new trustee and we have suggested either Riley Taggart or Conor Taggart."

"I'm confused, Mr. Cooney. Doesn't the trust provide for a successor trustee? Isn't it the Bank of Antrim?"

"Ah, but that is the problem. Because of the rash of violence that has arisen since Liam Taggart's appointment, the Bank of Antrim has informed us that it will not accept an appointment as trustee. It will decline. If it pleases the court, the property is failing due to Liam Taggart's absent management, causing deterioration and disrepair."

Judge McNulty took a deep breath. There was no way she was going to avoid this hearing. "I see. I hope this time you are prepared to offer *evidence* of the alleged *deterioration* and *disrepair*. And I mean *evidence*, Mr. Cooney. You may proceed. Call your first witness."

"Well, there's a minor problem this morning. Our main witness, Riley Taggart, is temporarily unavailable. I request a short continuance, perhaps until next week."

The judge put her hand on her forehead. "After all that, you don't have a witness?"

"I didn't say that. I said our *main* witness is unavailable. I mean, we do have a witness, but not our main witness."

The judge shook her head and looked at O'Neill. "Mr. O'Neill, as we all noted earlier, Liam Taggart is present in court this morning. Did he come in from Illinois especially for this hearing?"

O'Neill stood. "He did indeed, Your Honor. Specifically for this hearing. His wife and child were hospitalized after their home was struck by an arsonist. His wife suffered serious injuries. Indeed, that is why Liam returned to Chicago a few weeks ago. Now, because of Mr. Cooney's repetitive motion practice, he has been forced to bring his wife and child back with him. They could not be left alone."

Judge McNulty looked sternly at Cooney. "Did you inform opposing counsel that Riley Taggart would be temporarily unavailable and that you would be seeking a continuance, Mr. Cooney? Did you do that before you forced Liam Taggart to travel from Chicago with his wife and child?"

"Uh, no, Your Honor, I did not. I was unaware of Riley's unavailability until I appeared in court this morning. I hope and pray that nothing untoward has befallen my client."

Judge McNulty shook her head. "I'm not going to continue this hearing, Mr. Cooney. You're either going to proceed, right here and now, with or without Riley Taggart, or I will deny your motion, assess costs against you, including Mr. Taggart's travel expenses, and I will not entertain these issues again without a showing of good cause. That means *solid* evidence, Mr. Cooney, not the kind of speculative claptrap I've heard from you before. Am I making myself clear to you, Mr. Cooney?"

He cleared his throat. "Yes, of course, quite sorry, Your Honor, very clear. We will proceed. The petitioner will now call Conor Taggart to the stand in support of the petition." He looked over at Conor and nodded, but Conor remained in his seat and shook his head. "Get up, Conor," Cooney said under his breath, "get up and take the witness stand."

Conor shook his head again. "Nope. You don't want me to testify. I'm not going to lie and say that the property is deteriorating. It's not true."

Cooney talked through clenched teeth. "For heaven's sake Conor, she's going to assess costs against me. Get up."

Conor just smiled. "I will, but I'm going to tell the truth and testify against the petition."

"Mr. Cooney?" Judge McNulty said. "Are you going to present a witness?"

"Uh no, I'm afraid I must renew my motion for a continuance."

"Then your petition is denied. Court will assess costs. Mr. Taggart, please prepare a list of your expenses. Good day everyone." The judge stood, whirled around and quickly left the courtroom.

Conor looked at me and shrugged. "I'm not going to lie," he said.

A world of surprises. I was as confused as the judge. Riley's absence and failure to support his petition seemed to confirm previous fears. Was Farrell right? Was Riley complicit in the violence, the murders and arson? Or had he gone into hiding fearing arrest by the government for financial crimes? Or, heaven forbid, was he himself a victim? I thanked O'Neill for his service and left the building. It was time to get back to Fortress Deirdre.

ONE THING I WAS sure to find when I walked in the door—a plate of tasty food. Living at Deirdre's was going to do a number on my waistline. Deirdre was feeding the baby and Catherine was stirring something on the stove. Old Wicklow was lying under the table hoping someone would drop a morsel in his direction. The five-second rule didn't apply in Fortress Deirdre. Old Wicklow was a two-second dog.

"I made you a plate of bangers and mash," Catherine said, smiling proudly. "Irish pork sausage, mashed potatoes and onion gravy. Isn't that cool? I've been schooled by the best."

"You're turning into the perfect Irish homemaker," I said. "You're not going to want to go back to Chicago."

"It's tempting. How did it go in court?"

"Petition denied. Riley didn't show and Conor refused to lie for Cooney. As far as Judge McNulty is concerned it's a dead issue."

"Conor wouldn't testify? I thought Conor was the moving force behind the petitions to remove you."

"Well, he was definitely behind the first petition and probably the second petition as well. There's no doubt he was furious when I was appointed trustee. He called me names and threatened me. He challenged the legitimacy of the trust and even his father's sanity. But he told me that the most recent petition was Riley's idea. He said Riley is frantic over the stock."

"But Riley didn't show. Did his lawyer have any explanation?"

"Cooney hadn't heard from him. He was totally embarrassed. He suggested that maybe Riley was ill, or worse. After all, his wife filed a missing person's report."

"Oh, I hate to think . . ."

"I know. We all hate to think that. The anxiety level is high enough."

Catherine nodded. "True, but Deirdre is holding up pretty well. She's planning a big dinner. She plays with the baby. Her spirits are lifting, and she's not as depressed today."

A FEW HOURS LATER, the doorbell rang and my nerves reminded me that, it being Friday afternoon, it was time to introduce Catherine to Annie. And vice versa. I had told Catherine about the appointment right after the phone call. I was anxious, even though it was Catherine who'd suggested that I talk with Annie. As much as I intended to conduct the meeting in a very businesslike manner, introducing my wife to my former almost-wife was a business I was unfamiliar with. Other than saying hello at the graveyard and Wednesday's brief phone call, I hadn't spoken to Annie in sixteen years.

It was a warm afternoon and Annie was in a light blue shift. Her sun-bleached auburn hair was pulled back in a loose knot. Rebellious blond wisps escaped her barrette and fell gently on the sides of her face. Her smile, her soft dimples and her green eyes, at once reminded me of bewitching times and for the briefest of moments, pulled me back to 1999 as though she was coming over for Sunday dinner. She leaned forward and gave me a hello kiss on the cheek.

I brought her to the kitchen where Catherine and Deirdre were sitting. Deirdre greeted Annie with a hug and a kiss. Old friends.

"Cat," I said nervously, "this is Annie Grossman. Annie, this is my wife, Catherine." My two women appeared totally at ease and exchanged handshakes, warm smiles and casual banter about travel and the weather.

I told myself it shouldn't be so difficult but it was patently uncomfortable for me. I was standing between the two episodes of my life. It was a clash of epochs. Annie was a former life. Catherine was my present life. For the last several years, I had been able to neatly compartmentalize those eras, but now my two lives were colliding and it made me feel damn uneasy. Somehow, I think that each of them was amused by my discomfort. These two graceful women had one thing in common and it was standing in the room between the two of them feeling as clumsy as could be. I quickly suggested that Annie and I withdraw to the living room to talk.

We sat opposite each other at the coffee table. I offered her a cup of tea or something stronger, which she declined. Finally, it was she who bridged the chasm. "I'm happy for you, Liam," she said. "Catherine's a lovely woman and Deirdre tells me that your son is adorable. I'm so pleased that you found all this happiness in your life."

I felt like saying, "You didn't give two shits about my happiness sixteen years ago," but I didn't. Truth be told, I felt apologetic. I had everything that she and I were planning sixteen years ago and I sensed that she had none of it. It's not that I felt guilty; after all, it was she who made those choices. It wasn't me who ran out at the last minute. But as she said, I had a lovely wife and an adorable son, and she seemed unhappy. I felt sorry for her.

"Thanks," I said. "Ben's sleeping right now, otherwise I'd introduce you. What's going on in your life?"

"As I told you, I'm still teaching. I have a cozy little house in east Belfast where I've lived for the last six years. My health is good. I can't complain. I suppose you want to know about my social status?"

I shook my head. "It's none of my business."

She smiled. "I'm not married and I'm not engaged. I've had my share of relationships, off and on, but not with a man that I could spend the rest of my life with." She smiled at me: a soft, sad smile.

"The vow to your father? Not to go outside the community?"

She shrugged. "That and . . . we set the bar pretty high, you and I. I wouldn't be content to settle for something less."

Oh God! She's going to blame me for setting the bar too high? Enough of this intimacy, I thought. It's getting way too personal. "Annie, I want to ask you about your conversations with my uncle. Maybe we can come across a sentence here or there that would give us a clue to solving these murders."

"I spent many an hour with Uncle Fergus. I loved him deeply, but I don't know how much help I can be."

"Did you notice, during the last few months, that he was acting nervously or anxiously?"

"Yes, I did. He asked me not to tell Deirdre, but he was sure that a person, or a maybe a group of people, were posing a threat. Whether it was to him or to the family, he wasn't clear. He tried to recall events over the past several years, allowing for the possibility that there was an altercation or an argument left unanswered from years ago. You know, dormant for years but not forgotten? That seemed to make the most sense to him. And there were certainly plenty of suspects to choose from, according to Uncle Fergus."

"What made him feel threatened?"

"He wouldn't say. He spent time on the computer—well, let me correct that—*I* spent time on the computer with him sitting next to me, researching companies, researching people, tracing events, and looking into newspaper accounts of the arrests and convictions of people on both sides of the conflict. He seemed to narrow his search down to half a dozen scenarios."

"Did he actually receive any threats?"

Annie nodded. "I think so."

"Written threats?"

"I don't know. He was never specific about the threats. Maybe the threats themselves were not specific. I'm sorry, I don't know."

"Annie, when he talked about persons or groups of people, did he mention the name Walker to you?"

"Oh yes. Many times. Archie Walker."

"He was killed forty years ago. Did he mention any other Walker to you? A brother perhaps?"

"Not that I recall."

"Thomas Walker?"

She shook her head. "I don't think so. He asked me to get copies of newspaper articles on two men: Seamus McManus and somebody named Lefferty."

"Sean Lefferty?"

"That's right."

I showed her the newspaper clippings from Fergus's folder. "Are these the articles you got for him?"

She nodded.

"Lefferty and McManus, were they two of the people he feared?"

She nodded. "In a way. Both Lefferty and McManus were dead, but they were prominent in his analysis. What troubled him the most was his suspicion that there was a connection between one of them and someone he knew. That was one of his theories."

"Who, Annie?"

"He didn't share that with me."

"Think about it, Annie, did he ever bring up a family member in a bad light, a suspicious light? Did he ever express distrust or unhappiness with any of his brothers, his nephews or his children?"

Annie pinched her lips and wrinkled her forehead, as I'd seen her do so frequently years ago. She sat in thought for a moment, then shook her head. "Some of the time he'd express his exasperation over this one or that, but you should know that the times I spent with Fergus were mostly pleasant times, full of laughter and warmth. Sunday night dinners were special occasions. Afterward we would often sit on the porch. Fergus and I shared a bond and he would open his heart to me on many occasions, especially where you were concerned. He'd reveal deeply personal thoughts and I was honored that he trusted me so well. But I don't want to sound like I was his priest. Almost all of what he had to say was positive."

"He talked to you about me?"

She nodded with a little raise of her eyebrows. "He loved you very much and would usually say things like, 'Do you think I should I give the little rascal a call?' Of course, I would urge him to do so right away. He'd nod and then shake his head. 'What would I say? How could I undo the words we exchanged?' I would tell him, 'You don't need to backtrack. Talk about the weather. Tell him there's a new pub in town. Tell him he should come for Sunday dinner.'"

"I would have come," I said, with a lump in my throat. "In a minute."

"He would always say he was going to make the call, but the first step is the hardest, right? Such a stubborn old goat. So, in the end he didn't call and it's a shame."

"Yeah, he didn't call and neither did I and it's something I'll have to live with. We could have talked through the whole thing. Maybe he had forgiven me."

"Oh, Liam, don't doubt that for a second. He had, and in many ways he blamed himself for sending you away. I remember one time, not so many months ago, we were sitting on the porch, Fergus, Janie and I. Somehow the conversation got around to you, like it always did. We talked about the falling-out, the last time you were at the house. And you know what he said? He said you were *right* to do what you did, and he was going to tell you so himself. He said McManus was trash and the names McManus gave you allowed the police to take a bunch of killers off the street. He was proud that you turned in all those IRA street thugs. He was going to call you and tell you that himself. You can ask Janie."

"That's really good to know, Annie. Thank you for that. But what about other people, other times he might have shared feelings of distrust or disappointment? Something that he may have said where he thought there was a connection between the threats and a member of the family?"

"There were times when your uncle Fergus could be irascible. Some would say downright disagreeable. And he would grumble, but mostly it would be about insignificant incidents. In the last few months, his complaints were more focused. His suspicions had heightened He had become wary of someone close to him. You ask me who? He never said. Though I hate to even mention it, I suppose Conor and Riley would both fit into that category. Goodness knows, Riley and Fergus got into it a lot during the past several months."

"The Global stock?"

"Oh, for sure the Global stock, but it wasn't just the stock. I think Fergus was more disappointed in what Riley was doing at Global. There were rumors. Riley is an investment consultant, you know, and I think Fergus believed he was crossing over the line."

"The line being unlawful?"

She nodded. "That and unethical. You know your uncle Fergus."

"What was Riley doing that Fergus thought was unethical?"

She shook her head. "I'm sorry. I don't know. I just saw them arguing a lot."

"Anyone else, Annie? Anyone else close to him that comes to mind?"

"Well, he sure didn't like Charles."

I smiled. "Me either."

She smiled back. "Me either. And the feeling is mutual. Charles hates me."

"Why?"

"I told you, I'm good friends with Janie. They have a stormy relationship. I told her to leave him several times. Many an evening she'd spend on my couch rather than go home to him. Charles knows I counseled her to break up with him. He's told me to mind my own business on more than one occasion. He calls me a meddlesome bitch."

I nodded. "I saw her with a black eye."

"Charles is an emotional and physical abuser. I think if Uncle Fergus had caught him red-handed, he would have walloped him right then and there. But all we ever saw was the aftermath and Janie always offered some lame excuse. I've tried to talk to her over and over, but it's no use. Recently, Janie had been coming to Sunday dinners alone. Fergus said he didn't want Charles coming over."

"What else did Fergus say about Charles?"

"He thought he was sneaky. He didn't like the way he flaunted his money or his status. Fergus could never understand how a boy from the Belfast neighborhoods could amass so much money in the linen business, such a small, boutique industry. But mostly it was the rude way he treated Janie."

I took the picture of the guns and laid it on the table. "Annie, have you seen this picture before?"

She shook her head. "It's a crate of automatic weapons."

"Is there any reason you know of that Uncle Fergus would have saved this picture?"

"No, I didn't know he had it. He never discussed weapons in my presence."

"One more thing, Annie. Do you know anything about a person named Bridget McGregor?"

"Why do you want to know that?"

"I can't tell you. It's confidential. Does Bridget McGregor mean anything to you?"

"Yes, it does."

"Who is she, Annie?"

"Bridget McGregor was an intensely private matter to your uncle. I'm afraid that's all I can tell you."

"All you can tell me or all you want to tell me? It's important, Annie. It has something to do with the trust."

"I'm sorry, Liam. I must respect your uncle's wishes."

"Is that another one of your *vows*, Annie?"

"Please don't."

I was sorry I'd said that, it just slipped out. I guess I wasn't as over my resentment as I thought. It was time to bring the conversation to a close. "Annie, if you think of anything else, you have my number. Please call me."

She started to get up but then reached over and gripped my arm. There were tears in her eyes and I could see tension in her face. "Liam, you have no idea how hard it was for me to come over here today. It took everything I had. For sixteen years I've thought about what I would say to you if we ever met again. And now all I can say is I'm sorry. I'm sorry for the hurt. I'm sorry for what I did to you. I'm sorry for what I did to us. There isn't a day that's gone by for the last sixteen years that I haven't been sorry. It was the sorriest thing I ever did in my life, and as bad as I felt over losing you, I felt twice as bad knowing I had hurt you and that I made you hate me." She buried her face in her hands. "I loved you so much and I made you hate me."

I closed my eyes. I didn't want to open that door. That door was locked. "I don't hate you, Annie."

"I should have been stronger. I should have stood up to him. I'm so sorry, Liam."

"Listen to me, Annie. I forgive you. I forgave you a long time ago."

Her tears were flowing. "Thanks for that, but I know you hated me for what I did; anyone would have."

"It was hard for a while, I won't lie. But I got over it and I moved on and I don't think of you in a bad way."

"That's sweet. I wish I thought it was true."

"It's true, Annie."

Now both of us were choked up. She brushed away her tears and said, "Right up to the last minute I thought I would be able to gather up the courage, change my mind and run to the airport to join you."

I smiled. "I was standing there. I was waiting at the gate."

"I knew you would be."

"It was another life, Annie. It was a long, long time ago."

"It was. But that wonderful year, it was a magical year. Please tell me that I'm not the only one who remembers those days."

I nodded. "I remember them too, Annie. The same as you."

She sniffed. "I better go. It's been good seeing you, Liam, and I'm so happy for your successes. Really, I am. Can I say good-bye to your wife?"

We returned to the kitchen where Annie said good-bye to Catherine and Deirdre and left. I watched her walk away,.

"She's crying," Deirdre said. "I knew this session would be difficult for her. She's carried that guilt for many years."

"I forgave her, Aunt Deirdre. Really, I forgave her a long time ago. I told her I don't hold any hard feelings."

"It's not your clemency she lacks. She seeks forgiveness from the one person who won't give it to her. Herself."

IT WAS LATE AFTERNOON and I was bouncing Ben on my knee when my cell phone rang. The caller ID read "Unknown."

The voice was harsh and trembling. "Liam, it's Riley. I need to see you. Immediately."

I signaled to Catherine and mouthed Riley.

"Okay. Where are you?" I said.

"My life's on the line. They're trying to kill me. I had to leave my house and my family."

"Okay, let me bring you in. Inspector McLaughlin will give you protection."

"Oh no. Not a chance. I'm not going to give myself up. But I need to talk to you in private. Just you and me, Liam."

"Where are you, Riley?"

"Will you be coming, yes or no?"

"Yes, I'll come. Where?"

"Alone, Liam. I can't trust anyone. You have to come alone."

"Okay, I agree. Where?"

"I don't want to say over the phone. People could be listening. You remember where we had lunch? The restaurant? Just get in your car and start driving in that direction and I'll text you. No funny stuff, Liam, I'll be watching." The phone went silent.

"You're not going, are you?" Catherine said. "That's crazy. Riley's our prime suspect. It's an obvious trap."

"I'm going."

"Why?"

"Because I have to find out who is responsible for all this. I have to put an end to it. If it's Riley, I'm going to bring him in."

"It could be someone else, someone with a gun to Riley's head."

"Yes it could, but this is a break in the case. Cat, we agreed I would come back here to stop the murders, to flush out the killer and protect the family. Yourself included. That's why we came. Well, this is a chance. If nothing else, I'm sure I'll learn something."

Catherine was angry. She had her hands on her hips. "Yeah, you'll learn something but you won't live to tell anyone. He's the number one suspect, the one responsible for the fire."

"I know that, sweetheart. I'll be careful."

"You're not going. And if you do, you're taking McLaughlin with you."

"I can't. Riley said to come alone."

"So, why does he get to call the shots? Maybe he just wants to get you out of the house. Did you think of that? Maybe he plans on coming over here when you're gone and you won't be here to protect us."

She had a point. There was a PSNI officer on the front porch, but he was solo and he was becoming complacent. Maybe we needed to beef up security.

I called McLaughlin, filled him in on the phone call. "He wants to meet with me alone, right now. His voice was tense and he spoke in short bursts. He sounded out of control. I'm going to go."

"His voice was tense?"

"Frantic. He definitely did not sound like someone who was coldly planning serial murders. I got the feeling that someone else is involved."

"He could be out there. I'll go with you."

"No. He insisted I come alone. He wouldn't even give me the address. He's going to text it to me when I'm on the way."

"Are you sure you want to do this? Your wife is right; it smells like a trap. When you get the address, text it to me and we'll catch up to you."

"I don't think he's the killer, but I think he has information and I'm the best one to get it. You have to give me a little time alone with him. Riley and I were as close as brothers when we were young. I can't believe he would try to harm me. If I'm wrong, I'll have my gun and I can take care of myself. But just in case this is a ploy to get me away from the house, I need you to increase security here. With Robert living here now, it's a bigger target than ever. I think we should post a second patrolman. Maybe the peaceful rural setting is lulling your patrolman into a sense of complacency. I've noticed that he's not even wearing his body armor. Remember, there is a sniper out there somewhere."

"I'll send an extra man and make sure they know to wear their armor. Be careful with Riley; he could be our man. Let me know where the meet is when you get the text. I'll see you later."

H ARBOR HOUSE WAS THE restaurant Riley was referring to, and it was on the western shores of Lough Neagh, twenty miles away, just south of the town of Ballyronan. As I drove around the north end of the lake, I tried to get my mind around the possibility that Riley was the killer. Could the Riley I know be the one who killed his father, killed his uncle, tried to kill my wife and child, firebombed my house and hired a sniper to take out Uncle Robert? Try as I might, that just didn't fit into my brain. I couldn't accept the proposition that quiet, gentle Riley was the mastermind of all this viciousness.

I had almost reached the restaurant when his text came in. "Shore Rd. 6 Km past Ballyronan. Take dirt road left toward the water. Wooden boathouse at end of road. Alone. I'm watching."

A broken rail fence lay on the side of the entrance to the dirt road. Lumps of clay and stones. My Audi wasn't going to like it. The road wound through thick woods toward Lough Neagh, past an abandoned shack and ended at the water's edge. "Boathouse" was a generous description of the broken-down hut, which appeared to be in a terminal stage of neglect. Several of the gray siding boards had rotted away. Windows were fogged or broken. Spiders had spun their webs all over the structure. Frogs were croaking in the marsh. It was creepy.

When I parked the car and looked around, it didn't seem like anyone was there. Riley's car wasn't in the drive. I didn't see any footprints or tire tracks. I called out, "Riley," but there was no answer. I decided to enter the darkened, wooden hut. Boathouse, indeed. It was ten by twenty, maybe enough room for a small rowboat. I didn't see Riley. I took a seat on a stool and checked my phone to see if there were any further texts. There weren't.

As the seconds ticked, a variety of scenarios played out in my mind. Maybe Catherine was right, maybe this *was* a ploy to get me out of the house. Maybe something had happened to Riley. Or maybe Riley was the bait and someone else was coming. If so, who was pulling his strings? In any event, I wasn't going to stay any longer. I started to leave when I heard Riley say, "Sit down, Liam."

I turned around and there he was, standing in the darkened corner with a double-barreled shotgun pointed at my head. Shame on me for not seeing him.

"Sorry to keep you waiting, Liam, but I had to make sure you were alone and you weren't followed."

"Okay, I wasn't followed. Now put down the rifle."

"I don't think so."

"Why did you bring a shotgun to this meeting, Riley?"

"Because civil conversation doesn't work with you. And I don't want to die. Take your gun out and put it on the floor."

That was a foolish request by a man with no combat or law enforcement experience. He was letting me put my hands on my gun. I could have easily shot him, but I didn't want to kill him or hurt him, I just wanted to get to the bottom of the murders. I did what he asked and he kicked the gun to the side.

"Now put your cell phone on the floor."

I laid my phone at his feet, hoping he would turn the wrong way or bend down and give me an opening to swat his rifle. "All right, I'm here. What's this all about?"

He stomped his heel on phone, cracking it open. "Someone's after me and it's a damn good guess that it's my boss, Ross Penters. He's in a rage, out of control, and you know why, don't you? It's because I haven't been able to get ownership of *my* stock certificate. Can you blame him? He needs the stock to save his ass and I can't give it to him. First my father blocks me, and now it's you. Why the hell did you come back for my father's funeral? Why couldn't you have just sent a damn condolence card, Liam? We hadn't heard from you in sixteen years. Why now? Why couldn't you have stayed in America where you belong? Why did you have to stick your meddling ass in the middle of things? Why?"

Riley was raising his voice, he was twitching and getting more frenetic by the minute. His speech was racing. The veins in his neck were bulging. He was sweating profusely. I was pretty sure he was speeding.

"After you learned that my father appointed you as trustee," he said, "why didn't you just turn it down? You could have said, 'I live in America, I can't do this,' and no one would have blamed you. Why the fuck didn't you just go home? Goodness knows, I tried to get you to go home. Why couldn't you take a hint?"

"It was you?"

"Yeah, Liam, it was *me*. Surprise, surprise. I needed you to get the hell out of Antrim. But no, you stayed, screwed things up and now my boss is all over me."

"Your boss is after you?"

He laughed loudly. "After me? Oh yeah, and he's no lightweight. He's powerful enough to cut down anyone in his way. He's got the money to hire people to get things done, like the sniper who shot my uncle, like the guy who plowed into Uncle Eamon."

"He did that?"

"Of course he did."

"Who shot your father?"

"Shut up, Liam. This is my show. I'll tell you what I want you to know and when I want you to talk." He stepped forward into the light, a little closer now, and I could see he was a wreck. He had a four-day stubble and he clearly hadn't bathed. What was once a well-tailored gray wool suit and white shirt was now torn and filthy.

"Riley, have you been taking anything? Any pills?"

"Shut up, I said! None of your business. Because of you, Penters is my problem, not a few Adderalls. I need them to stay sharp, I have to keep my edge. Penters is after *me* now. Me, the good soldier, who always did what he was told. I was sure there was a tail on me when I left the office four days ago. I got into my car and there they were, right behind me. I'd turn left, they'd turn left. I'd speed up, they'd speed up. I couldn't drive home and put my family in the crosshairs, so I gave 'em the slip. I'm pretty crafty. A damn lot craftier than you think I am, Conor."

"I'm Liam."

"I know who you are," he screamed. "Shut up! I managed to lose them near Castle Court and I made my way out here. No one will find me out here." He waved his arm around. "My father's fishing hole was right off this shore. Remember? Don't you recognize this place?"

I shook my head. "So you shook the tail and ended up out here?"

"Right. I've been sleeping on the goddam floor, Liam. The floor! I went into Ballyronan for supplies, but I can't go back. Not looking like this."

"You want me to get you supplies?"

"No, Liam, you're here for a reason."

"Why would your boss want to kill you?"

"The goddam stock, Liam. Aren't you listening? Without the stock, we're all going to jail. Why do you think everyone's getting killed? It's for the stock. Why couldn't you have just handed over the stock to me at lunch, or gone home and let someone else be trustee? Conor would have given me the stock. Why did you have to stay? Didn't I make it plain enough that you weren't wanted here?"

"Did you hire the guy to firebomb my house, Riley?"

"What?"

"Did you hire the guy to set the fire to my house and kill my family?"

"Jesus, Liam. I wouldn't do that. How can you think that was me?"

"You said it was you."

"No, I said I tried to get you to leave Antrim. I slashed your tires, I wrote a note and I rifled your hotel room. I made a few phone calls to your wife. Jesus Christ, anybody else would have taken the hint and gone home. They'd have been scared for their wife. But not Liam. No, not Liam. Why the hell didn't you go home?" he screamed and kicked at the dirt floor. He was unhinged. "I wouldn't have stayed. Not when someone started phoning my wife. But I didn't kill any-body or set any fires. That was all Penters. Don't you see? He'd do anything. He'll stop at nothing to get that stock. And now he's after me!"

"What about the pictures? Walker's house and his wake? Were you the one who delivered all those calling cards?"

"No, Liam, how would I get those? It was Penters. Had to be. He even put one in my mailbox to scare the shit out of me."

His nerves were firing out of control and while I didn't think he would shoot me, he was manic enough to tense up and squeeze the trigger. If he made the slightest move with that rifle, I'd have to lunge at him. I hoped he wasn't a good shot. He didn't look comfortable with a rifle. I made the distance to be about eight feet.

"Riley, why would Penters want to kill you? Think about it. With you dead, he'd never get the stock. It would go to the remaining beneficiaries."

"Revenge, Liam. He's a vicious man. He blames me for screwing up the whole company. He blames me for making bad investments, which was never my fault. How was I supposed to know what the short-term market would do? Am I a fucking prophet? I'm a long-term investor." Sweat was pouring off his forehead. He was speeding, he was out of his element and I was waiting for my chance. However, even with all this going on, I felt bad for the guy. This was Riley, my cousin, my childhood playmate. There had to be some way I could talk him down.

"Riley, let me help you. Let me take you in to Inspector McLaughlin. We'll get your family protected and then we'll go after Penters. You haven't really done anything wrong. McLaughlin will help you. We'll all help you. What do you say? We'll do it together."

"It's too late for that. Penters is a madman. The only way out is to give him the stock. Penters is ruthless. You can't imagine what pressure I've been living under."

I looked at the barrel. Close, but not yet. "Getting the stock won't prevent the government from prosecuting the case. The stock means nothing. You need help and we can do this together. Hand in hand, Riley, just like the old days."

Riley was screaming so much he was getting hoarse. "You think you're so smart? You know nothing! If Penters gets the stock, he'll refinance the company. It'll buy us some time. That's all we need. Just some time. Ross thinks we can use the stock to nail enough financing to get us all out of Northern Ireland. My family and I will be safe, resettled somewhere far away. But you're stopping us from doing that, aren't you?"

"You're wrong, Riley. It won't work. No bank is going to loan money to a company that's running from the regulators."

"You don't know anything!" he screamed. "Global's got hard assets. Hard assets, you know: realty, inventory, equipment. You can borrow against hard assets, and after we get the money, who cares? The bank forecloses and gets the assets, we have the money and we're out of here. Works out for everyone. Everyone's happy. But only if you give me the stock."

Then he got quiet. "Help me out here, Liam, and everyone will be okay. I'll reach Ross and tell him I've got the stock and all the killings will stop. Everything will be fine. Your family will be safe. You'll never hear from me again. Go back home and enjoy your life."

He took a folded piece of paper and a pen out of his pocket. "Sign it, Liam, and then I'll let you go."

"Riley, please."

"Sign it!" he screamed.

"Okay. Okay. Give it to me."

He stepped forward to hand me the paper. It was my opening. I knocked the barrel to the side and leveled Riley with a left cross. His head hit the wooden floor and he was out cold. I sat him in the chair and tied his hands.

"You're an asshole, Liam!" he said when he opened his eyes. "You've ruined everyone's life including your own!" He started crying. "Conor's right, you're a rat. You'll always be a rat. And here you are, turning on your family again."

I stood there looking at him and shaking my head.

"What are you going to do now?" he said. "Are you going to kill me? You should. You really should. Put me out of my misery. My life's not worth a damn anymore."

"No, I'm not going to kill you, Riley. Believe it or not, I still think of you as a brother. We're going to wait until McLaughlin gets here and then you're going to help us catch Penters."

He went into a frenzied laugh. "Wait for McLaughlin? That's funny. We'll be waiting a long time. I smashed your phone, Liam." Then he heard the car door slam. "What?"

I shook my head. He was pitiful. He looked like he could just slump down and melt into the floorboards. McLaughlin came in and I handed the shotgun to him. "Riley wants to chat with us about his boss, Ross Penters. He thinks Penters may be the one we're looking for." Riley's head was lowered. He was sobbing. "And then he needs a room for the night."

"Ross Penters?" McLaughlin said. "Get in line, everyone's looking for him." He pulled back the bolt on the shotgun. "There are no cartridges, Liam. The rifle's not loaded."

"I wasn't going to shoot you, Liam," Riley said quietly. "I just needed you to sign the transfer. Without the stock, there'll be more killings. You have to stop Penters."

I looked at the shotgun and shook my head. All that over an unloaded gun. But it made me feel better. As crazy as he seemed, as far as he was out over the edge, Riley never intended to do me any harm.

"The Office of Financial Regulation has had a subpoena outstanding for the last month and they haven't caught Penters," McLaughlin said. "No one knows where he is. OFR thinks he's left the country."

"Riley thinks he can reach him," I said. "We have something Penters wants: Fergus's stock certificate. Riley tells me that Penters wants to use the stock to secure a loan to Global, and as you might imagine, it's unlikely that his motives are pure. I think there was a plan for these guys to skip out on the loan and plant themselves somewhere far, far away. Right, Riley?"

He nodded.

"Riley also told me that he wants to do everything he can to help us catch Penters and stop the violence, right, Riley?"

He nodded again.

"Mr. Taggart," McLaughlin said to Riley, "you're lucky. I advised Liam not to come out here, that it was too dangerous, but he was confident in your relationship. And after holding a gun on him, he still wants to help you. This may be your only chance to do yourself some good. Help us bring in Penters. I'll give you a nice clean room while you think about it. You look like you could use one."

Riley looked at me with the eyes of wayward child. "Would you really help me, Liam? After all I've done? Did you mean it? Can you see me through this?"

"I did mean it and I'll do everything I can."

. . .

WHEN I RETURNED TO Fortress Deirdre, I saw two officers—one in a patrol car at the end of the driveway and one on the front porch—nicely dressed in body armor. Catherine was relieved to see me and threw her arms around me. "Thank God. Is everything in one piece?"

"Everything but my phone. Riley's now McLaughlin's houseguest. We're going to question him first thing tomorrow morning."

"It was dangerous though, wasn't it? I was right, wasn't I?"

I nodded. "You're always right. Poor Riley is a mess. He's been hiding out for four days in a dilapidated fishing shack, high on amphetamines. He's also in the middle of a nervous breakdown. He had an empty shotgun pointed at me for an hour." I shook my head. "It's really quite sad. He's in way over his head and now he's totally lost. I feel bad for him. He says his boss is the one behind all the killings."

"Why?"

Again I shook my head. I think I'd been shaking my head more in Northern Ireland over the past two months than I had in my entire life in America. It was that kind of place. "Riley insists that all the violence has been over the stock certificate. Maybe Penters has a contact inside the bank who will actually loan him money on the stock, I don't know. McLaughlin wants to use the stock as bait to grab Penters."

"Do you think Riley's right? Is it Penters?"

"It fits. Everything falls into place. According to Riley, he's ruthless. He has the money to finance the crimes. He has a strong motive. If he can't get the stock transferred over, he intends to kill off the beneficiaries one by one until Riley's the only one left. It all makes sense."

Catherine looked like she wasn't convinced. "There's some pieces in this puzzle that don't fit," she said. "In order for Riley to inherit the stock, he would have to be the last man standing. How would Riley and Penters accomplish that?"

"They're picking them off one at a time. First Fergus, then Eamon, then an attempt is made on Deirdre, then Robert. Don't you see that progression?"

"And Janie and Conor, they're going to kill them as well?"

"Both of them said they didn't care if Riley got the stock. Maybe their deaths aren't necessary."

"What about the McGregor Trust?"

"I don't know. I don't know how they were going to deal with that. I don't know who Bridget McGregor is or was. It could just be a foundation, a charity."

"Why would Penters hire someone to firebomb our house? How does that advance their cause?"

"It gets me out of Northern Ireland. Riley sees me as the stumbling block. If Conor became the trustee, he would gladly hand over the stock. Riley admitted to me that he was the one who ransacked my hotel room and slashed my tires. He even said he made the prank phone calls to you. It was all in an effort to get me out of Antrim. But he denies responsibility for the firebomb. He says that was Penters."

Catherine scrunched up her face, a clear sign she didn't accept my explanations. "Annie said that she and Fergus sat at the computer and researched names from the Troubles. Fergus had her clip two newspaper articles, one on Seamus McManus and one on Sean Lefferty. Why would Fergus do that? There must be something about those two people. Shouldn't we know more about them before we decide it's Penters?"

"What more do you need to know? McLaughlin has searched for a McManus or a Lefferty and come up empty. They don't exist. Penters is a big break in the case. Why don't you see that?"

"I have to tell you, Liam, I've had experience with white-collar criminals. They may be heartless thieves, they may defraud their best friends and steal their grandmother's pension money, but they're not the kind that firebomb houses or hire snipers. And the ones I know, the financial criminals I've met, do not have the detached coldness to stand in front of a living, breathing person and fire a bullet into his heart. That's a whole different mentality. Look at Riley; just as desperate as it gets and he doesn't have any bullets in his gun. At this time I'm not buying into the financial guy."

I love Catherine. No one thinks like she does. She has visceral logic. If something feels wrong to her, it usually is and she finds out why. I'm going to tell McLaughlin we need to keep the door open and follow up on McManus and Lefferty.

THIRTY-TWO

• • •

WHEN I WALKED INTO PSNI headquarters Saturday morning, McLaughlin was waiting for me in his office. "Riley's in the interrogation room. He's scared. I don't know where he got the courage to confront you with a shotgun."

"In a pill."

"Well, right now he's shaking like a leaf." We walked down the hall and looked through the one-way mirror. Riley was fidgeting and tapping his foot.

"So, you think he can lure Ross Penters into the open with the stock certificate?" McLaughlin said.

"Riley thinks it's in play. He believes there's still a plan to pledge the stock."

McLaughlin smiled. "Let's see what we can do. Let me go in first. I want to make sure he knows what he's up against."

I watched from behind the glass as McLaughlin entered the room. Riley turned his head. He was obviously full of shame and unable to make eye contact. "I don't have to talk to you, Inspector. I know my rights. I have the right to immediate access to counsel. I want to talk to a solicitor."

"I think you should, Riley," McLaughlin said. "You'll need a good attorney for all the charges against you. But you can hire the Lord High Commissioner and you're still going to serve a life sentence. Kidnapping, assault with a deadly weapon, intimidation, coercion, and those are just the crimes you committed against Liam in one afternoon. Add to that conspiracy to murder, arson, attempted murder, murder for hire, and well, you understand, things aren't looking too good."

"I didn't do any of that, except hold an empty shotgun on Liam. I want to talk to Cooney."

"I don't blame you. He's done a great job for you so far. How's that working out for you in Judge McNulty's courtroom?"

"I'm not talking."

"How about listening? I don't believe the statute says anything about having an attorney present before any conducting any *listening*. Here's the deal. Even for a man in as much trouble as you, opportunity knocks and a door can open, but only for a very short time. If I were sitting in your chair, chained to the table, peeing in my trousers, I would want to hear about that opportunity."

That was enough time for me, standing behind the glass. McLaughlin had suitably scared him and I thought I could talk him into helping us. "Listen to him, Riley," I said as I entered the room. "There's a good chance the court would look favorably on a person who cooperated. Farrell, don't judges in Northern Ireland have discretion to lower sentences if an accused person shows remorse and cooperates with the police?"

"They do indeed. Happens all the time. If Riley were to help bring in a fugitive like Penters, I would expect there to be a significant difference in the number of years he was separated from his wife and children."

"You asked me to help you, Riley," I said. "Well, the best help I can give you is to tell you to cooperate. Farrell, if he cooperates, I'm not going to press charges against him for the nonsense at the fishing shack or the phone calls to my house. The only beef Riley will face is the financial one and if he flips on Penters, can we get him probation?"

"It's up to the prosecutors and courts. I can't make any promises, but if he helps us catch Penters, I'd go along with it. Listen to him, Riley. Your cousin is making you a hell of an offer."

"What do I have to do?" he said softly.

McLaughlin smiled. "Are you in contact with Penters?"

Riley nodded. "We exchange emails and I have his cell phone number. Sometimes he'll pick up, but not always. He always reads his emails."

"Did he know that you were going to meet with Liam?"

"No. Actually, I was surprised when Liam agreed to show up."

"All right, I want you to email Penters. Tell him you got the certificate."

"Then what? He's going to want proof."

"That's not a problem. Liam, don't you have the physical stock certificate?"

"I do."

McLaughlin left the room to get Riley's cell phone and Riley turned to face me. "I don't know how to thank you, Liam, you're a great friend. I wouldn't have done the same. I don't have your strength of character. Never did."

"Don't worry about it. Let's just grab Penters, and then we'll work on getting your life back on track."

He started to tear up again. "It's just like the time when I took Mike Kelly's bike, do you remember that?"

I had to laugh. "I do. You were mad at Kelly because he embarrassed you in front of Maggie Dunn."

Riley nodded. "My father was going to whip my bum, but you stepped in and pleaded for me. You bailed me out, just like now."

I did remember that. Fergus was furious, but he lightened up when I told him what had happened. "Riley, let me ask you a question. Did Uncle Fergus know Ross Penters? Had he ever met him?"

"No. Ross is a very private man."

"Can you describe Mr. Penters for me?"

Riley shrugged. "Nothing special. He's kind of skinny with a full head of white hair that covers his ears. He's very tan because he plays a lot of tennis. He's in pretty good shape for a sixty-year-old man."

"How tall is he?"

"I don't know. A little under two meters. A little taller than Inspector McLaughlin." I did the math: that would make him six-two or -three.

"Can you tell me why your father would let this stranger walk up to him and stick a gun in his chest?"

"No, how would I know? I wasn't there."

McLaughlin brought Riley's cell phone and laid it on the table. "Email Penters and tell him you have the certificate. Nothing more."

McLaughlin looked over Riley's shoulder as he composed the email. He nodded his approval and the message was sent. "Now we wait."

Riley was taken back to his cell and I sat with McLaughlin. I mentioned Catherine's analysis, that she doubted that the killer was a financial criminal. I also told him what Annie had said about Mc-Manus and Lefferty.

He shook his head. "I think chasing Penters is a much better use of our time than looking for someone related to McManus or Lefferty. So far, we haven't come across any relatives of either family in Northern Ireland. There's just that one Lefferty who lives in New Jersey. He has a family, no record with the police and he hasn't been back here in twenty years. I think you are looking at a dead-end. I believe McLaughlin's first theory of relativity has been validated again."

"I hope you're right, and I hope we catch Penters and solve the case, but my wife has uncanny instincts and Penters doesn't feel right to her."

"I prefer to rely on criminals who are sitting in my jail who point their fingers at other criminals who will soon be sitting in my jail more than relying on uncanny instincts, if you'll pardon my obstinacy."

I smiled. "You don't know my Catherine. She's been right in the past."

THIRTY-THREE

...

I ADDED EXTRA DISTANCE to my Sunday morning run in a futile effort to work off the calories I was sure to ingest at Deirdre's special Sunday dinner. There was an Irish mist in the air and my run was pleasant and cooling as I hoofed it toward the village of Templepatrick. I estimated the round trip to be eleven miles and I was gassed and soaking wet when I returned. During my run, one thought kept going through my mind. It was Thomas Walker's description of the man who bought the pictures—tall, taller than McLaughlin, with a white cap and plenty of money.

When I asked Riley to describe Penters, he said he was very tan, thin, tall and had a full head of white hair covering his ears. Wouldn't some of those features stand out to Walker as well? Why wouldn't Walker remember a tan face and a full head of white hair, even if the guy wore a cap? Catherine discounted a white-collar criminal like Penters, and she had great instincts. If not Penters, then who? Conor wasn't that tall, I've never seen him in a cap and as mercurial as he was, I didn't think he was a killer. Charles was tall enough. He could have worn a white golf cap, like the one he gave to me. Was Walker describing a man like Charles? Maybe, but Charles had never done anything to make me think he was a suspect. What possible motive could he have?

Charles didn't need the money. Charles had his own business unrelated to Global. As far as I could tell, Riley and Charles weren't even friendly, let alone business partners or coconspirators. The only connection Charles had to the Taggarts was Janie. He didn't even attend the Sunday dinners. Was he mad because my uncle didn't like him? Annie didn't like him either. Maybe a lot of people don't like him. He's a pompous jerk.

I tried hard to think of reasons why Charles could be a suspect, but I couldn't come up with any. I just had that feeling. Catherine told me to have faith in my instincts and so did my uncle in my dream. I decided to get Charles's picture and show it to Walker. The best place to take a picture would be Deirdre's Sunday dinner. I had to make sure he would be there.

When I returned to the house, I called Janie. I hate that I'm so deceptive, duplicitous and dishonest, but hell, that's my job. "Janie, it's Liam."

"Please don't tell me you have more bad news."

"Oh no, not at all. I was calling to make sure you were coming to dinner tonight."

"Deirdre's Sunday dinner? I wouldn't miss it. I need to see my dad, and besides, I want to meet Catherine and your little baby."

"Terrific. Is Charles coming with you?"

"I doubt it. He never comes to the Sunday dinners. You know, Uncle Fergus never made him feel welcome."

"So I heard, but I want Catherine to meet him. I had such a nice time going to the country club with you two, I told her all about it. She'd love to meet Charles."

"Really? Well, I'll see if I can horse collar him and bring him out."

I FINISHED MY SHOWER and went down to the kitchen for a cup of coffee and a light meal. What is it with the Irish and their breakfasts? Two eggs and a grapefruit would have suited me just fine, but Deirdre laid a plate on the table that had to weigh ten pounds. Sausage, potatoes, pudding, tomatoes, eggs, bacon and black bread. Jam and butter on the side. Large cup of Americano. She stood there proudly and smiled.

"You ran for such a long time, you should eat lots of breakfast," she said, nodding her head.

"That run was to make up for the dinner you're going to serve me tonight, Aunt Deirdre."

She shrugged. "So, then you run tomorrow."

Hard to argue with that logic.

Catherine and I talked about Riley. "I'm proud of you," she said. "I don't know many men who would have been so generous and forgiving. He put us all through hell for an entire afternoon, not to mention the damn phone calls he made to my house."

"The stuff he pulled—the tires, the phone calls—they were nothing but juvenile pranks to get me out of Antrim. I don't think he has a mean bone in his body. He's never been a serious threat to anyone. I still have a lot of affection for him."

Just then, my new cell phone rang and I could tell it was a PSNI number.

"Liam, are you busy?" It was Megan.

"I'm just sitting down to breakfast. Considering what's been placed before me, I may not be able to get up."

"Riley received a response from Ross Penters. Inspector McLaughlin would like to set up an exchange for this afternoon. Can you bring the stock certificate after you finish your breakfast?"

"If I *finish* this breakfast, probably not. If I eat judiciously, I can be there in an hour."

RILEY WAS BROUGHT INTO the interrogation room in his prison greens. He was seated at the table and McLaughlin came in holding Riley's cell phone. "Your boss has replied to your email." McLaughlin held the phone up and read, "'Good work, Riley. There's a hefty bonus in store for you. Meet me at Brian's. Two p.m. Bring the certificate.'" He set the phone down in front of Riley.

Riley shook his head. "Oh, no. No way I'm doing that."

"You're not backing out on us now, are you, Riley? We'll catch up with him eventually, but your window to cooperate will have slammed shut along with any chance at reducing your sentence."

"I'm not trying to back out, but what you're suggesting is suicide. Penters is telling me to go to Brian Lonnigan's house. The place is protected by a fence, a dozen cameras, guard dogs and Lonnigan's bodyguard. The email tells me to bring the certificate to Lonnigan. I don't trust a deal that goes down at Lonnigan's. Penters won't be there, they'll take the certificate and I won't survive the afternoon."

McLaughlin slid the phone across the table. "Reply to Penters. Say, 'I don't want to hand the certificate to anyone but you. I don't trust Brian. I think he'll call the police.'"

"He'll know that's bullshit," Riley said. "Lonnigan is his right-hand man, his CPA."

"The CPA has a bodyguard?" I said.

"He's a security freak."

"What's the name of the CPA's bodyguard?"

"Jenkins. Kurt Jenkins."

"Tell him that you heard Jenkins was cooperating with the regulators," I said. "Tell Penters to meet you in a public place." I looked to McLaughlin for approval and he nodded his head.

McLaughlin added, "Tell him to meet you at three o'clock at the Ulster Museum. First floor, in the back, the Ice Age exhibit."

I wrinkled my forehead. "Ice Age?"

"It's an enclosed area, out of the way, more secure. Besides, it's my favorite," McLaughlin added. "The museum has metal detectors at the entrance, just in case Penters and his friends get any ideas."

Riley nodded and sent the text. We waited a few minutes and the phone buzzed. "See you there at three."

"Jolly good," Farrell said. "Dooley, I'll want you up there on the first floor in plainclothes. Tell Rothschild and Berger I'll need them on the perimeter." Looking at Riley, he said, "We've had your clothes laundered. You need to change and clean up. We'll leave in half an hour."

THE ULSTER MUSEUM HAD changed since I was there in the nineties. It was always a magnificent building sitting alongside Belfast's botanical gardens, but it was closed to the public for three years, totally remodeled and reopened in 2009. The four-story museum was divided into three zones: a nature zone, an art zone and a history zone, with an in-depth exhibit on the Troubles, which one would expect in a Belfast history museum. The Ice Age exhibit was on the first floor, which meant it was one floor up from the ground floor. McLaughlin wanted the arrest to take place in the exhibit and not on the ground floor in case Penters had friends waiting outside or in the lobby coffee shop.

Riley was wired and coached. He was given a script to memorize. McLaughlin hoped that Penters would incriminate himself. Maybe we'd get a confession. Wouldn't that be dandy?

Megan was in jeans and a T-shirt, looking every bit like a student at nearby Queens College. She had a notebook and was seated next to a storyboard on the life of the woolly mammoth. McLaughlin stationed two plainclothesmen outside the building on either side of the entrance. Farrell and I were positioned in a first-floor overlook, surveying the ground floor lobby. Riley was nervously pacing behind us.

Precisely at three o'clock, a tall, thin, white-haired man in slacks and a sweater strolled into the building. He was alone. Riley nodded and whispered, "That's him." McLaughlin alerted his two patrolmen and we took our places in the Ice Age room.

Penters didn't look around. He didn't check with anyone on his cell phone. He didn't seem nervous at all. He just walked up the steps to the first floor and into the Ice Age room as confident as could be. Contrast that with poor Riley who was shifting his weight from foot to foot and his eyes from Megan to me and back again. Sweat was forming on his forehead.

Penters saw Riley standing by Megan. With an air of confidence he walked directly to Riley and shook his hand.

"Great work, buddy. Do you have the certificate?" Penters asked. Riley nodded and handed it to Penters along with an assignment of the stock from the trust. His nerves made the papers shake.

"Did he just hand it over to you?" Penters said quizzically. "I mean you didn't have to do anything illegal to get it, did you?"

Riley shook his head.

Riley cleared his throat and said, "Now that you have the stock, all the violence will stop, right?"

"What violence, Riley?"

"Oh, you know what I'm talking about. The shootings, the arson. Right? No more killings, right? I mean you have the stock now."

Penters shook his head as if to clear the confusion. "Are you drunk or something? I don't know what the hell you're talking about. This stock is going to save our ass. You struck gold here."

"But now you have the stock, no one else has to die, right?"

"Die? What the hell . . ." Penters looked at Riley who was glancing from side to side, a bundle of nerves. He saw Riley's phony smile and the sweat dripping from his forehead, and it all came together for him. "Aw, Jesus. What the hell is going down here?"

Penters made eye contact with Megan who had come to her feet and was positioned directly before him. He grabbed Riley by the collar. "You prick, what are you trying to do here? Are you wearing a wire?" He shoved him back and spun around to leave.

McLaughlin stepped in front of him and Penters lowered his shoulders as he realized there was no escape. "Riley, you bastard. You are such a fool. What did you tell them? Don't you understand that our solicitors are filing a petition to quash that subpoena? We can beat this bullshit regulatory charge."

"Ross Penters, you're under arrest," McLaughlin said. "Put your hands behind your back."

"For what? For ducking an illegal subpoena?"

"No, sir, for murder, arson, attempted murder and conspiracy."

"Are you insane? What has this man told you? Are you all crazy? Murder who? Arson? What the hell are you talking about?"

Farrell nodded to Megan, who walked Penters down the stairs and out the door. He complained bitterly the entire way, which, in my mind, served to support Catherine's doubts that the financial guy was the killer. If he was actually the mastermind, he was a first-rate actor as well. He had come to the museum alone. In fact, he had taken a taxi. And his protestations seemed authentic. I turned to McLaughlin. "It's pretty obvious, Farrell, it's not him. Catherine was right. I told you she has uncanny instincts. How's that theory of relativity holding up?"

"You mean because Penters is so righteously indignant? Wait till I get him to the station. Relativity still stands. To me, it's likely that Fergus thought it was Riley and his cohorts all along."

WHEN WE RETURNED TO PSNI headquarters, and before they could send him back to his cell, Riley asked McLaughlin if he might have a few minutes alone with me.

McLaughlin nodded. "Use the interrogation room. Take all the time you need."

I brought in two of cups of tea and sat across from him at the table.

"I've really made a mess of my life, haven't I?" Riley said sadly. "It's what ambition can do to you. I was handed all the advantages. Supportive family. Good schooling. Trinity University in Dublin. And I was a damn good investment counselor, Liam. Why wasn't that enough for me? If I'd only stayed at Gershman & Templer, I wouldn't be sitting here today. I could blame Penters, but I'd just be kidding myself. It was me. It was all greed. I was romanced by Penters's high life and all I wanted was to be just like him. Make the big trades, buy my wife fancy jewelry, drive the fast cars, live in a house that I never could afford. I was a fool.

"Working for Penters was life in a pressure cooker. 'Find me the next option, Riley, the next thirty-to-one return, where five ticks can mean millions.' We'd throw the money out there, and if it failed this time, we were sure to make it up on the next trade. Only where do you find the fresh money? You have to con some clueless investor—maybe an elderly person, a widow living on her husband's life insurance. Shame on all of us. I deserve whatever happens to me."

"Riley, you're not a bad guy. You've got a good heart. We're going to put your life back together. Me and you. You're going to testify and the prosecutor's going to give you a break."

"Even if he does, how do I patch it up with Susan and the kids? How can I ever hold my head up again?"

"She'll understand because she loves you. Your kids love you. People make mistakes. I'll go talk to Susan."

Riley stood, threw his arms around me, hugged me and buried his tears on my shoulder. I felt so bad for him. This was my childhood brother. I intended to do whatever I could for him, but I was afraid that his testimony wasn't going to be as valuable as I'd previously thought. Not if Penters wasn't behind the serial killings, and I had my doubts.

Still, providing testimony against Penters and assisting in bringing him in was worth something and I held out hope for probation.

"Penters looked surprised when McLaughlin accused him of murder and arson today, didn't he?" I said.

"Oh, he's good, isn't he? That's why he's the quintessential confidence man. No one ever doubts Ross's sincerity or his ability to bring it home. Not for a minute. Including me. That's why I'm sitting here."

"Let me ask you very bluntly, Riley, what evidence do you have that Penters was behind the murders, the fires or the sniper? Is there anything you can give us? Anything you've seen?"

Riley shook his head. "No, he's too slick. Penters didn't get where he is without covering his tracks. I just know he is."

"But how do you *know* Penters was behind the violence? You seem so sure."

"Because I work with him every day. I've seen his rage. I've seen him blow up at me and other financial advisors if we didn't bring home the big trade. He's ruthless. He ordered me to get the stock from my father. He screamed at me. 'Do whatever you have to do!' He stressed *whatever.*"

"Did you ever see him become physically abusive? Ever see him with a weapon? Does he even own a weapon?"

Riley snickered. "He's far too clever for any of that. He hires people to do his dirty work."

"Who, Riley? Who does he use to do his dirty work?"

Riley shrugged his shoulders. "I don't know. He's too slick."

I had one more question. "Riley, how well do you know Charles Dalton?"

"Janie's boyfriend? Not too well. I know one thing—he was smart enough not to give me any of his money to invest in Penters's wild schemes. Lord knows, I tried many times to get his account. He would just give me that big smile of his and say he'd think about it. Personally, I think he's an asshole."

"Because he wouldn't invest with you?"

"Nah. Because he smacked Janie around. Once I saw him backhand her outside my father's house as he was getting into his Porsche. I don't know why she stays with him. The night my father banned him from the house, there was a blowup at the dinner table. Charles had driven Janie to tears. My father declared that Janie would be welcome in the future, but not Charles." Riley shook his head. "He's an arrogant asshole. I know if I smacked my wife, she'd be long gone." He looked around the room and then lowered his head. Tears were falling. "Liam, I'm afraid Susan will leave me now and who could blame her? I've really made a mess of my life."

I tried to console him and told him we would get through this to-gether and that I'd talk to Susan, but both of us knew it would be a long road back for him. I checked my watch. It was six o'clock and Deirdre's dinner was starting in one hour.

"Riley, there's lots of people that love you. We'll be rooting for you. We'll help you get your life back together. Just remember that."

I bid Riley good-bye and watched the guard walk him back into the lockup. Damn, I felt bad for him.

THIRTY-FOUR

. . .

I RECOGNIZED CONOR'S CAR as I pulled into the driveway. I suppose I should have figured, after all it was a family dinner and he was family, but I wondered who'd invited him. Was it Janie? Either she or Charles might have mentioned that they were coming out for dinner and just assumed he was invited. Or was it Uncle Robert? Conor had visited Robert every day in the hospital. They were close. I'm sure they kept in touch on a daily basis. I doubted that Deirdre had invited him, even though she was his mom for forty years. Conor had tried to evict her and throw her out onto the streets. In fact, I recall him referring to her as the *"girlfriend"* and saying that she's *"had a free ride for too long."* Not exactly endearing words.

Catherine met me in the hallway and told me that it actually was Deirdre who'd invited Conor because she thought it was time to patch things up. She wanted to "make amends." God bless that woman. What a saint.

Cat whispered, "Deirdre said that Conor had called her earlier today and asked if it would be all right to come over and visit his uncle Robert. He was very polite, not like the Conor you describe. He didn't say, 'It's my house and I'm coming in whether you like it or not.' On the contrary, Deirdre said he was very contrite and asked for her permission. He even said, 'I understand that my father wants you to have the house and I'm not going to fight you on it.'"

I didn't understand this turnaround in Conor. I didn't understand it at the hospital and I didn't understand it now. Still, I wasn't about to trust Conor, that's for sure.

Conor and Uncle Robert were both sitting in the living room. Robert was leaning forward in a tufted chair, his left arm still taped to his body and locked up tight. Nevertheless, he had that patented Uncle Robert smile that puffed his cheeks and squinted his eyes, as pleasant a man as God has ever made. But he also looked like he'd gone twelve rounds with the champ.

Conor got up when I came into the room and stuck out his hand. "Hello, Liam."

This from the same Conor who told me that he didn't like me and screamed that if the judge didn't kick me out, he was going to do it himself. I shook his hand.

"Uncle Robert's looking much better, don't you agree?" he said. I agreed.

"I understand Janie and Charles are coming this evening," Robert said. Conor made a face. I guess no one likes Charles. Except Janie, of course.

"Actually, I was the one who told her to bring him along," I said. "He was nice enough to take me for golf and dinner at his country club. I wanted Catherine to meet them both. As you say, maybe it's time to bury the hatchet."

"Hmm. It depends on where you bury it," Conor said with a sly smile and pointed to the middle of his forehead. Now that's the Conor we know and love. You can't hide for long.

A few minutes later, Charles's Porsche rolled up to the house. Janie hopped out, a spring in her step. There seemed to be joy in everything she did. How a person could backhand Janie was as foreign and vile an act as I could imagine. Unforgivable.

Charles opened his door and took a moment to compose himself. He wore a navy sport coat over light tan trousers and a white polo shirt. Tan shoes with no socks. He walked into the house with his million-dollar smile. I wish I had his teeth.

Catherine came out of the kitchen to greet Janie and Charles. Catherine could make anyone feel welcome—as gracious as they make 'em. It gave me the creeps to have her shaking hands with someone I loathed. And still suspected, although I didn't know why. "I understand you treated Liam to a lovely day of golf and dinner," Catherine said. "I'm so glad he insisted that you come tonight."

"Liam insisted?"

"I certainly did," I said. "I can't repay you with golf and we don't have that spectacular view of the North Atlantic here, but Catherine's been sous-chefing Deirdre all day, and she tells me the dinner is spectacular."

Catherine nodded enthusiastically. "I wouldn't say I was a sous-chef, more like a stargazer, but I've been learning. I'm going to fatten Liam up when we get home."

Janie asked about Riley and I said I had just visited with him this afternoon. "His boss, Ross Penters, has hired a top-notch lawyer and they're hopeful that this whole financial regulation mess is just a big misunderstanding," I said, lying through my teeth. I didn't want anyone else to know about the incident at the fishing shack or the sting we ran on Penters.

"I never cared for his boss, you know," Charles said. "Penters was always trying to get his hands in my pockets. You have to be wary of these fellows who offer to make you a fortune overnight."

"Not like a solid linen business handed down from your father, right?" I said.

Charles wasn't sure how to take that and he looked at me sharply, but then smiled. "Exactly," he said. If Charles were the dark knight, this was going to be an interesting evening. Either he knew I was playing him or he felt confident he could fool me. Or perhaps he just took delight in the bandy.

"I say, your wife seems to be on the mend," he said, looking at Catherine. I didn't like his eyes on my wife. "Dreadful incident at your home," he said. "One always expects there to be a sense of security in one's abode, don't you agree?"

"You're dead-on there, Charles. The asshole responsible for the fire better pray that the police catch him before I do."

He raised his eyebrows. "Do him in, would you, Liam?"

"Oh yes. In the most barbarous way possible."

Charles laughed quite loudly. "Barbarous. How monstrous of you."

Deirdre ended the conversation by summoning all of us to the table.

DEIRDRE AND CATHERINE HAD outdone themselves. My goodness, how this dinner brought back memories. Leek soup for a starter, followed by a cucumber, squash and kale salad, and then the pièce de résistance: poached salmon sitting atop Irish boxty under a covering of crème fraîche. I hadn't had Irish boxty, those Irish potato pancakes that Annie used to call "fat latkes," since I was here sixteen years ago. Of course, Irish soda bread, made with sour cream and raisins, complemented the main course.

Catherine laid the plates on the table beaming with pride. "Deirdre taught me an Irish poem," she said. "Boxty on the griddle, boxty in the pan, if you can't make boxty, you'll never get a man."

"Well, your worries are over," I said.

Dinner conversation was light, and for the moment the fears and anxiety of the past few weeks were set aside. Old memories were in play and we were careful to reminisce about joyous times only, though tears would form when stories recalled Eamon or Fergus. Out of respect, Riley's circumstances didn't come up. Wine was flowing, people seemed more at ease, so I thought I'd try my hand at probing Charles.

"So tell us, Charles, with a degree from Princeton, you must have been wined and dined by a lot of American companies who wanted to hire a suave British graduate. Did you go through all those on-campus interviews?"

I got that wide Colgate smile and he said, "You sure seem interested in my younger life, Liam. Are you writing a book?"

"I'm just curious," I said. "And a little fascinated. You've done so well."

"Curiosity? Well, you know what they say about that and the cat?"

"No, Charles, what do they say about the cat?"

He made a pistol with his forefinger and thumb. "Bang," he said, and laughed.

I laughed as well and turned to Catherine. "I've got to have some pictures to remember this fabulous dinner." I took out my cell phone and handed it to her. "Would you snap a few pictures, please?"

Catherine made little groupings and took pictures of everyone. I left the table for a minute, ran back to my bedroom and retrieved the golf cap that Charles had given to me. I told Catherine to take a picture of Charles and me, the two golf buddies. Charles was happy to oblige.

I took my hat off. "Charles, you should be the one wearing the Dunluce Links golf cap. I mean that is *so you*." He hesitated, knowing I had something up my sleeve, but not to be outdone or the least bit intimidated, he nodded and put it on. Catherine snapped the picture.

Deirdre brought out a bottle of port and a strawberry whipped-cream cake, which everyone agreed was impossible to eat after such a big meal, but which mysteriously disappeared by the end of the evening. Another Aunt Deirdre masterpiece. I do love that woman.

THE NEXT MORNING I called McLaughlin to ask if he wanted to accompany me to Walker's apartment. I was anxious to confront Walker with the photo I'd taken of Charles. As they say in the CIA, I had *high confidence* that Walker would ID Charles as the person who'd bought the photographs.

"I'm tied up in meetings this morning, Liam. I'll send Dooley with you," McLaughlin said.

"I don't think Walker will talk to me if Megan is present. He knows I'm not a cop so maybe he'll open up to me if I'm alone. And if Walker's not at home, he's probably gone to the pub. Megan would be too conspicuous in that crowd."

"I wouldn't recommend you go poking around in those loyalist pubs, Liam. They're not exactly friendly to outsiders."

"I'm not worried. I can take care of myself."

"Well, don't take a gun in there. Too many things can go wrong and I'm the one who gave you the gun, okay? No guns."

"Okay, but I'm hoping to catch Walker at home."

Walker had given his address as 14 Bootle Street, a block and a half from Shankill Road in an area of tightly compacted, redbrick row houses. No army ever squeezed more barracks into a one-block area than were packed into Walker's block in the Lower Shankill. There were forty-two town houses—what locals called the "two up, two downs"—in the one square block bordered by Bootle, Tennent, Eccles and Orkney Streets. Number fourteen was in the middle of the block. The curtain in the front bay window was pulled back and I could see a sparsely furnished living room: chairs and a sofa with cloth slipcovers and a small tube TV on a metal stand. I knocked on the door.

An elderly woman in a white robe and plush slippers, her hair in pink rollers, opened the door a crack and asked me what I wanted. "I was hoping Tom Walker was at home," I said. She shook her head. "You'll find him at Willy's. He worked yesterday and he never works two days in a row. When you see him, tell him he needs to pay this week's rent before his wages are tossed on the bar and spent on drink."

I thanked her kindly and headed off for Willy's. It was just this side of noon and the bar was busy. Apparently, there were a lot of men who had also worked yesterday. Walker was standing at the end of the bar, just where McLaughlin and I had encountered him. He saw me and turned to duck out, but the back door was bolted and he really didn't have anywhere to go.

"Why don't you leave me alone?" he said. "I already told you everything I know. I sold the pictures to some fancy chap who came looking for me at my apartment. Now leave me be, I ain't sayin' nothing more. I don't have to."

I signaled to the bartender. "One for me and one for my friend here." The bartender nodded.

"Well, then, as long as you're buying, *friend*, add a shot of Bushmills," Walker said to the bartender with a smile. He nodded, drew the beers, poured the shots and set them on the bar for us.

"Tom, I want to ask you about the guy who bought the pictures."

He twisted his mouth in annoyance. "I told you everything I could remember."

"Well, *now* you say he's a fancy chap. Why is that?"

"He took the pictures and handed me three hundred quid like it was pocket change. I guess that qualifies, don't it?"

"Sure does."

"Anything else fancy about him?"

"Nah."

I pulled out my cell phone and showed him Charles's picture, the one in the golf hat.

"What's that supposed to be?"

"Is that the fancy chap?"

He took the phone and held it close, squinting and scrunching his face, and moving the phone back and forth, not more than inches from his eyes. "I don't know. I suppose it could be."

"Do you wear glasses, Tom?"

"When they ain't broken. Social services will only give me one stinkin' pair a year. That's the piss-poor care we get living here in Belfast."

"When's the last time you had your glasses?"

"Can't remember. April, I think. Maybe March. A long time ago. Way before I sold the pictures."

"Look closely. The guy in the photo, does that look like the man who bought the pictures from you?"

He tried to focus, blinked several times, shrugged and then looked away. "Yeah, it could be. Sure, why not?"

That was totally unconvincing. "What do you remember about the man's hair?"

"Told you, I couldn't see his hair. It was under his cap."

"Did he have a car?"

He shrugged and shook his head. "Dunno."

That's about as much as I could get, and it wasn't going to improve with any more alcohol. "All right, thanks for your help," I said, slipping my phone back into my pocket.

"You know, I might be real sure with another shot of Bushmills."

I smiled and nodded to the bartender. I might as well treat him to an extra drink. I think he would have given me the information if he could. "Give him another," I said, laying a couple of bills on the bar, and I turned to leave. As I approached the door, two hefty men stood in my way. The one on the right had a white T-shirt rolled up at the sleeves, baring his ample biceps. The one on the left was more bony and covered in tattoos.

"Excuse me, gents," I said.

"What do you think you're doing in here?" said the muscle man on the right with his arms folded across his chest.

"Nothing. Just having a conversation. Excuse me, please."

"*Excuse me please*," he mocked. "Listen up, buddy, this is an Ulster bar. You don't barge in here bothering one of my friends."

"Maybe not. I just bought him a couple of drinks and he drank them, so I don't think he feels bothered. Now get out of my way."

He took a swing at me. I ducked and hit him flush with a solid right. He stumbled backward into the door, straightened up, wiped the blood off his face, smiled and bull-rushed me. Now the bar was coming alive and I was in trouble. Someone hit me from the side and I fell into the bar, smacking my head against the wood. In a moment I was down on the floor and there were kicks to my rib cage and blows to my back. I scrambled to my feet, fought through a couple of swinging drunks, grabbed the tattooed man, spun him around and put him in a power half nelson. "Take one more step and I'll break this man's neck," I said.

"Back off," the first man said to the pack of bar-wolves who had encircled me. "I don't know who the foock you are, but you got no business in this bar. Let Jerry loose and we'll let you go, but we don't want you coming around here anymore. Understand? You don't be coming in here and you don't be hassling with old Tommy."

I was taking a chance letting him go, but it wasn't going to get any better. I backed up to the door, released the tattooed man, pushed him forward, and quickly left the bar, lucky to leave with only bruises as souvenirs of my unproductive afternoon at Willy's.

I PHONED MCLAUGHLIN ON my way back to Antrim. "Next time you give me advice, would you also tell me to take it? I had a very unpleasant visit to Willy's Pub this afternoon."

"Any broken bones?"

"No. Not mine anyway. Before all hell broke loose, I met with Walker at the bar, bought him a drink and showed him the cell phone photo of Charles Dalton in his golf hat."

"And?"

"Walker's useless. He can't see his hand in front of his face. Maybe if he saw Charles in person he could ID him, but I doubt it."

"I figured Walker would tell you anything you wanted to hear to get you to buy him a drink. He's full of crap."

"I doubt he paid much attention to the guy who gave him the

money, even if he could see him clearly. I'm sure his focus was on the bills and not the guy."

"So now what?"

"I still think we need to keep an eye on Dalton. There's something there, I know it."

"Hmm. Do you suppose that fits into my theory of relativity? He's a Taggart boyfriend. Maybe he doesn't like his girlfriend's family. Didn't you say that he was barred from Fergus Taggart's house?"

"I did and maybe that's not a bad starting point, Farrell. Maybe a feud between Dalton and Fergus? It seems as though nobody likes him but Janie. Feuds seem to get out of control in this part of the world. Still, that would hardly be motive enough for a series of murders, would it? Why would Dalton give a damn what Fergus thought of him? Even if Fergus despised him, it didn't seem to affect his relationship with Janie. And I don't think he gives a damn about Fergus's estate. He surely doesn't need the money."

"Have you counted his money?"

"Of course not, but he lives very well. Fancy car, fancy clothes, fancy country club and he's got a booming business. Didn't you send Megan out there? What did Megan see when she went to Dalton's plant?"

"Not much; she didn't get in. A security guard met her at the gate. Big guy in a uniform. She didn't have a warrant and he wouldn't let her in."

"What could be so damn secret about a linen factory?"

"Good question. It's not even a factory. It's a distribution center. From what I understand he gets his linen products from local suppliers and ships them to the continent."

"Can you go back out there and get me in?"

"Not without a warrant and I don't have probable cause. Why are you so focused on Dalton anyway?"

"Just a feeling. Do you think he might be connected to Penters? Maybe he has an interest in the Global stock? What are Riley and Penters saying today?"

"Absolutely nothing. Penters hired Farley, Block and Hopkins as his attorneys. They've had him transferred to Belfast lockup and they're filing a petition to have him released on bond. All he's charged with at this time is skipping out on a subpoena in a financial investigation. Riley's a different matter. He's retained the eminent Mr. Cooney, who has advised him to keep his mouth shut. We're not learning anything new from either of them."

"Farrell, he held an unloaded gun on me, hardly a deadly weapon. It wasn't really kidnapping, I went there voluntarily. You know I won't press charges. He should be let out on bond."

"You might have gone voluntarily, but you weren't free to leave. That's kidnapping. He did commit assault, whether there were bullets in the gun or not. Whether he gets probation is up to the prosecutor and the judge. Bond's been set, but it's high and Riley has no way of making it. Everything he's got is leveraged. I'm afraid he's here for a while."

"Well, keep an eye on him, will you? He's really in a bad way. Put him on suicide watch."

"I'll let the warden know."

I ARRIVED BACK AT Fortress Deirdre and made my way to the kitchen. Where else? The baby was in a high chair with a tray of Cheerios and Catherine was receiving instruction in the fine art of baking Irish soda bread. The aroma of warm soda bread was intoxicating. I think a person could gain weight on the smells alone. It would be disrespectful not to devour a manly portion of freshly baked bread and I didn't intend to disrespect my wife and aunt. I bent over to grab a handful of that bread right out of the oven when Catherine slapped my hand.

Then she looked up and eyed my bruised and battered self, my dirty, torn and blood-stained clothes, and she said, "Jesus, look at you. What the hell happened to you this morning?" She grabbed a wet washcloth. "Deirdre, I'm going to need a first-aid kit."

"I ran into some contrary folks," I said, and winced as she pressed the cloth to a bruise, "but can't I get a piece of bread first?"

Catherine knew I suspected Charles, and she knew that I was taking Charles's photo into Belfast for a possible identification, but I hadn't disclosed my suspicions to Deirdre or anyone else in the family. Like my uncle, I didn't want to wrongfully defame an innocent person.

Charles had had a hard enough time ingratiating himself with this family without somebody implying that he was a serial killer. I held my finger to my lips and tilted my head toward the doorway.

"Okay," she said. "Why don't we get you upstairs into the bathroom to clean you up?" Deirdre said she would watch Ben and the two of us walked up the stairs to some privacy.

"Walker," I said, "he's drunk and blind. I thought maybe there was a moment of recognition but as an eyewitness he's useless. There must be some other way to investigate Dalton. I don't know why, but I'd bet my ass he's involved."

"If it makes you feel any better, I wouldn't be surprised if he was. I have the same feeling about him that you do, and I can't tell you why. What is it about him that makes you think he's involved?"

I shook my head. "I wish I could pinpoint it. I don't have a solid theory, just a feeling, like you. It can't be about the money, he's a high roller. I don't believe it has anything to do with my uncle's property or even Riley's Global stock. McLaughlin brought up the concept of a feud with Uncle Fergus and I know he and Fergus didn't get along, but nobody's crazy enough to start killing people because he's been banned from Sunday dinner."

"You've just given me a lot of reasons why he's not involved. What makes you think he is?"

"My gut. He's a phony. He flaunts his riches. A guy like that wants everybody to know he's got money, as though money establishes character. And he abuses Janie, which is enough to put him at the top of my enemies list. I asked Megan to look into Dalton, find out whatever she could about him, and she told me he doesn't exist. There's no record of Charles Dalton in Northern Ireland before he suddenly shows up with a Princeton degree. No record of him at all, Cat. How can that be?"

"What do you mean he doesn't exist? He has a Princeton degree."

"And the diploma's genuine, but with his application to Princeton, he submitted a transcript from St. Patrick High School. St. Patrick has no student records for Charles Dalton. He never went there. He's an athlete, he plays semi-pro Gaelic football for the Belfast club and yet there are no records of him playing sports or anything else at St. Patrick. No records of his attending classes. Don't you think that's strange?"

"Yes. Could the application have been mistaken as to the name of the high school?"

"No, Megan got a copy of the Princeton application. It's a St. Patrick High School transcript. It says he got straight As and played football. Obviously a phony. And that's not all. There are no birth records for Charles Dalton in any of the six counties at or about the time he would have been born. There are no elementary school records for Dalton children in the area where he supposedly grew up. And every time I ask him about his youth, he's quick to change the subject."

"So maybe he wants to hide something from his younger days. It's not a crime to change your name."

"It's a crime if he submits a phony application to Princeton."

"True. But that doesn't make him a suspect in a series of murders."

"What if my uncle discovered Dalton was a fraud? What if he threatened to expose him? It puts the two of them in a confrontational situation. It might give Dalton motive."

"To shut up your uncle? Maybe. But a *series* of murders? Why would your uncle want to expose Dalton anyway?"

"For Janie's sake. He'd do it to protect Janie from a bad relationship."

"How effective would such a threat be? From what you tell me, Janie seems very committed to Charles. I doubt exposing him for identity fraud in filing a false college application would make any difference to her or to the business world. Dalton owns a multimillion-dollar company. Who would care if he faked a college application in America? After all, he did go to Princeton and he did graduate. With honors."

I shook my head. "I guess so. I just know he's involved somehow."

Catherine finished doctoring me and I decided to take a rest. I lay down and quickly fell asleep.

SOMETIME LATER, I WAS awakened by the sound of a car pulling into the driveway. I lifted my bruised body out of the bed, looked out of the window and saw a PSNI Rover. I first thought it was a changing of the guard, but then I saw Farrell get out of the car. He started walking toward the house, but not with his usual spritely gait. His pace was slow. Something was wrong. I walked out to meet him.

"What's wrong?" I said.

"I'm so sorry," he said, kicking at the stones in the driveway. "I'm very sorry to tell you this, Liam. Riley Taggart died this afternoon."

I felt his words in the pit of my stomach. I immediately thought of Deirdre. She had lost her husband, her brother-in-law and now a son. How much more could the woman endure? And Robert, how was he going to handle this? Or Conor, or Janie? Riley had become unhinged, but since the confrontation with Penters, I was hopeful he would get back on track. Hell, I loved him. He'd been despondent and I knew he was in a bad state of mind. I'd asked McLaughlin to put him on suicide watch, but I guess we were too late.

"Damn," I said, "I could see it coming."

McLaughlin shook his head. "You're wrong, Liam. It wasn't suicide. I called over to Warden Sheldon after we spoke and he told me that Riley was found in his cell this morning, stabbed right between the shoulder blades. Prison shiv. I'm really sorry."

"Penters?"

"No, he was moved to Belfast yesterday."

"Then Penters paid someone."

"We're considering that."

All at once I felt overwhelmed. Another loved one was murdered and the great Liam Taggart had failed to stop it. I was totally ineffective. "How could this have happened in Riley's cell? Did he have a cell mate? Was the cell unlocked? Where the hell were the guards?"

"Take it easy, Liam. He was found in his cell shortly after the inmates returned from lunch."

"What about the cameras? What do they show?"

"We'll be studying them, but I'm not optimistic. We only have a single camera in the block and it doesn't show much. The inmates have a morning break and they always hang around in bunches. We give them a little leeway, a short time for socialization. The problem is, when they're standing in a group, the coverage is obscured. Warden Sheldon questioned the group, but of course no one saw anything. I'm very sorry."

"This is going to send some of my family over the edge."

"And 'tis true there's cause for that. I wish it were otherwise. Let me know which mortuary will be coming to pick him up."

CATHERINE HAD BEEN WATCHING us and when McLaughlin turned to walk back to his car, she came outside to meet me. My expression must have said it all because she began to weep.

"Who?" she said.

"Riley. He was murdered in the jail and I was the one who put him there."

"No, Liam, this isn't your fault. He put himself there. He alone bore responsibility for his actions."

"Now it's up to me to break the sad news to Deirdre and the rest of the family."

We walked inside, my wife and I, our arms around each other. When we reached the kitchen and Deirdre saw us, she knew to expect the worst.

"What is it?" she said.

"Riley," I answered and lowered my head.

"How did he die? Did he take his own life? Jesus, God forgive him."

I held Deirdre. Her every muscle was tensed and she was shaking. "I'm sorry. It wasn't self-inflicted. He didn't take his own life."

"How? In a prison? Who killed him?"

"You don't want to know any more, believe me. Just know that his journey is over and he's in a better place, a much better place."

Poor Deirdre. Another blow, just as she was fighting so hard to get back on her feet. She retreated to the living room, to her chair in the corner, with a glass of whiskey—once again the solitary person I encountered when I first returned to Antrim. "Give her some time," Catherine said. "Let her be for a while. I'll come sit with her later."

I found Robert sitting in his bedroom reading a book. I can only describe his reaction as fatalistic. He spoke in a monotone. "They're taking us down one by one, Liam. Nobody's safe. You'll not know the killer till he's the last one standing."

I tried to reassure him. "Riley was in a lot of trouble. His death could have come from any number of sources—his boss, an unhappy investor, or even another crazed inmate. His death wasn't necessarily part of a series, he was different." But neither one of us believed that.

I couldn't reach Janie and I texted her to call me. Conor was next.

"Conor, it's Liam. I'm afraid I'm the bearer of very sad news. Inspector McLaughlin just stopped by to tell me that your brother died today and . . ." The line went dead. I redialed in case it was my phone that dropped the call, but it immediately went to voice mail. I guess each person is entitled to deal with tragedy in his own way.

THIRTY-FIVE

· · ·

LL WAKES ARE SAD and lamentations are painful, but where the death has been sudden and shocking, there is a chilling realization that drifts from person to person—life is ephemeral. The next day is not a given but a gift. Mortality is parked just outside the door. I recalled how mourners attending Eamon's wake moved about the parlor as though low-hanging clouds were passing through the room. Now at Riley's wake, the mood was repeated, coupled with the frightening knowledge that each Taggart had been the victim of a vicious murder and each had been served with a calling card. Marked for death.

In fact, it was at Eamon's wake where Riley came running in, waving the photo with the legend on the back: *Two down. How many to go? As many as it takes! Up the Union. Down the murdering Taggarts.* At the time we all believed it was a photo delivered by one of the Walkers. If not from a Walker, then surely from some unionist taking up the Walker cause. Now, some weeks later, I had come to believe that these photos were a classic misdirection. It was highly unlikely that Walker or some unionist would be firing up the vendetta forty years later. Nevertheless, there was no disputing Robert's statement—the Taggarts were being taken down one by one. We had all been served with calling cards. Myself included. We were all in the crosshairs. Who would be next?

Though many were in attendance, Murphy's Funeral Home was as quiet as a library. If you spoke at all, you whispered. The line of people waiting to express their condolences wound around the room. And what was there to say? Susan and the children were seated on a couch near the open casket. The other day when I left Riley at the jail, I spoke briefly with Susan as I had promised Riley I would. She knew he was in trouble. I told her I hoped he would receive a minimal sentence and I asked her if she could give him a second chance. She said she loved him and she would try. I respected her for that. Unfortunately, the next day I had to deliver the sad news, and she took it hard.

I was looking at a poster board of pictures when a voice behind me said, "He was such a quiet, gentle soul." I instantly knew the voice and turned around to say hello to Annie. I didn't want to tell her that she should have seen this gentle soul a few days ago with a shotgun in his hand and the look of a wild man.

"A million good qualities," I said. "We'll all miss him dearly. But lately he was at the end of his rope."

"I know. I witnessed the strain between Riley and Uncle Fergus. There were harsh words."

"So you said. You told me that Fergus was critical of Riley's investment practices."

"Not just that. Riley had changed. He was preoccupied with his perceived social status. Fergus knew that Riley was living beyond his means and was measuring his self-worth by what he could buy, and that distressed your uncle greatly. They had some mighty arguments. But I don't want to speak ill of Riley, not tonight. In his heart he was a lovely man."

While we were talking, Janie and Charles walked into the room. "Mr. Wonderful," I said quietly to Annie.

She nodded. "Janie's grief is nothing but an inconvenience for him. She was devoted to both of her uncles and to Riley, and their deaths are very hard on her. And she's frightened. She could use Charles's support, but doing for others never seems to enter his psyche." Annie uttered an expletive under her breath and said, "What does she see in that phony?"

"I think that mystery is universally held. I understand Uncle Fergus banned him from the Sunday dinners."

"Oh, it was more than that. You have to understand, Janie was like a daughter to Fergus. He was protective of her. He witnessed the discord between Janie and Charles, the spats, the angry words. He saw the marks on her pretty face. Recently Fergus told me that he had started looking into Charles and his company. 'I'm going to find out what this guy is all about,' he told me. I think Fergus was trying to build a case on Charles to let Janie know what she was in for. I don't know whether Fergus ever found out anything, but you'd have been proud of him. He was a very good spy."

"Did he look into Northern Exports?"

"He did. Like all of us, Uncle Fergus was suspicious of Charles amassing wealth from a linen export business. He wanted to make sure, for Janie's sake, that her boyfriend wasn't up to something nefarious. Not too long ago, Uncle Fergus told me he was going to take a ride into Belfast and see Northern Exports for himself."

"And what did he find?"

"I don't know."

Standing there talking to Annie, I decided I would follow up on what Uncle Fergus started. I'd look into what Dalton was all about. I was certain that the man who didn't exist would have a shadow, leave a footprint. I'd follow it.

I saw out of the corner of my eye that Megan and Farrell had entered the room and joined the line. After they had kneeled at the casket and expressed their condolences to Riley's family, I walked over to talk to them. I should say *whisper* to them.

"It's awfully nice of you to come," I said. "Riley's family is in a bad way. When he left home last week, they didn't know where he'd gone. He didn't call. First they file a missing person's report. Then they learn he's in the Antrim jail and the next thing they know he's been murdered."

Farrell nodded. "It was a nasty murder, Liam. Not only was he stabbed, but his shirt was ripped open and 'RAT' was written on his chest. Written in Riley's own blood."

"It has to be Penters. Is there any doubt? He did it to shut Riley's mouth."

McLaughlin shook his head. "Why would Penters need to make a statement? A rat makes a statement. Penters would know we'd immediately finger him for the crime. Why would Penters want to draw attention to himself if all he wants to do is shut Riley's mouth? Riley's death would ensure his silence. Penters wouldn't need to brag about it. No, this is someone who wants the whole world to know that Riley Taggart has been executed."

"McManus was found in the yard with his throat cut and a rat painted on his chest. Just the same."

McLaughlin nodded. "I know you're focused on McManus because your uncle saved that clipping, but we have no evidence that any McManus relative exists."

"Maybe you didn't look hard enough. Or maybe it's someone seeking revenge for McManus," I said. "A friend or a social club member? Wasn't McManus active in some RIRA bunch? Couldn't it be one of them who would seek revenge?"

"Who indeed? We have no leads."

Conor, who had been standing by the casket talking to a group, saw McLaughlin and walked straight over. I feared this could get ugly. McLaughlin extended his hand and Conor took it. His eyes were red. His brother's death had hit him hard. He didn't have the look of someone who intended to start a scene with McLaughlin. He nodded in response to Farrell's expression of condolence and said, "What's it going to take to catch this guy?"

McLaughlin shook his head. "Conor, you have to believe we are doing everything we can. It's my top priority. I have two men posted at your father's house. I have a patrolman on the street outside your home. Sooner or later, we'll get this guy, I promise."

"I've seen the car sitting on my street. I thank you for that. I understand you had a talk with Walker?"

"We did. We're keeping an eye on him."

"But you're not picking him up?"

McLaughlin shook his head. "Nothing to hold him on yet. He says he sold the pictures and we believe he probably did."

Conor nodded and walked away. I looked across the room and saw Janie. She was sobbing and Annie was consoling her. Dalton was out in the hall on his phone. Annie was right; Janie's sorrow was an inconvenience for him. He was a classic study in egocentricity. There was nothing that would connect him with Riley's murder, but my instincts were in sync with my uncle's.

Father Sweeney entered the room and led us all in prayers. When he concluded, Conor addressed the gathering on behalf of the family and expressed his gratitude for everyone's thoughts and wishes. Then, quite unexpectedly, he turned to McLaughlin.

"Inspector, we have lost yet another family member and I know that many of us here are frightened. They are scared that the PSNI, which is sworn to protect Northern Ireland's citizens, has turned its back on us. Just a few minutes ago, you told me it was your top priority and I want to believe you. If you wouldn't mind, I'd like you to say a few words and give us all comfort that the police are doing everything they can to protect us and that you care about each of us."

McLaughlin nodded and strode to the center of the room, his cap in his hands. "Conor, I thank you for what you just said. It is indeed our top priority and I give you my word that we do care. I know that old biases die hard and it's easy to believe that the PSNI is insensitive to your family. I want to assure all of you that I take Riley Taggart's death personally. I arrested him and he died in my jail while under my care. I wouldn't fault you for holding hard feelings against me and my department. You have that right. But in this situation, you'd be wrong to think us insensitive. I deeply mourn his passing.

"Many of you know me, I'm an old-timer. I've been a policeman for fifty years and my wife has told me for the last ten years that it's way past time to retire. But I've continued to stay on because I love my country and I want to serve. As with many of you, I've watched the Troubles rob us of some of our brightest and most promising youth. It never mattered to me whether the death came on this side of Divis or the other. It was always a tragedy. Northern Ireland is wounded by the loss of each and every one of its children. Do I care about each and every one of you? Aye, that I do.

"I am not an eloquent man, and it's not easy for me to express my sincere belief that the loss of a single life is a loss to us all. Long ago, witnessing the senseless deaths on the streets of Belfast, I listened to a minister recite a poem and I committed it to memory. I'm sure many of you know it. It was written four hundred years ago by John Donne and it's particularly poignant when applied to our country and the lives taken by the Troubles. If you will permit me:

No man is an island,
Entire of itself,
Every man is a piece of the continent,
A part of the main.
If a clod be washed away by the sea,
Europe is the less.
As well as if a promontory were.
As well as if a manor of thy friend's
Or of thine own were:
Any man's death diminishes me,
Because I am involved in mankind,
And therefore never send to know for whom the bell tolls;
It tolls for thee.

McLaughlin walked slowly to the back of the room. I saw water in his eyes. So did everyone else. They nodded to him and whispered their thanks.

Before Farrell and Megan could leave, I thanked them for their presence and their concern. But there was one more thing on my mind.

"Megan, when you inquired at St. Patrick High School about Charles Dalton, did they tell you they had no records?"

"Correct. None at all."

"Who did you talk to?"

"A woman in the attendance office. First she said that the school has a firm privacy policy. It will not provide any information about any of its students to anyone other than a parent or legal guardian without consent of the student. I told her we had seen an application for admission we obtained from Princeton that showed his graduation from St. Patrick. Would she just tell us if he graduated? She reluctantly ran his name through the computer. 'I don't find anything," she said. 'No enrollment, no degree, no evidence of matriculation.' She had no information to give us."

I turned to McLaughlin. "I'm not satisfied. I want to go out to St. Patrick tomorrow morning. I want to talk to an administrator. Maybe the principal or the dean of students. Will you go with me?"

"I can't go and I think it's a waste of time, but you can go. This time take my advice and let Dooley go with you."

I looked at Megan. "I don't think they'll give us information without a warrant. Can you get one?"

She nodded. "Come by at ten o'clock."

I turned to McLaughlin. "Riley's funeral is Thursday morning, the day after tomorrow. The entire Taggart family will be present. We're going to need extra police coverage."

"It'll be there."

To my right, I saw Catherine take the baby out of the parlor. Ben was fussing and I needed to get them home. I said my good-byes and drove back to the farm.

C ATHERINE AND I SAT in the kitchen long after midnight. The house was quiet. I told her how Riley's body was found.

"McManus was killed the same way," Catherine noted. "It's macabre. Ghastly. I've been thinking, maybe we're not giving those two newspaper articles the proper attention? Wasn't there another killing in prison?"

"Lefferty."

"Right. And what's the connection between McManus, Lefferty and the Taggarts?"

"Me. I'm the connection."

"Weren't McManus and Lefferty both IRA, both Catholic?"

"Yes."

"Could Charles be related to either of them?"

"Well, Megan can't find the connection, but let's say he is. Let's say he's a McManus or a Lefferty and he changed his identity. McManus didn't know who I was. Lefferty never heard of me. Neither one knew I existed or could make the connection between their misfortunes and the Taggart family. They were both killed in prison. Even if Charles were a relative how would he know to blame the Taggart family? How would he know to plant pictures of Walker's house as a calling card? How could he connect the dots between the Taggarts and the Walkers if he didn't even know about the Taggarts? Someone would have had to give all that background information to him."

Catherine gave me that look, that spontaneous look that said she knew the answer and didn't like it. "Janie," she said. "Didn't Annie tell you that she and Fergus and Janie would sit and talk?"

I was stunned. Why hadn't I realized that? Annie said he'd discussed it all on the porch and wasn't Janie present as well? He'd talked about McManus. He'd talked about my turning in the names of the RIRA operatives. Would she have unwittingly passed these stories on to Charles? Was Charles really a McManus?

THIRTY-SIX

...

GOTHIC SPIRES, RESIDENCE HALLS, acres of green grass and a good-size high school soccer stadium stood in sharp contrast to Charles's description of St. Patrick as a small Catholic school. As soon as we walked into the entrance hall, Megan and I were greeted by Sister Maria, the assistant dean of students.

"We'd like to talk to you about Charles Dalton, who claims he was a student here twelve years ago."

Sister Maria smiled sweetly, but shook her head firmly. "I'm afraid we're not allowed to divulge information about any of our students. We have a strict policy here at St. Patrick that requires us to honor our students' privacy. We have our reputation to uphold."

Megan tendered the search warrant and Sister Maria read it carefully. She gave us an indignant stare and said, "Well, this search warrant requests production of St. Patrick's records for Charles Dalton. While I resent your coercive intrusion into St. Patrick affairs, I have no problem cooperating with the warrant because we have absolutely no records for a Charles Dalton. And I believe we already told you that."

She handed the warrant back to Megan and offered a plastic smile as a final exclamation point to this obtrusive visit. She started to walk us out when I took out my cell phone and showed her Dalton's picture. "This is Charles Dalton," I said.

Her eyes widened and she nodded. "Hmm. I do recognize him," she said softly. "One moment, please."

She moved into an anteroom and picked up the phone. We saw her talk quietly for a few minutes and then return to us. "All right. We do have records, but not for a Charles Dalton. The man in the picture is Michael Charles Lefferty. He was an excellent student and an accomplished athlete. He got straight As and played football. His father died quite tragically. His tuition was paid by an endowment."

Megan responded, "The father, the one who died quite tragically, was that Sean Lefferty, the convicted criminal who was killed by an inmate while serving a twenty-year sentence for possession and sale of illegal weapons?"

"Unfortunately for Michael, yes. Is there anything further, Officer Dooley?"

"Yes, the records, please," Megan said, "and who did you just call on the telephone?"

Sister Maria's lips were tightly sealed and she shook her head.

"Who, Sister Maria?"

"That is none of your business," she snapped.

"The man in the picture is a person of interest to the PSNI for a multitude of crimes. If you don't answer my questions here, you will have to answer them at the PSNI station in Antrim and explain why you are obstructing our investigation."

She took a deep breath and said, "Well, if you must know, I called Mr. Lefferty, of course. St. Patrick will defend our students' privacy at all costs. He has a right to know you are inquiring about his status. He has a right to know that someone is forcing us to violate our sacred policy of confidentiality."

Megan and I exchanged glances. That was going to be troublesome. "What did Mr. Lefferty say?"

Sister Maria raised her chin and folded her arms across her chest. "I suppose I have to tell you or you'll take me to jail?"

Megan nodded.

She made a face at us, as though she had just bitten into a lemon. "Mr. Lefferty wanted to know who was asking. Naturally, I told him the truth. I said Officer Megan Dooley and Mr. Liam Taggart. And they had a warrant or I wouldn't have told them a single thing. He said thank you very much. That was all."

"What number did you call?"

"His office number. I should tell you that Mr. Lefferty is a generous alumnus and St. Patrick appreciates his yearly donations. And he insists they be credited *anonymously*. He seeks no glory."

She printed out the records and happily showed us the door.

W E NEED TO GET into Lefferty's plant," I said on our way back to Antrim.

Megan was not optimistic. "We'd need a warrant to get into the property of a private corporation and Inspector McLaughlin doesn't think there's probable cause. We were lucky to get the warrant this morning. I had to tell the judge that we suspected the fraudulent use of school records. But for his business, we really have no basis at this time. It's not illegal to own a business under an assumed identity and we have nothing that ties Lefferty to any of the murders."

"But you and I both know it's him. Through Janie, he'd have learned everything: my sting at the jail, McManus, even the feud between the Taggarts and the Walkers. He knows it was me, a Taggart, that turned his father in. What better motivation for picking off the Taggarts one by one? He's Lefferty's kid, and I'll also bet he's carrying on the family business of running guns. My uncle must have suspected that as well. That's why he wrote, 'God help this family if I fail.' That picture, the crate of guns, has to be tied to Lefferty. If silencing my uncle wasn't a strong enough reason for Lefferty to kill him, then avenging his father's death surely would have been. Isn't that sufficient enough to get a search warrant?"

"It's Inspector McLaughlin's call."

"Megan, I'm worried about Janie. Thanks to Sister Maria, Lefferty knows we've uncovered his identity. I'm sure that Janie doesn't know who he really is. And she's a Taggart." I dialed Janie's phone and it went immediately to voice mail. "We need to get to her," I said.

Megan nodded. "I agree. Where does she live?"

I shook my head. "I don't know. I don't know where to find her. Hell, most of the time she lives with Charles. Wait. Annie's her best friend. She would know."

I called Annie's number but she didn't answer. I texted her, "Call me right away. It's an emergency." With the knowledge that his false identity was blown, there was no telling what Charles would do. As we pulled into the Antrim PSNI, Annie returned the call.

"What's the matter, Liam? Is everything all right?"

"No. Do you have any idea where Janie is?"

"She's right here. We're at the mall. We just ordered lunch."

"Don't let on what I'm about to say to you. Whatever you're doing, stop doing it and bring her out to the Antrim police station immediately. Don't let her call Charles. We have reason to believe that Charles is the man behind the murders. Just get in the car and bring her out here. Use whatever excuse you need to."

"Oh my God. Is she okay?" I heard Annie say. There was panic in her voice. "Poor Deirdre. Tell her we'll be right out. Janie, cancel our order, we have to drive to Antrim right away. Deirdre's had a bad fall." And she hung up.

Good work, Annie.

MEGAN GAVE MCLAUGHLIN A full report of our visit to St. Patrick and the revelation that Charles Dalton was really Michael Charles Lefferty. As Megan had feared, McLaughlin didn't feel we had enough to get a search warrant. "I can't bust in there just because his father was a criminal," he said. "As to his assumed identity, if my father was Sean Lefferty, I'd want to change my name as well. Still, I'll alert the patrolmen guarding Deirdre's house to be on the lookout for Dalton. If he shows up, I'll bring him in for questioning."

Annie and Janie walked in a few minutes later and Janie was angry. "What's this all about?" she said. "Why did Annie lie to me about Deirdre and bring me to the police station?"

"Janie isn't very happy with me," Annie said. "You need to explain why."

"I'm sorry," I said. "Blame me, not Annie. I forced her to get you out here, and I asked her not to give you the real reason. You wouldn't have come if she told you the truth."

"What's this all about, Liam?"

"It's about Charles. He may not be who you think he is. We think he could be the man we're looking for, the person behind all the murders."

"What are you talking about? Are you all nuts? Every one of you?" She clenched her fists. "Oh, I see it all now. None of you ever liked Charles. Uncle Fergus told me to leave him a hundred times." She turned and gave a glaring look at Annie. "You told me to leave him a hundred times too. And I thought you were my friend." She started to walk out but I jumped in front of her.

"Wait, Janie. Let me explain."

"You all hate him because sometimes he acts out when he's under stress. You have no idea the pressure he's under. Running a huge company takes a lot out of him. None of you would understand that. Yeah, sometimes he acts out, okay? But a serial murderer? Are you all crazy? Go to hell, all of you! I'm leaving." She tried to push by me but I held her arms.

"Please, Janie," I said. "Just give me one minute. Let me explain and then if you want to leave I won't stop you." Janie stood with her arms folded on her chest and a furious look on her face. I felt so sorry for her, sorry for the hurt and disillusionment she would soon feel. But she needed to know. She was a Taggart and possibly Lefferty's next target.

"Please sit down," I said. She shook her head, remained standing in her defiant posture, tapping her foot. I took a breath. "Charles Dalton's real name is Michael Charles Lefferty. His father was the convicted arms merchant, Sean Lefferty. Does the name ring a bell?"

Janie nodded. "Uncle Fergus told me about Sean Lefferty. Both Lefferty and McManus and what happened sixteen years ago. But Charles's name is Dalton. He's an honest businessman and he loves me. And I love him. Now can I go?"

"Charles always told us that he graduated from St. Patrick High School, right?"

Janie nodded. "That's right."

"But St. Patrick has no record of him ever being enrolled."

"So, their records are screwed up."

I took out my cell phone and showed her the photo Catherine took of Charles in his golf cap. "Remember this? I've had suspicions about Charles, so I took this picture and brought it to St. Patrick this morning. The assistant dean, Sister Maria, identified this picture. She said she recognized him."

"He's right, Janie," Megan said. "I was there. But she ID'd this photo as her former student, Michael Charles Lefferty, who she knows well. She also told us he's a large benefactor and the son of Sean Lefferty."

Janie's eyes were tearing, her cheeks were twitching and her lips were quivering. She took quick breaths. "I don't believe you," she said in a quavering voice, barely audible. "The dean must be confused. Charles is a wealthy businessman. I have no doubt he's a benefactor; he's very charitable. She must have gotten the name wrong. He's not a Lefferty and he's not a killer."

"Janie, have you been inside the Northern Exports plant?"

"Part of it. Charles tells me that because they ship overseas, it has to be secure. I was only in the offices, not the warehouse."

"How is it secured?"

"Well, I don't really know the details. Montgomery is in charge."

"Who's Montgomery?"

"Northern's security officer. He used to be a sergeant in the British army. He's very large and very stern. He rarely smiles. Charles hired him to make sure that his competitors don't sneak in and get access to Northern's products and sales programs. You know, corporate espionage and all. Charles is always worried about that."

"That's what Charles told you?"

She nodded. I opened Fergus's folder, took out the picture of the guns and laid it on the table. "Do you recognize anything in this picture?"

Janie shook her head and said, "It's a wooden box full of rifles. I've never seen this box before. Should I have?"

That was disappointing, but I suppose Lefferty wouldn't have kept boxes of guns lying around where anyone could see them. "Not necessarily. We believe it's a box of illegal assault weapons."

"Well, why would I know anything about illegal assault weapons?"

"Did you ever hear Charles talk to anyone about guns?"

"No. And I really want to go home. I don't care if he fudged some school records."

I sighed. This was going nowhere. She'd never believe me.

"Wait a minute," Janie said suddenly. "Let me see that picture." She picked it up, held it close to her eyes and squinted. "The floor beneath the box of guns—it's blue swirly tile."

"Does that mean something?"

She held her hand on her mouth. "That's the tile on the floor at Northern Exports. This picture was taken there. Who took it?"

"We think Uncle Fergus."

"He said he was going to visit the plant."

McLaughlin and I locked eyes. "Is that enough?" I said. "She's tied the box to the Northern. Does it get us in?"

He nodded. "I think so. Let's take a ride out there and see what Mr. Lefferty has to say." Turning to Megan, he said, "I'll want three cruisers. We'll need warrants. Judge Collins should be at home, and he'll sign them. Bring them back and we'll go." Turning to me, he said, "Do you want to ride along?"

"You better believe it."

I turned to Janie, who was sobbing on Annie's shoulder. "I'm sorry, Janie, truly I am, but please don't call Charles."

"It doesn't mean he's a killer. Just because he has a box of guns doesn't make him a killer."

T WO HOURS LATER, THREE PSNI Land Rovers pulled up to the gate at Northern Exports. An armed guard came out of the gatehouse and approached the lead vehicle where McLaughlin and I were seated. Several PSNI officers jumped out and stood with their rifles at the ready.

"Take your weapon by the handle and lay it on the ground," McLaughlin demanded. The nervous guard slowly lifted his pistol from the holster, gently laid it on the pavement and walked over to our car. McLaughlin showed him the warrant and instructed him to open the gate and not to make any calls, though we were certain the cameras would alert Northern's personnel. Moments later the mechanical gate rolled to the side.

We entered through the main office door into a reception area. Seven of us. The young lady sitting at the reception desk was shocked to see a police force march in and she quickly rose from her seat. McLaughlin waved for her to be seated. "Relax. We're here to see Mr. Dalton."

She shook her head. "Mr. Dalton's not here. He received a telephone call this morning that he described as quite urgent and he left to attend to an emergency. He told me he'd be out of town for an indeterminate amount of time. That's all I know."

"Where did he go?"

"I'm afraid I don't know. I didn't make the arrangements. He drove out about ten thirty."

"Will you please show us into the warehouse?"

At that moment, a thickset man with a buzz-cut and a closely cropped beard walked into the reception area. His shoulders were broad. His hips were narrow. He wore khakis and a white polo shirt with NORTHERN EXPORTS stitched in script over the pocket. "What's going on here?" he said with a growl.

"I assume you are Montgomery?" McLaughlin said.

"*Mister* Montgomery. What is this all about? Why are the cops busting into my plant?"

"Is it your plant, *Mister* Montgomery?"

"I'm responsible for security. I will ask you again, what are you doing here?"

McLaughlin handed the search warrant to Montgomery and said, "Step aside, Mr. Montgomery, and let us do our job."

"Not so fast. How do I know this is genuine? I need to call our lawyers and get their advice before I let you into my warehouse." It seemed obvious that Montgomery knew the purpose of our visit and was determined to do what he was hired to do—keep us out.

"Last time, Mr. Montgomery. Step aside or I will arrest you for obstructing a police officer."

"You think that scares me? I was a combat officer in Operation Telic. On the point in Iraq, three deployments. I've faced much tougher opponents than a skinny old cop in civilian clothes."

McLaughlin looked back at the five officers that stood behind him. "Arrest him," he said.

The first officer who approached Montgomery with cuffs in his hand went down quickly with a right to the midsection. All told, it took four of the officers to bring Montgomery down, cuff his hands behind his back and chain his ankles. Once he was subdued, we entered the warehouse.

Rows of wooden crates with IRISH LINEN and NORTHERN EXPORTS

stenciled on the sides, sat on pallets ready for shipment. As Janie had noted, the floor underneath the pallets was blue tile. McLaughlin ordered the workers to stand along the walls. Then he instructed an officer to open one of the boxes.

The young officer kneeled down, pried open the top and looked up at us. "It's linen, sir. The whole box is full of linen."

"Open another one."

Crate after crate revealed only bolts of linen cloth. McLaughlin looked at me and shrugged.

"This can't be everything," I said. "There has to be another part to this warehouse."

McLaughlin turned to the workers standing along the wall. "Is there another part of this plant where crates are stored?" The men looked from side to side and said nothing. Finally, one string bean of a man near the end of the line jumped forward and raised his hand.

"I ain't going to jail," he said. "This ain't the only part, Commander. There's another area filled with different boxes. The ones you're looking for."

"Take me there," McLaughlin demanded, and turning to a patrolman, he said, "I want the rest of these men processed. Call for additional backup."

We walked through a door into another portion of the plant where more rows of crates were stacked on pallets. Those crates were marked FINE CLASS-A IRISH LINEN—NORTHERN EXPORTS. As we all knew they would, under a thin layer of linen they each contained military assault rifles and ammunition. Once a Lefferty, always a Lefferty.

McLaughlin radioed in an alert for Charles Dalton, aka Michael Charles Lefferty, and his photo was sent to public and private airports and harbors. "We're on an island," Farrell said. "Unless he got out this morning, we'll catch him."

THIRTY-SEVEN

• • •

THE MORNING SKY WAS dark, the wind was hard from the north, and intermittent rain fell at an angle, as though the weather gods felt our sorrow. We were at Deirdre's, preparing to attend another funeral mass for yet another family member. No one had heard from Charles, and McLaughlin called to say that he hadn't been found. It was likely he had made his way to the continent before we could get the notice out. In some ways, I was glad he was out of Northern Ireland and out of my life. One day he'd make a mistake, take a wrong turn, slip up at a border entry and he'd be apprehended. EU authorities would return him to Northern Ireland for trial. He'd get what he deserved. Today our thoughts and prayers were with Riley, his wife and children and the grieving Taggart family.

There was an extra PSNI car to escort the black limousines to St. Michael's. Once again there would be a gathering of black umbrellas standing on the hillside. Catherine felt it would be unwise to take the baby out in the bad weather and I concurred. She would stay at home. PSNI would post a guard in the front, though with Charles gone and Montgomery in prison the level of danger was negligible.

To see Riley's young wife and children dressed in black and following the casket into the church was heart-wrenching. As I had at Fergus's and Eamon's funerals, I sat next to Janie. Life had certainly taken a shocking reversal for her. She was consoled by Annie, who sat on her other side. Conor took a seat in the first pew with his arm around Susan. She had lost her husband. He had lost his father and his brother.

Once again, Uncle Robert stepped up to the pulpit and delivered a poignant eulogy. His arm was still bound tightly in a sling. The Taggarts were a battered clan, what was left of us.

I had come to the realization that I was wrong about Conor. Irritable, irascible, and bad-tempered? Yes. But he was never the evil-hearted person I imagined. There was no question that he resented my duplicity when I was with the CIA, or that he had carried that grudge forward. In my mind, I believed he was hurt that his father had chosen me as the trustee and had said I was the only person he could trust. I was sorry the two of us got off on the wrong foot. I hoped we could be closer in the future.

Deirdre had buried her lifelong partner, her brother-in-law and now a boy she had raised from infancy. In a day or two, when Robert returns to his condo and we leave for home, she will truly be alone. Catherine and I will offer to move her to Chicago, but she will most certainly decline. I hoped that Annie would look after her.

As the service ended and we stepped outside into the rain, I noticed that one of the officers was trying to reach someone on his radio. He waved at me and beckoned me over to his car. He said he couldn't reach his partner, the man assigned to guard Deirdre's house. He wondered if Catherine had changed her mind and asked to be driven into town. I shrugged and took out my cell phone. Catherine didn't answer. I dialed again. Voice mail. My nerves fired up. I had seen too much in Northern Ireland to believe in coincidences. "Take me home, please. Right now."

"I can't," he said. "I can't leave my post."

"Call inspector McLaughlin. Tell him to get a car out to the house as fast as he can." I ran to find Annie. She had driven Janie to the church earlier this morning. I found her walking down the hill, into the cemetery, and I grabbed her arm. "Annie, please drive me home. Something's wrong."

She didn't ask what was wrong, she didn't ask why, she didn't hesitate, not even for a moment. Our mutual vibes were still intact in that curious, metaphysical way. She immediately understood, turned and ran with me to her car.

We drove out to the house at breakneck speed. The PSNI car was still parked at the end of the driveway. I exhaled a sigh of relief. We drove up to the house and my heart fell. The PSNI officer lay dead on the front porch in a pool of blood, shot several times. Old Wicklow lay beside him, also riddled with bullet holes. From inside the house, we heard the baby crying. I ran in shouting, "Catherine? Cat? Catherine, where are you? Please answer me, baby. Oh, please say something, honey."

Ben was standing up in his crib, grabbing the sides and screaming. I picked him up, hugged him and ran out into the living room. Catherine was nowhere to be found. Annie and I searched all over the house, including the basement. There were no signs of a struggle and thankfully no more bodies. Just then, two PSNI cruisers pulled up to the house, sirens blaring. Megan and Farrell had arrived.

"He's got Catherine," I shouted with panic in my voice and in my heart. "I never should have brought her here to Antrim. I never should have left her home alone."

"No time for recriminations, Liam. We have to get her back. He's taken her for a reason. He hasn't left the country and he needs safe passage."

Annie reached for the baby. He was soaking wet. "Let me have Ben. I'll take care of him," she said gently.

"I'm going to go after Lefferty," I said. "I'm going to kill that son of a bitch."

McLaughlin put his hand on my shoulder. "Liam, he's not at the plant and we don't know where he is. We don't know where he's taken her."

"I have to find him. He'll kill her."

He shook his head. "If he was going to kill her, she'd be lying here like my young officer. No, Catherine is his ticket out. We have to wait for his call."

Megan came in from the yard. She held a plastic bag with several spent shell casings. "Five-five-six NATO," she said. "They came from one of Lefferty's AR-15s. I called for the homicide unit and the coroner."

McLaughlin exhaled slowly through pursed lips. "What a shame. Bobby was a good man. From the looks of his body and the holes in the front wall siding, he never had a chance. It must have been a surprise attack out of the woods. I'll have to tell his father."

"I can't just sit here," I said.

"We don't have a choice."

"What about Montgomery? I'll bet he knows where Lefferty is. Give me a few minutes alone with him."

McLaughlin shook his head. "You know I can't do that. I can bring him into the interrogation room and we can do it the right way, but this guy isn't about to flip on his boss. You saw him at the plant. He was ready to take on a dozen armed policemen."

"What do we know about him?"

"He's the real deal. British Special Forces with three tours of combat in the Middle East. He received field decorations and was discharged in 2011 when British units left Iraq. He had his share of internal discipline problems but the file is silent as to why."

"So, he was Lefferty's muscle?"

"Undoubtedly. We'll take a look in his apartment and I'm confident we'll find the rifle that was used to shoot your uncle, along with other military hardware. I wouldn't be surprised if he was also responsible for Eamon Taggart's murder. Northern Ireland is immeasurably safer with Montgomery off the streets."

People started to file back to the house from the funeral. Deirdre, Robert and Janie returned. As each of them came in, Annie took them aside and quietly filled them in on the details. Other than an exchange of quick empathetic glances and terrified shock, they pretty much gathered in the kitchen and left me alone to confer with Megan and McLaughlin in the living room. Deirdre and Annie took to the task of caring for Ben.

I was pacing. My nerves were getting the best of me. "Why hasn't he called?"

"If he's smart, he'll let you stew for a while and increase your desperation. He knows we're all here waiting. Sooner or later, he'll make the call. He needs to get off the island."

"Then why do we need to wait here? If Lefferty calls the house they can give him my cell number. I want to talk to Montgomery. We have nothing to lose. Humor me, I can't sit here and do nothing."

MONTGOMERY WAS BROUGHT INTO the interrogation room in handcuffs and leg irons and was quickly chained to the interrogation table. He had a smug smile on his face. "What's the matter, boys? Something I can help you with?"

"Where's Lefferty?" I said.

He feigned a pouty face and mimicked, "'Where's Lefferty? Where's Lefferty?' Like I'm going to tell you."

I was ready to explode. "He kidnapped my wife."

"You're breaking my heart. Boo-hoo."

I lunged across the table, put my hands around his thick neck and squeezed as hard as I could. He squirmed from side to side until McLaughlin pulled me off.

"Take these chains off me, garda," Montgomery said, coughing. "Let's see this punk come at me again. You're a real brave honcho while I'm tied to a table."

"Give him his wish, Farrell," I said. "Cut him loose." Every muscle in my body was contracting and all my anger was on the surface. I met his stare. I wanted his blood.

McLaughlin walked me back into my chair. "Liam, sit down."

I stared at Montgomery and spit out my words. "He's nothing but a hired killer, an indiscriminate murderer who kills without conscience. He's the lowest of the low."

Montgomery smiled. "Really? Am I that bad? Am I so different from when I was a hired killer for the British government? Was I acceptable then because I was killing Iraqis indiscriminately without conscience for her majesty the queen? Look around, pal, you're in Northern Ireland. Indiscriminate murder is our national pastime."

McLaughlin interceded. "The game's over, Montgomery, your boss doesn't give a damn about you. Why protect him? Just tell us where he went."

"Why should I? What's in it for me?"

"Cooperation could go a long way. You weren't the head of this operation, Lefferty was. He used you like he'd use a tool and then discarded you like he'd discard a tool. He took off and left you holding the bag. Northern Ireland appreciates remorseful felons who help us prosecute the real responsible parties."

"Northern Ireland don't appreciate shit. I was a decorated war hero. What good did that do me after I was discharged? I couldn't find a freakin' job in this dogshit country until Charles took me on. He paid me well for services rendered. I'm not about to rat him out. And don't give me the cooperation bullshit. I'm sure you've already got your minions snooping around in my apartment, grabbing my guns and hardware and collecting all your evidence. I'm never getting out of this can, and you and I both know it. So what can you offer? Are you going to set me free, Inspector? Ha!"

"No. You're going to go to prison for the rest of your miserable life. But there's prison and then there's prison, if you know what I mean. Work with us and it will benefit you in the long run. Lefferty's kidnapped an innocent woman. He took her as a hostage so he could get away and leave you here. That's how much he cares about you. Just tell us where he is. He never needs to know it came from you."

Montgomery shrugged his massive shoulders. "Well, even if I wanted to, the truth is I don't know. Charles doesn't exactly share his itineraries with me. How am I supposed to know where he went? Somalia, Bosnia, Chechnya? Probably anyplace he ships his guns. Why don't you check with his social secretary?"

"He must have had a plan in the event his operation went south. Why don't you help us out and we'll help you out?"

"Operation? I call it a business. Supply and demand. There's a market with a strong demand out there, a demand that no one can supply legally, and we serve that market. And they pay very well. Our clients in Somalia and Syria will buy everything that we can ship and pay top prices. Charles's family's been running this business for forty years. The street demand in Belfast has dried up, so Charles markets to areas of the greatest demand. To me, that's a good businessman. That's not an *operation*. I've been in operations. This is business and we're good at it. I'm done talking to you assholes."

McLaughlin turned to me. "He doesn't have the answer."

I nodded and we left.

DEIRDRE WAS TENDING TO the baby when we returned. Our house was becoming a PSNI communications center. There were open lines to headquarters in Belfast and to districts all over the six counties. Janie and Annie had set out some tea and pitchers of water. Conor had arrived and pulled me aside. "Just tell me what I can do and

I will do it, Liam. Wherever you want me to go, whatever you want me to do."

"I wish I knew what to do, Conor. I wish I had a clue. But I thank you for your offer."

The phone hadn't rung since we left and it was almost three o'clock. I became less and less convinced that Lefferty needed Catherine to make his escape. It was more probable that Lefferty was exacting further revenge on the Taggarts. Each hour that passed made it more likely that I'd lost my wife.

The PSNI set up equipment to track the location of a call, whether it came in to the house phone or my cell phone. Given enough time, they could pinpoint his exact location unless he had some sophisticated scrambling device, which McLaughlin felt was not available to Lefferty on the run.

The house phone rang at three forty-five. I quickly picked up the phone.

"Liam, so nice to speak to you. There's someone here who misses you."

"If you hurt her, I will hunt you down no matter where you go and I will kill you."

"My, my, such bold words from a man with so little bargaining power. Didn't anyone ever tell you that's not the way to begin a negotiation? Here's how it works: you have what I want and I have what you want. In such situations, between men of reason, a bargain may be struck."

"What do you want, Lefferty?"

"Actually, I prefer Dalton. I've been Charles Dalton for such a long time that I've really become quite fond of the chap. So let's stick with Dalton. Or Charles. By the way, how is my little girlfriend? Is she there with you?"

"What do you want?"

"Well, I surely don't want Janie anymore. I'm tired of her petulance."

"Come on, Dalton, let's get on with it."

"We will, we will. We're just beginning. I'll call you back in a bit. Toodle-oo."

We looked at Megan, who shook her head. "He wasn't on long enough."

Janie and Annie came into the room. "I think I know where he is," Janie said. "I think he's at Dunluce Castle. It's near his country club and we used to go there late at night. We'd sneak into the towers and . . . well, we'd sneak into the towers. He said it made him feel like the Earl of Antrim."

Fifteen minutes passed and the phone rang again.

"Dalton," I said. "I just want my wife safely returned. What do you want?"

"Oh, let's not be so formal. Charles, just Charles. I want my freedom and I want my property. I also want each and every Taggart dead and underground, but I guess I fell short in that regard."

"What property?"

"Why, my inventory, of course. I bought and paid for all those rifles. They belong to me."

I looked at McLaughlin. He shook his head.

"Out of the question and you know it," I said. "Let Catherine go. She's done nothing to you. Let me take her place. Use me as a hostage instead. I'm just as valuable to the PSNI as Catherine."

"Perhaps that's so, but a bird in the hand, as they say. Besides, she's easier to handle than you are, aren't you, sweetie?" I heard a muffled scream.

My blood was boiling. "I'm warning you Dalton, if you hurt my wife in any way there won't be an inch on this planet where you'll be safe."

"How gallant. Well, Sir Galahad, if the PSNI won't give me my property back, then it must pay fair value. Don't you think that's reasonable?"

"What do you want?"

"You always come back to that, don't you? You keep repeating yourself. I can see you don't enjoy the art of negotiation. Or you're just shitty at it. Well, the bottom line is this: I want one million euros and a helicopter with a range of twelve hundred kilometers. Call you back soon." The line went dead.

"That would put him somewhere in Belgium or France to refuel," Megan said.

We paced for fifteen minutes until the phone rang again. McLaughlin said, "Tell him you don't have the money and you need to talk it over with me."

"I don't have a million euros, Charles, you know that."

"Of course, I know that, but I'm not selling the guns to you, Liam. I'm selling them to the PSNI and they're worth every shilling. The lovely state of Northern Ireland isn't going to lose a single pound sterling on the deal. The government buys guns every day and mine are just as good as the next fellow's. We'll keep it quiet where the guns came from and the government can take the money out of its general accounting office to make the purchase. Or out of some slush fund, and don't tell me there's no such thing. It will all be quite legal. Talk to whatever police official is standing next to you and I'll call you back in fifteen minutes. But don't take long because your wife is probably hungry and thirsty and doesn't look very comfortable at the moment. Am I right, sweetie? Do you have to use the toity? Aww, how inconvenient. Bye-bye."

I put the phone down and walked outside with Megan and McLaughlin. "Someday, somehow, I'm going to kill that man," I said.

"Just stay cool. As long as we're still talking she'll be all right."

"Farrell, you have to protect my wife. Whatever you have to do, you can't let this bastard hurt Catherine or take her out of the country. We'd never see her again. You have to make a deal with him. If we have to go out there with a bag of money, then that's what we have to do."

"Liam, I'm going to do everything I can, but think about it. He's demanded money and a helicopter. He's committed three murders, and how many countless others are dead because of his guns? I don't want this guy getting away."

Annie, who had been standing behind us, said, "I think I can keep him on the line. He despises me. I've counseled Janie to leave him numerous times; I've even had her stay at my house when they were fighting. He resents my intrusion. He calls me a meddlesome bitch. I get under his skin. I may be able to keep him on the line long enough."

The phone rang again and my inner rage shook my hand so badly I could barely push the speaker button. "I want to talk to my wife," I said right off. "I want to know she's okay."

"Well, 'okay' is a relative term, Liam. I don't think she would go along with the characterization. She's bound and tied and has a gag in her mouth. Would you say you're okay, sweetie?" I heard muffled anger from Catherine. "She says no."

"I'm going to kill you, Lefferty."

"Oh, God, stop, will you? What about my demands?"

"We can get you what you ask for, but it's going to take time."

"You don't have much of that, Liam. Neither does your wife."

Annie stepped forward. "Charles, it's Annie."

"Well, if it isn't the world's most meddlesome bitch. Fuck you, Annie."

"Same to you, you misogynist bully. I want you to let that woman go. She's innocent."

"And why would I do that?"

"Because I'll make a deal with you."

"A deal? What could you possibly have to offer?"

"Me. The meddlesome bitch in exchange for Catherine Taggart."

"No, Annie, you can't do that," I whispered. "He'll kill you."

Annie grabbed my arms and squeezed hard. "Please, Liam, don't interfere. He'll make that deal; he hates me. I don't have a family. I don't have anyone. Let me do this for you, for Catherine, for your baby. It's what I should do. It's what I need to do."

"The slate is clean, Annie. There are no debts to pay."

McLaughlin shook his head. "I can't let you do it. I'm not sending in another hostage. That's not what we do."

Annie wouldn't back down and she leaned forward to speak into the phone. "Charles, I'm offering an exchange. Catherine Taggart means nothing to you. But me, I'm the bitch. I'm the one you can't manipulate. I'm the one who tells the world what a complete asshole you are."

"Well, all that's true and it's certainly an attractive offer, very tempting, but I've grown quite fond of sweetie here, and she's a Taggart. So . . . no."

Megan nodded and quickly jotted down that he was calling from a road four miles east of his country club along the Antrim coast. Janie was right. It was the Dunluce Castle. "We can have him surrounded within twenty minutes," Megan said. McLaughlin nodded and motioned for me to continue. "We have to make him believe we're going to meet his demands. Tell him it'll take time to get the money and the copter, but we can get them. Get the details on the exchange."

"Charles, I'm told that we can meet your demands. We ordered the money and we're trying to get the copter, but it will take time."

"You don't have time. I want to talk to whatever police commander is standing next to you. I'm upping the ante."

I nodded to McLaughlin. "This is Inspector McLaughlin."

"Farrell, is that you? My goodness, I went right to the top, didn't I? A fifty-year vet just for me. I feel so honored."

"Let her go, Charles. We can talk after you let her go. We can work things out. We know where you are."

"Of course you do. I've been on the damn phone for ten minutes. Tell Janie I'm the Earl of Antrim." He laughed. "And please don't try any of your psychological police negotiator crap on me. It won't work. I have only one way out. I'm not going to die in your prison like my father. But I want to tell you that I have additional items to bargain with now. Before we go any further, I need for you to know that I'm upping the ante."

"What does that mean?"

"What are your names?" he said, and we heard other voices. "They are Mr. and Mrs. Goodston and their two children Steven and Emily. They've traveled here all the way from Ohio and had the misfortune of visiting the castle while I was in charge of the tower. They are now my guests. We're having a party."

"You're going to take this out of my hands, Charles. I'm working on getting you a helicopter. Now I'm going to have to turn this over to headquarters. You'll be talking to someone else. Let your hostages go before we have an international drama. Do you want to see this on CNN or Sky News? That will limit my ability to get you what you want."

"I'm calling the shots here, Farrell, and I'm only going to talk to *you*. So, you're still in the game and you can get me what I want, just like you were planning to do. If you make it an international crisis then the blood will be on your hands."

"Let the hostages go and we can talk further."

"*Au contraire.* You will promptly supply the helicopter and a million euros or you will have the deaths of five innocent people on your hands. It's nonnegotiable, Farrell. I'm not going to let you lock me in your prison so I can die like Sean Lefferty did with a knife in his back. I've got five hostages and I'll take them all down before I let you grab me. At least I'll go out in a blaze of glory. Let's see, it's five fifteen. Have the money and copter here by ten o'clock. Bye-bye."

"Dooley," McLaughlin said between clenched teeth, "Call the visitor center. Make sure the area is clear. Then call Huntley at HQ. We'll need to set up a command post. Tell him to shut down A2 and A26 on the coast, all roads going in and out. Tell them to send the mobile trauma unit. Dunluce is dark, we'll need spotlights."

My heart sank. There was no way this would end without bloodshed. My only hope was that it would be Lefferty's and not Catherine's or those innocent tourists.

As we prepared to leave, McLaughlin turned to Megan and said, "I'll want you on the point. Tripod, night vision scope, range finder. Bring everything you have."

"Megan's going to be the sniper?" I said.

He nodded. "She's not only the best we have, she's the best in the UK. If there's an opening, Dooley's the one to take it."

"Farrell, I'm not the kind of guy who relies on other people. I don't have to tell you that my whole world is in your hands."

"I know it is, Liam. Let's go get her."

THIRTY-EIGHT

...

THE COMMAND POST WAS established on Dunluce Road outside the visitor center, and McLaughlin and I stood by the side of his Land Rover fifty yards away. Before us lay an open grassy field leading to the ruins of the historic Dunluce Castle. Farrell had an intra-department mic clipped to his shoulder pad with an open channel to his units. Spotlights and barricades were set up before we arrived. Thankfully, no news crews were present along the road or on the grassy perimeter of the national heritage site, and McLaughlin had closed off the highways so that none could approach.

Spotlights were focused on the medieval castle, lighting the gray stone structure as though it were daylight. The sixteenth-century castle had not survived the years intact. Large chunks of the castle were missing and gaps were notched in the imposing fortress walls, resembling a mouth of broken teeth. Portions of the walls had crumbled to the sea below, but two of the towers remained in pretty solid shape, and Lefferty was cloistered in one of them with his hostages.

The castle was built on the flat surface of a rocky, windswept outcrop, stretching far out over the swirling North Atlantic. Though the castle was only a shell of its former self—there were no roofs intact and the northern walls were merely stubs—the front walls stood at least fifteen feet high, a fortification solid enough for Lefferty to defend. The original design was brilliant—the castle walls were constructed right up to the edge of steep precipices on all sides, a vertical drop hundreds of feet to the sea and the rocks below. The only ingress to the castle was by a narrow stone bridge over a deep, sloping crevasse that lay between the castle and the grassy field. If an advance were to be made on the castle it would have to be over the bridge, one person at a time, an easy target for the castle's defender.

As I stood there I couldn't figure out Lefferty's plan. It was obvious that a helicopter couldn't land on the castle and there was no other flat surface on the outcrop. There wasn't even five feet between the castle walls and the edges of the cliffs. A helicopter's only landing spot was the grassy field. To reach the helicopter, Lefferty would have to march his hostages over the bridge and out to into the field. There might be a good chance to take him down when he did that and I was momentarily heartened. It seemed as though Lefferty had boxed himself into a corner.

But my hopes were dashed when McLaughlin laid out a diagram and an overhead photo on the hood of his car. Lefferty was one step ahead of us. The photo depicted a large open courtyard inside the walls at the rear of the castle where it extended farthest out over the sea. If a copter were small enough it could land in the open courtyard, pick up passengers and fly north over the sea and out of sight.

Cell phone negotiations between Lefferty and McLaughlin seemed to be at a standstill. Lefferty was demanding a million euros and a helicopter, and McLaughlin was asking for Lefferty to release the children as a show of good faith.

"How lucky am I that the Goodstons came along?" Lefferty said. "People always seem to care more for children than adults, though why that is I don't understand. They annoy the hell out of me. But as long as *I've* got them, and *you* care about them, they serve their purpose. Especially when they're bound and gagged. You know the old saying: seen and not heard?" He laughed loudly. "Where's my copter, Farrell?"

"C'mon, Charles, we need a sign of good faith. Let the kids walk. You'd still have three hostages."

"I'll show you my sign of good faith, Farrell. If the copter's not here in an hour, I'll throw one of these kids over the wall."

McLaughlin spoke softly into his shoulder pad, "Dooley, do you have a sight line on him? Is he near a window or an opening?"

Megan, who had stationed herself on a grassy hill directly southeast of the tower, was lying in the darkened shadows looking through her scope. "Occasionally, sir. He'll pop his head into the tower opening and then duck back. It's a risky shot unless he's standing still."

McLaughlin went back to his cell phone. "Charles, you don't want to kill those kids. All you want to do is get away, and I'm going to help you do that. The copter's on its way."

"Good. You have forty-eight minutes. If the copter doesn't come, I'll have to toss a kid. My credibility's at stake. If I don't toss one of these little monsters, then you won't believe me and I'll lose my bargaining strength. I'm a better negotiator than that. Thank goodness I've got hostages to spare."

McLaughlin studied the drawing and the dimensions of the back courtyard of the castle. "A small copter can land in the courtyard," he said. He looked at me and shook his head. "And that's a bad idea." He spoke into his radio, "Harris, send the Sikorsky, the large one, twenty meters in length."

"You can't land an aircraft that large in the courtyard," I said.

"I know. If we land the small copter in the back of the castle where we can't see him or the hostages and he loads it in the dark, and flies out over the sea, we've lost the game."

The phone buzzed. "Seven minutes, Farrell. I've got the little girl in my hands. She'll make quite a splash, don't you think?"

"Hang on, Charles, the copter's on its way. Just be patient and you'll get what you want. All I care about is the safety of the hostages; you can have your money and your copter."

Suddenly there was buzz of utterances among the policemen and on the castle, a figure emerged. It was Lefferty standing on a ledge behind the front wall and he was holding a squirming little girl high above his head.

"Dooley, do you have a clear shot?" McLaughlin said.

"Negative, sir. He's holding the child in front of him."

Screams echoed through the night.

"Now he's holding her over the wall, sir. I'm clear on his head, but . . ."

"Take the shot."

"I can't. He'd drop the child. She'd fall a hundred meters."

"Farrell?" Lefferty shouted, shaking the child. "Do you see me? Do you think I'm kidding? Your time is up."

"It's coming, Charles," McLaughlin said calmly into his cell phone.

"Listen. You can probably hear the chopper. Give me a few more minutes. You don't want to kill a child."

"Oh, you're wrong. I don't give a damn about this child. Of course, I'd rather kill a Taggart. That's my only regret—I didn't get all the Taggarts. Should have had Robert Taggart. I don't know what got into Montgomery; he never misses. It must have been Robert's lucky day. But talk about lucky, along comes Liam Taggart. King Rat, himself. The biggest prize of them all. The bastard that turned in my old man. And now I've got his wife. How fortuitous!"

McLaughlin spoke into his radio, "Harris, where's my Sikorsky?"

"Two minutes out, sir."

"All right, Charles, the copter is minutes away. Hold tight. I'm keeping my end of the bargain."

"Where's my money?"

"Got it right here. Do you want to come and get it?"

"Funny, Inspector, I see you're keeping your sense of humor."

Screams from the child traveled through the windy night and echoed off the hillsides, as Lefferty shook her and dangled her from the wall far above the rocks below. "Let's keep on joking, Farrell, although I have my doubts the little girl appreciates the levity in all this. I want my money."

"Dooley, if he steps back or lifts the child inside the wall, and if you're at all clear, take that shot."

Watching this play out and doing nothing was killing me. "I'll take the money to him," I said. "Give me the bag of euros and let me go."

Farrell looked at the large duffel bag filled with fake bills and shook his head. "I can't let you do that. He'd like nothing more than to kill you."

"I've got my gun."

"I can't put my hostages in the middle of a gunfight."

"If he doesn't get the money, he'll kill Catherine."

"I'm not going to give him money early, that's a mistake, and he's not getting the copter just yet either. He's a cold-blooded killer. The Sikorsky's too large to land in the courtyard. I have to lure him out of the castle, maybe onto the bridge, maybe into the field, just far enough to let Dooley take her shot. That's our best play."

I stood there feeling helpless. It was an impossible shot. The wind was howling, the distance was significant, he was a moving target, and if Megan missed, Lefferty would go berserk. He'd already threatened to go out in a blaze of glory. If he thought he couldn't get away, he'd kill everybody. My whole world was hanging on the sharpshooting skills of that twenty-six-year-old policewoman lying in the grass.

The chopping noise of the helicopter's rotor was heard in the distance. Lefferty pulled the child back and disappeared behind the wall. The large Sikorsky landed in the grassy field two hundred yards in front of the castle.

"There, you see, I kept my word," McLaughlin said. "Now let the hostages go."

"Don't insult my intelligence, Farrell. Do you expect me to walk out of Dunluce and stroll into a field? Wouldn't that be dandy for you? I'm not leaving the castle. Send the bird up here."

"All right. But when it's on its way, I want you to let the kids go. I'm doing my part. I need to see some good faith. You still have three others. We need to work together here."

"All right, I agree. And Liam, I want you to take notice. This is how you negotiate."

The copter lifted off the field and slowly flew up toward the castle.

"Sir, there are two children running over the bridge," Megan said. I watched the children dash off the bridge and into the arms of two patrolmen who took them into the visitor center.

The copter hovered a bit and then turned around and headed back to the field.

"What the hell?" Lefferty said.

"Charles," McLaughlin said, "my pilots tell me the aircraft is too large to land in the castle's courtyard. My guys can't set it down."

"You transparent asshole. You intentionally brought an oversized helicopter. And you broke your word. Bad mistake, Farrell. Now I'll have to kill one of the hostages to show you that I mean business. This one's on you."

"Wait, Charles, you said you needed a helicopter with a range of twelve hundred kilometers. The Sikorsky's the only one we have with that range. Charles? Charles, are you listening?"

A shot rang out and reverberated off the walls of the castle. We heard a woman scream.

"What did you do, Charles?"

"And then there were two," he said calmly. "Now do you get a sense of what I'm willing to do? Can you see that I'm serious? Do you know that I would take out every single person? I care nothing for them. The only life I care about is mine and I'll give that up before I'll let you take me to your jails." Demonically, he sang, *"If you take me back to Texas, you won't take me back alive."* Then he burst into crazed laughter.

He was a raving maniac. Catherine could be next. "Give me a gun and let me climb up the western bluff," I said. "I can make it up that hill and scale the wall. I can get in there, I know I can. Just stall him."

"Liam, you can't. There's no cover and if he sees you he'll kill another hostage, maybe Catherine. It's too risky."

McLaughlin picked up the phone. "Charles, you've got your cell phone. Google helicopters and their ranges. I'm not lying to you. The Sikorsky is the only copter I have that will satisfy your distance demands."

The phone was silent. I kept urging McLaughlin to consider an attack from the west.

"Even if you could make the hundred-meter climb," he said, "you'd have to scale the castle wall in plain sight. Unprotected. It's a bad idea."

"You could distract him."

"Liam, it can't physically be done, but even if it could, what would you do when you got up there? He's got two hostages that we can't secure. Do you want a gunfight with a guy who's hiding behind stone barriers holding hostages? I have to keep trying to talk him down. I have to work with him."

It was true. I was panicking. Thank goodness McLaughlin was thinking for both of us.

"Farrell?" Lefferty said, "I've done a little research on your helicopter. You're right about the range, I'll give you that. It's too large to land in the courtyard here, but the Sikorsky has a very stable hover. They use it in rescues all the time, especially over the ocean. It can drop a rescue basket while hovering over the castle courtyard. So here's my final offer. Send the helicopter up here, lower the basket for me and my sweet lady, and I'll let Mrs. Goodston go. Liam's wife is going to go with me for safe passage."

"Let them both go, you don't need her for safe passage. You've got my two pilots."

"I said that was my final offer. I know you've got this figured out, at least partway. I can't get to my final destination without stopping to refuel and when I do, I'm going to change pilots. But even when I have my own men piloting the copter, I'll need a hostage. Otherwise you'll blow me out of the sky. I'll take sweetie with me and let her go when I get to my final destination."

"No, he won't," I said. "You can't let her get in that helicopter."

"I may not have a choice, Liam. As long as he thinks he needs Catherine for safe passage, he won't hurt her. And he'll be freeing Mrs. Goodston. We're buying time. We need that time and I'm getting another hostage. I'm hoping he'll let his guard down long enough for one of my pilots to take him out."

"Then put me on the copter. Let me be one of your pilots. I'm the one who should be up there protecting my wife. I can't let her get into that helicopter without me."

"He knows you, Liam, and he knows you're not one of my pilots. He'll panic when he sees you."

"Where's my money?" Lefferty shouted. "Send it up here." He laughed loudly.

"The money's on the copter."

"Farrell, if one of your men has a gun, if I even see a gun, I'm taking everyone out. If one of your men makes a move in my direction when I'm on the copter, I'm taking everyone out. Understand? The pilots, Mrs. Goodston and sweetie. I'm not going to be taken alive, and if I go down, so does everybody else. Are you following me, Farrell?"

"I understand, Charles."

I was as desperate as I'd ever been. "Listen to me, Farrell. When he goes into the back courtyard, he'll lose sight of the front of the castle and the bridge. I can make it across the bridge and take him down before he gets into the rescue basket."

Farrell put his hand on my shoulder. His face was inches from mine and he had a solemn look in his eyes. "Lefferty's an insane killer who can start shooting wildly at any moment. The castle grounds, the copter, the landing zone, are all exposed and unprotected. You couldn't get close. You and I, we both know the score here. There's a good chance that the people up there—my pilots, Mrs. Goodston, even your wife—may not come back. Liam, you have a baby and that baby needs a parent. You want to stay right here for your son. You need to stand down."

Farrell's words drove home the anguish of the moment. I was forced to come face-to-face with the likelihood that I would lose Catherine and would be left to raise Ben alone. Of course, he was right. I was out of options.

"Charles," McLaughlin said. "You're going to get your helicopter and your money. All I care about is the health of the hostages. I'm going to send the copter up now and when I do, I expect to see Mrs. Goodston." McLaughlin spoke into his radio, "Send the Sikorsky up to the rear of the castle."

The large helicopter lifted off the field and headed back toward the castle. When the Sikorsky was hovering in position over the back court-yard, I heard Megan say, "There's a woman running across the bridge."

McLaughlin spoke into the phone. "Charles, the helicopter is there for you, just like I promised. I'm pleased you let Mrs. Goodston go. You kept your word and I kept mine. Now let Mrs. Taggart go and I give you my word we will not follow you to the continent. You can change pilots and we won't interfere. You still have my unarmed crew as hostages until you get there. You have my word and you know I keep my word."

"What don't you understand about final offer, Farrell? Sweetie's going with me. I like her company. She's kinda cute in a tied-up sort of way." He started laughing hard, an insane laugh. "Some might say she's fit to be tied." More laughs. "Nope, I need her. Your pilots are only hostages until I change pilots. Then what? You shoot me down? Nope, nope, nope. She stays. We're going on holiday together, right, sweetie?"

McLaughlin gave me a sympathetic look. "I'll let you make the call, Liam. Catherine's the only one left up there. If you think we stand a better chance of getting her back with further negotiations, I'll tell the Sikorsky to turn around and return to the field. We can always keep talking to him. Maybe we can work something else out."

How could I do that? How could I make that decision? If we with-draw the helicopter, if McLaughlin didn't keep his word, Lefferty might conclude the game is over. He might shoot Catherine and himself. But if I let her get on that copter, I'll never see her again, I'm sure of it.

"Farrell, what should I do?"

"Liam, if it were me, I'd let her board the copter. I have my two men up there and there's a chance Lefferty will make a mistake."

"Do you think he'll let her go when he gets to where he's going?"

McLaughlin sadly shook his head. "I can't say. Still, if it were my wife, I'd let her get on the copter. He's deranged and at the end of his rope. There's no telling what he'd do if we turned the copter around. My instincts tell me he'd go berserk."

My heart sank. He was right. We had done the best we could in the hostage negotiations. We lost one out of five, but three were now safe and Catherine was still alive. We were buying time and hoping. Maybe Lefferty would look the other way and one of McLaughlin's men would overpower him. After all, they were professionals. Maybe we'd get lucky when he exchanged pilots on the continent. With GPS we'd follow the helicopter and we'd know where the refueling would take place. Maybe he would still need her for safe passage like he said. I gave McLaughlin the okay.

The black Sikorsky hovered over the rear of the castle. I watched as it lowered a wire rescue basket slowly down to the castle's courtyard, behind the wall and out of our sight. I felt as powerless as I had ever been in my life. I felt so bad for Catherine. Her predicament was all my fault. I never should have brought her to Northern Ireland to begin with. I certainly shouldn't have left her alone at the house. I wished there was something I could do. I held onto the slimmest hope that Lefferty would keep his word and let her go, although I knew that was foolish. Other than his freedom, Lefferty wanted nothing more than revenge against the Taggarts. Especially me. King Rat.

The Sikorsky moved from side to side as it hovered thirty or forty feet over the castle. I heard McLaughlin say, "David, take her up a few more meters." And the response, "Roger that."

The Sikorsky rose twenty feet higher. The orange basket came into view, rising slowly into the air above the walls of Dunluce Castle. I saw Catherine sitting beside Lefferty inside the metal basket. I feared this might be the last time I'd ever see her. I blew her a kiss. I said a prayer.

The basket swayed from side to side as it slowly rose beneath the belly of the Sikorsky, Catherine on one side and Lefferty on the other, his gun in his left hand pointed at my wife. Lefferty got to his feet and began laughing and waving at us with his right hand, a final punctuation to his victory. "Bye-bye, Farrell," he shouted, laughing loudly. "Bye-bye, King Rat." Back and forth he waved his arm. Back and forth. Suddenly, his head snapped to the left, he stumbled backward, tumbled over the edge of the basket and windmilled down through the dark night into the sea. I looked to the side, to the field where Megan was lying. She smiled and gave me a thumbs-up.

The Sikorsky finished raising the basket into the aircraft, turned and headed back in our direction. McLaughlin breathed a sigh of relief and patted me on the back. "Like I told you, Dooley's the best."

I hugged him. "I don't know how to thank you," I said.

He smiled broadly. "Just another day at the office. Go get your wife."

He unclipped his radio from his shoulder lapel and set the cell phone down. "Now I have to go and talk to Mrs. Goodston."

The Sikorsky heading back toward the visitor's center was the sweetest thing I ever saw. I willed it to hurry up. I needed Catherine in my arms again. I dashed to the landing zone and watched the copter settle gently onto the pavement. Two officers helped Catherine disembark. I could see that she was weak. I lifted her into my arms and kissed her a thousand times. Her first words, barely audible, were, "How's the baby?"

"He's fine, Cat. We're all fine now. I love you so much."

"He was a monster, Liam."

"I know, but he's gone. Are you okay? Did he hurt you?"

She shook her head and the tears started coming. "Oh, Liam, he shot that young father. For no reason."

I couldn't hold back the tears either. "I thought I'd lost you, Cat. I knew if you got into that helicopter, I'd never see you again."

"He was a madman. I had just put the baby to bed when I heard the dog bark. I heard a number of shots going off and the dog squeal, and then the door burst open and Charles, he had a crazed look on his face and . . ."

I shook my head. "Stop. It's over. We don't need to revisit it. Ever."

I carried Catherine to the paramedic van where they examined her and gave her water. They said she seemed physically all right but they wanted to take her to the hospital for further evaluation. She declined. "I want to be with my husband and my baby," she said. "I don't want to go anywhere else."

THIRTY-NINE

• • •

ITH LEFFERTY DEAD, THE trust's preconditions were satisfied. It was time to settle the estate, distribute the assets and return home. To that end, we gathered in O'Neill's office a few days later, all that was left of us. According to the terms, only those beneficiaries alive at the time of distribution were entitled to receive their shares, but Deirdre suggested that Riley's share be given to his widow and children. Everyone agreed.

"I have no objection," I said, "but can we do that legally? The Bridget McGregor Trust is a beneficiary. Wouldn't we have to have unanimous consent? Wouldn't her trustee have to agree as well?"

O'Neill nodded. "Liam's right. We need the concurrence of the trustee for the Bridget McGregor Trust."

"And we don't know who that is, do we?" I said.

"We certainly do," O'Neill said. "I drafted the instrument."

I was peeved at that answer. "All along I've been under the impression that no one knew who the trustee was. Why did you leave me in the dark?"

"I'm sorry I was unable to correct that impression, but I was following my client's instructions. So long as there were enemies of the Taggart family, so long as a threat remained, the Bridget McGregor Trust and the identity of the trustee were to be confidential."

"Who is Bridget McGregor?"

O'Neill smiled in an apologetic way. "I'm not authorized to divulge that information."

"Well, who is?"

"The trustee."

I was getting frustrated by this merry-go-round. "And I take it you're not authorized to divulge the name of the trustee."

"Liam, my good man, if you were listening, I just told you that I couldn't divulge the name of the trustee while there were enemies outstanding. Given the events of the last few days, that impediment has been removed. The trust instrument provides that during his lifetime, Fergus Taggart was the trustee of the Bridget McGregor Trust. Upon his death, Ms. Ann Grossman was appointed successor trustee."

"Annie?"

"Quite. Any further disclosures are at her discretion."

I looked around the room. Robert, Conor and Janie all shrugged. "We didn't know," they said. Deirdre, however, had a Cheshire smile.

"You knew?" I said to her.

She nodded. "I'm an old woman. Annie's young. She can take care of the trust for years to come."

"I would like to know who Bridget McGregor is."

Deirdre nodded her understanding. "I think you should, but the decision is not mine to make. Talk to Annie."

I shook my head. "I haven't spoken to her since the afternoon of the kidnapping. What she did, what she tried to do, offering to sacrifice herself, it took the air out of me. It still does. I've left messages, but she hasn't returned my calls."

"Annie's a wonderful woman, but she still blames herself for what happened years ago. I suppose if she had ever picked up the phone and talked to you, found out about your life, found out you didn't hate her, it would have lifted that burden, but as you know, those calls are hard to make."

Didn't I know that! Hadn't the fallout with my Uncle Fergus left me with the same guilty feelings for sixteen years? A phone call would have given me peace of mind. The same is true for Annie. While there's still time to make amends, while there's still time to set things straight, you've got to make it happen. That's the lesson we've all learned.

"She didn't need to punish herself. I moved on a long time ago."

"I think she knows that now. I'll call and tell her to come over to the house, that you want to talk to her about the Bridget McGregor trust."

. . .

CATHERINE WAS DOING HER best to rebound. She was staying busy tending to Ben and spending time with Deirdre in the kitchen. They were good for each other. Catherine had faced death twice in the past month, and a woman could not be expected to suffer those traumas without scarring. Yet, I knew that if anyone could right the ship, it was my Catherine and I could see that she was working on it every day.

Annie arrived after the lunch hour. I greeted her at the door, immediately hugged her and tried to tell her how overwhelmed I was by what she'd done and what she'd tried to do, but she waved me off with a smile. "Would it be all right if we just didn't talk about it right now? It doesn't need words. We were all working for the same result. Let's leave it at that." She immediately went into the kitchen to inquire about Catherine and Ben.

In a little while, Annie and Deirdre asked me to step into the living room. "You want to know about Bridget McGregor?" Annie said. "Some years ago, Uncle Fergus made me promise that I wouldn't disclose anything about the Bridget McGregor trust to anyone other than Deirdre and your uncles. But that is a promise I will no longer keep. Given what we've all been through, I think you have a right to know and I think Uncle Fergus would now agree. If you want to know who Bridget McGregor is and what the trust is all about, come with Deirdre and me and we will show you."

I told Catherine I would be gone for a little bit, and Deirdre and I got into Annie's car for the drive to Dublin. When I tried to raise the subject, off and on, she told me I should wait until we get there.

Some two and half hours later we drove through a gated entry, down a tree-lined lane and into the parking lot of a large brick-and-stone building. The chiseled name above the oak doors read ST. ELIZABETH HOME.

"Is Bridget McGregor in this facility?" I said.

Annie nodded. "In a manner of speaking."

We walked into the entry hall where Annie checked with the receptionist and beckoned me to follow her down a long corridor to the right. "Come this way. She's in the sun room." The sign on the entrance to the corridor read BRIDGET MCGREGOR WING.

We came to a community room where several patients were seated in wheelchairs and at tables. Annie looked around the room and led me to a group by a far window. A woman was seated with her back to us, staring out the window at the gardens below. She had curly red hair tied with a ribbon in the back. I knew in a minute who she was.

Annie walked up to her and tapped her on the shoulder. The woman slowly turned her head. "Molly, there's someone here to see you."

I had a hard time holding it together.

"Molly, it's your brother, Liam. He's come to see you today." But she didn't seem to understand.

Annie beckoned me forward with her index finger. "It's all right, Liam. Come on."

I swallowed hard. This was my sister, who for all these years I had been told was dead. I leaned over and kissed her on the forehead. She looked up at me and smiled. Then she turned her attention back to the window.

"Why wasn't I told? Why didn't my mother tell me that my sister was alive? Deirdre, you lied to me. You told me she was shot and killed by Archie Walker."

"I'm sorry I deceived you, but that was a decision that was made by your uncle Fergus years ago. Molly *was* shot by Archie Walker. That's true. But as you see, she survived. Unfortunately, the injury, the loss of blood and the delay in getting her to the hospital left her in this condition. You have to understand how it was back in those days. In the Lower Falls, there were no ambulances, no cars, no police or firemen to help you, no way to get emergency medical care. Your father ran through the streets, carrying her to the hospital."

"That doesn't answer the question. Why wasn't I told?"

"You remember when you were sent to live with Uncle Fergus on the farm?"

"Of course. I was four."

"You were sent because you didn't have a parent to look after you. Your father had been killed by the Shankill Butchers. Your mother witnessed her daughter being shot and her husband slaughtered within a matter of hours. She suffered a total breakdown. She was incapable of caring for herself, let alone four-year-old Liam. She was confined in a sanitarium. She was suicidal. She blamed herself for leaving Molly alone on the stoop. Four years later, when she was released, she denied she had a daughter. She actually *believed* she'd never had a daughter. The doctors told us that confronting her with Molly, who was then in need of special care, would likely put your mother back into the sanitarium, maybe for good. So, Fergus had Molly placed in a facility where they would take very good care of her. She needed more care than any of us could give.

"Because of the feuds between the Walkers and the Taggarts, Fergus decided to take Molly out of Northern Ireland entirely, move her down here to Dublin and keep her existence a secret. Only five of us knew: Fergus, Eamon, Robert, Annie and I. Over the years, we've visited her quite often. We make sure she receives the best of care."

Deirdre put her hand on my shoulder and said, "While your mother was still alive, Uncle Fergus didn't risk telling her about Molly. We all feared your mother would suffer another breakdown. When you returned here in the nineties, we talked about it, but we decided to keep it secret. We still didn't want it to get back to your mother. She was a delicate soul."

"My mother died in 1995. Why wasn't I told afterward?"

"Again, that was your uncle's decision. You're a Taggart, Liam," Deirdre said. "Fergus decided that the tragedy of your father and your sister should be kept from you because he didn't want you running off to settle the score. You were a young man and embarking upon your career. In retrospect, that was unfair. You had a right to know. I told Fergus that myself."

Molly's hands were folded on her lap. I reached down and took her hand. She tilted her head and smiled at me. "You're so pretty, Molly," I said with a lump in my throat, and it was true. She had a darling face and it brought back memories of when she and I were very young. I could see her dancing in the living room in her black patent leather shoes. The very same Molly. Did she see the young Liam when she looked at me? She was smiling. I chose to believe she did.

"Is she physically healthy?" I said.

"As a horse," Annie said. "There just seems to be a little disconnect between what she experiences and what goes on around her."

"She's squeezing my hand," I said with a little excitement. "I think she knows I'm here. I think she knows I'm her brother."

"I'm sure she does, Liam."

FORTY

...

MY BUSINESS IN NORTHERN Ireland was finished and Catherine and I were preparing to return home. I took time to visit Molly again and I promised her that I would stay in touch and come to see her again soon. Did she understand? I think so. She squeezed my hand and gave me a beautiful smile to remember.

Deirdre would not think of our leaving without one more grand dinner. And grand it was. Her guests included Conor, Robert, Janie, Annie, Megan and Farrell. The tragic set of circumstances that had brought us together had also forged a strong bond. We would all be family for the rest of our lives. We'd not let distance get in our way again.

Deirdre's dinner was lavish, and though our family had been bruised and bandaged, we were constrained to make our conversation gay. None of us felt a need to revisit the details of the past several weeks. By tacit agreement, those memories were barred from entering the kitchen. Wine was flowing, Bushmills was pouring and there was a warm glow of camaraderie. There was talk of visits to America, of summer vacations in Northern Ireland, of legends and castles and kings. And when we had all eaten too much, someone—Janie, I believe—suggested we all go into Antrim town and enjoy a Guinness at Conway's Pub.

Catherine was immediately all over that idea and bundled up the baby for the ride into town. Conway's set a large table for us in the center of the room. The band was striking up traditional Irish songs and the beer and Jameson shots were there for the taking. The band was getting ready to start its second set when the fiddle player looked down at me and waved for me to come up to the stage.

"Oh no," I said. "I played all my cards last time. You guys are much better without me. I'd rather listen than make another fool of myself."

With that, the band struck a hard C chord, and the leader pointed at me with a stiff arm and loudly sang, *"Oh then tell me Sean O'Farrell, tell me why you hurry so?"* Then he tilted his head and waited for my response.

I shook my head, but Janie poked me in the side with a sharp elbow. "Get up there, cousin."

"Go on," Catherine said. "Don't be a chicken, I want to hear this."

I had to smile. Here I go again. I stood up and belted out, *"Hush me Buchall, hush and listen, and his cheeks were all aglow."*

The bandleader turned and nodded to his players, who took up their instruments. The glorious music filled the room, and he sang, *"I bear orders from the captain, get you ready quick and soon."*

I walked up to the stage. In for a dime, in for a dollar. *"For the pikes must be together by the Rising of the Moon."*

McLaughlin stood and shouted, "You'll not do this without me." He strode forward and joined me on the stage. *"Oh then tell me Sean O'Farrell, where the gatherin' is to be."*

Deirdre stood and pointed at the band. *"In the old spot by the river, right well known to you and me."*

"You're not leaving me out," Annie said. *"One more word for signal token, whistle up the marching tune."*

Janie jumped up. *"With your pike upon your shoulder by the Rising of the Moon."*

When I think back to that time in Antrim, I see my Uncle Robert in his sling, dancing up an Irish jig. I see Conor spinning Megan. I see the whole room standing and singing the chorus. And when that night comes back to me, I hear the echoes:

By the Rising of the Moon
By the Rising of the Moon
For the Pikes must be together
By the Rising of the Moon